On Grounds of
Honor

RebeKah Colburn

MY BROTHER'S FLAG
BOOK 1

On Grounds of
Honor

BY REBEKAH COLBURN

Other Books
by <u>Rebekah Colburn</u>

OF WIND AND SKY SERIES
Through Every Valley
The Whisper of Dawn
As Eagles Soar

MY BROTHER'S FLAG
On Grounds of Honor
For the Cause of Freedom

Dedicated to my Mom and Dad,
For teaching me faith,
And for always showing me unconditional love.

Acknowledgements

I would like to extend special thanks to the following:

Bill and Ann Turpin for generously allowing me to use their home, Locust Hill, in the cover art (the inspiration for "Laurel Hill"), as well as for their information and assistance in this endeavor.

Becky Marquardt of the Queen Anne's County Historical Society for invaluable help with researching the Civil War in Centreville, and for pointing me to Emory's *Queen Anne's County Maryland*, a historical account.

My parents, Leroy and Mary, for their enthusiasm and support in this endeavor, and for always believing in me.

My husband, Ben, and daughter, Grace, for tolerating my constant preoccupation with research and writing, and allowing me to hide away in my office at all hours of the day and night.

I would also like to thank the following for their feedback, creative suggestions and editing assistance: Sarah Smedley, Nikki Link, Lisa Peterson and Teresa Martinoli. I couldn't do it without you!

And my gratitude to Jody Christian for another beautiful cover!

Finally, to all my readers who've sent notes of encouragement and appreciation, you will never know how much it has meant to me.

All My Best,

Rebekah Colburn

"Is anyone among you suffering?
He should pray."
James 5:13

Prologue

April 15, 1861
Centreville, Maryland

Jeremiah Turner deftly managed the wooden handles of the plough, the leather reins leading the mule looped over his right shoulder and around his neck. The loamy smell of freshly tilled earth drifted on the spring breeze, cooling his brow beneath the wide brimmed hat. Behind him trailed the slave, Henry, pausing to plant golden corn kernels at the appropriate intervals and cover them over with a layer of soil.

The muscles in Jeremiah's shoulders bunched beneath his cotton shirt as he steadied the blade to keep the furrow straight. His dark hair was damp beneath his felt hat, his beard scratchy against his skin. The sun was as yellow as freshly churned butter in a sky as blue as a robin's egg. Squinting his brown eyes against the brightness, Jeremiah followed the sorrel haunches of the mule.

Suddenly a cry sounded behind him, and Jeremiah jerked his head to see his younger brother riding hell-bent up Turners Lane, flying at breakneck speed past the stately white edifice of Laurel Hill. Bringing the mule to an abrupt stop, Jeremiah watched Charlie gallop the buckskin gelding toward him, black mane waving like a banner in the wind.

Old Joe, at the other end of the field, followed Jeremiah's lead and halted his mule-drawn plough. Eli, his eldest son, likewise stilled his work at planting. Behind him, driving a wagon loaded with a tub of water and a siphon to spray the freshly planted corn, the boy Silas also came to a stop.

In a smooth, athletic leap, Charlie vaulted to the ground, waving a newspaper wildly over his head. His hat fell to the ground, sandy brown hair tumbling into his blue eyes as he held tightly to Buck's reins, snorting and prancing from the run.

"It's happened!" Charlie cried. "The Rebels have taken Fort Sumter! The President's calling for seventy-five thousand men to volunteer to stop them!" he gasped, breathless from the excitement as much as from the wild ride.

Their father, Francis Turner, supervised the planting from his perch atop the chestnut mare. A man as broad through the shoulders and thick through the chest as any man half his age, Francis studied his youngest son beneath thick white eyebrows which sprouted in as many directions as weeds in a fallow field. His blue eyes were solemn as he rubbed a weary hand over his face and lowered his head.

"I'd hoped this day would never come," his voice was hoarse with regret as he spoke.

"What are we going to do?" Jeremiah queried, removing the reigns from his neck and stepping forward as he searched his father's tired eyes.

Francis shook his head resolutely. "We will wait and hope Lincoln can crush this rebellion without help from my sons."

"I hope he *can't*," Charlie retorted, the newspaper crinkling in his hand as he clenched his fist passionately. "We fought Britain to be a free country only to have Lincoln trample our Constitution. I say Godspeed the Rebels and may they make it a free country once again!"

"Stop such traitorous talk and help your brother with the planting," Francis snapped. "I'll take that," he extended his right hand to accept the newspaper, waving his left hand at Jeremiah to resume his work.

Charlie handed over the *Centreville Times* obediently, but his blue eyes flashed as he declared, "I think you and Lincoln have both underestimated the Confederacy. This isn't just a band of rebels causing trouble. They aren't going to be easily defeated."

"Time will tell," Francis answered quietly.

Straightening, Jeremiah leveled his dark eyes on Charlie. "You want to join this rebellion? Do you really think it wise to sting a slumbering giant?" His eyebrows, black as a crow's wing but just as unruly as his father's, drew together in challenge.

"Better to sting the giant than to be trampled under its feet!" Charlie glowered at his older brother. "There's always a price to freedom!"

Jeremiah draped the reins over the wooden handle and stomped angrily toward his brother. "You're not seeing the whole picture, Charlie! If Maryland sets herself against the Federal Government, we'll lose everything we have!"

"So you would just give in to the tyrant, instead of fighting for what's right?"

"Peace!" Francis cried, placing himself between his two sons just as he had positioned himself between the two factions at town meetings many times before.

He clenched his fists and barked out the word once more: "*Peace!* How many times must we fight for it before it is finally ours to keep? Peace must not be lost at every disagreement, but carefully guarded as something fragile and prized. We must learn to compromise! The only thing standing in the way of peace is man's pride and stubborn ego."

Charlie side-stepped his father to glare at Jeremiah. "Well, if one man demands and the other complies, I don't call that compromise. I call it tyranny."

"Enough!" Francis nearly growled, his bushy white brows drawn together violently as he stared down first one son and then the other. "You, go take care of your horse," he dismissed Charlie. To Jeremiah, he pointed to the plough. "Back to work."

Jeremiah plodded through the thick black soil to take up his position behind the plough, snapping the leather reins on the mule's rump and setting her into motion. He saw the belligerent glare his brother shot him from beneath the hat he shoved onto his head before swinging up onto Buck and riding toward the barn.

Behind him in the field, like shadows unnoticed by those whose eyes are not downcast to the ground, the slaves stood silently waiting for the signal to resume their labors.

Chapter One

The staccato rhythm of horse's hooves outside the window drew Clara's head up sharply from her needlepoint. Placing it aside, she moved to the window to observe the scene in the field below. A sinking feeling grew in the pit of her stomach as she watched the exchange between Jeremiah and his brother. From the way Charlie brandished the newspaper, she knew the war they'd been dreading had finally come.

Her father-in-law would discourage rash enlistment, she was certain. Francis Turner was a level-headed man, always pointing to compromise and embracing peace. Her husband was like him in many ways, and she found comfort in that. Perhaps the conflict would end quickly, and Jeremiah would never need to be involved in it.

Although attention to politics wasn't considered a feminine pursuit, there had been no avoiding the rants and discussions which had engrossed first her father's home, and now her husband's. Like any mistress of the house, Clara had been taught the value of needle-point and the necessity of managing household affairs with efficiency and grace.

But these accomplishments did not preclude her from reading the newspaper when the men left it behind, or listening with an attentive ear to the discussions which ensued during meals. While intelligence wasn't commonly celebrated as a feminine attribute, Clara saw no reason not to gather information and come to her own conclusions.

Her father, George Collins, was a merchant involved in the trade of goods at the Centreville Wharf. He had a successful business, and Clara had often watched the cargo ships as they were loaded or unloaded before sailing off to ports in Baltimore and Norfolk. Like most men of Queen Anne's County, her father had sided with those in favor of States Rights, the Democratic Party, and the continuation of the social structure which predominated Maryland's Eastern Shore, if not the majority of the state.

Her father-in-law took a more moderate approach and argued from both sides of the disagreement in pursuit of a peaceful compromise. Jeremiah was naturally inclined to agree with the general climate but was heavily influenced by his father's perspective. Jeremiah didn't favor war, but hoped that men's ability to reason would allow them to settle on an acceptable resolution to the disagreements which seemed to grow greater with each passing month.

In Clara's mind, the use of force to maintain order seemed barbaric in the present age when trains flew over steel rails and telegraphs clicked out messages over wires, where sewing machines could weave the needle and thread for you and images could be captured for all time through use of a camera. They were a civilized people, and killing one another to resolve a conflict seemed both primitive and senseless.

The threat of war had been hanging over their heads for years now, although for most of that time Clara had either been too young or too preoccupied to pay attention to it. But when South Carolina had seceded from the Union only five days after her wedding, she felt as if a dark thundercloud had scudded over the blue skies of her world, threatening to shatter life as she knew it.

When South Carolina withdrew from the Union, she declared herself as separate and sovereign. The controversy which had boiled beneath the surface for years had finally turned from rhetoric into action, a spark which would invariably detonate a catastrophic reaction.

Clara remembered that day very clearly. With her hands folded numbly in her lap, Clara had listened to the Turner men analyze this pivotal turn of events.

"I don't see how war can be avoided now," Francis had told his sons sadly. "Other Southern states will secede, and I don't think Lincoln's going to let them break away as easily as that."

"They've found ways to compromise and restore peace in the past," Jeremiah offered hopefully, "perhaps they will again."

"Not this time," Charlie countered, shaking his head. His hair glimmered bronze in the candlelight, and his eyes, as blue as his father's, were sincere as he continued, "It's bigger than just South Carolina this time. It's bigger than just the South. The Federal Government's not playing fair, not following the Constitution, and not considering the welfare of all the people under it. It's time for change. And if it can't come peacefully, change will come with a heavy hand."

"We'll see," Francis answered evenly, evaluating the wisdom of his son's words. "I say let us pray that whatever change must come, can come peacefully."

Clara had bowed her head and earnestly prayed for war to be averted.

But within a matter of months, six states had followed South Carolina and seceded from the Union to create a new form of government under The Articles of Confederation. First Mississippi, then Florida and Alabama, followed by Georgia, Louisiana, and finally Texas.

A peace conference was held in February to try to mend the rift between North and South, but without success. The seceding states took claim to the Federal properties within their boundaries, and the incumbent President Buchanan took no action against them. Both sides felt justified in laying claim to Fort Sumter, and all efforts to resolve their dispute resulted in increasing the tension rather than alleviating it.

After Lincoln took office, his efforts to resupply Fort

Sumter were met with resistance, and full-scale military engagement resulted on April 12th. The battle had continued to wage for two more days, with the whole of the nation holding their breath to see which side would claim the victory in this epic battle of new government against old.

As Clara watched Jeremiah snap the reins and fall into step behind the mule-drawn plough, her stomach knotted with fear. Clara could only surmise from Charlie's excited response that the Rebels had taken Fort Sumter. Her view through the glass faded into a tearful blur as her eyes followed Jeremiah in the cornfield below, the sun golden on his bare forearms and his face shadowed beneath the wide-brimmed felt hat.

Her hand fluttered to her heart as an ache grew in her chest at the very thought of her husband marching into war. They hadn't even been married six months.

~

If Jeremiah's mother, Henrietta Turner, had still been alive, talk of politics during mealtimes would have been strictly prohibited. However, in the five years since she had passed, the gentility of her influence had slowly disappeared.

"Now every state's going to have to choose which side they're on," Francis reflected as he scooped a helping of Mamie's chicken pot pie onto his plate. "Lincoln's put the choice on the table: Either send volunteers to fight the insurrection, or join it."

Reaching for a biscuit, Jeremiah narrowed his thick brows as he asked, "What do you think Maryland will do?"

"All the talk I've heard is for secession," Francis admitted. "It appears we'll be siding with the South."

Charlie forked a mouthful of the steaming pot pie into his mouth, talking around it. "As well we should!"

"I'm not so sure," Jeremiah countered quietly, his earlier zeal having lessened with reflection. "It all depends on how much support the Confederacy gets. If it's a question of seven states against twenty-seven—a handful of rebels against a trained military, it doesn't seem like a wise gamble."

In response to his brother's calm reply, Charlie's temper also cooled. "If Maryland joins, that'll be eight. It's likely North Carolina and Virginia will go, and there's talk of Tennessee following. That makes eleven. And I wouldn't be surprised if others followed. It's possible that the nation could split right down the middle—unraveling like a flag whose seams are frayed around the edges of the stars being cut from it."

Francis slathered a biscuit with butter, conceding, "At this point, I'd say anything's possible."

Jeremiah observed his wife's expression across the table as her delicate brows drew together in concern. Rather than being offended by the political conversation, Clara seemed engaged and curious. Her almond eyes flitted from one face to the other, taking in the information quietly.

He reached between the basket of warm biscuits and the blue Wedgewood butter dish to lay his hand over hers, gently squeezing her fingers. He wished he could offer words of comfort: "Don't worry. Everything will turn out all right." But he knew such assurances to be a lie, and false comfort was no comfort at all in the long run.

Jeremiah didn't blame Clara for being afraid. Truth be told, they were all afraid. None of them wanted to see the nation divided, afflicted with war and painted red with blood. The men hid their dread behind bluster and bravado, not wanting to be perceived as cowards. But Jeremiah didn't want to take up arms and fight any more than his wife wanted him to. He was content with the life of a farmer, always having assumed he would live out his days at Laurel Hill, fattening hogs and turkeys and growing corn and wheat.

Clara's lips parted as if she wished to speak, but Charlie's continued discourse silenced her.

"If the Confederacy can get enough support, it has a fighting chance," Jeremiah's younger brother insisted. "There's more than just cotton that comes from the South, although that alone is enough to give them some leverage. Not to mention that farmers, hunters, and cowboys are far more experienced with a gun than a bunch of New England scholars. And don't forget that the President of the Confederacy, Jefferson Davis, served as Secretary of War for four years."

Clara parted her lips again, but still hesitated. "What is it?" Jeremiah encouraged.

She blushed, unsure about participating in the conversation. "I just—I wondered, is secession Constitutional? I read in the newspaper that there's nothing saying a state can't leave the Union in the same way it joined—by choice. If that's the case, why is it being called insurrection?"

Jeremiah felt a flush of pride at the intelligence her question revealed. Not every man would find his wife's interest in politics appealing, but Jeremiah didn't want a woman who could be no more than an ornamental attachment on his arm.

"That's an excellent question, my dear," he replied. "And that's part of the problem: the answer isn't clear. Since the Articles of Confederation predate the Constitution—and it was not a vote by Congress, but by the individual states, which replaced it—it stands to reason that each state could choose to revert back to the Articles if they so wished. However, others argue that by accepting the Constitution, the states forfeited their sovereignty and became an inseparable part of the Union forever."

"Keep in mind," Charlie interjected, "that Texas was annexed—they didn't join voluntarily. Likewise, Missouri was bought from France in the Louisiana Purchase."

"So..." her brows scrunched together in consideration, "it's not illegal—it's just not allowed?"

Francis leaned his elbows on the table, expanding on his

son's answer. "Divorce is legal, but if an abusive man refuses to let his wife leave him, she's either going to have to run away in the night or hit him over the head with a frying pan. Sometimes it's more about power than it is about legality."

"Ah," Clara nodded in understanding.

"So we're using the frying pan," Charlie grinned at his father's domestic analogy.

Francis offered his daughter-in-law a sheepish grin, then added, "The question of power verses legality is key. Is President Lincoln like that husband, holding on to his wife's wrists simply because he doesn't want to let her out from under his thumb?"

"I'm worried he's going to go after her and drag her back by the hair," Jeremiah admitted. "It doesn't mean it's morally right for her to stay; just that it makes more practical sense and offers her a better chance of survival."

Silence fell heavily around the table as everyone considered the implications of this possibility.

The following day's newspaper announced that Virginia had indeed broken away from the Union to join the Confederate States. "More will follow," Charlie promised.

Four days later, a riot erupted in Baltimore. Union troops were traveling through the city en route to secure Washington when a Massachusetts regiment in the process of transfer between railroad stations was blocked passage by Southern sympathizers, who threw cobblestones and bricks at the troop. When the harassed soldiers fired into the mob, those with weapons fired back and full scale pandemonium ensued. The Baltimore police arrived on the scene and tried to restore order, but before it ended four soldiers and twelve civilians were dead.

Charlie read the newspaper to the family over breakfast.

"Doesn't Lincoln know that Maryland's sympathy is with the Confederate States?" Jeremiah wondered. "If he didn't before, I suppose he does now."

"Since Virginia joined the Confederacy, Maryland's all

that's standing in the way of the Rebels taking Washington. I don't think Lincoln's going to let us get away with breaking free," Francis worried. "If Maryland wants to survive this war unscathed, she needs to avoid choosing sides. The tyrant's boot will take a heavy toll."

Chapter Two

As she listened to the men talk of surviving the war to come, Clara couldn't help but shake her head in protest. This wasn't the way it was supposed to happen.

She had first lost her heart to Jeremiah Turner when she was nineteen years old, five and a half years ago. The Collins and Turner families had intermingled many times through the years, but he'd always been merely a boy in the background. It wasn't until she was in attendance at a party at Laurel Hill that Clara observed an admirable quality in him which secured his place in her heart.

The beautiful white house was alive with conversation and laughter, crowded with women in colorful satin gowns and men in black linen suits. The spring breeze drifting through an open window had been inviting as she stepped back from the press of bodies and the hum of voices. Slipping away from the melee and down the hallway, Clara had let herself out onto the back porch, breathing deeply the cool evening air and enjoying a moment of solitude.

The moon overhead in the starlit sky was full and bright, casting a white glow over the grassy lawn and draping the trees in shadows. The brick smokehouse was visible from her position on the porch, and Clara's attention was snagged from the ethereal beauty of the night by the sound of hushed voices in the yard.

She spied a man, dressed formally in suit and cravat, crouching over the plump figure of a black slave woman.

"Are you all right?" she heard the masculine voice ask in concern.

"I so sorry, suh! I done dropped the ham!"

"I'm not worried about that. Did you hurt yourself?"

In response to his insistence, the husky voice of the woman replied, "My hands..."

Clara watched as the young man took the Negro woman's hands gently into his own and studied them. "You scraped your palms up pretty good, didn't you? Go inside and let Phoebe tend to you."

The woman made an attempt to kneel down but the man caught her by the elbow. "Don't worry about the meat, Mamie," he assured her. "You go on inside and I'll dispose of it. No one ever need be the wiser."

Mamie's sigh was audible even at a distance. "You a good one, Mistuh Jeremiah. I thank you."

"Well, I'll just expect my favorite supper tomorrow as an expression of gratitude," his deep voice teased. In the moonlight, Clara could make out the contours of his handsome face as he smiled.

A deep chuckle came in reply. "Steak with mashed potatoes and gravy? Yes suh. I do that for you," Mamie promised as she bustled back into the kitchen.

Jeremiah Turner, heir to the estate, knelt down in her place and carefully gathered the slices of soiled meat onto the tray and made his way to the barn to eliminate all evidence of the mishap. It was an act of both humility and compassion, rare qualities to be found in a man. And in that moment, Clara knew exactly who she wanted to one day become her husband.

The question was how to let *him* know.

Her opportunity came two years later, at the wedding of Margaret Palmer and Colin Ferguson. The violin had played a merry tune as couples swished and twirled on the dance floor. Jeremiah had noticed her, dressed in a gown of lavender satin with her auburn hair styled in ringlet curls, watching him from the sidelines. Her breath had caught in her throat as he'd purposefully strode toward her, bowed, and offered his hand.

The next thing she knew, one strong hand was resting on her corseted waist, the other warm and callused against her right palm. Clara had peered up at him through her lashes, aware of his solid form beneath her left hand. As far as she was concerned, Jeremiah was the most handsome man in Centreville, in Queen Anne's County—or the entire Eastern Shore, for that matter.

Dark hair tumbled over his tanned forehead, thick brows shadowing eyes the color of amber honey. A smile hovered around the corners of his full lips, partially hidden beneath his beard. Her heart stuttered in her chest as she smiled up at him, letting the adoration in her eyes say everything for her.

Before their marriage, Clara had tried to ignore all the predictions of war. She'd focused on preparing for her wedding day: the purchase of a white silk gown that flattered her small waist, laced tight in a corset, and flared out into a wide hoop skirt decorated with lace and ribbons; the purchase of an elaborate and beautiful trousseau; and the excitement of planning for bridesmaids, guests, and decorations.

After all, a year ago there had been talk of war erupting after John Brown's raid on Harpers Ferry, Virginia, but nothing had ever come of it. The abolitionist had reputedly organized a small army of twenty-one men and captured the armory there with the grand scheme of arming local slaves and heading south to draw more Negroes into his army. He had hoped to eventually bring about the economic collapse of the institution. But it was an overly ambitious plan, though some said he may have met with greater success if his Canadian supporters hadn't been prevented from joining him in the raid.

In the end, the mission was a failure and Brown was hanged. The event, however, had sparked fear of slave uprisings led by abolitionists inspired by his fanatical efforts. In Centreville, the local militia reorganized under the name of the Smallwood Rifles to ensure the safety and social order of the town's occupants.

Clara had looked at the family's slaves with new eyes after the incident, wondering if they were as content as they appeared or if they would murder her in her sleep if given the chance.

But after the initial uproar, life quieted down and resumed its normal pattern. Clara's thoughts had turned back to celebrating this time in her life of being young and in love, dreaming of all the future would hold. She hadn't given it another thought until the Presidential Election of 1860 was discussed at the breakfast table by her father and her younger brother, Eddy. Abraham Lincoln—the Republican candidate who would turn their world upside down—had won the election without a single vote from the residents of Queen Anne's County.

It had seemed so far and removed from her own life and dreams. But suddenly all of Clara's wedding details had blurred as she listened to the rise and fall of her father's voice. He leaned forward, the biscuit in his hand dropping crumbs as he suspended it in the air over his plate, brown eyes narrowed. "This is just the beginning of the end," he'd predicted.

"What do you mean?" Eddy's dark head tilted quizzically. Although only seventeen, he took an avid interest in both his father's business and in the political affairs of the era, largely because they effected his allowance and the standard of living the family afforded.

"We've been teetering on the brink of war for some time. Lincoln's a Northerner, through and through. The scales have just tipped, and the South is going to react."

"You think there's going to be a war?" Eddy worried, more inclined to ledgers and business negotiations than to violence.

George Collins had never looked more solemn as he met his son's gaze across the table. "I do, son."

"But... when?" Clara had asked breathlessly.

"Now, don't you worry about such things, dear," her mother, Naomi, had patted her hand. To her husband she'd suggested, "Why don't you save such talk for another time?"

George had nodded in compliance, draining his coffee cup as he pushed back his chair, directing a look at his son which said it was time for the men to retire to his office. Ignoring his mother's disapproving glare, Eddy finished his bacon in a single bite then quickly gained his feet and followed his father from the dining room.

Clara watched their hasty exit, their eagerness to resume talk of the approaching war obvious. Always immaculately dressed in the finest materials and modish designs, George cut a stylish figure with his gray hair neatly combed and his chin defined by grizzled whiskers. Just as well dressed, Eddy's smooth face revealed his youth and inexperience as he trailed along behind his father.

"Mama, will the war ruin Clara's wedding?" Jane turned anxious eyes to her mother. Three years younger than Clara, Jane was her closest friend and confidante.

"Of course not," Naomi assured both her girls. "Men love to talk of fighting, but it doesn't always come to it. Now, let's finish our breakfast and make sure the rooms are set up for Aunt Martha and the cousins. They should be arriving any day now."

Clara had taken her mother's advice and turned her thoughts back to the joy of her upcoming wedding. She'd giggled with Jane as they sampled pastries and cakes in the kitchen with the cook, dreaming of the day when the house would be filled with guests to celebrate her marriage.

It had been a Christmas wedding, the church decorated with evergreen boughs and sprigs of red holly berries. The twinkling flames of the candles burned with hope and the promise of a bright future. The wedding ceremony was held at the Methodist Protestant Church on Commerce Street, just a few minutes by carriage from the Collins' home on Chesterfield Avenue.

A light snow fell, covering the roofs and the grass with a powdery dusting. The sky above was gray as gunmetal, contrasting against the colorful Christmas decorations on the houses they passed. Evergreen boughs draped wrought iron gates, and many doorways were dressed with a fan of green magnolia leaves, the pineapple in its center accented by red pears or yellow lemons.

Drawing her cloak tighter about her shoulders, Clara suppressed a shiver. Her mother observed her reaction to the chill and commented, "I remember suggesting a summer wedding, dear." She smiled indulgently as Clara blushed in remembrance of the conversation. Everyone knew she was too in love with Jeremiah Turner to wait another six months to become his bride.

They would have married sooner if her mother could have been assured that the arrangements would have been satisfactory and all the necessary family in attendance. Jeremiah had courted her for a year before proposing in July of 1860 with her father's permission. Clara had been delirious with happiness as she'd recounted every detail of the moment to her mother and sister. Jeremiah had been both poetic and sincere as he'd promised his undying love and asked for her hand in marriage.

When she finally walked down the aisle of the church on December fifteenth of 1860 in her white silk gown, the stately figure of her groom obscured by the lacy veil hiding her face, Clara had felt as if her greatest wish had been granted. She was to be Mrs. Jeremiah Turner, and the man she respected and loved was to be hers forever.

~

"I've joined the Smallwood Rifles," Charlie announced, pouring himself another glass of fresh milk from the porcelain pitcher on the table. "Captain Goldsborough is enlisting men to prepare to defend Maryland," he continued as all eyes fell upon him. "We march beneath the Confederate flag with nine stars."

"Nine?" Clara questioned.

Jeremiah sighed as he explained, "They must be counting Maryland as the ninth state."

Francis regarded his youngest son from beneath his shaggy

white eyebrows. "I wouldn't be in such a hurry to fight, son."

"I'm not in a hurry to lay down my liberty, father," Charlie retorted. "There's going to be a war, and there's no avoiding it. Peace isn't an option anymore, and I see no reason to surrender our rights without a fight. I'd rather be killed as a rebel than live as a prisoner."

Clara's eyes flew to Jeremiah as Charlie's impassioned declaration hung in the air. "I agree with Father," he assured his wife, while also trying to reason with his brother. "Rash action can ruin all chances of eventual victory. It's an elaborate game of chess, and Maryland needs to look at all the pieces on the board before she throws her lot in with the South."

"I've already made my choice," Charlie insisted. "I'm drilling with the Rifles this afternoon on the Courthouse Green."

The remainder of breakfast was consumed in silence. Mamie's buttermilk pancakes, scrambled eggs, and spicy sausage made delicious fare, but the food didn't settle well in Jeremiah's stomach. War was coming, Charlie was right about that.

But who to side with didn't seem as clear to him as it did to his impetuous brother. Jeremiah didn't want to surrender the freedom his grandfather had fought to gain for them in the War of 1812. Nor did he wish to see that flag—the stars and stripes of freedom—rent in two. He was loyal to his country and felt constrained to fight for her and never set himself against her as a rebel.

Yet wasn't that what the Patriots had done when they fought to be free of British rule?

Lifting the yellow linen napkin to his lip, he stood and pushed back his chair. "Clara, would you like to walk with me for a moment?"

She hastily dabbed at her mouth as she came to her feet and followed him from the dining room, through the front door, and down the brick walk toward Turners Lane. He laced his fingers through hers, looking down at her upturned face, studying him with a worried expression.

"I'll never fight on either side unless I have to," he promised. "Put your mind at ease about that."

A small sigh escaped her lips. "There's some consolation in that, but if you are *forced* to fight, what comfort is there for me?"

"That I will always love you," he promised, turning to face her and lifting her hand to brush a kiss across her knuckles.

The morning sunshine was warm and golden, its fiery rays touching her auburn hair and setting it aglow. Her skin was smooth and fair as she stared up at him, brown eyes framed in dark lashes, her full, bow-shaped lips parted as she released a heavy sigh.

"Jeremiah," she whispered. "I can't bear the thought…"

He slid an arm around her slim waist and encouraged her to walk with him down the lane, the spring breeze stirring the green leaves of the birch trees which lined it. She wore a dress of blue plaid cotton, its wide skirt swaying over the tips of her black boots with every step she took.

Jeremiah couldn't bear the thought of leaving Clara any more than she could—either for a time, or indefinitely, should death claim him in his prime. But she needed to understand that such sacrifices were sometimes demanded. Though his desire may be to stay, duty may call him elsewhere.

"Whatever comes, Clara, we must face it bravely. Life doesn't ask what we want of it, otherwise I would never leave your side," he vowed sincerely.

Behind the sheen of tears which glistened in her eyes, he saw both understanding and resignation. She nodded silently.

As if by mutual understanding, they simultaneously turned and began walking back. Turners Lane curved as it made its ascent up the gradual incline toward the two story white house, black shutters dressing the windows. The pitched gable roof was accented by twin brick chimneys, the front façade dominated by a white pillared portico over the entrance. Flanked by towering laurel trees on either side, it overlooked the acres of fields and the creek called Gravel Run with quiet nobility.

Laurel Hill had been in the Turner family since it was purchased from the Nicholsons in 1812. As the eldest son, Jeremiah would inherit the farm and he'd always hoped to one day produce an heir to carry on the family's legacy. Clara's hand slipped through the crook of his right elbow, and he covered it protectively with his left hand.

This was his home. Here, at Laurel Hill with Clara. And he would never leave them if there was any other possible alternative.

He'd been born within those walls. He and Charlie had scraped their knees on the wood floors of its hallways learning to walk. His mother had breathed her last in the master bedroom where his father now slept alone. Even the familiar faces of the slaves, Old Joe and his wife Mamie, and their children, Phoebe, Lena, Eli and Silas, were part of what made Laurel Hill home. Phoebe's husband, Henry, had come to live with them about a year ago, and had quickly integrated into the Turner household.

The house faced west, toward the town of Centreville. Its shell-paved streets were as familiar to him as the grounds of Laurel Hill. It too, was home. And he would do all he could to protect his family, his farm, and his town from whomever threatened it. Whichever side that decision required him to take.

Reaching the house, Jeremiah kissed his wife's hand as they parted ways, Clara returning inside while he continued to the barn. "Try not to worry," he reminded her. "My greatest loyalty is to my wife and my family."

The smile that curved her lips was grateful, even if worry still lurked in her eyes. "I'll see you tonight," she replied.

Within the shadowy interior of the barn, Jeremiah strode to Archie's stall and reached for the curry comb. He could hear Charlie in Buck's stall, swinging a saddle over the gelding's back and tightening the cinch. Setting the comb aside, Jeremiah went to join him.

"You make me crazy," he stated plainly, "but you're my

brother. I just want you to be careful."

A crooked smile softened Charlie's features. "You drive me crazy too, you know." He placed the bit into Buck's mouth and slid the bridle over his ears, fastening the buckle under his chin.

"I'll be as careful as I can, Jeremiah. But just as Grandfather Turner answered the call to keep this country free for us, I have to answer the call for those who will follow us. Sometimes our ideals demand a sacrifice. I don't want to raise my children in a country where the government dictates their lives, suppresses their rights, and limits their freedom. What made this country great was its liberty, each state making the laws which suited it best, rather than one man ruling over every state and every individual like a king.

"We rid ourselves of the monarchy and established a republic. I don't want to believe that the bled shed in the Revolutionary War or the War of 1812 was for nothing," Charlie finished passionately, fists clenched by his side. Buck nickered in response and stamped his hoof.

Jeremiah sighed wearily. "I respect your position." He shrugged as he admitted, "I guess I'm just hoping we can find another way to keep her a great country without shedding more blood."

Charlie absently rubbed the gelding's tan neck beneath his black mane. "I'm going to tell you something, but I don't want it go any further than this," he lowered his voice, checking over his shoulder to be sure they were alone.

"What is it?" Jeremiah wondered.

Charlie's blue eyes appeared darker in the dim lighting as he leaned forward, speaking just barely above a whisper. "Colonel Emory and James Earle are going to Baltimore to find weapons and ammunition to defend the county. There are rumors that Union troops are moving this way. We need to be prepared."

Jeremiah glanced through the open barn doors at the proud lines of the white house set against the pale blue canvas of the sky. "I don't want Clara to hear of this," Jeremiah agreed with his brother on this one point. "She's worried enough."

The following day Charlie brought the report that while fifty kegs of gunpowder and a large quantity of lead and shot had been acquired, there were no weapons to be had in Baltimore. Everyone there feared another invasion by Northern troops.

"We stored the powder and shot in the courthouse," Charlie confided. "I sure wish we could have put our hands on some more rifles."

Jeremiah felt as if his insides were twisted in half. If he had to defend his town against Federals, he'd be pitting himself against his own government.

He closed his eyes, praying it would never come to that.

Chapter Three

Clara sat on the pink cushioned settee before the mirrored vanity, a beautifully carved piece of walnut furniture Jeremiah had given her as a wedding present. Her long auburn hair cascaded over her shoulders as she brushed it with the ivory handled horse-hair brush she had brought from home. The pale candlelight glinted in the mirror, through which she could see the reflection of her husband lying in bed, arms folded over the quilt across his chest, eyes fixed on the ceiling.

When she had finished plaiting her hair into a waist-length braid for the night, Clara padded silently across the wood floor in her bare feet and white shift, setting the candle on the nightstand as she slid beneath the blankets warmed by Jeremiah's body heat. He seemed oblivious of her presence, and she rested her chin on his shoulder as she asked, "What's on your mind?"

Startled from his reverie, Jeremiah opened his right arm to enfold her against his chest. "I'm sorry, just distracted tonight."

"What is it?" she pressed, suspecting he was withholding something from her.

His hesitation made her wonder if his reply was only a half-truth as he answered, "I'm worried about Charlie. He's always been one to act first, then think about it later. I just hope he won't do anything foolish."

"I know he's drilling with the Smallwood Rifles, but you don't think he would actually join the Confederate Army, do you?" Clara pushed herself up onto her elbow. "And if Maryland secedes, won't we all be considered rebels anyway?"

Jeremiah's heavy sigh was answer enough.

Clara studied his strong jaw in the pale light, his lips

pressed together in a tense line. She leaned over to extinguish the flame, then sank back into the soft pillow, her hand resting on her husband's chest. She wished she could push all thoughts of worry and war from her mind, but they refused to let her rest. Finally she fell into a fitful sleep plagued with distorted images that slipped away from memory when she awoke, but left her unsettled and exhausted.

A vague feeling of apprehension accompanied her into the morning. At the table, she learned that General Robert E. Lee had resigned his commission with the United States Army in order to command the Confederate forces of Virginia. Additionally, after the riot in Baltimore and at the request of its Mayor, President Lincoln had rerouted his troops through Annapolis to secure Washington.

Clara felt as though she was holding her breath, waiting for the next development and desperately hoping it wouldn't spell doom for those she loved. Bent over the stove in the kitchen, her thoughts were drifting on a tide of worry as she absently poured the melted paraffin wax from the saucepan into the candle mold. A sound behind her—no more than the subtle shuffle of feet on the wood floor—made her jump, nearly spilling the hot wax onto herself.

Gasping, she turned to find Mamie's daughter, Phoebe, regarding her with a dark hand on her slim hip. "You all right, Missus Clara? I just come in the kitchen to see if you need more wax. I awful sorry. Didn't mean to startle you."

Laughing at her own foolish jitters, Clara assured the young Negro woman, "You didn't do anything wrong, Phoebe. I was just lost in my own thoughts."

"All everybody thinks 'bout now is that war, huh, Missus Clara? I sure hope none of our boys gots to fight," she added vehemently as she shooed Clara from the stove and took over the business of pouring the hot wax. Clara smiled indulgently, both at Phoebe's assumption of the work and her reference to the Turner men as "our boys."

Phoebe had grown up with Jeremiah and Charlie. They had played together as children and matured side by side into adulthood. Although there was a clear distinction between the whites and the blacks, there was also mutual affection and respect.

Behind the big house was a brick building known as "the quarter," where the slaves resided. Jeremiah told Clara that it was nicer than the original pioneer cabin built on the property, which now served as the kitchen. The slave quarter boasted a fireplace and chimney, plank flooring, and a loft. Although it was snugly occupied, as it housed all seven of the Turner's slaves, they seemed happy enough to sleep under the same roof.

Ever since Frederick Douglass had published his accounts, rumors of the cruelty against slaves had been widely propagated. Douglass had been owned by a family in Talbot County, on the Eastern Shore, in his early years and later relocated to Baltimore. Although Clara had never read his work and did not doubt the truthfulness or sincerity of his writings, she had not personally witnessed any hostile treatment of slaves either in her family's home or the Turners.

In fact, Phoebe had become something of a friend. Before she married, Clara had benefited from the companionship of her mother and, most especially her sister, Jane. Once coming to Laurel Hill, she had found herself in an unfamiliar environment dominated by men. Phoebe had taken pity on her and made sure that if there was anything Clara needed, whether it was understanding the workings of the house and the expectations of the mistress, or a pat on the hand when assaulted with homesickness, it was provided. And for her kindness, Clara was grateful.

She guessed Phoebe to be around the same age she was, and as Phoebe was also recently married, they had a lot in common. Her husband, Henry, had been purchased from a neighbor at the request of the young Negro woman, who wanted to marry but also wished to remain with her family.

"I wish there *never* had to be any fighting," Clara agreed with Phoebe as she wiped her damp forehead with the edge of her apron. "Why can't men talk it out in a civilized fashion instead of killing one another?"

"Well ma'am," Phoebe moved the mold to the table to cool, "I reckon it's cause every man think he *right*, and ain't a one of 'em willin' to think maybe he *wrong*!"

Clara laughed as she nodded in agreement. "Just don't let them hear you say so!"

Phoebe grinned, her white teeth contrasting against the darkness of her skin. She was as slender as a willow, though where she had inherited these proportions was a mystery. Both her parents, Mamie and Old Joe, were as stout as the old laurel trees in the yard. Her younger sister, Lena, was only reaching her teen years and had yet to leave girlhood behind.

Clara surveyed their handiwork and offered Phoebe another sack of paraffin beads to melt into wax, wanting to make enough candles to last them through the month. She sighed as she considered Phoebe's conclusion.

What was it that made men so stubborn and prideful? Whenever she and her sister had disagreements, it usually ended in a tearful apology and reconciliation. It didn't matter who was at fault when both girls were upset and missing one another. It only mattered that they mend the rift and restore their friendship.

Only a few months ago Clara had heard of a man in Baltimore who'd been killed in a duel over some senseless issue which he had considered a question of honor. Why couldn't a man simply say, "You want to be right? Go your way with that belief and I'll go my way believing you're wrong. Life and peace are more important than forcing my opinions."

Some things were, in fact, worth dying for. But only matters of faith and ethics, neither of which seemed to factor largely into politics.

"You gots to stop thinking about it, ma'am," Phoebe advised. "Ain't no use in it. We's just goin' to have to live with whatever them men decides for us, nohow. 'Sides, ain't a woman's place to be worryin' over pol'tics."

Clara sighed. "Well, I disagree on that point, Phoebe. Though not enough to fight with you," she added, flashing a grin. "Let's finish up these candles and then I'd like to visit my parents. Can you ask Eli if he can drive me over?"

"Well, I ain't going to fight with you either, Missus Clara, long as you knows I right," Phoebe winked.

~

Jeremiah wielded the hoe in his hand with unnecessary violence. It was as if he took personally the impudence of the weeds that dared to grow in his cornfield. The spring showers and cool breezes of April had yielded to a glaring sun as May moved into the calendar. He removed his felt hat and used his sleeve to mop the sweat from his brow. Breathing heavily, he resumed his attack on the weeds.

It was simply the way of farming to combat the growth of unwanted plants to leave the space and nutrients of the field for the desired crop. Truth be told, Jeremiah was grateful for an avenue to release his pent-up frustrations in useful exercise.

He'd felt a measure of relief when he learned that Governor Hicks and the General Assembly had taken a stance of neutrality, declining secession while at the same time requesting Northern troops vacate the state. While they did not side with the rebellion, they declared that the state of Maryland "desires the peaceful and immediate recognition of the independence of the Confederate States."

Charlie, however, was furious with this attempt to straddle the lines. "Hicks held the session in Frederick on purpose, because the vote might have been different had it been held in Annapolis! It doesn't sound like neutrality to me at all—it sounds like cowardice! Since we're too afraid to take a stand, we'll just try to stay out of the way. Well, I can promise that it was a failed maneuver. Mark my words, Lincoln will force us to choose sides!"

But Maryland wasn't really being given the freedom to choose to stay in the Union or secede from it. It had already been chosen for them.

The President had made that much clear when he sent General Butler with a thousand Federal soldiers into Baltimore, setting up position on Federal Hill with their guns trained on the city. Furthermore, General Butler, once taking possession of the city, had declared martial law and assumed control of the local government, ordering its current officials—including the mayor and city council, the police commissioner and the Board of Police, and even Congressman Henry May—imprisoned at Fort McHenry, even though no formal charges were brought against any of them.

Ross Winans, a member of the House of Delegates, had been jailed a second time for his pro-South rhetoric, and was only released after signing an oath declaring his loyalty to the federal government.

Another man, Lieutenant Merryman, had been arrested while executing orders given by Governor Hicks and Mayor Brown of Baltimore to dismantle two state railroad bridges in order to prevent passage of Federal troops moving south. Merryman was charged with treason and duly imprisoned.

When a judge issued a writ of habeas corpus, contesting that the incarceration of the Lieutenant was unlawful, it came to light that the President had suspended the writ in the state of Maryland. Anyone who might be viewed as a threat could be arrested and imprisoned without the necessity of following lawful procedures.

To complicate matters further, Supreme Court Judge Taney ruled that Lincoln's suspension of the writ was unconstitutional.

Maryland was forcibly under control of the federal government. And while those like Charlie raged against the measures taken to suppress any inclination toward secession—or as it was perceived by the President, "treason"—Jeremiah understood Lincoln's desire to hold the country together as a unit. The President believed that drastic measures would bring a quick end to the insurrection and the Union would be preserved. But as the cry was against tyranny, Lincolns' efforts to gain control merely supported the accusation and cost him support.

Striking the weeds with renewed vigor, Jeremiah considered the position of the man who had held office before Lincoln. President Buchanan had determined that *"our Union rests upon public opinion, and can never be cemented by the blood of its citizens shed in civil war. If it cannot live in the affections of the people, it must one day perish. Congress may possess many means of preserving it by conciliation, but the sword has not been placed in their hands to preserve it by force."*

Though Jeremiah's anger may have appeared to be directed at the unruly weeds threatening the fragile green corn stalks, it was in fact directed at the founders of the country and the writers of the Constitution for not being far-sighted enough to consider every eventuality and build guidelines into it which may have prevented civil war.

He was angry at both sides of the political arena, Democrats and Republicans, and all those who fell in between, for not having enough wisdom and humility to find a satisfactory means of compromise. He was angry at his brother, for drilling with the Smallwood Rifles under a flag boldly bearing the "Stars and Bars."

And perhaps, he had to admit, Jeremiah was also angry at himself for not having a strong position in this conflict which threatened to rend his beloved country in two.

Up until now, the only position he had held was that of peace. But peace was no longer considered a position. There were only two sides: North or South; Union or Confederate. Some would say the choice was between Slavery and Abolition, although such individuals were primarily from the Northern states which only knew about slavery from the likes of Frederick Douglass and Harriet Tubman. But slavery was only one distinction between the North and the South. It wasn't the true cause of controversy.

Dissension between the two sections had existed for over a decade, the gap between them widening with time instead of narrowing. The cultural differences between the North and the South were as starkly contrasting as the speech of a man from Boston was from that of a man born and bred in Atlanta. The North was industrial in its production and liberal in its thinking. The South's economy depended on the production of cotton and tobacco, and its mindset was rooted in tradition and old-fashioned concepts of gentility and honor.

Dead center between North and South, Maryland was influenced by both polarities, representing the division of the nation on a smaller scale.

Just as Charlie was passionate for States Rights, Jeremiah's friend, Will Downes, believed with equal passion that the nation should remain intact. And the Turners weren't the only family with differing viewpoints under one roof. The Pacas, Goldsboroughs, and Tilghmans were divided in loyalties as well.

His shirt clung to his back with sweat, and Jeremiah paused to lean on the hoe and catch his breath, running a hand over his beard. As the oldest son, he felt a sense of responsibility not only for Laurel Hill, but for Charlie, to protect and guide him. Part of Jeremiah's frustration and anger stemmed from his utter helplessness.

His hands were tied. Charlie was twenty-five years old and past the age of influence. And while Jeremiah was determined to do all he could to protect his family home, he had no way of predicting what forces would challenge its continuance.

With a ragged sigh, Jeremiah removed his hat and raked his fingers through his damp hair. Perhaps hoeing weeds was the only thing he could accomplish for today. In adjacent fields, Charlie, Old Joe, and Henry were bent over their own swinging hoes, chopping out the threats to their livelihood.

If only life were as simple as farming.

Chapter Four

Eli, the eldest of Old Joe and Mamie's sons, was waiting outside on the driver's seat of the carriage with the white mare, Nan, hitched and ready as Clara closed the front door behind her. As she rode along the crushed shell streets, she considered the implications of being declared traitors to the United States government. If Maryland seceded, and all its inhabitants were regarded as rebels, what would become of them?

Since the President had decided the secessionists were guilty of insurrection, Clara hadn't spoken with her father or brother to determine their position. And although she expected they would be reluctant to discuss the matter with her, holding the same opinion about women and politics as Phoebe, she needed to know which side they were on.

"'Morning, Missus Clara," said Mercy, one of the household slaves. She smiled as she opened the door. Mercy was barely a woman, no more than seventeen, but hard-working and affable.

Clara smiled in response as she entered the foyer. "Good morning, Mercy."

"Clara!" Jane's squeal could be heard in the upper hallway, then in a flurry of petticoats she descended the stairs to throw herself at her elder sister. "I've missed you so much!"

Clara laughed. "I've missed you too, Jane," she laughed, surprised at her sister's exuberant greeting. Clara's family attended the same church as the Turners, so they saw one another routinely every Sunday morning.

"I'm sure you've heard the talk about Maryland joining the

Southern states," Jane's voice was hushed as she leaned in close to Clara conspiratorially. "I've been listening in the hallway to Papa and Eddy talking in the study. I'm scared of what's going to happen."

Clara reached for her sister's hand as she admitted, "I am too, Jane. Do you know what position Papa's taking—for or against secession?"

"Oh, he's for it," Jane answered. "Just like most everyone else."

"Well, my husband and father-in-law think it will be a mistake. They're afraid it will just spell our downfall."

Jane pinched the bridge of her nose as she closed her eyes with a regretful sigh. "I'm twenty-two years old. I should be worried about ball gowns and beaus, not politics! I wish you were still at home with me. I feel so alone without you here."

"Let me say hello to Mama, then let's go for a stroll down to the river and try to forget about all this nonsense. It hasn't happened yet. Maybe things will settle down and blow over," Clara said hopefully, though she feared the time for optimism was past.

Naomi was bent over her writing desk in the bedroom, the nib of her pen bent to a page of floral stationary. She looked up from her letter with a smile of delight as her eyes settled on her eldest daughter. "Clara!" she stood, drawing her into an embrace. "What an unexpected pleasure to see you today."

"I needed an afternoon with my mother and sister," Clara confessed. The four-poster bed with its ornate headboard and pink and white quilt, the Persian rug covering the wood floor, and the white muslin curtains at the window all brought a sense of comfort with their familiarity. Nothing in her parents' room had changed since she was a girl. This would always be home, no matter how much she loved Jeremiah or how long she lived at Laurel Hill.

"Is everything all right?" Naomi worried, studying her carefully for signs of illness or distress.

"Oh, yes," Clara forced a relaxed smile, knowing that if she confessed her worries, her mother would brush them off with a reminder that it was the business of men to handle matters of finance and safety, and a woman's place to manage hearth and home. "It was such a pretty day, I wanted to walk down to the Corsica," she added truthfully.

"Your father and Eddy are there now, overseeing a shipment of coal. Perhaps you can ride home with them for lunch?"

"That sounds like a perfect afternoon," Clara replied sincerely.

Once on the brick sidewalk of Chesterfield Avenue with Jane's arm linked through hers, Clara found it impossible to worry about the nebulous threats of the future. The spring breeze carried the fragrance of azaleas and rhododendron, and the green leaves of the oak and birch trees rustled softly. In the flower bed, yellow daffodils danced, and in the yard robins hopped through emerald grass in search of earthworms.

The tassels of her crocheted shawl fluttered as she held it firmly around her shoulders. Despite the warmth of the sun, there was a chill to the air. Jane, too, seemed to be freed from the clutch of anxiety as they walked toward the river. She gushed about her latest interest, Louis Bland, a young man she had met at a friend's dinner party.

"He's undoubtedly the tallest man I've ever met," she praised. "Why, my head barely reached his chest! And he has the broadest shoulders—he could barely fit through the doorway! He had to duck his head and turn sideways to exit the porch to the flower garden…"

Clara suppressed a smile. While she had fallen in love with Jeremiah Turner at nineteen and never had eyes for anyone else, Jane fell in and out of love with men as often as the weather changed.

"And what of his character?" she nudged her sister gently in the ribs with the point of her elbow. "Now that I know what a fine specimen of masculinity he is."

Jane laughed good-naturedly. "He is as gentlemanly as he is attractive!"

"Well then, he sounds like quite a catch," Clara agreed. "When will you see him again?"

As Jane babbled on about the young man who currently held center-stage in the drama of her young life, Clara listened with only half an ear, praying that one day Jane would find a man who could be to her everything that Jeremiah was to Clara.

Passing Chesterfield Plantation, its brick residence overlooking fields freshly planted with corn and wheat, she indulged in a moment of fancy as Jane's list of the gentleman's attributes didn't require her close attention. She paused to wonder what it had looked like when it was three thousand acres of fields, forests and marshland. The town of Centreville had been incorporated in 1794, built on land sold to Queen Anne's County by a widow named Elizabeth Nicholson.

The county seat was then moved from Queenstown to Centreville, which was not only more centrally situated, but its proximity to the Corsica River made it a prime location for trade and settlement. From the Corsica, one could sail down the Chester River to the Chesapeake Bay, and across the Bay to Annapolis, Baltimore, or even down into Virginia.

Clara's thoughts were drawn back to the present as they reached the river. The wharf teemed with activity as men unloaded cargo from sail powered schooners and onto freight wagons, while others loaded empty schooners with goods to be taken to Baltimore and Norfolk. Grain, produce, lumber and tobacco were carried onto the schooners which had arrived carrying coal, textiles, and farming supplies. If they had arrived an hour earlier, the sisters could have watched the steamboat *Balloon* take on passengers to Baltimore.

Avoiding the congestion of the wharf, the young women found a grassy spot to settle where the Corsica River narrowed into Mill Stream. On the opposite bank, a willow tree's delicate branches swayed in the breeze like a woman's unbound hair flowing gracefully around her shoulders. Above them, the sky was pale blue with wisps of white clouds, like the brushstrokes of a water painting.

"How long do you think it will be before they build the railroad?" Jane wondered aloud. "Won't it be fun to have a train station right here in town? Not only could we catch the rails for a day trip somewhere, but there'd be visitors coming into Centreville," she exclaimed enthusiastically.

Assuming the anticipated visitors must be of the opposite sex, Clara chuckled. "I thought Louis Bland already lived in Centreville? What need do you have of visitors?" she teased.

Jane blushed as she hastened to explain, "I just mean that it would make this town more interesting if there were new people coming and going." At Clara's raised eyebrows, she admitted, "Well, there's no guarantee Louis will want to court me. It wouldn't hurt to have a few more options."

"Fair enough," Clara laughed, sobering as her thoughts drifted out into the future once again. "Although the railroad might be postponed by the war."

She regretted the words as soon as they passed her lips. She had hoped to hold the demons of worry at bay, both for herself and her sister. But she had just invited them back into the conversation with her careless comment.

Jane sighed in disappointment. "I hadn't considered that."

"I'm sorry," Clara apologized. "I didn't mean to—"

"It's all right," Jane patted her hand. "I suppose if the United States are no longer united, everything's going to get ruined anyway." Her shoulders slumped and she leaned against Clara for support. "I understand fighting against the British or the French, but I don't understand why we would fight one another. If there's a civil war, nothing and no one will be left undisturbed."

The sun glinted off the rippling surface of the river as a breath of cool air blew over them, setting the cattails and grasses dancing on the bank, and the willow bowing gracefully beneath the azure sky. Clara gazed out at the serene picture, a chill of premonition skittering up her spine. Everything was about to change, not only for her and her sister, but for the country. There would be no going back.

~

A movement from the corner of Jeremiah's eye caught his attention. Clara was walking toward him through the rows of sprouting corn, her pink muslin dress sashaying with the swing of her hips as she managed the weight of a water bucket. Without speaking, she offered him a wooden ladle and extended the bucket.

Jeremiah sighed his gratitude as he took a long drink, the coolness refreshing as it slid down his throat and into his middle. He could feel her eyes upon him, watching. They both felt as if there was a clock ticking down the minutes until their separation. Since he had challenged her to bravery, Clara had not spoken again of her fear. But her silence and the constant furrow between her brows said it for her.

"Thank you, darling," he said as he returned the ladle to the bucket. "You're an angel."

A smile ghosted her lips. "I'll remind you of that should you forget."

Leaning on the hoe, Jeremiah paused to study his wife's expression. Her full lips were pinched together and she studied him as if looking for an answer to some unknown question. Moisture dotted her upper lip, and a tendril of auburn hair at her temple which had escaped the snood lay wet upon her cheek. She bent over and rested the water bucket on the ground.

"What is it?" he demanded, sensing that there was more than compassion to credit for her visit.

"I don't, I mean, well..." she stammered. Then, with reluctance, Clara reached into the front pocket of her white cotton apron and retrieved a paper, folded into a neat square.

"Phoebe was sweeping Charlie's room," she said in a near whisper, "and she accidentally knocked his coat onto the floor. When she picked it up, this fell from the pocket."

Dread mingled with curiosity as Jeremiah reached for the paper. Opening it slowly, Jeremiah let his eyes drift across the scrawled penmanship. It was an invitation for Charlie to cross the Potomac River with one of his colleagues in the Smallwood Rifles. The author wished them to go to Richmond and join the Confederate Army.

"I thought you'd want to know," she said, peering up at him solemnly. "I didn't mean to interfere but I thought that if he was going, you would want a chance to talk him out of it."

Jeremiah scrubbed his hand over his face as he let out a sigh. "You did the right thing, darling. And thank Phoebe for me. I just don't know how to bring it up to him. And if he's already made up his mind, I doubt there'll be any talking him out of it."

"Maybe you can persuade him to wait," Clara suggested. "Perhaps the Southern states will be brought into submission as quickly as Maryland has."

He could hear the disbelief in her voice even as she spoke the words, and he smiled his gratitude for her efforts to encourage him. "I can try," he agreed.

"Would you like another drink?" she offered as she took the handle of the bucket and lifted it.

Accepting the ladle, Jeremiah took another swallow. His gaze drifted across the fields to where his brother worked the hoe nonchalantly, as if it was any other day, as if he wasn't planning to join the Rebel Army and placing the family in danger as a Southern sympathizer. Vaguely aware that Clara had spoken, he looked up to realize she had already walked away. Luckily he knew she wasn't the sort of woman to be upset by petty matters.

Stuffing the folded square into his pants pocket, Jeremiah resisted the urge to confront his brother then and there. But good sense told him it was better to wait until they were seated at the supper table and address it with his father present. He wouldn't give away Phoebe or Clara's involvement in the discovery, and he wanted to be careful that his resistance didn't push Charlie in the very direction he was trying to steer him away.

As he resumed his labors, his force with the hoe was not what it had been. His movements were slowed and distracted as his thoughts raced ahead to arguments which might convince Charlie to, at the very least, postpone enlistment. Perhaps Clara was right and he could buy some time for Charlie to be prevented by other means.

With the arrests of the authorities in Baltimore, Ross Winans, and Lieutenant Merryman, it was clear that being associated with the Confederacy was now a dangerous proposition. Anyone who aligned with the South would be considered guilty of treason, a crime punishable by hanging, as in the case of John Brown. If Maryland had seceded and joined the Confederacy, it wouldn't have been quite the same risk to enlist. But now that they were firmly attached to the Union, any Confederate soldier was on enemy soil.

Jeremiah watched the progression of the sun, equally nervous as relieved when the hour came to wash up for supper. Once in the dining room, seated at the long oak table which filled the space, he studied his brother as he helped himself to Mamie's fried chicken, green beans, and mashed potatoes. Charlie was unusually silent, as if his thoughts kept him deeply occupied.

The fireplace was hidden behind a decorative screen for the summer months, and Jeremiah found himself studying the birds flitting across the painted powder blue sky and the pink blossoms on the trees with great interest as he searched for the least provoking way to admit his discovery.

With a regretful glance at his father, Jeremiah produced the folded paper as he announced, "Charlie, I believe this belongs to you. It must have fallen from your coat pocket."

Charlie glanced up from his plate as if jarred from great contemplation, then his eyes narrowed as he recognized the missive in his brother's hand. "Hey, what are you doing with that?" he demanded.

"Are you going to do it?" Jeremiah asked quietly.

"What is it?" Francis looked from one son to the other, his unruly snow-white brows drawing together furiously. "Going to do what?" he barked.

Charlie's blue eyes flashed as he challenged, "I doubt that fell out of my pocket without help."

"I asked if you are going to do it," Jeremiah repeated, working to keep his voice calm and even.

"I'm considering it," Charlie admitted, chin lifted defiantly.

"Considering what?" Francis banged his fist on the table impatiently. "Will someone tell me what's going on here?"

Clara spilled water down the front of her, jumping like a startled cat at the sudden noise. Her exclamation of surprise punctuated the angry thud.

"Joining the Confederates," Charlie answered his father, his expression one of belligerence though his tone was more uncertain.

Francis Turner studied his son wordlessly. The unexpected silence was even more nerve-racking than an outburst. "I see," he said finally.

"I'm not asking you to change your position," Jeremiah began the argument he had carefully formulated while hoeing the weeds. "I'm only asking you to take time to carefully consider the risk and the consequences before you do something which could endanger the entire family."

"Father is the head of the household and I'm merely the second son," Charlie answered as if he had already given the matter great thought. "I doubt my defection will be of great consequence."

"If the rebellion is as quickly suppressed as the North boasts it will be, there's no use in endangering yourself for a lost cause," Jeremiah persisted.

"The capital of the Confederacy is Richmond, Virginia,"

Charlie replied, meeting his brother's gaze steadily. "Home of the Tredegar Iron Works. The North thinks that because they have the Springfield Armory, the South will be unequipped. But even now they're producing artillery to defend themselves against the aggressor."

"How do you know this?" Francis wondered.

"I have friends," Charlie answered vaguely.

"Like this one, who wants you to cross the Potomac with him?" Jeremiah indicated the invitation in his hand.

"When I joined the Smallwood Rifles, I believed in the cause of freedom, in the right of each state to determine its own domestic institutions and laws. Just because Lincoln has imprisoned all those who would have voted for secession, my position hasn't changed," Charlie insisted, coming to his feet. "I'm sorry if you don't understand my dedication to this cause. But our grandfather didn't die in the name of freedom for us to surrender it without a fight—even if it is our own government who would take it!"

Clara's eyes fluttered to Jeremiah's briefly then fell back to her lap, where her hands were clasped tensely together. Jeremiah felt the words she didn't say: tread carefully or you might push him away.

His father hadn't received the warning glance and was ready to blast his son with the voice of authority as he stood, shoulders squared, glaring across the table. "Charles William Turner, I absolutely for—"

Jeremiah jumped to his feet, raising his voice to cover the challenge before it exploded like a grenade in the dining room. "Father, we have to agree that we respect Charlie's love of freedom, even share it. But to wage war against one's own government is a perilous venture. All I ask is that you take more time to carefully consider it before you act."

Francis huffed, but did not argue.

Charlie's jaw was clenched in stubborn resolve, but he slowly lowered himself back into his chair. He waited until his brother and father had done the same before conceding, "I have already given the matter considerable thought. But if that is the only promise you demand, I can swear to give it more."

"That is all I ask," Jeremiah hurried to assure.

But when morning dawned, Charlie's place at the breakfast table was notably absent. As Jeremiah rushed up the stairs, he bumped into Lena in the hallway.

"His bed was still made up like he never go to sleep," the Negro girl reported anxiously. "And he left this layin' on his pillow."

Lena offered the sheet of paper to Jeremiah, who held it out for his father to read over his shoulder. It was the lyrics of the song, *"Maryland, My Maryland,"* written by a Southern sympathizer after the riot in Baltimore.

In his own hand, Charlie had penned in the upper right hand margin: *"Upon further reflection, I am convinced of the rightness of this cause."*

Scanning the words of the song, Jeremiah's eyes fixed upon the sixth verse:

"Dear Mother! Burst the tyrant's chain.
Maryland!
She meets her sisters on the plain—
"Sic simper!" 'tis the proud refrain
That baffles minions back again.
Maryland!
Arise in majesty again,
Maryland, my Maryland!"

Likewise, the ninth verse also proudly declared:
"I hear the distant thunder-hum,
Maryland!
The Old Line's bugle, fife, and drum,
Maryland!
She is not dead, nor deaf, nor dumb—
Huzza! She spurns the Northern scum!

She breathes! She burns! She'll come! She'll come!
Maryland, my Maryland!"

Francis leaned his broad shoulder against the wall for support. "It's nothing but treason... God help him."

Chapter Five

Behind the men on the stairwell, Clara watched her father-in-law sag against the wall as if the weight of a thousand tons had been placed on his shoulders. Jeremiah's features were shadowed in the flickering lamplight cast by the wall sconces, but she could see the disappointment and apprehension etched into the beloved lines of his face.

"His sources are wrong," he told them quietly. "They're overly optimistic. There are far more foundries and armories in the North than there are in the South, and they have access to new and modern weapons. The South's arms are only what they have on hand—old muskets used for hunting squirrels and deer. They have no navy to protect their harbors; no manufacturers of gun powder to replenish their supply when it runs out; not to mention being sadly outnumbered. It's madness."

Francis looked at Jeremiah quizzically. "You sound well informed."

"I have friends too," Jeremiah replied, sighing wearily. "William Downes is a devout patriot. His uncle is a senator in Connecticut."

Clara rested her hand comfortingly on her husband's arm. "Is there nothing we can do to bring Charlie back?" she wondered.

Jeremiah shook his head.

Francis replied, "It's too late now. He's a grown man and he's made his decision. There's nothing to be done now but pray for him."

Clara was tempted to reply that all of their prayers for peace had been fruitless, but she bit her tongue.

One thing alone was clear to her: her husband would never join the Rebel Army. He had sworn he would not join *either* army unless forced, but she still found little solace in this promise. What exactly had he meant when he said "forced"? What circumstances would impose upon him a sense of requirement?

Clara sought comfort in the familiar routine of her life as she worked alongside Phoebe and Mamie in the kitchen as they churned butter, pressed it into molds for the table, made fresh cheese, or stepped out into the sunshine to gather vegetables from the garden. Clara could allow herself to believe that the world continued as she had always known it. She could daydream about raising babies and growing old with her husband.

But reality crashed into this sweet fantasy as brutally as the butt end of a rifle and sent Clara spiraling into a whirlwind of fear and anxiety. Union troops marched into two local towns, Easton and Queenstown, arresting citizens for perceived crimes and seizing arms from the residents there.

Jeremiah was sent word that these same troops, a detachment from General Butler's forces, were advancing on Centreville.

"What will they do to us?" Clara gripped Jeremiah's hand, searching his eyes for the truth.

"You've nothing to fear," he reassured her. "They're just making a show of force and securing the state for the Union. They need Maryland. They need our roads, railroads, and rivers. Just as General Butler secured Baltimore and Annapolis, he wants to secure this county."

"But will they know that Charlie...?"

"I don't know," he admitted, and Clara saw the flicker of concern carefully hidden behind a mask of confidence. "If we cooperate with them fully, they'll have no reason to mistreat us."

Clara swallowed down the knot growing in her throat. The very idea of soldiers marching through the streets of Centreville, searching for rebels and seizing weapons, made her blood run cold. "When will they arrive?"

"Tomorrow, I suspect. I'll be here with you, don't worry."

Clara nodded, grateful for his presence, but terrified just the same.

She spent the following morning at the parlor window, watching for the soldiers' arrival. What had before been mere phantoms of the imagination became flesh and blood as she glimpsed the blue uniforms of the men riding up the hill toward the house. She called Jeremiah to the window, and both he and his father were quick to join Clara in peering through the glass at the approaching soldiers.

"Stay here," Francis instructed, his gazed riveted on Clara. Turning on his heel, her father-in-law strode to the front door and met the Union soldiers at the end of the brick walk before they had time to dismount.

With her husband's arm encircling her waist, they stood back from the window where they could not be seen keeping watch on the developments outside. Francis shook hands with the commanding officer, greeting him cordially and nodding his head in concession as he swept an arm of invitation to the house. Four soldiers followed him through the front door and into the foyer.

Clara sank down into the armchair, both so as not to appear that she had been spying, but mostly because her knees suddenly felt weak. At the sight of Jeremiah, the leader of the unit marched briskly into the parlor, a Minie rifle conspicuously visible in his right hand.

"On orders of Governor Hicks, we are searching the residences of this town for weapons which may be used in the act of treason. Your father has already given his permission for us to investigate the premises, and I assume that you also have no objection?" he challenged disdainfully, as if assuming by their residence in Queen Anne's County that they should be counted as traitors.

"I have no objection," Jeremiah replied coolly.

The officer nodded curtly to his men and each parted in a different direction to search the house.

Clara's hands trembled in her lap. Charlie had taken his rifle when he left for Richmond, as well as the gelding, Buck. But Francis and Jeremiah were both in possession of muskets used for hunting, if not for protection. Whether there were other weapons lying about, she had no idea. How these soldiers could know the intended use of any arms they uncovered was also beyond her. It was well within their rights to own as many guns as they desired.

Sounds of tromping feet, slamming of drawers, and the scraping of furniture as it was dragged across the wood floor filled the house. Beside her, Jeremiah ground his teeth, the muscle in his jaw flexing angrily.

After what seemed an interminable amount of time, the officer and his men reappeared in the parlor. He held an old, rusty musket in the air as if it were a prize. "I'll be taking this with me," he announced to the Turner men. "I suggest you choose your affiliations wisely." Then, with a curt nod, he took his leave.

It wasn't until the rhythm of their hoof beats had faded into the distance that Clara's heart resumed normal beating. "What—" She stopped, her voice coming out high-pitched and breathy. *Bravery*, she reminded herself. "What musket was that? I'm sure we had more guns than that."

Jeremiah joined his father on the sofa. "It was my grandfather's. We knew they wouldn't leave unless they had something to take with them."

"The others?" she pressed.

"Safely hidden in the cellar, thanks to Mamie," Francis replied. "Let's go survey the damage," he stated grimly as he came to his feet.

Investigation revealed that the soldiers had gouged the wood floor in their efforts to move furniture, ransacked the private bedrooms and strewn clothes from the wardrobes onto the floor. Francis and Jeremiah seethed as they looked around at the insulting calling card the Federals had left behind. Clara could only cover her mouth in shock.

~

The following week, a letter arrived from Charlie. He had safely reached Richmond and enlisted in the First Maryland Infantry of the Confederate States. Jeremiah sagged onto the bench outside the Centreville post office, the letter in his hands trembling in the breeze.

His brother was safe for the moment, but he was afraid that condition was only temporary. Folding the letter back up and returning it to the envelope, Jeremiah couldn't suppress the surge of anger that flared at Charlie for the way he had chosen to run off under cover of night to follow a course of action he knew very well his family disapproved of.

Had Charlie even taken the time to consider the position he had placed his brother in? Should Jeremiah decide he wished to serve in the Union Army, he would be choosing to fight against his own flesh and blood.

Leaning back against the wooden bench, Jeremiah tucked the letter into his coat pocket to share with his father and Clara when he returned home. A sound in the street caught his attention, and he looked up to watch the Union Zouaves round the corner onto Water Street, their brisk double-time march matching the beat of the drum carried by a young boy at the front of the company. At the rear of their unit a soldier carried the American flag, the bold red and white stripes with a rectangle of blue and thirty-four white stars waving proudly over his shoulder.

The sight of that familiar pattern—the stars and stripes— stirred a deep sense of patriotism within Jeremiah. His heart beat quickly as the flag rippled in the wind, the symbol of an independent nation and a strong people who had bravely fought to make it free and to keep it free. A nation forged on the principles of religious freedom and autonomy, the right of the people to govern themselves.

It was a sacred compact, this union which bound the states together into one greater whole: The United States of America.

Jeremiah remembered his father's analogy of a woman wishing to escape an abusive husband. But what if there was a way her marriage could be saved by convincing her husband of the error of his ways? Instead of leaving him or hitting him over the head with a frying pan, could she convince him of the sacredness of the vow they had taken to become one—the union of man and wife into one flesh until parted by death? Was it possible that this husband could be reminded of the commitment inherent in their vow to treat one another with respect and affection?

Like the Southern states, Charlie had given up on the hope of ever achieving peaceful reconciliation. He was convinced that the Federal Government was beyond being convinced of its errors and the only way to claim liberty was to break free. Jeremiah understood this desire, yet something within him was dissatisfied with the idea that liberty could only be achieved by disunion.

Why couldn't there be a way to keep the nation whole, flawed and in dissension, but together? Perhaps the threat of divorce (or secession) would be enough to spur the unyielding party to reconsider his position.

Francis Turner often said that wherever conflict existed, neither party could be found wholly blameless. In the case of the North-South disagreement, Jeremiah knew that wrongs had been committed by both sides. Neither section could truthfully claim to be innocent of insult or crime.

The North was guilty of unfair tariffs placed on Southern goods, of efforts to impose their views in matters which had been left to the state to decide, and of publicly and frequently demeaning their agricultural counterparts. As example, their recent behavior in Queen Anne's County had been disrespectful and unconstitutional.

However, the South was guilty of antagonism toward the North in retaliation for these acts. The incident of Senators Sumner and Brooks five years earlier immediately came to Jeremiah's mind.

Senator Sumner had delivered an anti-slavery speech rife with disgraceful sexual imagery suggesting that all slave-holders were guilty of forcing relations with female slaves. In retaliation for this shameless degradation, Senator Brooks beat Sumner unconscious with a cane in the Senate chamber. His act of violence was then used to confirm that Southerners were intolerant of free speech and inclined to control by force.

However, Southerners supported Brooks' defense of their honor and it was reported that he received hundreds of new canes as an expression of support. One of them was reputedly inscribed: "*Hit him again.*"

Episodes like this only served to further polarize the country. As far as Jeremiah could tell, both sides were right in some things and wrong in others. Indeed, neither was blameless.

Charlie was moved by a passionate desire for freedom. Jeremiah agreed with the premise of the Southern argument, but he was devoted to his country and to its preservation. While on the one hand, he hoped the flaws within its government could one day be eradicated, he also recognized that any institution operated by man was destined to imperfection.

In the end, if one had to choose, it seemed to him that the honorable course was to uphold the Union—the country his grandfather had fought to preserve. If the war continued, and if the fate of Maryland was in the balance, wouldn't it be best for his home and his family to demonstrate loyalty to the government?

Captain George H. Steuart had resigned his commission with the United States Army after thirteen years of military service to join the Confederacy. He was a resident of Baltimore, and in response to his act of treason, supported by his father, the family home known as "Maryland Square" had been confiscated by the Federal Government. Rumor had it that he was commanding Charlie's unit, the First Maryland Infantry Regiment of the Confederate States Army.

Jeremiah was determined to never let Laurel Hill fall into the hands of strangers for any reason. The mere thought of Laurel Hill being taken away and overrun with soldiers strengthened his resolve. He was loyal to both his family and his country.

He didn't want to fight, but should he ever feel compelled to don that Federal blue, Jeremiah would pray with intense fervency that he never faced his brother across a field of battle. Even if he were not otherwise reluctant to fight, that horrible possibility alone was a terrific deterrent.

Standing, Jeremiah shoved his hands into his pockets and directed his feet homeward. If he did fight with the Federal Army, it was more than likely that he would encounter others he knew and respected on the battlefield.

It was reported that in the month of May six hundred Marylanders had been sworn into service in the Confederate Army and a quarter of the officers at the Naval Academy in Annapolis had resigned their positions to join the Confederate States Navy. Those remaining were detached and ordered to sea or transported to Fort Adams in Rhode Island, and the Annapolis campus had been converted into an army hospital for the United States.

To enlist on either side meant fighting against friends and family. As long as he could stay out of it, Jeremiah would. He simply wasn't in a hurry to risk his own life or to take that of another man.

Almost every week in the news there was a list of those killed or wounded in the most recent battle, all but one of which had been fought in nearby Virginia. The other had taken place in Missouri, securing that state for the Union and gaining control of the Missouri River.

As they settled at the table for breakfast, Jeremiah produced the letter for his father. Francis frowned as he read Charlie's brief missive. "Well, now we know something," he said quietly, handing the letter to Clara.

"He's still in Virginia," she commented softly. "Isn't that where most of the fighting is?"

Jeremiah nodded bleakly. "I'm afraid so."

"That's what he signed on for," Francis huffed as he reached for his mug of coffee. "To fight."

Chapter Six

Clara found breakfast had lodged in her throat. Swallowing down a gulp of cold milk, she tried to shake off the fingers of dread closing around her neck. But she had no words of comfort to give herself. They were living in perilous times.

No sooner was breakfast finished than Phoebe announced the arrival of a visitor. It was Jeremiah's friend, Will Downes. He was broad shouldered and tan from working the fields, and Clara found him a friendly and likeable fellow.

Sitting on the back porch with a glass of lemonade in his hand, Will announced, "The soldiers took the five kegs of powder left in the Courthouse. Somehow they got wind of the thirty kegs that mysteriously disappeared before their arrival."

"Mysteriously, eh?" Jeremiah chuckled. "I imagine it's no mystery who took them."

"I'm afraid not," Will agreed. "Madison Brown and John Palmer have been arrested."

Clara sipped her lemonade to keep her mouth from asking questions. She resolved to wait until their guest had left to request more information from her husband.

"Any other arrests?" Jeremiah questioned.

"Not that I'm aware of, but anyone suspected of sympathizing with the South has had their house ransacked and every weapon the soldiers could find was taken. Judge Carmichael and some others are submitting an appeal to the State Legislature in Frederick to stand against this infringement of liberty. And I don't blame them for it. After all, we *do* have the right to bear arms." He raked a hand through his hair, which had conformed to the shape of the hat now resting on a peg by the door. "It's a mess. I love this country. I don't want to see it go to the dogs. We're a nation—thirty-four states unified into one nation—and that's the way we should stay. And, it seems that the only way to remain whole is by force."

Jeremiah sighed wearily. "We've reached that fork in the road where to turn to the right or to the left is just as sure to lead us to destruction. There's no turning back. No way to make things right."

Listening to the resignation in her husband's voice, Clara felt any lingering hope she may have clung to sinking. She felt it sinking down into the pit of her stomach, turning into a lead weight of fear.

Will agreed with Jeremiah, "That's right. It's too late now. The South is proud. They'll have to take a beating before they'll surrender and come back like a dog with its tail between its legs, begging to be readmitted to the Union. It shouldn't take more than six months, but then we'll still need to settle the issue of slavery."

"If each state were free to decide, there'd be no need to fight over it," Jeremiah reminded him.

"You have to forgive my New England roots," Will laughed good-naturedly. "We're abolitionists at heart. I know you don't mistreat your slaves, and most don't, but it's the matter of regarding a human being as property. It goes against the laws of God."

Jeremiah shrugged in reply. "Inequality and class distinctions have existed since time immemorial. No one will ever change that. Not even abolitionists and philanthropists. It's just the nature of this world."

"Well, I guess there may be some truth in that," Will Downes agreed, "but I guess we feel an obligation to try. No reason why that black man out there," he pointed to Henry in the yard, "shouldn't have a chance to own property and raise his own crops and livestock. As a slave, he'll spend his whole life working hard, only to die with nothing to his name. Just because his skin is dark."

Jeremiah countered, "It's the only life he knows. It's how his parents and grandparents lived before him. He has a roof over his head, clothes on his back, more than enough food to fill his belly, and the weight of responsibility lies on *our* shoulders. He does his part, and we provide all he needs. I don't know that he's as unhappy with his lot as you abolitionists suppose."

Will smiled in reply, a crooked half smile, as he answered, "And I'm not so sure he's as content as you slave-holders suppose."

Jeremiah extended his hand with a conciliatory laugh. "Fair enough," he conceded as Will clasped his hand. Watching the exchange, Clara wished that the dissenting factions in authority could disagree as amiably as these two men.

After Will had taken his leave, Clara turned to Jeremiah with curiosity. "He said thirty kegs of powder were missing. Isn't that a lot of gunpowder to keep in the courthouse?"

"It's part of the supply Captain Emory brought back from Balti—" Realizing his inadvertent disclosure, Jeremiah suddenly clamped his jaw shut. But it was too late, and a guilty look crept over his face.

"Oh." Clara might not have thought any more about it, except her husband looked as if he had been caught. "I didn't know about that. You didn't tell me on purpose, didn't you?"

Jeremiah took her hands in his, his expression apologetic. "I'm sorry. Charlie said there was concern that it might be needed to defend the town, and I didn't want you to worry."

"I appreciate that. But I'd rather know what's coming so I can be prepared for it," she replied steadily.

"I'll try to remember that," Jeremiah drew her against his chest and dropped a kiss onto the top of her head where her hair was parted evenly down the middle. "I want to take care of you in whatever ways I can. But everything is changing so fast. I'm not sure what's expected of me anymore. Not just with you, but... my country."

Clara closed her eyes, resting her forehead against his neck. There was nothing to say. He was considering enlisting in the Federal Army. He was letting her know in advance so she could begin to prepare herself for it. *Bravery*, she reminded herself. *I will not beg him to stay. I will not cry.*

"I'm sure you will find your answers," she replied, though her throat felt constricted as she pushed the words through. "In time," she added, encouraging him in the same way she had proposed that they delay Charlie's enlistment, by asking only that he wait and give the matter further consideration. Of course, her tactic hadn't succeeded with Charlie, and she suspected it wouldn't work with his older brother either.

"I'm sure you're right," Jeremiah agreed, his voice solemn against her ear. His arms tightened around her waist, and Clara clung to him, praying desperately that this rebellion would end before her husband felt compelled to join the fray. And that Charlie would be safe, wherever he might be.

The visitation of the Union soldiers had apparently worked its magic in inspiring the men of the county to patriotism in the face of insurrection. A second company of ninety men was formed under the Stars and Stripes, calling themselves the "Maryland Zouaves." Jeremiah explained that the Zouaves were a light infantry military unit inspired by the French. They employed different tactics than the traditional infantry, marching in open-order formations with several feet between them, rather than touching elbows in close formation, and at double-time cadence.

To reward their loyalty, the U.S. Government supplied the Maryland Zouaves with Hall's breech-loading carbines with bayonet attachment. Their uniform consisted of Navy-blue flannel shirts trimmed with black, loose fitting red flannel trousers which buttoned below the knee, black leggings and dark blue caps trimmed with red. They were a dashing group as they marched briskly down the streets of Centreville, rifles resting against their shoulders.

When Jeremiah first mentioned their establishment, Clara feared he intended to join them. She was relieved when he never suggested any such idea. But the presence of the two opposing companies, the Smallwood Rifles and the Maryland Zouaves, only sharpened the awareness of the great division growing wider and deeper, not only in Maryland, but in Queen Anne's County.

On the first of July, the Union's 8th Massachusetts regiment surrounded Captain S. Ogle Tilghman's house on the Wye River, demanding he relinquish the guns in his possession for use by the Smallwood Rifles. Tilghman refused and was arrested.

Sitting on the back porch to feel the afternoon breeze, Clara sat with Phoebe on the wicker divan weaving baskets for use in the kitchen. Lena sat cross-legged on the floor, attentive to her task.

"You all right, Missus Clara? You lookin' a bit peaked to me," Phoebe observed.

"Oh Phoebe, I'm so worried," Clara confessed, grateful for a feminine ear to confide in. "Charlie's off fighting with the Rebels, and any day Jeremiah's going to join the Federal Army. I feel sick with worry. I wish it was just a bad dream, a nightmare, and I could wake up and life would be normal and happy again. That sounds so foolish, I know. And I can hardly say that to the menfolk, but I hate this constant black cloud hovering over our heads, waiting at any moment to unleash a furious storm on all of us."

"Now, that don't sound foolish to me," Phoebe's dark slender hands moved adeptly as she weaved the reeds over and under into the shape of a basket. "Sound like what any woman gonna wish. And if a man had any good sense in his head, he wish for it too. But you right that it ain't gonna do no good wishin'. If dat war ain't ended soon, Mistah Jer'miah gonna join up for sure. And you just gonna have to be strong and let him go. We gonna take good care of you, Mamie and me, don't you worry none."

Lena looked up from her lap to add, "And me too, Missus Clara," with a sweet smile. Her black hair was braided into tight rows against her scalp, accentuating her round forehead and wide brown eyes.

Clara reached out and grasped the girl's hand. "Thank you," she smiled, tears glistening in her eyes.

Lifting her chin, Clara admonished herself for her weakness. She wasn't the only young wife in the nation who would have to let her husband go. She could see the same fear mirrored in the eyes of all the women at church on Sunday, worrying over husbands, sons, and brothers. They had come to depend on the men in their lives, but very soon they might have to learn how to live without them.

At least until they came back... *if* they came back. Quickly Clara shut her mind to this morbid consideration. Jeremiah hadn't even enlisted yet. Today's troubles were enough without worrying over what might come in the weeks or months ahead. *One day at a time*, she instructed herself sternly. *Just take your troubles one day at a time*.

~

Since Charlie had run off to enlist with the Rebels, their marriage had suffered and Jeremiah knew it was his own fault. He was preoccupied and withdrawn, churning over his own internal arguments and concerns. Seeing Clara so forlorn, Jeremiah immediately regretted not only leaving her to deal with her worries alone but undoubtedly adding to them.

He committed to spending time with her, time focused on enjoying her company and not on mulling over politics and loyalties. But the farm demanded his time and by the day's end, Jeremiah was exhausted and unable to produce the necessary energy for light-hearted conversation.

"Tomorrow," he told her as he slid beneath the sheets, his mind humming with fatigue, "let's take a day and go into town. We can visit shops or simply walk. I think it would do us good to just have time together."

Sitting at her vanity brushing her hair, glimmering like bronze in the pale lamplight, Clara's expression softened. "I would like that," she admitted. "I feel like you're a thousand miles away even when you're next to me."

"I'm sorry," he ran a weary hand over his face. "I don't mean to neglect you."

Setting the ivory brush aside, Clara approached the bed as she plaited her hair. "You don't need to apologize. I know you're being pulled in many directions. But I do miss you... I miss the easy laughter and conversation we used to share." She sighed as she secured the braid, "I suppose those days are gone for good."

"Not for good," Jeremiah hastened to assure her, pulling back the wedding ring quilt and patting her side of the bed. "Just for a little while."

Clara stood, pausing to retrieve the oil lamp and carry it to the nightstand before joining Jeremiah beneath the quilts. Then turning the key, she plunged the room into darkness before nestling into his shoulder. Jeremiah pressed a kiss onto her forehead, wrapping his arms around her slender form and holding her tightly. He wanted to share a hushed conversation in the shadows with her, but his eyelids felt weighted with lead and before he could speak he had fallen into a gray fog of sleep.

In the morning, their plans were disrupted by a steady downpour of rain and skies obscured by gloomy clouds. Clara agreed that they would wait for the following day, providing that the weather cleared. With a disappointed sigh, she left Jeremiah to review the ledger with his father while she returned to the bedroom for an afternoon nap.

The weather cooperated, and the next morning dawned clear and golden, the sky a flawless powder blue stretching over the summer foliage of the trees and the green stalks of corn growing in the fields. Jeremiah was pleased to see a smile on his wife's face as he helped her into the open carriage. Today, he vowed, he would leave their burdens behind and celebrate that they were still together and there was still peace in Queen Anne's County.

Clara's brown eyes had a sparkle in them as she settled her lavender skirt around her, mindful of the full crinoline beneath. A straw bonnet covered her hair, accented with flowers in the front and a plaid lavender bow in the back. Her hands, covered in white cotton gloves, were folded primly in her lap.

No sooner had Eli flicked the reins and Nan pulled the carriage down the hill toward town, than Jeremiah watched her hands flutter with animated gestures as she came to life with conversation. He couldn't focus on her words, but Jeremiah felt the tense muscles of his shoulders relax as he listened to the rise and fall of her voice and watched the rapidly changing expressions on her lovely face as she chattered about the weather and which kinds of flowers were in bloom. He'd forgotten just how much he enjoyed being with Clara, the ease of their companionship, until this very moment. Leaning back into the cushioned seat, Jeremiah drank in the pleasant picture she presented.

"What would you like to do?" he asked as she felt silent, the wheels rolling over the dirt road of Turners Lane and onto the crushed shell of Commerce Street.

"I'm happy just to have you to myself," she answered, the smile she offered making Jeremiah wish they were truly alone. "Could we take the steamer *Balloon* to Annapolis for the afternoon?"

"Whatever your heart desires," Jeremiah answered, leaping from the seat facing her to the empty place on the cushion beside her, bunching her voluminous skirts into a mountain of fabric on her lap. He cherished the sound of her giggle as she ineffectually attempted to smooth out the exaggerated curve of her crinoline.

"Jeremiah Turner! We *are* in public!" she reminded him, but her stern tone was unconvincing and punctuated by a pleased smile. Lifting her hand to his lips, Jeremiah kissed it and elicited another giggle with the flirtatious wink he offered.

Eli turned the carriage onto Academy Lane en route to

Liberty Street, urging Nan to carry them toward the Wharf by way of Broadway Avenue. As they approached the white-washed brick structure of the courthouse, Jeremiah's attention was captured by a group of men standing on the lawn in front of it.

William Downes was among them, and spotting Jeremiah, he flagged him down with a frantic wave.

Eli obeyed Jeremiah's instruction and pulled the carriage over. A throng of townsfolk was clustered in front of the newspaper office, spilling onto the street and the Courthouse Green. They seemed to be intently studying the latest edition of the paper or engrossed in conversation about it. One woman sobbed into her daughter's shoulder.

"What is it?" Jeremiah demanded as Will handed him the paper.

"There's been a battle near Bull Run Creek in Manassas, Virginia. The casualties are still coming in. Losses were high on both sides. Your brother's regiment was brought in by train with the reinforcements from Johnston's Army in the Shenandoah Valley."

Jeremiah's heart squeezed with fear as his eyes scanned the long list of dead and wounded men. It stuttered to a brief stop, then slowly resumed beating as he realized Charlie's name was not among them. "The casualties are still coming in?" he repeated, afraid to release the sigh of relief which he longed to exhale.

Will nodded. "The clean-up may take days," he admitted grimly, then glanced regretfully at Clara as the full brunt of his words soaked in. She paled and swallowed. "I think the tide has turned for the Rebels," he continued gravely. "This isn't going to be over in just a few months."

Jeremiah nodded as if he understood, but his mind was reeling. The incomplete list of casualties occupied two full pages of the paper. He tried to imagine what the clean-up from a battle of this proportion would look like, but his brain refused to produce such an image.

"I hope he's all right," Will left Jeremiah with the paper as he rejoined the group of men gathered on the Courthouse Green.

Turning to Clara, Jeremiah asked, "Do you want to—"

"Let's just go home," she answered before he could complete the question. The twinkle in her eye had been replaced with a stricken look of dread. He slipped his arm around her waist and pulled her close.

Once home, Jeremiah sent Clara inside to change while he accompanied Eli to the barn to saddle Archie. Then, carrying the newspaper, he rode the path around the perimeter of the field in search of his father. He found Francis with Joe and Henry, hoeing the weeds at the far end of the property.

Immediately upon observing Jeremiah's attire, still dressed from his outing with Clara, Francis knew something was wrong. Dropping the hoe, he ran toward Jeremiah, his thick white brows shadowing worried eyes as he demanded, "Is it Charlie?"

Jeremiah swung down from the saddle, answering as he did, "He could still be all right. His unit was sent to fight in Manassas. It's the bloodiest battle we've seen yet..." He opened the paper to show his father the long list of casualties. "Charlie's name isn't here, but they still haven't finished bringing in all the men."

Francis opened the newspaper reluctantly. "Who claims the victory?"

"The Confederacy."

Francis squinted at him uncertainly. "The Rebels won?" he repeated, as if unsure he had heard the answer correctly.

"I haven't read it, but that's what Will Downes told me."

Heads together, father and son read over the newspaper reporter's account of the battle. It was clearly an imprecise and disjointed retelling of the event, making it difficult to piece together exactly what had happened.

It seemed that the Union had the initial advantage, but were eventually beaten back and forced into retreat with the arrival of

Johnston's reinforcements.

Removing his hat, Francis ran a callused hand through his thinning white hair. "After all that boasting, the Federals were soundly beaten," he shook his head. "Pride goes before the fall."

Returning to the house, Jeremiah found Clara sitting pensively on the settee in the parlor. Against the red damask, she was white as a sheet. Jeremiah joined her, covering her clasped hands with one of his own.

Her expression was solemn as she looked up at him. "The Rebels won. What happens now?"

"More fighting," he answered with a bitter sigh.

Chapter Seven

Clara shifted her position on the hard wooden pew. Behind the pulpit, the preacher pursed his lips as he continued to deliver a message he knew was both unpopular and uncomfortable. Had he been the church's regular minister, his message would have certainly decreased the number of bodies in the pews in the weeks to come, as well as the money left in the offering plate. But everyone present knew he was only there for the day.

Reverend Miller, whose preaching they were usually blessed to hear, had taken a brief leave of absence to visit his daughter in Tennessee after the birth of her child. The Conference had sent Reverend Webster to fill in, and there was no doubt the man was a Yankee. He unapologetically denounced the practice of slave-holding, which if it counted as a sin, more than ninety percent of the congregation was guilty of committing.

Glancing around the sanctuary, Clara observed the varied responses of those in attendance. Most appeared outraged while some studied their laps intently, and only a small handful nodded their heads in zealous agreement.

The sermon came in the wake of the Battle of Bull Run. With the dead being numbered around eight hundred and fifty, the total of wounded men at well over two and a half thousand, and over a thousand men still missing or captured, the war was at the forefront of everyone's thoughts. There was still talk of secession, though with Maryland firmly in the grip of Federal soldiers, it no longer seemed like a real possibility. And with the defeat of the Union Army came the call for more volunteers to stop the rebellion.

Since one of the key points of dissention between the North and South was the issue of slavery, it was a subject which the Reverend felt must be addressed during his time in Centreville. His scriptural text was Philemon, a letter written by the apostle Paul to a slave-holder regarding a runaway slave.

Reverend Webster's booming voice echoed off the plaster walls and wooden beams as he read from the open Bible in front of him about Philemon's reputation as a man of faith and love. The Reverend explained that it was because of this reputation Paul asked a great favor of the slave-holder. Paul was sending the slave back to his master, but not in accordance to any Fugitive Slave Law or to be punished for having escaped. Paul challenges Philemon to welcome the slave as he would welcome Paul, not as a slave, but as a "brother beloved."

The Yankee Reverend peered up at the congregation over the rim of his wire glasses. "Yes, the slave was sent back to his master. But the master was instructed to do more than merely treat his slave with kindness. He was instructed to *love* the slave as a brother. Jesus said, *'By this shall all men know that ye are my disciples, if ye have love one for another.'*

"Paul's request was that Philemon accept this runaway slave back into his household as an equal. If we claim to know God, we must treat people with love, not hold them as property to be bought and sold, to perform labor so that we may profit by it."

Clara's jaw slipped open a little at the bold statement. As if in response, Reverend Webster continued, "As this may very well be the last time I darken the doorsteps of this church, I want to say that we are all—every one of us—sinners. One sin is not greater than another. And forgiveness is free to all who ask. So if you are here today in agreement with me, search your heart for that which you must repent of, whether you are showing love to those who do hold humans in bondage.

The Reverend removed his glasses and placed them on the pages of the Bible. "And to those who own slaves, I challenge you to consider the words of William Lloyd Garrison: '*Enslave the liberty of but one human being and the liberties of the world are put in peril.*'"

At the conclusion of the service, Reverend Webster took position at the exit of the sanctuary to shake hands with the parishioners on their way out. After being snubbed repeatedly, he finally folded his hands in front of him and offered a nod to the few who bothered to glance his way.

Clara nodded politely as she brushed past, afraid to hesitate for fear of the censure she would receive if seen associating with him, though her conscience chided her for such poor manners. She noted that the preacher held his head high, apparently undisturbed by the cold reception. Clara suspected he had anticipated such a reaction.

Even within the church, the conclusion on slavery was determined by geographical influence. The Northern abolitionists in the Methodist Church had officially denounced the practice of slave-holding the year previous, and the General Conference had voted to add to the *Book of Discipline* a new chapter which outlined this position. The local church however, whose congregation associated with the South, had reacted by calling a meeting to evaluate this declaration and determined that it was anti-scriptural, and therefore, null and void.

The committee which thus voted, of which Centerville's Reverend Miller was chairman, resolved that "*the system of slavery as it prevails among us is in its main features but the due degree of subordination of an inferior race to a superior race and that while the two races exist together it is the best adapted to promote the temporal and spiritual welfare of both and particularly of the inferior race.*"

Clara had no doubt that the Yankee Reverend would be the topic of conversation in every household represented at the church that morning, and she was curious what the Turner men would have to say about him and his abolitionist message.

"Discretion is the better part of valor," Francis grumbled as the carriage rolled over the streets on the way home. "I don't begrudge the Reverend his opinion, but I would say he chose the wrong place to share it."

Next to him on the seat, facing Clara, Jeremiah nodded his agreement. "I don't think anyone would hurt a clergyman, but he might want to keep a lookout over his shoulder."

Clara mulled over the sermon quietly. What if Reverend Webster was right and not Reverend Miller? What if slavery *was* an abomination in the eyes of Providence, as the abolitionists insisted? It was a disturbing thought.

In support of slavery, Reverend Miller had pointed his congregation to Leviticus twenty-five, which not only granted permission for the Israelites to purchase and own slaves, but specifically referred to them as property. There were numerous passages throughout the Bible which supported the assertion that slavery was a God-given social institution. *"Servants, be obedient to your masters…" "Masters, give unto your servants that which is just and equal…"*

But the story of Philemon and the runaway slave had planted a seed of doubt in Clara's mind. Yes, Paul had sent the slave back to his master—validating Philemon's ownership of him—but he had asked the master to treat him the same way he would treat Paul, as a brother and not as a slave. It wasn't a conclusive argument, but it merited consideration.

Watching Mamie and Phoebe quietly set the table for the afternoon meal, Clara wondered what they thought of the war and the argument over slavery. She marveled at the good fortune which had allowed her to be born as the daughter of George Collins, with white skin and a privileged future.

Her husband had told Will that inequality and class distinctions had always existed and always would exist. But did that make it right if one had the power to change it?

And, if it could be changed, was war the best means of accomplishing it? So many opposing ideas were circulating that Clara sometimes wondered what the war was really about. Some, like Reverend Webster, seemed of the opinion that the Confederacy was fighting to preserve slavery and the Northern states to abolish it. But Charlie had never once mentioned it as the reason he'd enlisted with the Rebels. It had been about freedom, about preserving the rights of the state, keeping the Federal Government as an umbrella authority and not a dictator.

And no matter what the cause of the war, was it worth the loss of life—almost nine hundred men in one day?

Thankfully, in the days following the battle as the list of casualties poured in, Charlie's name remained absent. They hoped to receive a letter affirming his safety soon, even though there was no reason to doubt it.

If Jeremiah had seemed distant and preoccupied before the battle of Bull Run, he was even more so afterward. Clara couldn't begrudge him the ruin of their day out together, but she was bitterly disappointed. He was still at home with her, but she felt as if he was slowly slipping away in front of her eyes. How could she miss him so much when he was lying next to her in bed?

She wished there was a way to tie him to her, to keep him close. But what man wished to be tied by his wife's apron strings? Clara had no choice but to stand beside him in silence and watch her marriage and her world slowly disintegrate into mere ashes of the dream she had once cherished.

The summer days stretched on. The July humidity dampened her dress with sweat, frizzed the loose tendrils around her face, and brought on an acute case of irritability. The heat from the cast iron stove in the small kitchen as they worked to store fruits and vegetables for the winter did nothing to alleviate it.

Mamie seemed immune to the sweltering discomfort, standing over the stove humming as she stirred the paraffin wax that would be used to seal the glass jars. A large pan of lima beans rested on the table between Phoebe and Clara, who spooned its contents into the containers. Lena worked with

Mamie to fill the jars before screwing the zinc lids on tightly and setting them aside.

The tomatoes and carrots had already been canned and stored in the cellar. Next week they would prepare the peach preserves. Using her apron to dry the sweat beading her upper lip, Clara reached for another empty jar to fill.

"You go on out this kitchen an' get a break, Missus Clara. Get you a drink of water," Mamie instructed in her maternal way. "You look 'bout ready to faint."

"I'll wait until we're finished," Clara insisted. She wished she could be insulted by Mamie's fussing as if she was weaker than the Negro slaves, but they appeared to be enduring the misery far better than she was.

"I swear I waited all winter for spring to come, and now all I can think about is the fall," she laughed at her own foolishness. "I guess every season has its worries."

"Now, I don't know about that," Mamie argued, her round face glistening. "I don't remember hearing you complain in the spring."

Clara smiled weakly, but lacked the energy for a smart retort. She wished she could pause to take a long drink of cool water, but she didn't want to stop until the other women did. Even young Lena offered no complaint as sweat trailed from her temples to her neck.

When at last the day's work was complete, Clara felt a twinge of guilt leaving the women to prepare supper as she retreated to her bedroom to freshen up. She sighed as she mopped her face and neck with a damp handkerchief, relishing the faint breeze which stirred the white lace curtains at the window.

With a sigh, she sank down into the blue velvet armchair by the window. The wedding ring quilt on the bed reminded her of home. Her mother and sister had made it for her as a wedding gift. Against the white background, the circles of colored fabric stood out in cheerful relief.

Naomi and Jane had come calling to inquire after Charlie once the news had spread of his presence at the battle. There was no mention of her brother enlisting, and Clara hoped that such a thought never entered his mind. Although rumor had it that the Rebels won the battle only because of disorganization and miscommunication in the newly formed Union Army, the victory still bolstered the confidence of those who believed in the Southern cause.

Afraid she might drift off if she remained sitting, Clara pulled a clean dress from the armoire and stepped behind the dressing screen. Phoebe appeared just in time to assist with the buttons and help her into an airy muslin the color of jade. Once dressed, Clara sat before the mirror at the oak vanity. Unpinning Clara's auburn hair, Phoebe ran a brush through the frizz until it could be twisted back into a sleek bun. The result of her efforts was rewarding. Clara looked more like a pretty young woman than a weary kitchen maid.

When the men came in from cultivating the fields, they looked even more wilted than Clara had felt, and dust and soil clung to the dampness of their skin and clothes. Clara waited in the parlor while they went upstairs to wash and change. She wished that just today she could have supper alone with her husband and find something to laugh about.

But as they descended the stairs, and Clara rounded the corner to greet them, she noticed a newspaper in her father-in-law's hand. To expect the conversation to include anything but politics and the war was clearly hopeless.

"I hope Reverend Webster reads today's paper," Francis commented wryly as he turned the page.

"Why's that?" Jeremiah wondered, his damp hair falling over his forehead.

"Here, read it. Congress has made it official: the war *isn't* about slavery." Francis passed The Centreville Times across the table to his son.

Jeremiah's thick brows drew together in curiosity. "The

Crittenden-Johnson Resolution," he read aloud. "I take it that this is supposed to be some sort of compromise. Meant, no doubt, to deter any more Southern states from leaving the Union."

"You guessed it," Francis replied wryly.

"What does it say?" Clara wondered.

Jeremiah cleared his throat, then read: *"'That in this national emergency, Congress, banishing all feelings of mere passion or resentment, will recollect only its duty to the whole country; that this war is not waged on their part in any spirit of oppression, or for any purpose of conquest or subjugation, or purpose of overthrowing or interfering with the rights or established institutions of those States, but to defend and maintain the supremacy of the Constitution, and to preserve the Union with all the dignity, equality, and rights of the several States unimpaired; and that as soon as these objects are accomplished the war ought to cease.'"*

"The 'established institutions' mean slavery, right?" she verified.

"Yes, exactly," he nodded. "They're clarifying their position, making it clear that the Federal Government is fighting only to preserve the Union. As soon as the errant states return like contrite run-aways, war will cease. Slavery has nothing to do with it."

"The abolitionists will never let this stand," Francis asserted. "Mark my words."

"I thought Lincoln was an abolitionist," Clara commented.

Francis laughed dryly. "He's a politician, my dear."

"Everything in politics serves a purpose," her husband agreed. "This resolution is meant to dissuade the states sitting on the fence. But to those who've already left, it means less than the paper it's printed on. It doesn't promise States Rights. It merely clarifies that to the Federal Government, the purpose of this war is to restore unity."

"Isn't *war* an odd way to bring about unity?"

"Beautiful and wise," Jeremiah winked at her.

Clara blushed, appreciating the praise. "But I thought you agreed with them?"

At his father's scowl, Jeremiah was quick to explain. "I never said I agreed. I believe in States Rights. But I also believe in preserving the Union as it stands, with thirty-four states. Well, I guess it's thirty-five now, since West Virginia's been admitted."

"But killing one another won't bring the nation together!" Clara insisted.

"No. I don't think there's any way to bring the nation together now," Francis agreed. "We're between a rock and a hard place."

Jeremiah released a heavy sigh. "The fact is, the government can coerce *legal* unity by force even if it can't command peace among its citizens. The states came together in a sacred compact to become one unified nation. We're far too diverse to ever agree on matters of religion or politics, but if we stay together, we're stronger than we are alone. Who says Britain or France will never wage war on us again?"

Clara bit her lip. She didn't want to contradict or disrespect her husband, especially in front of his father.

But Jeremiah leaned forward and placed a hand over hers. "What do you think?" he asked gently.

"I just don't understand why it would be such a terrible thing to recognize the Confederate States as a sovereign nation. If Britain or France ever wished to attack, we could join together against them in an alliance of the two American nations. A Union sealed with the blood of its own citizens can never be truly one," she declared passionately.

"For the record," Francis jerked a thumb at her, "I agree with your lovely wife."

Jeremiah leaned back in his chair. "I think the war could have been averted many times over. But it wasn't. The rightness of it has become almost irrelevant. Now it's a question of whether or not you regard the joining together of the States as a binding contract or not. And that is all."

"And you do?" Francis pushed.

"I do," Jeremiah admitted slowly. "Come what may."

Chapter Eight

The sun beat down on Jeremiah's shoulders through the sweat-soaked fabric of his shirt. August had been hot, but September was hotter still. He felt as if he were inside an oven, baking like a loaf of bread in a cast iron chamber heated by blazing fire.

The cornfield was scorched, the tips of the plants curling beneath the burning rays of the sun. It hadn't rained in over a week, with temperatures rising daily. If the crops were to be saved, they would need to be watered. The men divided into teams of two and worked from one end of the farm to the other, hoping to offer a healing drink to the plants withering in the fields.

No breeze stirred the green stalks topped with yellow tassels, the ears of corn hanging limply to them, glossy strands of silk dangling from the green husks. Jeremiah carried two buckets of water, suspended on either side of a wooden yoke balanced across his shoulders. With a wooden dipper, he poured water onto the parched soil at the base of the stalks.

Jeremiah paused to wipe the sweat from his eyes with the back of his hand. His neck and shoulders ached from the weight of the yoke, but even in his mind, he refused to complain. He wondered where Charlie was and what he was doing at that very moment. He wondered if Charlie would rather trade places with him, for despite the discomfort, at least he was safe.

No end to this wretched civil war was in sight. Two more battles had been fought since Bull Run, both of them attributed as Confederate victories. One of them had occurred in Virginia, the other in Missouri. It was the first major battle which had been fought west of the Mississippi.

The Federal Government was beginning to realize that they had severely underestimated their opponents from the South. President Lincoln signed a bill providing for the enlistment of another 500,000 men for up to three years of service, while coincidentally abolishing flogging as a punishment for disobedient soldiers.

He also issued the Revenue Act to fund the war. This act imposed a tax upon all citizens, requiring the payment of three percent on all incomes above eight hundred dollars, *"whether such income is derived from any kind of property, or from any profession, trade, employment, or vocation carried on in the United States or elsewhere, or from any other source whatever…"*

The tension in Maryland was steadily building, and in Queen Anne's County opposition to the war was rising just as steadily. On September third, a meeting had been held at the Courthouse to draft resolutions which would be presented by elected delegates at the State Convention in Baltimore on the tenth. The meeting was well attended, the overwhelming feeling being sympathy for the Confederacy.

The resolutions adopted at this meeting denounced the Federal Government for its violation of the Constitution, *"the suppression of the freedom of speech and of the press, the arrest and imprisonment of citizens without process of law, the search of private houses and seizure of private papers by military force, the denial of the privilege of habeas corpus and acts of a kindred character, all manifesting but one purpose and tending to one end, the subversion of civil liberty and the erection of military despotism."*

They also demanded that those citizens unlawfully imprisoned should be released, or if found guilty of a crime, handed over to the civil authorities for sentencing. Perhaps most importantly, it declared uncompromising disapproval *"of the present war with its train of ruinous taxation and destruction of life and property"* while expressing the desire for *"peace with the Confederate States on honorable terms."*

Jeremiah shooed a fly from his face, thumbing a salty droplet of sweat from his eye. He and Will were not alone in their favor of the Union, but they were by far the minority. While he didn't appreciate the income tax any more than anyone else, he understood why the President felt compelled to issue it. Lincoln loved his country the way Jeremiah loved Laurel Hill, with pride and commitment and uncompromising loyalty.

Extreme circumstances required difficult decisions, and every action Lincoln took from now on would be with the sole intention of preserving the Union, of preventing it from being fractured into separate nations.

After seeing how Baltimore and Annapolis had been secured by General Butler, Jeremiah wondered what the continued protest from the Eastern Shore would bring. That there would be a consequence, he was certain. The government had a right to demand loyalty and a responsibility to secure its territories, and the spirit of rebellion in Maryland would most certainly be quashed.

Jeremiah had been invited to attend a private gathering at Will's house in the evening, after supper. He had yet to tell Clara. He knew she would suspect the purpose of the meeting, and he preferred to wait until the last minute to save her the day spent fretting.

He too suspected the purpose of the meeting: to discuss with other supporters of the Union the merits of joining the Federal Army at this particular time. And Jeremiah was unsure what his answer would be. On the one hand, he felt that the sooner the matter was resolved, the better for the nation and all its citizens—North and South. On the other hand, he felt a strong sense of duty to remain at home and share the responsibilities of the farm. They were already one son short, and Jeremiah dreaded leaving his father to carry the burden alone.

And then there was Clara.

"I'll be going out this evening," he informed her as they took their places at the supper table. "I'll likely be out late."

"Oh," she said softly, her brown eyes searching his. "Where are you going?"

"Will's." There was no need to say more.

Clara nodded slowly, then quietly placed her napkin in her lap and directed her attention to the plate before her on the table. Jeremiah glanced up at his father. Francis wore an expression of regret and resignation. Supper was finished in strained silence.

By horseback, the Downes' farm was an hour from Laurel Hill. Jeremiah followed the narrow path between the fields, forded Gravel Run Stream, and continued through the forest until he reached Church Hill Road and followed it the remainder of the way. By the time he reached his destination the sky was dusky purple, tinged with a band of crimson along the horizon.

Will welcomed Jeremiah into the house and invited him to join the men gathered in the smoke-filled study. He accepted a glass of whiskey and took the empty armchair next to the desk. On the sofa, he recognized Amos Mosley and James Cecil. A third man lounged against the bookcase, vaguely familiar but still unknown.

"I assume we know one other, but allow me to perform the introductions," Will said, closing the door of the study and moving to take position in the leather chair behind the heavy mahogany desk.

"This is Sam Price," he indicated the man leaning against the volumes of history and agriculture which filled the bookcase.

William Downes was thirty years old, with sandy hair thinning at the front, a ready smile and a firm handshake. Having inherited his uncle's gift for oration, he conducted the introductions quickly before proceeding with the purpose of the meeting. Cigar in one hand, a glass of whiskey in the other, he began his speech.

"I have invited each of you here tonight because I have been led to believe that you share my desire to uphold the Union, having proclaimed your loyalty to this great nation, the United States of America." Nods and grunts accompanied his statement. Will continued, "Countless men from the Eastern Shore have crossed the Potomac River to join the Rebels in Virginia. Maryland—and especially Queen Anne's County—have positioned themselves against the Federal Government, a stance which will not be looked upon favorably by those in authority. I propose that it is our duty to uphold the honor of our families and to preserve the good name of our County by enlisting in the Federal Army as proof of our commitment to our country."

Amos and Sam nodded vigorously, while James leaned forward and rested his elbows on his knees, studying the cracks in his fingernails with great interest. Jeremiah nodded his agreement, although with far less enthusiasm.

"I intend," Will continued, "to enlist in the Eastern Shore Infantry now recruiting in Cambridge. I would like for you to join me in this noble cause."

Stepping forward, Sam declared, "You have my pledge. When will we go?"

"I'll go with you," Amos assented, his voice strong and certain.

Jeremiah noticed that the only other married man in the room shared the same hesitancy he did. James straightened, his hands resting casually on his thighs, but he said nothing.

Looking from one face to another, gauging the response of each man, Will added, "This is a critical decision. If you choose against it, there will be no hard feelings. Unless of course, you join the Rebels," he flashed his teeth in a grin. "I say we think on it and meet again next week. That gives us time to be sure of our decisions and to prepare our families should we choose to fight."

Jeremiah hadn't realized how tense he was until he felt his shoulders relax. He'd feared he might be cornered into defending his reluctance—not for the cause, but the timing. He accepted a second glass of whiskey as the recently adopted resolutions were analyzed and discussed.

"The assertion that Lincoln's suspension of habeas corpus is unconstitutional is unfounded," Amos was saying. "There is a suspension clause which states that *'the privilege of the writ of habeas corpus shall not be suspended, unless when in cases of rebellion or invasion the public safety may require it.'* Which means that the President was well within his rights."

"And as for the other accusations, what is the government in place for if not to govern those under its authority? Freedom of speech is an admirable ideal, but when lies and civil unrest are being fostered, there's a time to step in and say, 'Enough!'" Sam added. "The President and Congress have been entrusted by the majority with the power to run this country as they deem best."

"The key word there is 'majority,'" Will agreed. "There will never be a President, Congress, or governmental system which pleases everyone. But once one is in place, it is our duty to defend it."

Jeremiah lifted his glass. "To the greatest country on earth!"

"Here, here!" echoed around him as the men lifted their glasses to salute the United States of America.

Riding back to Laurel Hill, the sky was black as velvet, lit dimly by a crescent moon and a spattering of brilliant stars. Jeremiah followed the road into town rather than taking the forest trail in complete darkness. The sound of chirping crickets and humming cicadas filled the night, hiding in the grass below him or above him in the trees. Archie seemed to know the way, and Jeremiah held limply to the reins as his mind churned over Will's proposal.

Despite the promise that refusal to enlist would not be met with hard feelings, it still seemed to Jeremiah more of a challenge than an invitation. It wasn't as if the idea hadn't been weaving its way around in his mind for weeks, but now it seemed an immediate decision was before him. If like Will, Sam, and Amos, enlisting in the Federal Army would not require him to leave his wife or to risk facing his brother on the battlefield, the choice would have been far easier made. But Jeremiah did have a wife he dearly loved at Laurel Hill, and a brother who was fighting with the Rebels.

Approaching the bridge on Church Hill Road which spanned the narrow Gravel Run Stream, the chirrup of "peeper" frogs filled the night with their shrill and jubilant chorus. As Archie's hooves clumped over the wooden boards, the frogs ceased their song and the night immediately plunged into silence. Jeremiah listened as he plodded up the hill toward Turners Lane for the peeping to resume.

The church bells from the Episcopal Church on Liberty Street rang out the midnight hour as Jeremiah unsaddled Archie in the barn by the yellow circle of light provided by the lantern. Rubbing his tired eyes, Jeremiah made his way into the house and up the stairs to the bedroom. He turned the heavy brass knob slowly, slipping into the room as quietly as possible. After pausing at the washstand to wipe the sweat from his face and neck, Jeremiah shed his clothing and carefully slid between the sheets.

Clara stirred, but did not awaken. In the moonlit shadows of the room, he could make out the contours of her frame beneath the quilt, her long braid standing out in contrast against the white pillow where she slept. Rising up onto his elbow, careful not to disturb her, Jeremiah gazed down at her tenderly. He studied the curve of her cheekbone, dark lashes fanning out against them, and the pert shape of her nose. Her lips were slightly parted as she breathed with the measured rhythm of the dreaming.

So far, most of the fighting had been in Virginia, though it was extending into Missouri and Kentucky. As the war waged on, it would continue to spread into others states, both to the north and south. No one would be safe. And if Centreville fell under fire and Jeremiah wasn't there to protect his wife, his father, or his home, how would he forgive himself?

He recalled the day Union soldiers had come to Laurel Hill to search for arms, or whatever else their mission had been. Clara had been terrified, turning to him for refuge and protection.

Would she forgive him if he left her at the farm alone with her father-in-law while he went off to war?

And what if he was killed in battle?

Jeremiah leaned back against the walnut frame of the headboard. He was exhausted, but sleep eluded him. Thoughts and questions chased one another around in his head like a fox chasing chickens in a henhouse. He had no military training. His only experience with a gun was hunting deer, squirrels, duck or wild turkey. Could he choose to stop the beating heart of another man? Would he be able to pull the trigger when it was asked of him, or would he stand there stupidly to be shot like a sitting duck on a pond?

Jeremiah loved his country, there was no question about that. But did he love it more than his wife—more than his own life, if it came to that? These were the questions that gave him pause. And then there was Charlie.

Growing up, the brothers had been inseparable. Only two years apart, they had done everything together, from splashing in mud puddles as boys to learning the science of farming as teens. They had learned to ride on the same day, began to notice girls around the same time, and shared the same love for adventure and exploration.

A nostalgic smile curved his lips as a long buried memory rose to the surface. They had been learning about the famous explorers, Lewis and Clark, who had been the first to cross the western portion of the United States in 1804. These brave men had faced all the perilous dangers of the unknown: savage rivers, brutal winters, demanding terrain, and angry predators. To the young Turner brothers, this was the stuff of legends, to be acted out with great imagination.

The shallow waters of Gravel Run Stream had become the Powder River, raging over jagged rocks in white-water rapids. The snapping of twigs in the underbrush (likely made by squirrels or sparrows) was the footfalls of shaggy bears lurking behind the trees. Like Lewis and Clark, they carried notebooks to catalog their discoveries and to draw maps of the region. They had taken the game quite seriously, and played at it off and on for many years.

It was a fond memory, those days of boyhood solidarity, when the world was simple and their only loyalties were to one another: Jeremiah and Charlie, the Turner brothers.

Another memory, far less pleasant, followed. This one brought a sharp stab of pain. Five years before, their mother, Henrietta, had fallen ill with Influenza. She had always been a kind, sweet and energetic woman. Watching her lie against her pillow, pale and wheezing, had been a form of agony for all the Turner men. Jeremiah had been twenty-four at the time, and Charlie twenty-two. They were grown men, yet the fear which had clutched them at the possibility of her death had reduced them to boys again.

He remembered sitting with Charlie on the back porch as the doctor went upstairs to examine Henrietta. From where they sat, the tops of the gravestones in the family cemetery were just barely visible, separated from them by a garden of green shrubs and colorful flowers. Life and death were no longer merely words, but fragile concepts to be gingerly apprehended and respected.

"Do you think Mama's going to die?" Charlie had asked quietly, sounding more like a nine year old than a grown man.

Next to him on the divan, Jeremiah had wanted to lie. But the truth would prove him a liar, so he answered simply, "I don't know."

The air had a bite to it, the chill of autumn usurping the warmth of summer. The leaves were dressed in all their brightest colors: gold, crimson, and saffron. They fluttered in the breeze, making a brittle rustling sound in the tree tops and as they skipped about in the grassy lawn.

"I can't imagine home without her," Charlie's voice had cracked, and he'd leaned forward to rest his sandy head in his hands.

Jeremiah had looped his arm around his brother's shoulders. Tears had streamed down both their cheeks. "I can't imagine *life* without her," he'd confessed.

His younger brother had leaned into him, and they had wept together as they waited for those final words: she's gone. Jeremiah had cradled Charlie against him, feeling the shuddering sobs as they shook his shoulders. He bit his own lip until it bled, trying to keep the raw and angry cry lodged in his throat from breaking free.

"We'll always have each other," he'd finally managed in a hoarse voice. "Even when Mama and Daddy are gone, we'll still have each other."

And he had believed they always would.

Chapter Nine

The morning sunlight streaming through the curtains on the window left a shadowed pattern of lace across the quilt. Clara squinted against the brightness, rolling over to be sure her husband's side of the bed was occupied. Jeremiah slept soundly, unmindful of the rooster crowing in the yard. His dark eyelashes twitched as he dreamed, his breathing deep and even.

Clara wondered what time he had come home during the night. She had lain awake staring at the ceiling for what seemed like hours, listening for his return for so long that when she finally did succumb to sleep, she was oblivious of his arrival. He looked exhausted, as if he had been up most of the night.

She hoped Jeremiah would tell her about the meeting at Will's last night. She prayed that the conclusion wasn't what she feared. Ever since the day that news had arrived of the fall of Fort Sumter, she had felt as if there was an invisible cord tied around his waist, waiting for the right moment to pull him away. And she feared that moment had come.

This despicable war had only been waging for almost six months. It was early yet, and anything might happen. The Confederacy could surrender and request to be readmitted into the Union. Or the President could decide it would be best for the nation as a whole to simply let them go and declare them a sovereign entity. Why did her husband feel the need to get involved?

Jeremiah had obligations to his farm, to his father, and perhaps most importantly, to her. Why would he choose to risk his life for a cause that might leave his wife a widow, childless and alone? Anger flared within her, but was quickly extinguished by a tide of fear as she imagined how cold and empty the bed they shared would be without him. She pressed her lips together firmly and blinked away tears. She must be strong. If he chose to go, she could not keep him from it. She would have to let him go.

A bitter sigh escaped Clara's lips, and his eyes fluttered open. He stared at her blankly, as if still lost in the fog of dreams. Then he blinked, and his eyes focused upon her face. Jeremiah smiled lovingly at her, resting his strong and callused hand over hers. Anger and fear fled, swept away by a wave of tenderness as she gazed into those amber eyes.

"Good morning, beautiful," he whispered, fatigue etched into his features.

Clara felt a smile shape her lips. Oh, how she loved this man! "Good morning," she answered.

"I suppose I have to get up for breakfast?" he groaned.

"You probably should," she agreed.

"I hope Mamie made the coffee strong this morning," he said as he pushed himself up into a sitting position.

"You were out late," Clara ventured.

"I wasn't out very late, but once I was home, I couldn't sleep," he admitted.

"Should we talk about it?" she asked softly.

Jeremiah leaned forward and pressed a kiss to her forehead. "We will. Later."

She watched as he swung his legs over the edge of the bed and went to the washstand to splash water on his face. If he was putting the conversation off until later, he knew she wasn't going to be pleased by what he had to say.

Part of her was relieved. Until he said it, she didn't have to admit that it was happening.

"When?" she pressed.

He hesitated, as if unsure. She could see his eyes shifting as he considered possible answers. Finally he sighed, "After breakfast."

When the meal was finished, Jeremiah pushed back his chair and stood. "Father, I'll be out directly. I need some time with Clara first."

Francis nodded, without comment or question.

Clara followed Jeremiah to the back porch, taking the seat next to him on the divan. A lump had lodged in her throat, and she found it difficult to speak as he took her hand. He swallowed, as if the words did not come easily for him either.

He looked up, his gaze spanning the lawn and the flower garden, which boasted mostly green shrubs and leaves, the purple crocus blooms standing out in colorful contrast. His eyes settled on the family cemetery where his mother and grandparents were buried, and where he still took flowers every Mother's Day, as well as Henrietta's birthday and the anniversary of her death.

Unable to take the silence, Clara finally pushed the question out: "What have you decided?"

Her voice seemed to break the spell, and he turned to face her. "I haven't decided anything yet."

"Is Will joining the Federal Army?"

"Yes, and two others."

"And he wants you to join." It wasn't a question. Clara knew the answer.

"I told him I would give my answer next week," Jeremiah informed her, raking his fingers through his thick, dark hair. "I'm torn, Clara. I hope you understand that."

"I suppose I don't understand," she admitted reluctantly, grasping his hand more tightly. "Why do you feel you must do this?"

"I love this country, and it is under attack from rebels who would tear it apart. It is my duty to fight for my country, to preserve the honor of my family name and the state which I call home," he answered certainly.

"Duty. Honor." Tears glistened in her eyes as she looked up at him beseechingly. "What about me?"

Jeremiah laid a hand upon her shoulder and squeezed it gently. "What is a man without honor?" he questioned softly.

Alive, the answer screamed in her mind, but Clara kept her lips silent. If he felt that he must fight on the grounds of honor, all her arguments against it would only render him a coward.

"Well then," she said, by means of acceptance. But one thing had to be asked: "What will you do if you meet Charlie in battle?"

Jeremiah sank into the back of the wicker divan. His entire demeanor changed, softening from firm resolve to burdened resignation. "I don't know," he whispered. "But that is one rebel I don't think I can kill."

In this one sentence, Clara glimpsed the fullness of his agonizing decision. Although Jeremiah said he hadn't made up his mind, it was clear to her that he had, but needed to come to terms with it himself. And the heart-wrenching anguish clearly written on his face robbed her of any resentment she might have felt at his choice to fight. She feared he would suffer the most of all of them for this decision.

The silence between them lengthened. Clara blinked away tears, but her throat was too swollen to speak, even if she could have found the words.

Finally Jeremiah stood, pulling her to her feet and wrapping his strong arms around her. "I need to be going," he told her hoarsely. Then pressing a kiss to her cheek, he descended the porch steps and disappeared around the corner of the house.

Clara took a deep breath and slowly exhaled to regain her composure. Then she went to the kitchen to inform Mamie and Phoebe that she was going upstairs to lie down. "I have a headache," she lied. The woman nodded, their eyes understanding.

Once in her room, Clara collapsed onto the bed. Her head fell forward into her hands and her shoulders shook violently as all the tears she had held back were unleashed like a sudden summer storm. There was no stopping them once they had started, and she lay down and curled into a ball on her side, stifling the sound of her sobs with a hand over her mouth.

The casualty reports after each battle flashed before her eyes. What if one day her husband's name appeared among them? Wounded, of course, was better than deceased. But the moment he buttoned the uniform and saluted "Yes Sir!" his life was no longer his own.

A sound outside the window brought her upright. Running to the window, she peered down to see a carriage parked at the end of the brick walkway, and her sister stepping out of it. A quick glance in the mirror assured her that her emotional episode was no longer a secret. Dipping a cloth into the pitcher on the washstand, she bathed her face with cold water with the hope of soothing her eyes, red and puffy from crying.

A knock at the door brought her hurried efforts to an end. Opening it, she found Phoebe standing in the hallway. One look at Clara gave everything away.

The Negro woman's expression held compassion as she reached out with a slender hand to squeeze Clara's arm. "You is gonna be all right, Missus Clara. You just remember that. Now, Miss Jane's downstairs. What you want me to tell her?"

Clara bit her lip. "How bad do I look?"

Phoebe raised her eyebrows as if to say, "You sure you want to hear the truth?"

"Send her up to my room, please," Clara replied, not wanting the whole household to see if she fell to pieces again.

"Yes ma'am," Phoebe nodded before turning to descend the stairs.

Clara glanced in the mirror, wrinkling her nose at what she saw. A soft rap at the door announced their arrival. At her call, the door swung open and Phoebe stepped back to allow Jane entry before silently slipping away into the shadows.

"What's wrong?" Jane ran to her, grabbing her hands.

"It's Jeremiah... He's going to join the Federal Army," Clara confessed, trying to keep her voice calm.

"Oh," Jane sighed with relief. At Clara's obvious aggravation, she quickly added, "I thought someone had died or worse."

"Not yet," Clara sank down into the blue velvet armchair.

Jane pulled the ottoman close and arranged her skirts around it as she sat. Wrapping her arms around Clara's waist, she tried to offer what comfort she could. "I'm so sorry, darling. Let's just pray this war will be over soon."

"It won't be over soon enough," Clara produced a handkerchief from her sleeve and dabbed at her nose.

"Let's go out and get some fresh air," Jane suggested, coming to her feet and smoothing the wrinkles from her brown striped muslin dress.

Linking arms, the sisters crossed the back lawn to the peach orchard, strolling beneath the outstretched limbs of the trees, now barren of fruit. The warmth of the late morning sun was alleviated by the shade, and the rustling of the leaves in the breeze was peaceful and soothing.

"When is he leaving?" Jane asked gingerly.

"I'm not sure," Clara answered, feeling more in control of herself.

"Well, I came here today for a reason, though now I feel almost selfish saying it," Jane admitted, releasing Clara's arm and facing her.

She had the same auburn hair as Clara, and was very similar in height and build. But she had their father's square chin and straight nose, while Clara had inherited her mother's pointed chin and sloping nose. Clara noticed now that a twinkle had come into Jane's brown eyes, her cheeks were flushed with more than summer heat, and she looked as if she were curbing a smile.

"You didn't know," she dismissed Jane's guilt with a wave of her hand. "What is it?" Clara wondered.

"Do you remember the gentleman I mentioned?" her sister asked, the smile having taken full shape.

"Which one?" Clara teased.

Jane giggled, as it was a fair question. "Louis Bland," she answered as if there was something special in the name itself. "I saw him again recently and he invited me to go sailing with him. We had such a wonderful time, and he asked Papa if he could call on me again! Papa invited him for dinner this Sunday after church, and I was hoping you and Jeremiah could come."

Clara's head was spinning as she listened to the rapid rise and fall of her sister's voice, eyes sparkling with excitement. Perhaps Louis would be the final suitor. "You didn't go sailing with him alone?" she demanded.

"Oh, you're such a bore!" Jane huffed. "No, his brother was with us."

"Well, I had to ask. You know that it's my job as elder sister to take care of you," she reminded Jane with a playful elbow to the ribs, trying to suppress her melancholy emotions for the sake of her sister's happiness.

"Will you come? On Sunday?" Jane persisted.

"I'll have to speak with Jeremiah, but I think we should be able to," Clara had to chuckle at Jane's enthusiasm.

"I hope you can," Jane turned and began to meander through the orchard. "I know it's too early to say I'm in love… but Clara, he makes my heart race every time I see him! I could talk to him for hours, just listening to whatever is on his mind, listening to the sound of his voice. He's so handsome, but he's kind and good too." She laughed at herself. "I'm gushing, aren't I?"

"Just a little," Clara had to laugh at Jane's excitement. "Well, I will definitely have to meet this wonderful man," she promised. "I'm very happy for you."

Chapter Ten

The shadows beneath the green canopy of leaves were lengthening as Jeremiah rode the trail through the woods toward Will's house. Tonight he would give his answer.

He had invited Clara to walk with him after breakfast, leading her into the relative privacy of the peach orchard where he had seen her with Jane earlier that week. Her blue plaid skirt swayed like a bell as she walked beside him. Perhaps she had saved her female histrionics for her sister, as he had yet to witness her shed more than a single tear over the matter. But he feared that if she was to lose her self-possession, it would be either upon hearing his announcement or at his departure.

She had held herself together well at her parents' house, where they had supper on Sunday to meet Jane's new suitor. Although he knew Clara was struggling with her own worries, she kept a pleasant smile on her face for her sister's sake. Louis Bland seemed like a nice enough fellow, and since the setting was inappropriate to discuss politics, Jeremiah had no idea which side of the war Louis was on and whether or not he needed to worry of one day fighting him as well.

Taking Clara's hand, Jeremiah led her under the sprawling limbs of a great peach tree, its green leaves trembling with the breeze. "I've thought the matter over thoroughly, and I must join the Federal Army, Clara. My sense of honor compels me to defend my country."

He had expected angry tears and protests, but she had replied with acceptance, brown eyes dry as she lifted her chin to meet his gaze squarely. "I know," she said, her voice serene and strong. "I knew last week."

Jeremiah furrowed his brows. "How were you so sure, when even I wasn't?"

"You sounded to me like a man who had made up his mind."

Taking her hand, Jeremiah pressed a kiss into her palm. "Will you be able to forgive me for leaving you?" he worried.

"Only if you come home alive," Clara retorted. She looked away then, her lip quivering, and Jeremiah realized how much this show of bravery was costing her.

"I'll do my very best, darling," he vowed, though there was little reassurance in the promise.

"When will you leave?" Sadness underscored the question.

"I can only say soon. We'll decide more precisely tonight."

"Have you told your father?" Clara wondered. The angle of the morning sun sent a shaft of light between the trees, catching in her auburn hair and setting it aglow.

"I wanted to tell you first," he replied, his voice husky. "You know I wish I could stay with you," he added softly, enfolding both her hands in his and holding them tightly. There was so much more in his heart, but he could not find the words to express it.

She blinked away tears, straightening her shoulders. "I'm sure he already knows," she said. "He knows you as well as I do."

Jeremiah nodded at the truth of her words. "Will you be all right here with him?"

"Yes, I'm sure we'll be fine," she assured him.

Turning Archie onto the road, Jeremiah remembered the tilt of her chin as she lied. She was trying so hard to be strong for him, and he loved her all the more for it.

His father hadn't responded very differently. Quiet resignation was all he had offered as he said, "I'll miss you, son. I'll be praying for you and Charlie every day that you're away."

Jeremiah couldn't determine if his father was disappointed with his decision or if he supported it in his own way. There was no use in asking. If Francis was opposed, it would have only made leaving that much harder. And Jeremiah knew it was going to be hard enough.

Reaching Will's, he stabled his horse and reported to the study. The air was thick with cigar smoke as Jeremiah took the empty seat on the sofa, next to Amos Mosley. Will poured him a glass of whiskey from the decanter on the shelf. Sam Price and James Cecil had yet to arrive.

"Good to see you tonight," Will grinned. "I was afraid you wouldn't come."

"I don't know why," Jeremiah replied, not wishing to be judged as a coward or a pacifist.

"Have you made your decision?"

Jeremiah acknowledged the question with a nod. He still had his qualms, but having set himself upon this course, he must see it through. "I'll be riding to Cambridge with you," he answered.

Amos clapped him on the shoulder, the force of it sending the amber liquid in his glass rocking precariously. "Glad to hear it, man!" he exclaimed.

"I knew we could count on you," Will laughed as he raised his glass in salute.

Their boisterous approval was interrupted as Sam arrived, going straight for the cigar box on the desk. He leaned in toward Will for a light, gripping the cigar between his teeth as he said, "I heard you say you're going with us." He accepted a glass of whiskey as he added, "Never doubted it."

"Where's James?" Sam paused to look around the room, noting the other man's absence.

"On his way, I hope," Will replied. He glanced at the clock on the wall. "We'll give him a little more time."

"Did you see the story in the paper about the arrest of Francis Key Howard?" Amos asked as he settled back in the sofa and puffed his cigar.

"Arrested for the article he wrote in the paper criticizing the

President's suspension of the writ of habeas corpus," Jeremiah answered. "Sent to Fort McHenry."

"You know he's the grandson of Francis Scott Key, the man who wrote the poem which became *The Star Spangled Banner*?" Amos queried.

"He should have known better than to speak against the President of the very flag his grandfather celebrated," Sam declared.

"Isn't Fort McHenry where that poem was written?" Amos wondered.

"It was written about the flag flying over Fort McHenry, and the pride Key felt that his country had not lost the battle," Will answered.

"I'm sure you've all heard who else has been imprisoned there?" Sam leaned against the edge of the desk, rubbing his chin with his thumb. "I'm not sure if I agree with going that far."

"Twenty-seven state legislators... all in favor of secession," Amos stated.

"That's one-third of the Maryland General Assembly," Jeremiah added, shaking his head. "I admit, it seems extreme."

"I've been thinking it over, too," Will admitted, "and I've come to this conclusion. It forced the legislative session to be cancelled, preventing a vote for secession or other anti-war measures. It could be said that their arrests saved Maryland from stepping over the line to become a rebel state and facing the consequences that would come with it."

"It's all a game of chess with high stakes," Jeremiah commented. "Saving Maryland is just one move toward saving the Union."

"And we will take our place in history as those who fought to defend—" Will's impassioned speech was halted as the door to the study creaked open and James Cecil slipped through the door.

"James," Will acknowledged him with a pat on the back. "Glad you came."

As Will moved toward the whiskey decanter, James stopped him with an upheld palm. "I'm not staying long. I almost didn't come." The young man's lean features were sharpened with worry, a deep groove forming between his brows. "I just wanted to give my answer. I can't put myself at risk right now. I believe in this nation, and I will always be a loyal patriot. But my wife needs me. She's expecting another child, and her health is suffering. Our little one is weak, and I just can't leave Mary to do this on her own. I won't." His eyes moved from face to face apologetically, "I'm behind you all the way. This just isn't a battle I can fight right now."

Will stepped toward him, offering his hand in a conciliatory gesture. "There's no shame in that. Sometimes a man needs to choose deeper loyalties than country. Go ahead and have a drink before you head out," he said, offering him a whiskey.

James accepted it, standing a little straighter now that the weight was off his chest. "I'm glad you understand."

After James Cecil had taken his leave, Will turned to the three who had committed to enlist. "When will you be ready to go?" he asked them.

"I'm ready," answered Amos.

"I can go whenever you decide," Sam agreed.

Jeremiah swallowed. He could hardly say that he wanted more time, so he simply nodded his accord with the others.

"Let's give it three days to put all our affairs in order. We can meet here Thursday afternoon and ride to Cambridge," Will suggested.

And so it was decided.

Jeremiah stayed only a little longer than James, making his apologies as he left. He respected James' decision to stay and care for his wife in her time of need. No one could judge a man for choosing to attend to his sickly wife and child. He was thankful Clara was neither ill nor carrying a child. He suspected it would be painful enough to say good-bye as it was.

He wasn't surprised to find Clara waiting up for him when

he crept silently into the bedroom. A pale yellow circle of light flickered from the oil lamp on the nightstand. Leaning against the headboard, Clara sat in her white cotton shift with a novel in her hands, knees drawn up in front of her. Her tired eyes brightened as soon as she saw him.

"You're up late," he forced a smile as he removed his boots and padded to the bed.

"I couldn't sleep. I needed to know how much time we have left."

Jeremiah sighed wearily as he removed his clothes and sank down onto the bed. "Three days. We leave on Thursday."

Clara nodded, then reached over to turn out the lamp. She said nothing as she snuggled into the circle of his arm, but he could feel the dampness against his chest from her tears.

In the morning, Jeremiah instructed Mamie to gather the slaves on the back porch so that he might address them. During the night he had been disturbed by an owl hooting in the forest and was unable to fall back to sleep. He had lain awake thinking that if this was the last three days he had in this life with his wife, his father, or even the slaves who served his family, he wanted his last words to them to be meaningful and memorable.

Standing on the back porch, looking down at the black faces which were as much a part of home as the white portico at the front entrance and the laurel trees which flanked the house, Jeremiah was moved by deep emotions. Old Joe and Mamie stood with their youngest children, Lena and Silas, on either side of them. Next to the boy were Phoebe and her husband, Henry. The eldest son, Eli, stood by himself off to the side.

"On Thursday I will be leaving to join the Federal Army," Jeremiah announced. "I am confident that in my absence I can trust each and every one of you to care for my wife, my father, and Laurel Hill, just as you have in the past. When I look at you, I see home. Each one of you are as deeply rooted in the soil of Laurel Hill as I am, and from the bottom of my heart, I wish to thank you for all your labors. God willing, I will return to work alongside you once again, but until then, may God bless you and keep you."

"Yessuh, we gonna take care of things," Old Joe promised.

"Don't you worry none, we gonna take good care o' Missus Clara," Phoebe promised.

"I know you will," Jeremiah nodded to both of them gratefully.

He would wait until the last day to say his final good-byes to Francis and Clara, but there was someone else he wanted to visit. Pausing to pluck a few of the purple crocus blooming in the flower garden, Jeremiah carried the bouquet to the family graveyard and placed them against Henrietta's stone. Kneeling down on the grass, Jeremiah traced the letters of her name carved into the marble slab.

"Hi Mama," he said in an almost whisper. "You might know it already, but it looks like I'm going to war. Charlie's already left and he's fighting on the other side. It's a horrible time to live in, Mama, and it's just as well you aren't here to see it. But we miss you dearly and wish you were here, for our sakes. I'll do my best to take care of myself, and I promise I won't do anything to hurt Charlie if I can help it." He sat in the stillness for a moment, listening to the cicadas humming in the nearby trees. "I love you, Mama," he said finally before rising to his feet.

Jeremiah was thankful for these three days, but they sped by so quickly that it felt he hadn't been given nearly enough time. If he had felt a clock ticking before, now it seemed that he could hear every second as it ticked past, time lost that could never be brought back.

His father seemed to age before his eyes in those last days. Francis' white hair seemed thinner, and the creases and grooves of his face grew deeper than they were before. Gray circles developed under his eyes, as if sleep routinely eluded him. But perhaps the most disturbing change was his taciturn silence. It was as if a spark had gone out within him.

Wednesday evening Jeremiah found his father on the back porch, reclining in a rocking chair and smoking a pipe. Taking a seat on the divan, he waited to see if Francis would speak first, but when he continued to puff his pipe without a word, Jeremiah initiated the conversation.

"Father," he spoke softly, and when Francis did not reply, Jeremiah feared his voice had been lost in the strident chorus of late summer insects. He spoke more loudly, "Father?"

"What is it, son?" Francis clenched the briarwood pipe between his teeth as he spoke.

Before he could lose courage, Jeremiah blurted: "Tomorrow I leave. I just wanted to say once and for all that I love you. You've been a good father and I'm glad you'll be here to care for Clara while I'm gone."

A sad half-smile curved his father's mouth. "You've been a good son, Jeremiah. I'm going to miss you."

"About Charlie..." Jeremiah began, the subject causing his throat to close.

Francis removed the pipe and rested his elbow on the arm of the rocker. "I know you love him, son. I know you don't want to hurt him."

"I'll try to make you proud," Jeremiah cleared his throat as his voice broke with emotion.

"I already am, Jeremiah," Francis stated, coming to his feet and offering his hand, pulling Jeremiah into a hug as he accepted it. "I already am."

Thursday morning dawned bright and clear. The sunlight streaming through the lace curtains fell across Jeremiah's eyes, and he blinked against the brightness. Rolling onto his side, he took in the tranquil beauty of his wife as she lay sleeping, hand tucked under her cheek. Her long auburn braid fell across her shoulder, and he reached out to rub the silky strands of it between his thumb and forefinger. Watching the peaceful rise and fall of her breathing, Jeremiah felt an ache grow in his chest.

The knowledge of their imminent separation cast a pall over

the entire house. No one seemed to have much to say. Breakfast was a somber affair.

Jeremiah packed extra shirts, socks and utensils in a knapsack, unsure what the army would provide. Mamie gave him a sack filled with sourdough biscuits, jerky, and dried beans called "leather britches" to take with him.

"Don't want you goin' hungry," the plump Negro woman said as she handed him the sack.

Jeremiah nodded his gratitude. Eli had offered to saddle Archie, allowing Jeremiah a few more minutes to spend with his wife. Standing alone with her in the parlor, he drew her against his chest and held her tightly, his hand rubbing slow circles on her back. They stood this way for a moment, before she drew back, staring up at him with solemn eyes.

"Do you know how much I love you?" he asked softly, his eyes intense as they studied every curve and feature of her face. He noticed that she had worn the jade muslin dress he liked so much on her. It accentuated the reddish tint of her hair and her creamy complexion.

Blinking back tears, Clara whispered, "I do."

"Never forget," Jeremiah ordered gently, drawing her close and pressing his lips against hers. He deepened the kiss, wishing he never had to let go.

But the time soon came for him to leave. Francis and the slaves were all gathered at the front of the house, Eli holding Archie's reins. Jeremiah followed Clara down the narrow brick walkway, the sound of his boots on the stones echoing with finality.

He turned to take in the details of his home one last time, trying to memorize it for the long months or years ahead. He shook hands with Old Joe, Henry and Eli, and hugged Mamie, Phoebe and Lena.

Francis stepped toward him, gripping his hand in a firm farewell. "Take care of yourself, son," he said hoarsely.

Jeremiah nodded, then turned to his wife, standing quietly at his side. "Never forget," he whispered in her ear as he drew her close for one last hug.

Then swinging up into the saddle, Jeremiah lifted his hand and nudged Archie forward.

Clara stopped him with a hand upon his thigh. Her brown eyes were pleading as she looked up at him. "Come home to me," she ordered.

Chapter Eleven

April 1862

It was planting season again. One year had passed since the fall of Fort Sumter. By the blushing light of dawn, Clara could see the shapes of her father-in-law and Henry working in the field with mule and plough, along with Old Joe and Eli. This year, Phoebe drove the wagon hauling the tub of water for Silas to spray the kernels as they were buried in the soil.

Without his sons, Francis was short two pairs of hands. Six months had passed since Jeremiah enlisted in the Federal Army, and there was no indication that the wretched "War Between the States," as some called it, would come to a swift end.

Those with Rebel leanings referred to it as the "War Against Northern Tyranny." Although Maryland remained under the control of the Federal Government, the Eastern Shore harbored strong Southern sympathies even if it was not openly expressed for fear of the consequences.

Every few weeks, reports of a new battle appeared in the paper. The fighting had extended as far south as Florida and as far west as Indian Territory. A small skirmish had occurred in Maryland, but so far it had yet to see any real action. Although Virginia was still the site of frequent battles, Jeremiah had been spared direct combat. His regiment had been assigned further south on the peninsula to Accomack and Northampton counties in eastern Virginia. Their mission was to suppress Rebel influence, and they were able to effectively chase any committed Confederates from the peninsula without the firing of a gun.

Whenever fighting in the state of Virginia was reported, Clara's heart beat a little faster until she had confirmed that Jeremiah's name was not listed among the casualties, even though she had no real reason to believe he would be involved. The eastern shore of Virginia had seen no violence, but there was no way she could be sure his regiment hadn't been sent into the battle as reinforcements.

Although she had grown accustomed to Jeremiah's absence, Clara missed him painfully. She mailed him a letter once a week with daily entrees, almost like a diary. Writing to him every day helped her to feel as though she still had a way to share her life with him, and it helped to keep the loneliness at bay. It forced her to keep her eyes open to the world around her rather than retreating into herself as she was sometimes tempted to do.

She was always grateful to receive a letter from her husband, to see the unique scrawl of his penmanship. Her mind could hear his voice speaking to her as she read over the words. It was an inferior form of communication to be sure, but she was thankful for any means to remain connected to him.

During the day, Clara kept herself busy as an anecdote to the constant ache of loneliness and worry. But as she slid under the wedding ring quilt at night, the bed cold and empty, there was nothing to distract her from the awareness of her husband's absence. Used to falling asleep with her cheek upon Jeremiah's shoulder, the lifeless pillow under her head offered neither companionship nor comfort.

For his part, Francis tried to care for Clara as if she were his daughter. But never having had a daughter of his own, it was a role he was unfamiliar with. Clara appreciated his awkward attempts for the love and kindness they demonstrated, but was relieved just the same when he ceased the unnatural displays of concern and paternal protectiveness. Within a few months, they had found their own form of friendship, comfortable to eat together in silence or to discuss farming and current events.

Jeremiah wrote to his father as well, and Francis often compared notes with her to try to put together the full picture of his life in the army. He wrote of different things to them, perhaps to make it easier to write two letters, or perhaps because Jeremiah thought they would be interested in different aspects of his life. To Clara he wrote of simple, cheerful things, like the friendships he was forging with the men in his regiment or the beauty of the landscape where they camped. To his father, Jeremiah wrote about the routine and demands of military life and the daily activities required of him.

In her replies, Clara purposefully kept her own tone cheerful and brave. Only occasionally did she put to pen the sadness and longing she felt. She was confident he felt the same, but if they were to endure this separation, they must not make it more difficult for each other by issuing words of complaint.

She'd never known Jeremiah to take much of an interest in the Bible before, but the war had reminded them all of their immortality and put to mind questions about life beyond the grave. Jeremiah had attended church regularly, but more for the social opportunities than for the spiritual nourishment.

Now he often quoted scripture in his letters. His regiment had been assigned a chaplain and Jeremiah had been issued a New Testament. A worship service was held once a week and the chaplain ministered to their souls with words of comfort: "*And I give unto them eternal life; and they shall never perish, neither shall any man pluck them out of My hand,*' John 10:28."

Clara had to confess in her own private thoughts that although the words sounded reassuring, she wasn't entirely sure what they meant.

The Negro women were a great comfort to Clara. They hummed songs as they worked together in the kitchen baking bread, churning butter, or making cheese. In the fall, Clara helped them bring in vegetables from the garden, braiding onions together into a long rope by their tops, or threading red peppers to dry. Pumpkins, squash, potatoes, carrots, and turnips were all carried down to the cellar for storage.

She also participated in the most dreadful day of the year: the day of the hog slaughter. Old Joe wielded the butcher knife, and Clara hid in the kitchen until the squealing had stopped. The men built a large fire and heated a giant kettle over it, dipping the carcass up and down until it was well scalded. Then it was laid over the butcher table, which was little more than a roughly hewn log bench, and the bristles were scraped from it.

After that, the hog was suspended from a tree while its innards were removed, and there it remained until it had cooled. Once taken down, it was cut into hams and shoulders, side meat, spare-ribs, and belly. The heart, liver and tongue were salted with the larger cuts for preservation, and all the remnant pieces were set aside to make sausage. The hams and shoulders would be hickory-smoked, and the head of the hog was used to make a meat jelly called "headcheese."

Old Joe blew up the hog's bladder into a white balloon and gave it to Silas to play with like a ball. The nine year old bounded off into the yard, bouncing it into the air as he went. Mamie fried the pig's tail and it was shared by Lena and Silas, who treated it as if it were a rare delicacy.

Clara was determined to prove herself a valuable asset to Laurel Hill, even if she found the entire event disgusting. She grit her teeth as she watched Mamie boil the lard over an outdoor fire, the smell it produced as it smoked making her gag. Occasionally, Mamie skimmed the brown "cracklings" off the top and placed them in a cloth. Phoebe squeezed the lard out of them, wrapping them to be used for flavoring in cooking or baking.

Having been raised in a home where such food was purchased, not made, Clara admired the sufficiency of the farm even as she was appalled by the process. She found that she felt sorry for the hogs fattening in the pen, knowing what their end would be.

In Jeremiah's absence, Clara also established a new routine of taking supper with her parents on Sundays. She found the home she grew up in and the familiar faces of her parents and siblings acted as a balm to her aching heart. Often, Francis came with her. She hated the idea of leaving him to take supper alone, and her family provided a distraction and comfort for him as well.

After supper, George, Francis, and Eddy would retreat to the study to enjoy brandy and cigars while Naomi and her daughters settled in the parlor for feminine conversation. For just a while, Clara could forget that her world had tilted on its axis and might never be righted again. She could push her own life aside and step into the world of the Collins home, listening to Jane prattle on about Louis Bland or her mother's flower garden.

Eli didn't seem to mind driving her. In fact, she noticed that he appeared to look forward to the trip and was disappointed if they were unable to make it for any reason. Initially, Clara had thought he was just enjoying the break from his chores at Laurel Hill, but she soon discovered the real reason. She spied him in the kitchen leaning across the table on his elbow, flirting shamelessly with Mercy, whose cheeks were flushed beneath her dark skin. Since Mercy's mother was present to keep close watch on the situation, Clara had merely chuckled and left them alone.

When she mentioned her observation to Phoebe, a slow smile had spread across his sister's face and she had thumped her hand on her slender thigh. "I knew somethin' was goin' on with that boy! He been actin' like he can't keep his mind on nothing lately. Now I know what his mind on!" She'd laughed.

"Mercy's just barely a woman," she told Phoebe, "so I hope he'll give her a little time to grow up. But her mama was in the kitchen with them, so I'm sure she'll keep a firm hand on the romance."

"Don't you worry," Phoebe assured her, the indigo blue turban she wore bobbing as she nodded certainly, "*his* mama gonna beat him if he don't behave like no gentleman!'"

Clara laughed, imagining that was true enough. "How long did it take you to decide you wanted to marry Henry?" she wondered.

"About five minutes," Phoebe grinned, her white teeth gleaming against her dark skin.

"I think it took me less than that to know I wanted to marry Jeremiah," she reminisced, "and I wasn't much older than Mercy is now."

"How's that?" Phoebe wrinkled her dark brows, knowing when the couple had begun courting.

"Oh, he didn't even notice me for another three years," Clara blushed. "I saw him here at a party, and I waited until I was of age and he was ready to pursue me."

Phoebe leaned in, hand on her hip as she asked, "Now, how you get him to notice you, Missus Clara?"

With a nostalgic sigh, Clara admitted, "I just wore a pretty dress and smiled at him. Jeremiah did the rest."

"What would you have done if he hadn't noticed you standing there gawkin' at him?" Phoebe demanded, eyebrows raised. "Seein' how you'd already made up your mind to marry him."

Remembering the day very clearly, Clara giggled. "I had already asked a mutual friend to steer him in my direction if he didn't come on his own," she admitted.

Laughing out loud, Phoebe declared, "I reckon that poor man didn't stand a chance!"

Clara smiled in reply, even as she wiped a tear from her eye. She had spent countless hours during those three years of waiting praying she wouldn't lose him to another woman. Now she lived in fear of losing him to a Rebel bullet.

~

Jeremiah tapped his chin with the end of the cedar pencil, staring down at the stationary he had removed from his leather writing kit. He needed to send a letter to his wife, but he found himself staring down at the blank page, searching for something to tell her. Clara would consider the lack of excitement a good thing, as it meant he was out of the action.

This was the first time since he was a boy that Jeremiah had not helped his father at planting season. The sweet smell of new growth around him stirred a deep longing for the acres of tilled black soil and the satisfaction of a hard day's work. Jeremiah put the pencil to paper and confessed how the budding spring flowers and the trill of the birds from the treetops reminded him of home, and more importantly, of her.

He was thankful he had been spared direct engagement with the enemy, and could hardly consider the boredom he suffered a true hardship. When he'd enlisted and been sent to the southern tip of the peninsula to disperse the Rebels recruiting there, Jeremiah had naturally expected to face gunfire as the Confederates opposed their advance into Virginia.

He had been issued a .58 caliber 1855 Springfield musket and was drilled daily on the Manual of Arms, which included procedures for priming, loading and firing the musket. The infantryman were also drilled as squads and in company formations, learning to obey precise commands and execute them as a single unit. Additionally, he was drilled on the procedure of fixing a bayonet to the end of the musket in the case of close range hand-to-hand combat.

The repetition of these drills imbedded the commands and maneuvers into his brain until the quiet life of a farmer seemed like a distant dream. He learned to control his movements, executing the commands to "shoulder arms," or "present arms" with military precision. The musket became an extension of himself, no longer a foreign object, but a piece of machinery with which he was well acquainted.

Capable of firing up to three rounds per minute, the 1855 Springfield's effective range was three hundred yards, although a skilled marksman could hit a target up to a thousand yards away.

The .58 caliber minie ball was a soft lead bullet, cone-shaped rather than round, spiraling down grooves bored into the musket barrel to increase its velocity. Unlike a round bullet, which would remain in the flesh of its target, taking a winding path around tendons and bones, the minie ball cut a straight path. It went through the object it struck without deviation, shattering bones. The only way to treat such injuries was by amputation.

As the war raged on, more and more men were sent home without arms and legs, if they were lucky enough to be sent home alive. Although boredom was a trial, Jeremiah tried to count his blessings and be thankful that the mission of the Eastern Shore Infantry, joined with General Lockwood's Brigade, had been able to execute their mission without military engagement.

In an effort to limit Confederate influence and enlistment in Maryland, as well as to tighten the blockade on goods shipped from the Eastern Shore to the Rebel Army on Virginia's Western Shore, Major General Dix had gathered a force of five thousand men at Newtown.

The Confederate Colonel Smith responded to this show of aggression by assembling a force of eighteen hundred men at Oak Hall. However, when Smith learned he was badly outnumbered, he withdrew from his entrenchments and retreated down the peninsula.

Causing some to question his loyalty to the Union, General Lockwood, a slaveholder from Delaware, pursued the fleeing Confederates at such a leisurely pace that it took the Federal troops eleven days to march the sixty miles from Newton to Eastville. This pace allowed ample time for the Rebels to either return to their homes or cross the Chesapeake Bay to fight with other units of the Confederate Army.

Jeremiah, not as eager to spill blood as some, commended the General for allowing the enemy to retreat and disband. If only other commanders were capable of exercising the same wisdom, perhaps the war could come to a more rapid and peaceful end.

Although they were never directly opposed by Rebels, breastworks had been built at Oak Hall, and at Knappsville a battery for fifteen guns was found. In the town of Pungoteague, seven large cannons were confiscated which the Confederates had intended to send across the river to their counterparts engaged in active warfare. In Drummondtown, in addition to a large Confederate flag, were found a collection of rifles and muskets. However, they were of such antique quality that their usefulness was uncertain as some of them dated back to 1808.

Having secured the peninsula, Major General Dix began to withdraw troops, leaving only a few hundred men stationed behind as a Federal presence, guarding the telegraph wire and maintaining the blockade. The First Eastern Shore Infantry remained, setting up headquarters in Oak Hall using a church building seized by the government for this purpose.

At the onset of the occupation, Dix had issued a proclamation to the local people promising to respect "*your laws, your institutions, your usages.*" In addition, he had pledged, "*To those who remain in the quiet pursuit of their domestic occupations... peace, freedom from annoyance, protection from foreign and internal enemies, and a guarantee of all Constitutional and legal rights and the blessings of a just and parental government.*"

It was an eloquent and reassuring promise, however poorly kept. Jeremiah withheld from Clara the misgivings growing within him daily as he acted out his orders. Not only was property confiscated by any prominent citizens serving in the Confederate Army, but private citizens expressing Southern sympathy were often arrested without due process and sent to Fort McHenry. At times, the property of these individuals was also confiscated.

Freedom of speech no longer appeared to be a Constitutional right. Jeremiah suspected that just as in Maryland, the Eastern Shore of Virginia was largely occupied by Rebel sympathizers who had the good sense to keep their opinions to themselves.

More and more, Jeremiah began to ponder the concept of freedom. As far as he could tell, none of them were free: black or white, Union or Confederate. Everyone was under the rule of a greater authority imposed upon them, and forced by threat of consequence to follow commands whether these orders agreed with their conscience or not, and without any consideration for their personal feelings.

Finishing the letter to Clara as he always did, *"Never forget how much I love you,"* Jeremiah folded the stationary and slid it into the envelope along with three months' wages. His monthly salary of thirteen dollars was rarely paid on a regular basis. Sometimes as many as six months elapsed before he saw the money. Jeremiah sent most of it home, spending on himself only what was absolutely necessary.

Some of his comrades spent their wages on cigarettes and liquor, occupying the long hours of boredom with gambling and drinking. Others, like Jeremiah, found that the time left them undistracted to consider the deeper things of life, previously overlooked and taken for granted. The world was a different place in times of peace, and people were different too.

The War Department, understanding this sudden need for spiritual guidance, assigned an ordained chaplain to each regiment. Chaplain Davies had been assigned to the First Eastern Shore Infantry, and the soldiers who wished to avoid the Devil's workshop associated with him during their idle moments.

Davies wasn't much more than five feet tall, in his sixties, with a thinning crown of snow white hair and a disarming smile which took years from his appearance. As quick to humor as he was to compassion, Davies made for good company. A Baptist minister, Chaplain Davies had spent forty years serving in the church at his hometown in Chestertown, Maryland. Widowed just before the war broke out, he volunteered as a chaplain both to attend to the souls of the soldiers as well as to bring a sense of purpose back into his life.

When Davies first arrived, the men weren't sure what to make of him.

"I hope you're not one of those 'fighting chaplains,'" Private Phillips had sneered as he sized up the old man, who barely reached the middle of his chest.

"Don't be intimidated," Davies replied, lifting his small chin to meet Phillips' eyes. "As long as you stay on my good side, I won't have to hurt you."

Private Phillips cocked one eyebrow, studying the serious expression on the chaplain's face to determine if the man had escaped from a mental institution disguised as a church. But as a slow smile spread across Davies' face, laughter broke out all around them.

Stopping short of delivering a right hook to Phillips' gut, the little chaplain grinned, "I may look like all brawn, but once you get to know me, I'm really all heart."

With a loud guffaw, the private slapped Davies on the back approvingly, almost knocking the old man to his knees. Steadying him with a giant hand, Phillips stood Davies firmly on his feet.

After that, the men loved to challenge the chaplain to arm wrestling matches, accompanied by sarcastic pleas not to crush their hands and to take pity on them. Davies was always ready with a quick reply and his characteristic dimpled grin.

When Jeremiah learned that Davies had raised three sons, he understood why the chaplain had so easily established a rapport with the soldiers in his care. Two of his three sons were fighting in the war, one in North Carolina and the other in Kentucky. The third son was ineligible for service because of a injury he had suffered racing horses in his early twenties.

The question Private Phillips had posed to the chaplain had been valid, even if it had been intended as a slight to the man's small stature. Many chaplains, Federal and Confederate, carried weapons and participated in combat with their troops. Under normal circumstances, if a chaplain was taken as a prisoner of war he would be released immediately upon recognition of his duty. However, if he was found carrying arms, he could be held like a common soldier.

When asked his opinion of these fighting chaplains, Davies replied, "I figure that if God had wanted me to fight, he would have made me look a little more like Private Phillips."

Chapter Twelve

Clara eased down onto the plush sofa in the parlor of her parents' home, trying to suppress her irritation at her mother and sister. She knew she was being unfair, but even admitting it didn't give her the power to quell the feelings.

All Jane wanted to talk about was her blooming romance with Louis Bland. To listen to her, one would think the man walked on water.

Every morning, Clara awoke alone in the room she had shared with her husband, offering up a prayer for his safety. And while she was certain that during her courtship with Jeremiah, she was probably just as effusive about his superior qualities as Jane was now about Louis', the nation had not been torn with war at that time.

Romance seemed like a frivolous notion when throughout the country fields were being soaked with the blood of American citizens. Clara wondered how much her mother and sister even knew about the progress of the war. They never wished to talk about it with her, and if they didn't read the newspaper or discuss it with her father, they wouldn't know the dark realities of the situation.

Clara grit her teeth as Jane giggled again, recounting something sweet and charming Louis had said to her that week. Clara had to admit that Louis was a good looking man, and certainly he was the tallest man she had ever met. As far she could tell he was a gentleman of good breeding and manners, with a kindly nature. And clearly, he was as in love with Jane as she was with him.

Jane's cheeks were flushed, her hands dancing about in

animated gestures as she babbled on. Clara pasted a smile on her face and nodded as if she was listening to every word. Then a horrible thought struck her. What if her place and Jane's had been reversed—if it had been Jane who had married before the war and Clara who dared to fall in love while it raged?

Chastising herself for her selfishness, Clara tried to clear the resentment from her mind and share in her sister's joy. It was foolish to think that the war would bring an end to the most celebrated of human experiences. Truth be told, she had no desire for her sister to be deprived of the blessings of love and marriage simply because Presidents Lincoln and Davis could not come to terms of agreement.

Living at Laurel Hill alone with her father-in-law, where both sons were away fighting on opposing sides, the truth of the war was inescapable for Clara. But this one day, Sunday, she could set the newspaper's reports and speculations aside and focus on the things that the war *hadn't* taken away from her. She could and she must grab hold of these moments to forget the rising death toll and enjoy the beauty which still existed in the world.

Relaxing her shoulders and smoothing the crease from between her brows, Clara breathed out slowly and tried to concentrate her attention on Jane's monologue. Her sister wore a yellow muslin dress and looked as fresh as a rose, her spiral curls glistening like burnished copper in the lamplight. Jane was too young to give up on love, and Clara would be wrong to expect it of her.

After all, if she hadn't begrudged Eli and Mercy's budding romance, why should she begrudge her sister?

"You know, Jane," she teased, "if I didn't know better, I would think you were head over heels for this fellow."

Jane rolled her eyes in an exaggerated show of annoyance. "You don't miss a thing, do you?"

Clara laughed in response. "I just wonder if your mouth knows how to talk about anything else?"

A brief smile touched Jane's lips before she sobered. "You don't really mind me talking about him so much, do you?"

Realizing she had assumed Jane was too self-absorbed to notice her melancholy, Clara rushed to reassure her. "I'm very happy for you, Jane! Sometimes I just miss Jeremiah so much..." the words trailed off as her throat constricted with emotion.

"Oh, I've been so insensitive," Jane lamented as she reached over to grasp her sister's hand. "I should have remembered how hard this is for you."

"Have you received a letter lately?" Naomi asked, looking up from the needlepoint in her lap.

Nodding, Clara admitted, "He writes to me faithfully and promises he's in no danger. But that could change at any time... After all, he's a soldier no matter where he's stationed."

Jane nodded understandingly. "I can't imagine if Louis were away fighting," she mused, as if only now fully comprehending her sister's situation. "I hope for all our sakes this war ends soon and all the men can return to their homes."

"It's all in the hands of Providence," her mother reminded them sagely, setting her needle aside to study her daughters intently. "No matter where we are, every one of us is in the hands of Providence."

Naomi's expression grew far away as if her eyes had fixed on some place in the distant past. "I was just a child when my father and uncle fought in the War of 1812," she reminisced. "I was too young to understand what war meant, but my mother would often sit on the veranda to visit with my aunt, and I could hear the fear in their voices. When I asked my mother if she was afraid Father would be killed, she said, 'We're all in the hands of Providence.' I thought that meant everyone I loved would come home safely, but Uncle Richard was killed when the British invaded Queenstown."

"Mother!" Jane protested. "I don't think you're making Clara feel any better!"

The lamplight caught in the gray stands of Naomi's hair as she leaned forward to take Clara's hand. "I don't want you to misunderstand me as I misunderstood my mother. From birth to death, *and after*, we remain in God's hands. And there's peace and comfort in that."

Clara swallowed the lump in her throat with difficulty. "I've never heard you talk that way before, Mama," she admitted.

"I suppose I've never had a reason before," Naomi admitted, her brown eyes soft with compassion. "I wish my girls did not have to face such realities so soon. But truth be told, I see no end to this war in sight. I know I discourage talk of the war because it isn't ladylike, but I don't have my head in the sand."

Clara had thought talking about it would make her feel better, but it only validated her fear. Perhaps it was better to leave this time to lighter conversation.

Her mother squeezed her hand gently. "We shall pray every day for Jeremiah's safe return, my dear. Every day."

But Tuesday brought news of another battle, the bloodiest the war had known. Along the Tennessee River, in a place called Shiloh, the soldiers of the North and South had spent two days in a violent struggle resulting in over three thousand deaths with the combined wounded numbering close to fifteen thousand.

The Confederate Army had taken the Federals by surprise, concluding the first day of fighting with a presumed victory. But the following morning, General Grant launched a counter-attack with his newly arrived reinforcements and pushed the Rebels into retreat.

Although the Union was able to claim the victory, Grant was questioned for not having his troops adequately prepared for the attack. He had been warned of the enemy's approach, but failed to take it seriously. Instead of putting the men to work preparing entrenchments for battle, he had ordered them to drill.

When the attack came, it was suggested that Grant himself was drunk and, due to his lack of patrols on duty, his men had been bayoneted in their tents. The General claimed he was ten miles downriver in Savanah recovering from an accident he had suffered days before when his horse had fallen on him and he had been pinned beneath the massive animal.

Clara sat beside her father-in-law at the table reading the horrible account of the battle, struggling to hide the sudden nausea which clenched her stomach. General Grant had assured his men that they were safe at Shiloh, just as Jeremiah's commanders had promised that he was not in a position of danger.

How many of the soldiers who died in the Battle of Shiloh had wives, mothers and sisters praying for their safe return? Perhaps these dead were still in the hands of God, but Clara doubted that was of much comfort to their widows as they donned their mourning clothes.

~

Jeremiah sank down onto his cot, removing his forage cap and placing it on his chest. Although the tent was better suited to a dozen men, he shared it with nineteen others, their cots crammed tightly into the conical tent around the similarly shaped wrought iron stove used for warmth in the colder months. Today the flap of the white canvas tent was open to allow the breeze to move through and he closed his eyes, listening to the sounds of the bees in the clover nearby and the birds in the treetops.

This was a brief respite between drills. To fill the time and keep the men prepared for military action, should the need ever arise, they were drilled intermittently throughout the day. Sometimes Jeremiah found himself executing drills in his dreams, shifting the ten pound weight of the rifle from his right shoulder and sliding it to the ground, positioning it in front of him for inspection.

The commanding officers, Colonels Wallace and Keene, and Lieutenant Colonel Comegys, had converted the church into their headquarters and barracks. The two hundred men stationed with them enjoyed more rustic accommodations. The camp was arranged according to army regulations, the tents lined up in a grid in the same order which the unit would present for battle.

Jeremiah considered writing Clara, but there was nothing new to report and the afternoon sunshine and the hum of the bees was lulling him into sleep. Mornings in military camp began before sunrise, the reveille bugle call rousing the soldiers from their slumber to line up for roll call. After breakfast was the first of as many as five drills per day, each lasting about two hours.

When he didn't dream that he was completing the drills, Jeremiah dreamed of Laurel Hill. The cornfields rippling in the summer breeze, the yellow tassels of the cornstalks waving around him as he cleared away the weeds. His father and brother worked alongside him, and Clara stood waiting for him beneath the white portico at the front door, wearing her jade muslin dress.

In moments like these, when his mind was free to wander, his thoughts often turned to his brother. Jeremiah only hoped that Charlie was as far away from the fighting as he was, equally bored and homesick.

"You sure you don't want a swig?" Private Phillips asked, settling onto the cot beside him and procuring a flask from beneath the thin mattress. Although army regulations prohibited soldiers from purchasing alcohol, and any who were found to have violated the rule were punished, it didn't seem to discourage its presence in camp. Phillips took a draught, wiping his mustache with the back of his hand.

"No thanks," Jeremiah declined, pushing himself into a sitting position. Next to liquor, the most important beverage for the soldier was coffee. When they had run short on the substance during their march down the peninsula, it had virtually brought the campaign to a halt. Other substitutes were sometimes tried, such as chicory or peanuts, but as soon as supplies were replenished, there was a sigh of relief among the men.

Phillips seemed like a good sort of fellow, but like most of the soldiers, he struggled with the tedium of their mission. They had enlisted in the army with a great sense of purpose, only to wind up listlessly counting down the days until their term ended and they could return home. Any Rebels left on the peninsula had been effectively subdued, leaving the First Eastern Shore Infantry to keep watch over them as if they were wayward children.

"You want to play cards?" Phillips offered, retrieving his deck and shuffling it expertly as he waited for an answer. He knew that Jeremiah declined to gamble, preferring to send his money home where it would be well spent rather than lose it to a soldier to purchase whiskey. However, if there was no money on the line, Jeremiah was happy to pass the time playing a game of Spades or Poker.

"Sure. Let's see if anyone else wants to join in," he replied, coming to his feet.

They followed the sound of cheering to find a group of men gathered beneath the outstretched limbs of a giant oak, the sun filtering through the green leaves and leaving patches of golden light on the ground. Something in the center of the gathering held their attention, and they whooped and hollered with great enthusiasm.

Nudging a young private by the name of Cullen, Phillips asked, "What's going on here?"

Cullen shook his head in disbelief. "You aren't going to believe this. They're racing weevils."

"Turner, you hear that?" Phillips guffawed. "How am I supposed to see?" he demanded, elbowing his way through the crowd. As Phillips cleared an opening with his massive form, Jeremiah followed on his heels.

As if it were thoroughbreds thundering down the track instead of weevils inching slowly along, the men yelled and cheered for their pick, calling their bets. And there in the very thick of it was Chaplain Davies, fist in the air as he rooted his weevil on. Jeremiah leaned in to better see the "racetrack," a tablecloth folded into a narrow strip and placed over two card tables pushed together. The weevils required some direction to stay on the track, prodded back onto the runway by a helpful finger whenever they wandered off course.

When the smaller of the two weevils reached the end of the track first, a mixed chorus of applause and groans exploded around them. Money exchanged hands as victors claimed their winnings. Chaplain Davies grinned at Jeremiah, who raised his eyebrows as if to ask the chaplain if he approved of all this.

"Idle hands are the Devil's workshop," the old man shrugged with a grin. "Don't worry, I didn't put money in the game."

"I suppose there are worse vices the Devil could tempt us with," Jeremiah replied, shaking his head that they were reduced to using pests for entertainment.

"Boredom and verminous hard-tack make for an interesting combination," Phillips agreed with a laugh.

The hard-tack was also referred to among the men as "dog biscuits" because of its texture and lack of flavor. Made with flour, water and salt, the crackers were a staple to the military rations because they were virtually imperishable. But often, they were also near to inedible as they became infested with weevils from improper storage.

"Now that the excitement's over, who wants to play cards?" Phillips inquired of the men standing around him.

Davies, Cullen, and two others joined Phillips and Jeremiah, each man dragging a chair up to the small table. It was a good thing the chaplain didn't gamble, as he was invariably served a good hand and had a knack for bluffing on the rare occasion when he wasn't. Like Jeremiah, Cullen and Phillips sent most of their wages home to support their families while they were away. Jeremiah had no idea what Davies did with his money as he neither gambled nor indulged in the habits to which most of the soldiers donated their pay.

Jeremiah stroked his beard thoughtfully as he surveyed his hand. He'd played more games of cards in the last six months than in the entirety of his life prior to military service. Growing up on a farm, he had spent many long days working in the fields. When he was given free time, he and Charlie spent it horseback riding or sailing with friends on the Corsica River, once they had grown too old for games of pretend. Sitting still to play a game of cards had never held much interest for him.

Now there were few alternatives to pass the time. If he had been a gambler, Jeremiah would have lost every cent he earned. And Chaplain Davies would have been the one to take it from him.

"How long do you think we're going to be stuck here?" Cullen mused aloud as he drew a card from the pile on the table.

Phillips shrugged. "Till the end of the war, I guess. Somebody's got to keep the Rebels quiet here, and as long they know we're around, they'll be quiet."

Cullen was young, close to eighteen if Jeremiah had to guess. The boy had probably never been away from home this long before, and the dream of chasing glory had long since been replaced with the mundane reality of endless drills. Cullen sighed. "I'm sick to death of hard-tack, beans, and salt beef. I'm tempted to desert just to get a plate of my mama's cooking."

"Well, I'll have to shoot you if you desert," the chaplain warned with his poker face, "so I guess your momma could give me that plate instead."

The men laughed. There wasn't a one of them that wouldn't give his eye teeth for a chance to visit home, see loved ones, and get some real food.

"When I left home," Cullen tapped the cards against his chin in reminiscence, "my daddy told me to be sure to dodge those Rebel bullets. Now, I'm more worried about dying of boredom!"

"You and me, both!" Phillips sympathized.

"Jesus said, *'I am the resurrection and the life: he that believes in me, though he were dead, yet shall he live,'*" Chaplain Davies interjected with one of his random scripture quotations, his finger punctuating the air as he spoke.

The men had learned that he liked to sprinkle Bible verses into a conversation like a cook seasoned with salt. "The Word of God is too good to save just for Sundays," he always explained whenever his "weekday preaching" was questioned.

Chapter Thirteen

A summer breeze stirred the white lace curtains at the window as Clara bent over her writing desk. It was an elegant and feminine piece of furniture with a scrolled floral back and four small drawers for holding paper and envelopes, with an open compartment for ink and pens. The leather top was accented by spiral molding and contained a large rectangular drawer beneath it, where she had stored all of Jeremiah's correspondence for safe keeping.

The fountain pen was poised over the blank sheet of paper before her. Pinching the bridge of her nose with her left hand, Clara closed her eyes and tried to formulate the letter in her mind before she began to write. As much as she despised sending Jeremiah bad news, she could not bring herself to withhold events she knew would be of interest to him.

"*My Dearest Husband*," she began, "*I hope this letter finds you well. With each day that passes, I miss you more and pray daily for your safe return. The fields have been planted and the corn is sprouting in rows of green promise, but it doesn't seem fitting without you here. Nothing is as it used to be since this dreadful war has uprooted the life of peace we once knew.*

"*The entire state is now under the complete control of the Federal Government. Just as Baltimore was assigned a Provost-Marshall to replace the local authority there, Centreville has been assigned one as well. The position has been given to Captain Joseph Goldsborough, and it is his duty to quell any signs of rebellion and maintain order. While most anyone with a sympathy for the Confederate cause has the good sense to hold their tongue, this flaunting of military control has only aggravated the feeling.*

"Yesterday I learned from Jane's friend Emily, who attends St. Paul's Episcopal Church, that the Bishop had authorized a prayer of thankfulness for the recent Union victories. Reverend Stearns refused to offer it, and I agree with his decision. As I love men on both sides of this horrible war, I cannot feel glad for any deaths which mark a victory for either one.

"Another recent event involves Judge Carmichael, whom I'm sure you'll remember is known for his unwavering integrity and bold convictions, as well as his staunch belief in States Rights. In recent weeks he has been making his circuit through the local counties taking a stand against arrests of Eastern Shore citizens without warrants, as with Madison Brown and John Palmer. The Judge deemed it unlawful, and a crime subject to penalty. In Talbot County, the grand jury indicted Lieutenant Colonel Bailey and some others for illegal arrests.

"You can only imagine how that action was received. General Dix sent Deputy Provost Marshall McPhail along with eight of his deputies, including Bailey, to arrest the Judge! They interrupted Judge Carmichael in the act of trying a case and told him to consider himself a prisoner. When he demanded to see a warrant and be informed of the charges, he was told that he would learn the charge when he reached Fort McHenry. There was no warrant, though the Marshall made it clear that his arrest was authorized by the United States Government.

"When the Judge protested and informed McPhail that he had no right to interrupt the proceedings, McPhail announced to the spectators: 'This court stands adjourned.' Carmichael responded by ordering the crier to arrest the deputy who had attempted to arrest him.

"The deputy choked the crier and McPhail ordered Carmichael dragged from his bench. The deputies beat him over the head with their revolvers until he was too stunned and bloodied to resist further. He was then taken aboard the steamer Balloon, *along with others placed under arrest (including the*

State's attorney, Mr. Powell), and taken to Fort McHenry.

"In the very act of protesting illegal arrests, Judge Carmichael has become an example of one.

"My darling, I fear the world is going mad around us. When a kind and gentle soul like Judge Carmichael, a man dedicated to justice and truth, is treated in such a disrespectful and cruel way, it makes me wonder what hope there is for the war to end before we see much more bloodshed.

"I apologize for the dismal tone of this letter. I wish there were better news to share, but at least I can take comfort in knowing that you are safe and I am secure in your love. Until we see one another again, I remain faithfully yours." Clara scrawled her name at the bottom of the page.

Reading over the letter, Clara chewed nervously on her lower lip. She hoped she didn't sound bitter, angry or afraid, although she had to admit that each of these emotions warred within her. She supposed if her letter fell into the wrong hands, she could be accused of treason herself for siding with Judge Carmichael, whose arrest was authorized by the United States Government. But it just didn't seem right. Nothing seemed right anymore. It was as if hell had loosed all its demons of hate and rage to wreak havoc on the mortal world.

Creasing the letter, Clara tucked it into the envelope and wrote the address of Jeremiah's camp in Oak Hall, Virginia from memory. How she wished he could just come home.

At least there was still some good to be found in human nature. Watching Eli as he wooed young Mercy was something which brought delight to both Clara and Jane. Sunday mornings, he was nothing but smiles as he stood by the carriage, face scrubbed shiny and clothes brushed clean, waiting to escort Clara and Francis to church, and afterwards to the Collins' residence.

Whether Mercy's mama, Hattie, had threatened the boy's life or he was so smitten that all he could do was swoon in her company, Eli treated the girl as if she were a prize to be earned. Wildflowers always appeared on the kitchen table in a cobalt blue vase shortly after his arrival, and the two could often be seen sitting on a log bench near the quarter, engrossed in lively conversation.

Like most of the slave women, Mercy's hair was hidden beneath a cloth turban, and she wore a white apron over her brown cotton dress. She leaned forward to listen to Eli with a twinkle in her eyes, enraptured by every word he spoke. And Eli beamed in return, his teeth gleaming in a wide smile that split his black face from ear to ear.

Louis Bland was often in attendance for Sunday supper, and whenever he wasn't, he was all Jane could think to talk about. When present, he was charming and polite, and hung onto Jane's every word.

Although the two couples often inspired a twinge of jealousy or a pang of loneliness, Clara was glad to see evidence that there was still goodness in the world. It was reassuring to know that even though hate flourished as never before, love was still alive.

~

The water in his mug was lukewarm, but it was still refreshing as it slid down his throat. Jeremiah mopped his brow with his sleeve, thankful for the shade of his tent and the ability to remove his blue wool sack coat. The white shirt he wore beneath it was soaked through with sweat, which only made the coarsely knit wool fabric more uncomfortable against his skin.

Completing drills in the summer sun was torturous, especially since the Eastern Shore Infantry felt a bit like imposters as they acted out the part of a soldier. As they sweat, their slick palms made the ten pounds of musket more difficult to shift from shoulder to ground and back again, and complicated the process of fixing the bayonet to the muzzle.

In his heavy leather boots, his feet protested against the wool socks, which were wearing thin on the bottoms. Jeremiah had two more pairs he had brought from home in his haversack, keeping for when winter came again. Surviving the cold in a canvas tent had been more uncomfortable than fending off mosquitoes and other blood-sucking flies which feasted routinely on the soldiers in the summer.

The army had issued him one shirt, one pair of drawers (which he was also saving for cold weather), one pair of trousers, and one pair of socks. According to regulation, he would be given a new uniform after a year of service, although he feared the one he wore might not survive its demands to last until then. At least it didn't have any bullet holes in it.

Slipping his feet out of the boots and socks, Jeremiah leaned back onto his cot, wiggling his bare toes. Next to him, Cullen wrinkled his nose.

"Can we open that flap a little wider?" he asked. None of the men were as clean as they could be. Although occasional bathing and washing of the clothes occurred, it was not as regular as it could have been.

Phillips chuckled as he lit a cigarette, exhaling the smoke through his nose. His mustache twitched as the odor reached his nostrils. "I've met hogs that smell better than those feet."

Jeremiah grinned, scratching his chin through his beard. Sometimes he wondered if they'd have any manners left by the time they were sent home.

Suddenly a face appeared through the flap of the tent as Sergeant Thomas ducked his head in. He glanced around at the men reclining on their cots and announced, "Tonight after the evening drill, Westbrook's taking on a challenger. Any of you up for it?"

Cullen snorted. "I'd like to live to eat my mama's cooking again."

Westbrook was about three hundred pounds of solid muscle with fists the size of Cullen's head. One of the pastimes the men enjoyed was boxing, and Westbrook was the resident champion.

Thomas sized Phillips up and raised his eyebrows. "What about you?"

Phillips chuckled, "I thought I heard Chaplain Davies volunteer."

"Who's taking my name in vain?" the chaplain's voice cut through the resulting laughter as he entered the tent. He pointed a finger at Phillips, "I was passing by and heard you offer me up like a lamb to the slaughter."

"Guilty as charged," Phillips responded. "But I figured you could wear him down with Bible verses."

Davies offered his dimpled grin. *"But I tell you not to resist an evil person. But whoever slaps you on your right cheek, turn the other to him also,"* he quoted.

"Unless he's a Rebel. Then you can shoot 'im," Phillips added with an emphatic nod.

Young Cullen screwed up his face as he demanded, "If you're a pacifist, why are you here, Chaplain?"

"Put on the whole armor of God that you may be able to stand against the wiles of the devil. For we do not wrestle against flesh and blood, but against principalities, against powers, against the rulers of the darkness of this age," Davies replied without batting an eyelash.

"You have that whole book memorized?" Jeremiah wondered.

The twinkle in Davies' eye warned that another verse would be his answer. *"Therefore you shall lay up these words of mine in your heart and in your soul, and bind them as a sign on your hand, and they shall be as frontlets between your eyes. You shall teach them to your children, speaking of them when you sit in your house, when you walk by the way, when you lie down, and when you rise up."*

"Yeah, I say we put him in the ring with Westbrook," Phillips affirmed as he took another draw on his cigarette.

The impish grin which spread over Davies face made him look more like a ten year old boy than a man in his sixties. "Now, who'd want to damage a face as good looking as this?" he asked, patting his own cheek. "Even Westbrook can't be that cruel."

Jeremiah chuckled. "Something tells me you were a real charmer in your day."

The chaplain didn't deny it, simply winking in reply.

"Mail's here!" a cry sounded from outside the tent. Jeremiah reached for his socks, slipping them back on and shoving his feet into his boots. There wasn't a man present who didn't hope for a letter from home, and the Army Postmaster's call always drew a crowd.

Waiting with the others and hoping his name would be called, Jeremiah gathered around the tent designated as Post Office. He usually receive a letter from Clara at least once a week, sometimes more, and from his father a little less regularly. Without them, home would have seemed like a distant dream and not a real place to which he could one day return.

The chaplain's name was called, and when he received the letter, the look on his face drew Jeremiah's attention. "What is it?" he worried.

"Not his handwriting," the chaplain replied, his humor having evaporated. He ripped the envelope open and withdrew the letter with shaking hands. Tears began to course down his cheeks as he read.

"Your son?" Phillips asked softly.

Davies nodded. "Killed in action…" the words wheezed from the old man's lips in a barely audible whisper.

"I'm so sorry, Chaplain," Jeremiah placed a hand on the small man's shoulder, wishing he had something more to offer.

Compressing his lips into a firm line, as if afraid the terrible emotions rising up inside him would break free in a savage cry, the old man nodded his appreciation for the condolences. All the soldiers near enough to hear the news gathered around him in silent support. Davies clutched the letter against his chest.

"*The Lord gave, and the Lord has taken away. Blessed be the name of the Lord*," he forced the words through trembling lips. Then bowing his head, he somberly left the crowd to find a quiet place to grieve.

Chapter Fourteen

I brung you some more!" Silas sang out as he emptied a basket of freshly picked lima beans into the tub between Phoebe and Clara. His black cheeks were round as apples as he grinned, scampering back to the vegetable garden where his sister, Lena, knelt between the rows filling a basket of her own.

Shelling the beans was the part of the process Clara enjoyed most. Although it was tedious work, there was something peaceful about the repetition of the process and the satisfaction of seeing the empty pods pile up in one basket while the beans filled up in another. And the open air of the porch was far preferable to the stifling heat of the kitchen when it came time for canning.

Grasping the green pod in her hand, Clara took hold of the thick string at the top and pulled down, unsealing the shell. Squeezing gently, the pod split open to reveal the beans within. Using her thumb, Clara freed the beans, spilling them into the bowl on her lap. Once the bowl was full, she would add them to the basket.

Even under the shade of the porch, the afternoon was warm. Sweat beaded her upper lip, and Clara was grateful for the light breeze that stirred the tendrils of hair at her neck. Beside her at the table, Phoebe hummed a Negro spiritual, the words occasionally breaking through.

Clara was tempted to ask Phoebe about the rounded swell beneath her apron, but decided to wait until the black woman chose to announce it. Phoebe's slender frame made her early pregnancy impossible to hide, the conspicuous bump straining against the waistline of her dress.

The women worked side by side, the silence broken only by the throaty hum of Phoebe's song and the warbling of the birds in the trees. When she first noticed Phoebe's condition, Clara had felt a thrill of joy for her. But on its heels had come a stab of jealousy. Jeremiah had been away eight long months, and she had no idea when she would see him again. Sometimes she wished she had conceived before he left so that she would have his child to tend in his absence. At other times she was grateful she didn't have the worry of raising a child during this era of chaos and death.

In the garden, Lena suddenly stood, shielding her eyes against the sun as she stared out into the distance toward Turners Lane. Leaving her basket where she stood, she approached the porch. "Looks like you gots company, Missus Clara," she informed her. Clara followed her to the front of the house, recognizing the carriage immediately.

"Mother!" Clara cried as Naomi stepped down. Jane followed behind her. "Is everything all right?" she worried. It was out of the ordinary for them to make an impromptu visit.

"Yes, my dear," Naomi answered, although Jane's eyes said something different.

"Lena, can you prepare some tea and bring it to the parlor?" Clara asked the teenager as she motioned her guests to the front door. "Please come in," she forced a smile, wondering what news this visit portended. Removing her apron, she smoothed the skirt of her cotton day dress as she settled onto the sofa.

"Now, will you tell me what it is?" she demanded softly, searching Jane's face for answer.

"Your sister is engaged," Naomi informed her brightly, although the forced cheerfulness behind the announcement troubled Clara. "Your father gave Louis his permission just this morning."

Clara turned back to Jane. "You don't seem as pleased as I expected," she commented, waiting impatiently for the rest of the story.

"He's enlisting in the Federal Army," Jane supplied the missing information.

"Oh..." Clara searched her mind for something encouraging to say, but nothing came to mind. She remembered clearly the day that Jeremiah left, and the ache that had settled in her chest and never quite left since.

"He says it's better to enlist now, rather than wait to be drafted," Jane explained. "He says that the President has called for three hundred thousand more men to fight, and that if each state can't meet its quota, they'll resort to mandatory conscription. Lincoln thinks we can finish the war once and for all..." Jane's voice trailed off as they all wondered just how realistic such optimism was.

A bounty of one hundred dollars was being offered to any man who enlisted, not to be paid until after his term of service was complete and he was honorably discharged. It was meant to be an incentive as the fervor of patriotism had cooled in the face of the war's brutality.

"It's only a nine month term," Jane continued, her hands knotting in her lap. "The war might even be over by then."

Jeremiah had signed on for three years of military service. At the onset, the prediction had been that the South would be defeated in just six months. Now Lincoln was calling for more men.

Clara reached for her sister's hand. Poor Jane. What should have been a time of celebration was instead marked with sadness and fear. The war had taken so much from them already, but Clara suspected it would take much more before it was over.

All the traditional responses to an announcement of engagement seemed inappropriate. "I'm so happy for you," or "When will you have the wedding?" all sounded insensitive in light of the situation.

Clara was relieved when Lena arrived with the tea tray and interrupted the lengthening silence. She forced a smile, knowing her mother and sister would appreciate the effort while

145

understanding the insincerity behind it, as she proceeded to host the visit as if all was well and right with the world.

The following morning, Clara had just finished dressing when she heard her father-in-law calling her name and immediately rushed down the stairs to the study. Her heart thudded in her chest.

"Is it Jeremiah?" she demanded as she flew into the room, her skirt swirling around her legs as she came to an abrupt stop.

"No, no!" Francis assured her. "I didn't mean to scare you. It's Charlie," he held up the letter in his hands. "He somehow smuggled a letter through."

Sinking down into the leather armchair next to Francis' desk, Clara felt almost dizzy with relief. For a moment she had feared the very worst, and now her emotions felt like a runaway horse that could not be reined in.

"I'm so sorry!" Francis exclaimed as he observed her attempt to regain control of herself. "You look quite pale," he worried. "Would you like a brandy?"

Clara had to smile at his offered remedy. "I'll be all right," she promised. "I just..." But there was no need to explain. They both knew the possibilities. Pushing such thoughts from her mind, she asked, "How is Charlie? Is he well?"

Francis handed her the letter to read herself, although he related the contents to her as if he hadn't. "He didn't write much. I supposed he had to be mindful if it fell into the wrong hands. Says he fought in a battle at Front Royal and was wounded in the right shoulder, but it was just a flesh wound. He'll be all right."

Clara read over the brief missive, the stiff wording and sparse detail leaving her with the impression that Charlie was giving them bluster and bravado to shield them from the truth of his overall condition. But even if he was wounded, even if he was broken inside, he was still alive.

"I'm going to write Jeremiah," Clara stated as she came to her feet. "He'll want to know."

Francis nodded as she rushed from the study, hurrying up

the stairs to her delicate writing desk. Retrieving a fresh sheet of paper, Clara hastened to pen the words she knew Jeremiah longed to hear: "Your brother is alive and safe." No matter that they were formally enemies, they were first and above all family. And blood was a bond that even war couldn't dissolve.

~

Since the news of his son's death, Chaplain Davies had been unusually subdued. The stark contrast between the lively comedian they had come to know and this quiet, withdrawn man was unsettling. No one begrudged him this time to mourn, but they had grown accustomed to his wit and humor and the camp wasn't the same without it.

Jeremiah spotted the old man seated on the ground beneath the shade of an oak tree and went to join him. He squeezed Davies' shoulder silently as he took a place beside him. There was no need for words. What could Jeremiah say to a man who had memorized the entire Bible? All he knew to do was offer his silent support.

There were others in the camp who had lost friends or loved ones, but this death seemed to affect them all. If anyone's son should have been spared, it was this man of God who served with such joy and demonstrated love for everyone around him. If Chaplain Davies' prayers weren't effective to save his son, what hope did any of the sinners have?

Cullen dropped to the ground on the other side of Davies, crossing his legs in front of him. "You all right?" he asked the chaplain quietly. The stubble of a beard clung to his chin, a shadow that hadn't darkened despite days without a razor.

Davies eyes glistened with tears even as he nodded, "I'm all right. I know I'll see my son again."

"What was his name?" Cullen asked.

"Danny." Speaking his son's name brought a wave of fresh grief. He cleared his throat before he continued, "He was thirty years old and left two sons behind. Before the war, he was a teacher." The chaplain smiled tremulously. "He was a good man. I'm proud of him."

Lowering his large frame to the grass, Phillips rested his elbows on his knees, a cigarette dangling from his lips beneath his mustache. "He was lucky to have you," he mumbled gruffly. "Not every man can say that about his father."

With a sad smile, Davies nodded his gratitude. Jeremiah thought fondly of his own father, and vowed to tell him how much he valued and respected him before it was too late.

Cullen, too young to know better, said whatever came to mind. "It's a shame you can't attend a funeral for him. I guess they buried him at the battle site?"

Jeremiah cringed as he imagined how painful this loss must be for Davies, fearing that such questions were like rubbing salt into the wound. But Davies only nodded. "They buried him in the hospital's cemetery. Maybe one day I'll go to see it."

Usually cynical when it came to religious matters, Phillips leaned forward and asked in a hoarse whisper, "Chaplain, do you think God knows the name of every man who dies?"

"I do," Davies replied certainly.

Cullen picked at a piece of lint on his white shirt, his smooth forehead wrinkled with thought. "Why does God allow all this senseless killing? I just don't understand why He let your son die."

Lifting his hand, wrinkled and spotted with age, to thumb a tear from his eye, Davies sighed. "I once had an answer to that question," he admitted, "but I can't remember now what it was."

Phillips dropped the butt of his cigarette to the grass and extinguished it with the heel of his boot. "I don't even know what all the killing is for. Some say it's about keeping the Union together and some think it's about setting the slaves free. I can't even remember why I signed up," he admitted.

When they first arrived in Virginia with Lockwood's brigade in their Federal blue uniforms, wherever they camped as they marched southward down the peninsula, the slaves came to find them. The Negros had it in their heads that the soldiers were coming to liberate them and burn the houses of their masters. Of course, they had been gravely disappointed when they were sent back to their owners.

It had surprised Jeremiah how eager the Negros had seemed for their freedom. He hadn't believed they were so discontented with their lot in life. Perhaps the slaves at Laurel Hill were an exception, or maybe he had chosen to believe what allowed him to have a clear conscience. In any case, he hadn't heard any official talk of the war being for the purpose of ending slavery. The abolitionists would certainly push for it, but as far as Jeremiah knew, the President was only worried about keeping the South in the Union.

"My family owns slaves," Cullen mused. "I wouldn't have enlisted if I thought I was setting them free."

"My family does too," Phillips said. "I bet most of us here could say the same."

Cullen looked to Jeremiah, who nodded as he admitted, "We do, though not many, and we always treated them very well."

"What about you, Chaplain?" Cullen wondered.

Davies studied the boy's sincere expression before answering carefully, "I did once. But I haven't for a long time."

"Why not?" Jeremiah prompted, knowing there was more to the answer.

"I don't believe a person should be owned, like a horse or an ox. God created mankind, and I don't read in Genesis that He made one race better than another," he replied honestly.

"You don't think that Negroes are like us, do you?" Phillips demanded, disgust clearly written on his face. "You can't think they should be free, with the same rights as whites, to own property and vote?"

Without censure, the chaplain looked Phillips dead in the eye and replied, "Why not?"

"Because," the soldier sputtered, "everyone knows they're

Rebekah Colburn

inferior to whites!"

"You prove it to me from the Bible and then I'll believe it," Davies challenged, his mouth drawn in a firm line.

Phillips huffed, crossing his arms and resting them on his knees. Everyone present knew that he wasn't going to spend hours reading the Holy Scriptures in search of a proof text.

"If it looks like a person, thinks like a person, and talks like a person—it *is* a person," Davies expounded. "If you'd been born with dark skin, it wouldn't make you any less of a person than you are now. Just think about that," he finished gently.

"You're lucky I like you," Phillips retorted, and Jeremiah sensed there was truth in it.

The impish gleam the men had missed returned to Davies' eyes just for a second. "No, I'd say you're lucky I like *you*," he replied.

Their conversation was disrupted as the call went up that the mail carrier had arrived. Davies remained seated, as if he had no desire to receive another letter. Jeremiah followed the others to the makeshift Post Office.

Jeremiah waited as names were called, finally hearing "Turner!" he moved forward to receive the envelope. It was from Clara. He couldn't remember the exact shade of her eyes, but he had memorized the way her letters sloped and curled just slightly at the end of a word, and the way she crossed her t's and dotted her i's. He could hardly recall what it felt like to hold her in his arms, but every time he read a letter from her he felt that same profound and mysterious connection he had once felt in her company.

Retreating to his tent to savor the letter in some semblance of privacy, Jeremiah lowered himself onto his cot. He had learned to identify Clara's mood when she wrote based on the precision of her penmanship. If her letters slanted severely and she overlooked the use of punctuation, it meant she was feeling intense emotion as she wrote. He could hear her voice and the inflections of her tone as he read over her words.

150

His lips parted in surprise as he read that a missive had been received across enemy lines from his brother. Closing his eyes, Jeremiah offered up a prayer of gratitude for Charlie's safety. He exhaled slowly, thankful that his brother had survived another battle and had taken the effort to send communication home.

"Everything all right?" Phillips asked as he ducked into the tent and saw the look on Jeremiah's face.

"I just learned my brother's safe. I didn't know for sure."

"Is he fighting?"

Jeremiah nodded.

"Where's he stationed?"

"Virginia, on the Western Shore," Jeremiah answered, rubbing a hand over his face. "But he's fighting with the Rebels."

Phillips' eyes widened. "He's a Rebel?" he repeated incredulously.

"I'm afraid so," Jeremiah sighed, weighted down by the gravity of the situation.

"Sure hope our paths never cross," Phillips echoed Jeremiah's heartfelt conviction.

Chapter Fifteen

Jeremiah ran a hand over his face, enjoying the marvel of a freshly washed beard. He's wasn't exactly clean, but at least he was the cleanest he'd been in months. The regiment had been given permission to travel in small groups to bathe in a creek several miles away. They'd even been able to acquire soap, a rare luxury for the soldiers.

His hair was damp and curled at his neck. The August heat dried the clothes on his body as he marched back to the military camp at Oak Hall, the dust from the road instantly ruining his efforts. But he still felt better than he had in some time. The men had become so rank that they could hardly stand themselves, let alone one another.

Arriving at camp just before dusk, Jeremiah was grateful to have missed the evening drill. Life had become nothing more than a monotonous repetition of drills and aimless attempts at entertainment in between. Listlessness had set in between the continuous boredom and the oppressive humidity. A cool swim with a bar of soap had helped in alleviating it, even if nothing could cure it.

Reaching the camp, Jeremiah reported to his tent, wishing he'd had the opportunity to wash his bedding before taking a bath. The idea of sleeping on the filthy cot disgusted him, but there was nothing to be done about it now.

Retrieving his writing kit, Jeremiah went back out into the fading light and settled in a secluded place to write home. Ever since the conversation between Phillips and Davies, he'd been thinking about the necessity of communicating his respect and appreciation for his father before the time slipped away and one of them was gone. He retrieved a sheet of paper and the cedar pencil, rushing to form the words before darkness fell and he couldn't see the page in front of him.

Crickets chirped in the grass and above him, hidden in the branches of the trees, cicadas buzzed and hummed. Hosts of birds sang their goodnight songs, their varied melodies blending into one loud chorus. A deep longing for home stirred in his chest.

"*Dear Father,*" he wrote, "*I apologize for the sentimental nature of this letter, but I have recently come to understand the importance of saying what is in my heart while I still can. If I've never thanked you for all you taught me through your example, I would like to do so now. You taught me the value of hard work and how to be a man of integrity and character, to hold fast to my beliefs while respecting the beliefs of others, and to be a man of both strength and kindness.*

"*You instilled in your sons a love of country, a love of family, and faith in God. I am grateful to have you for my father, and it brings me comfort to know that you are caring for Clara while I am gone. I am relieved that word arrived from Charlie. I don't know if you can get a letter to him or if you've already tried, but if you can, send him my love and tell him he's in my prayers.*"

As the shadows lengthened, Jeremiah returned to his tent and tucked the letter into his haversack to mail in the morning. Lying on the cot, which smelled like an unwashed man had been sleeping on it for months, Jeremiah stared at the white canvas above him as he listened to the sounds of nature around him. An ache grew in his chest as he thought of Clara, his father and brother, and the time when they had been together at Laurel Hill. His deepest fear was that he would never know those simple times again.

He awoke to the drone of a mosquito in his ear, perspiration beading his face from the humidity even before the sun had risen in the sky. How wonderful it would be to end each day with a swim instead of wondering how long it would be before he could bathe again. Jeremiah lay waiting for the reveille to summon the men from their beds to dress and line up for roll call. He remembered a time when he was awakened by the crow of a rooster from the yard announcing the sun's ascent. It was a pleasant memory of life on the farm and a much more peaceful way to awaken than the call of the bugle.

When the morning drill was completed, Jeremiah returned to his tent to remove his blue sack coat and unbutton his shirt at the neck. He was soaked through, his beard and his hair beneath his cap damp with sweat. Seeking the shade of a tree and the hope of a gentle breeze, Jeremiah ducked beneath the flap and stepped out onto the tent-lined street.

Spotting Davies and Cullen in their usual spot, Jeremiah went to join them. Sitting cross-legged in the grass, he watched a wolf spider weave its way between the green blades in search of a meal. Its long gray legs moved rapidly across the ground, free to go wherever it wished. Jeremiah envied it.

"You ever think about deserting?" Phillips seemed to read his mind.

"Every day," Cullen replied with a grin, his boyish face ruddy from hours beneath the sun.

"Morning, noon, and night," Jeremiah echoed with a rueful laugh.

Davies wore a serious expression, his shoulders sagging as he confessed, "No. I'm where I'm supposed to be... and without my wife, I have nothing to return home to."

"Sorry, Chaplain," Phillips mumbled awkwardly.

"You're not looking so good," Cullen observed. "You look like you didn't get a wink of sleep."

A half-smile touched Davies' wrinkled face at the young man's blunt speech. "I didn't," he admitted. "I felt like Jacob— or Job, perhaps—wrestling with God. I spent half the night sitting out under the stars, trying to make sense of my life and the world we're living in. And I couldn't. And then, like God

155

was speaking, a verse came to me. But instead of giving me peace, it just made me angry."

Curious, Jeremiah asked, "What verse was it?"

A black leather Bible, dog-eared and worn, rested in Chaplain Davies's lap. He patted it now, reciting from memory: *"Rejoice always, pray without ceasing, in everything give thanks; for this is the will of God in Christ Jesus for you."*

Phillips reclined on the grass, plucking a blade and sticking it between his teeth. "I don't know, Chaplain. Sometimes I wonder if that Bible of yours is just a book full of nice thoughts that don't add up to much when you really need answers. God can't actually expect you to 'rejoice always' and give thanks when you've lost your wife and son."

Davies' gray brows came together as he considered his reply. "That's what made me angry. He does," he answered softly.

"Don't make sense to me," Cullen agreed with Phillips quietly.

"Doesn't make sense to me either," the chaplain admitted. "But God's ways are higher than our ways, and His thoughts higher than our thoughts."

No one replied. He figured Cullen and Phillips didn't want to argue with the chaplain or upset him in his hour of grief any more than Jeremiah did. After all, who were they to give an answer to the question of life's suffering?

~

Francis burst into the dining room, startling Clara as she sat down to breakfast.

"Look at this!" her father-in-law cried, waving the paper in the air. "There's been a battle here in Maryland!"

"Where?" she sprang to her feet and ran to his side. Spreading the newspaper on the table, they stood shoulder to shoulder as they read over the report.

"Sharpsburg, near Antietam Creek," he replied.

"Dear God!" Clara covered her mouth as she read over the account of the battle. The combined dead, wounded, and missing was over twenty-two thousand. It was the bloodiest single day of fighting the war had seen yet.

The Confederate Army had been slowly advancing toward Maryland, having recently taken Harpers Ferry in what was now called West Virginia. This strategic victory positioned the Rebels on the Mason-Dixon Line, the dividing point between North and South, and gave them access to the U.S. arsenal there. Additionally, when the Union surrendered, twelve and a half thousand soldiers became prisoners of war.

Confederate General Lee had first attempted to cut through South Mountain en route to Maryland, but had been defeated by McClellan's Army of the Potomac. Seeing an opportunity to take Harpers Ferry, he did so before continuing on to Sharpsburg. Unfortunately for him, although of great advantage to McClellan, a copy of Lee's battle plans fell into Union hands, allowing them to prepare for the attack.

Although severely outnumbered, the Rebels had fought valiantly and inflicted great losses on their enemy. The Union claimed the victory, however, as the Confederates had been the first to withdraw from the battlefield.

Over twelve thousand Federal soldiers had lost their lives; the Rebels had lost more than ten thousand. Clara couldn't even begin to imagine the horrifying scenes which must have surrounded the battle, or the aftermath as the bodies were gathered for burial. The very thought stole her appetite.

Then, as she turned the page to read the casualty list, she gasped in horror. "No! No, no..." she whispered. "Oh, poor Jane!"

Without a word, Francis turned on his heel and rushed from the room. Clara had spent enough time with her father-in-law to guess that he was sending Eli to ready the carriage. She was standing at the end of the brick walkway when he brought it around several minutes later.

Francis climbed down only long enough to assist her. As soon as he was seated, without waiting for a signal, Eli flicked the reins on Nan's white rump and sent her hurrying on her way down Turners Lane. Clara clutched the paper in her lap, on the off chance that her sister hadn't seen it yet. She was oblivious of her surroundings as they clopped at a quick pace down the crushed shell streets, her mind repeating over and over again, "Poor Jane!"

It wasn't until the carriage had stopped in front of the Collins House that Clara realized she was wearing her day dress and not a going out dress, as would have been appropriate for a social call. But then, this was no social call. She only hoped Jane had already been given the report and that Clara would not be the bearer of bad news.

The solemn expression on Mercy's face as she opened the door and directed them to the parlor gave answer to that question. Jane sat on the sofa sobbing brokenly into a handkerchief, her mother's arm around her shoulders. The cheerful lilac of her cotton dress contrasted against the pall which hung over the room.

At the fireplace, Clara's father stood puffing a pipe while Eddy perched on the edge of his armchair, staring helplessly at his sister's anguish. Francis quietly joined the men in their awkward audience of female histrionics.

"Oh Jane, I'm so sorry!" Clara threw herself to the floor, her skirts billowing around her as she knelt before Jane and wrapped her arms around her sister's waist. Naomi drew her into the circle of her arms, the two women offering what comfort they could through their shared grief.

"He's dead," Jane gasped out between great hiccupping sobs, her eyes swollen and red-rimmed from crying. "Oh Clara, he's gone!" she cried.

Tears dampened Clara's cheeks as she held tightly to her sister. There was nothing she could say to lessen the pain. And just as strong as her sympathy for Jane was the awareness that one day it could be her weeping over the casualty list.

As the death toll rose, so did the demand for black dye as clothing was darkened for mourning. The sight of mothers or widows in mourning was becoming more prevalent throughout the nation, and the Eastern Shore was no exception. As Jane was without formal mourning attire, Naomi left Clara to offer comfort while she went out to acquire the black crepe veil, gloves and undergarments, and an appropriately simple black dress.

In the days that followed, Clara went every afternoon to visit her sister. Jane had become a shadow of herself. Against the dark taffeta of her high-collar, Jane's face was blanched and lifeless. Always prone to strong emotions and an expressive personality, Jane wore her grief as passionately as she had displayed her joy.

Where she had been effusive before, Jane was now withdrawn and taciturn. Often the time spent with her passed without conversation. Clara brought needlepoint and sat next to Jane on the front porch as she worked, sometimes humming or singing to fill the silence. Jane stared vacantly at the carriages and passersby on the street or the birds swooping through the blue sky.

Several days after the Battle of Antietam, a letter arrived for Jane. It was sent by the doctor who had attended Louis' body. It included a kind word of condolence and explained that upon examination of the deceased, a message was found pinned to the inside of his uniform. It was addressed to Jane, and the doctor had seen to its delivery.

Louis' note was crumpled and blood-stained, the burned and fragmented edges telling a story of violence, fear and pain. Tears coursed down Jane's pale cheeks as she clutched Louis's last letter with trembling hands.

"*My Beloved Jane*," he wrote, "*If you have received this letter, I did not survive the battle and have been relegated to the past, to be nothing more than a memory to you. My deepest regret should be to have missed the chance to marry you and grow old beside you. I pray that you will remember me with a smile and that you will go on to find love and joy again. As I prepare for battle, my thoughts are of you. I vow to face the enemy with valor and make you proud. Forever Yours, Louis."*

A lock of Louis' dark hair was enfolded within the paper. Tenderly, Jane removed it and held it against her heart. When Clara took her leave an hour later, Jane was still sitting on the front porch in the wicker chair, the letter in one hand and Louis' hair in the other.

"She's not here," Naomi informed her the following day when Clara arrived for her visit. "She went to visit Mrs. Ferguson. She makes hair jewelry, and Jane's having her make Louis' into a cross pendant," she explained.

"Is she any better?" Clara wondered, accepting her mother's invitation to join her in the parlor over a cup of tea.

"Some," Naomi shrugged delicately, her brown eyes shadowed with the sadness a mother carries for her child. "His letter seems to have helped. Jane told me this morning before she left that if Louis could face death bravely, then she must face her future without him with equal bravery."

Clara's heart ached for her sister. After all Jane's dreams of love and romance, this was how it had ended. Tragic seemed the only word to describe it.

"I shudder to think how many women lost fiancés, husbands, and sons on that one dreadful day." Naomi shook her head, silver hair shimmering in the afternoon light streaming through the window. "What a horrible waste of human life."

Clara sighed, "Surely after the Battle of Antietam, President Lincoln and Jefferson Davis will see that the war can't go on like this. We won't have any young men left if it keeps going."

"I'm afraid that the more men who die, the deeper the hatred and resolve will run on both sides," Naomi admitted regretfully.

"How many men will have to die before this war ends?"

Clara lamented. "And what will our nation look like when it's over?"

Chapter Sixteen

To Jeremiah, it seemed that only a few minutes had passed since the morning drill before they were summoned to drill again. Afterward, they were dismissed to the mess tent for the noon-day meal. The fare was as tiresome as the routine, but compared to the men on the battlefield, they had it easy and they knew it.

"Hey Turner," Phillips called as he exited the mess tent, "you seen today's Tribune?"

Shaking his head, Jeremiah asked, "What's in it?"

"Read this," Phillips pointed to the front page. "Lincoln wrote a reply to the editor of the paper. Did you read Greeley's '*Prayer of Twenty Millions*' the other day?"

Jeremiah had missed it.

"Greeley's an abolitionist, and he wrote a letter criticizing Lincoln's failure to enforce the Confiscation Acts and challenging him to emancipate the slaves of the South to weaken the Rebels. Here's the President's answer." He offered Jeremiah the Tribune.

Jeremiah accepted the newspaper and went to find a quiet place to read. He had heard of the Confiscation Acts, the first passed in 1861 and the second one just having passed a few months before. It was an attempt by the abolitionists to free the slaves held by the Confederacy, stating that any Rebels failing to surrender within sixty days would have their slaves freed through a court of law. However, such a threat proved to be easier made than kept.

Scanning the opening paragraph which referenced the editor's letter, Jeremiah skimmed down to the brunt of the message. President Lincoln made his purpose undeniably clear.

"*I would save the Union,*" he declared. "*I would save it the shortest way under the Constitution. The sooner the national authority can be restored; the nearer the Union will be 'the Union as it was.' If there be those who would not save the Union, unless they could at the same time save slavery, I do not agree with them. If there be those who would not save the Union unless they could at the same time destroy slavery, I do not agree with them. My paramount object in this struggle is to save the Union, and it is not either to save or to destroy slavery.*

"*If I could save the Union without freeing any slave I would do it, and if I could save it by freeing all the slaves I would do it; and if I could save it by freeing some and leaving others alone I would also do that. What I do about slavery, and the colored race, I do because I believe it helps to save the Union; and what I forbear, I forbear because I do not believe it would help to save the Union. I shall do less whenever I shall believe what I am doing hurts the cause, and I shall do more whenever I shall believe doing more will help the cause. I shall try to correct errors when shown to be errors; and I shall adopt new views so fast as they shall appear to be true views.*

"*I have here stated my purpose according to my view of official duty; and I intend no modification of my oft-expressed personal wish that all men everywhere could be free.*" It was signed, "*Yours, A. Lincoln.*"

Phillips waited until Jeremiah had finished reading the President's letter to the editor to state his opinion. "So much for the abolitionists saying he's one of them. Lincoln just wants to keep the South in the Union, plain and simple. He doesn't care a whit about slavery."

"Well," Jeremiah noted, "as I've said before, he's first and last a politician. He's pacifying the Border States by claiming the purpose of this war is to save the Union, and trying to pacify the abolitionists with his '*wish that all men everywhere could be free.*' If that were true, and it very well may be, it only proves that he isn't the tyrant the Rebels make him out to be, because a tyrant wouldn't be bothered with the triviality of diplomacy."

"Well said," Cullen nodded approvingly. "I say we save the Union without freeing a single slave."

"If they do free the slaves of the Confederacy, it would weaken the Rebels. They need the slaves to do their planting and harvesting. Without them, they'll fall to their knees. And I wouldn't be a bit surprised if the freed slaves joined the Federals in fighting against their former masters. If the President only frees the slaves of the South, I'd support the idea," Phillips decided.

"He said it himself," Jeremiah assured him, "he won't do any more than he must to save the Union."

The familiar faces of Mamie and Old Joe appeared before his eyes, and the challenge Will Downes had once given came back to haunt him. *"No reason why that black man out there,"* Will had pointed at Henry, *"shouldn't have a chance to own property and raise his own crops and livestock. As a slave, he'll spend his whole life working hard, only to die with nothing to his name. Just because his skin is dark."*

The chaplain had set his slaves free. *"I don't believe a person should be owned, like a horse or an ox,"* he'd explained. *"God created mankind, and I don't read in Genesis that He made one race better than another."*

The uncomfortable feeling of guilt grew inside Jeremiah. Brushing it aside, he asked, "Where's the chaplain?"

"Napping," Phillips answered somberly. "Poor man's not doing very well."

"Wish we could do something for him," Cullen mused.

Thankful for a diversion from his burning conscience, Jeremiah furrowed his bushy brows in thought. "Maybe we could convince Colonel Wallace to give him furlough to visit the son who couldn't enlist. Maybe he just needs family right now."

"Hey, that's a good idea!" Phillips' mustache formed a grin. "And since it was yours, you get to ask the Colonel!"

Jeremiah laughed. "I nominate Cullen. He's better at persuasion than I am."

At that, they all laughed.

"If I survive this war, I think I'll take up politics," Cullen retorted. "Since I have the gift of persuasion."

"And diplomacy," Phillips added. "You always know just the right thing to say to everyone."

The young soldier cocked his eyebrow, "You know, Phillips, I'll be sure to tell Westbrook that you're looking for a fight. I'm sure he'd be happy to oblige."

"If we ever do go into battle," Phillips retorted, "I think I'll stay in Westbrook's shadow."

"You think we'll ever have to fight?" Jeremiah wondered. "I'm ready to just go home."

"You think you could kill a man if you had to?" Cullen grew serious.

"I don't know," Jeremiah confessed. "And I'd be just as happy to never find out." It was one thing to memorize the Manual of Arms, but to actually stop the beating heart of a man was another.

Phillips snorted. "If they're shooting at me, I think I could kill them," he replied. "And if you're sent into battle, you won't have a choice. Not if you want to live."

~

Clara was pleased to find Jane in the flower garden, reading over a copy of Godey's Lady's Book. Against the somber hue of her mourning dress, her pale cheeks had a touch of color to them.

"Clara!" she looked up, offering the first hint of a smile since she'd learned of Louis' death.

"Jane, I'm happy to see you looking so well," Clara admitted, relieved. "I was worried about you."

Clara took the vacant space next to Jane on the wooden bench situated in the center of the brick walkway that led through their mother's garden. Flowers of every kind and color flourished around them, the bees humming as they collected pollen and the butterflies fluttering above the blossoms in search of sweet nectar.

Jane closed the magazine and rested it on her lap, her billowing black skirt brushing against the dark plum of Clara's dress, worn out of deference to her sister's mourning. "I think his letter has helped me," Jane confessed. "It didn't seem real, just reading his name among a list of thousands of other names. I didn't want to believe it, but I was afraid to hope he was still alive. Now I know with certainty that he is gone and I have something to hold on to whenever I want to tell myself it isn't true. The gunpowder and blood on the paper remind me. And his hair is a part of him—like his final words to me—that I can hold on to and keep him close to my heart."

Jane tenderly touched the pendant dangling on a chain against her chest. Louis' dark hair had been carefully woven into an intricate design, shaped in the form of the cross and finished with gold beads on the tips of each of the four ends.

"I have to go on," she continued, her voice faltering and her face, beneath the shade of her black bonnet, pinched with pain. "A part of me died with Louis on that battlefield... But if I let myself die while my body still breathes, I dishonor his memory. If I am to make him proud, I must not let my heart stop beating with his."

Clara blinked back tears at her sister's speech. Jane was right, of course, but Clara wasn't sure that learning to live without a loved one was as easy making the decision. Perhaps because Jane and Louis hadn't been married, the loss would be easier to live with. Jane had never left home, never taken his name, never fallen asleep in his arms. Not that Jane's loss wasn't real, it just wasn't as deep as if they had already begun a new life together.

Perhaps one day Jane could still know the joy of marriage. If there were any men left to marry after the war.

"I'm happy to hear you say so," Clara reached over to clasp

her hand. "We need you. I need you, my little sister. We have to help each other through this time. One day there will be peace again and life will return to normal. We just have to hold on until then."

"Is Jeremiah well?" Jane asked, finally stepping out of the small circle of her own thoughts.

"Yes, he's fine. He's just not here with me," Clara felt guilty complaining about the distance separating them when at least he was still alive. "Would you like to walk with me?" she asked, thinking it would do them both good to shake this melancholy from their shoulders.

Jane nodded, coming to her feet. "I wouldn't tell anyone else, but I despise wearing all this god-awful black," she moaned. "And this horrible hat is beyond words."

Allowing a wan smile, Clara linked her elbow through Jane's. She had to admit the color didn't suit her sister at all.

"Did you take a lock of Jeremiah's hair before he left?" Jane asked.

"I never thought of it," Clara answered, pausing to admire Jane's pendant.

"If you had, I was going to say I could make something for you. I'm going to have a braiding table made so I can begin creating hair jewelry. I think it would be a comfort to women whose loved ones are away in the war."

"A braiding table?" Clara repeated, unfamiliar with the elements necessary to produce jewelry made from human hair.

Jane proceeded to answer in great detail, describing the smooth round table with a hole in its center, and the necessity of attaching lead weights to the separate strands before weaving them into a pattern. She explained that the tresses must first be boiled with soda, tied with pack thread, and gummed with cement composed of equal parts yellow wax and shellac melted together. Then, using the braiding table, any number of patterns and designs could be achieved.

Clara was relieved to see a spark of life returning to her

sister. Jane had found something to bring her out of her grief and give her purpose. And the hair jewelry truly was a work of art, requiring great patience and precision.

"Perhaps you could ask Jeremiah to send you a lock of his hair with his next letter," Jane suggested hopefully.

"I will," Clara promised, more for her sister's sake than her own.

"You know," Jane lowered her voice conspiratorially, "I'm not the only one who's enjoyed your frequent visits."

"Mother?" Clara wondered.

"Well, I'm sure she has too. But I was thinking of someone else," she nodded subtly toward the carriage house, although the dark bonnet she wore made the gesture seem conspicuous.

Clara squinted, spying the young couple shielded by the carriage house and hidden in the shade of a dogwood tree. Eli leaned casually against the white painted boards, hands shoved deep in his pockets. Next to him, almost too close for propriety, Mercy stood with her hands behind her back, swaying coquettishly. Clara couldn't hear their conversation, but the tinkle of soft laughter carried to her across the yard.

"Aren't they sweet?" Jane whispered, a slight catch in her voice.

Clara didn't reply, thinking that Laurel Hill couldn't sacrifice another pair of hands. If Eli decided he wanted to marry the girl, Mercy would have to come to them. But Clara had to admit that nothing was quite as sweet as the picture of young love, full of hope and tender dreams. If only life was as kind as the dreams of young lovers.

"I envy them," Jane confessed. "It's all still in front of them."

"Your life is still in front of you," Clara countered. "You still have a lot of living to do."

"Yes, I do... but without Louis, it isn't the same," Jane reminded her, and Clara immediately regretted her insensitive counsel. If her life stretched out before her alone, without

Jeremiah, how eager would she be to face the future?

"I'm sorry," she apologized, "I wish I knew what to say."

"I'm just glad you're here," her sister answered, her brown eyes forgiving. Jane had lost weight in recent days, and her square chin and straight nose seemed to dominate her pale face.

"I'll come as often as I can," Clara promised. "Although I'll be needed at home soon to help with harvesting the garden and storing for winter."

"Do you mind being a planter's wife?" Jane wrinkled her nose at the very idea of working in the garden. "I can't imagine it."

Clara had to admit, "I would have married Jeremiah if he had been a blacksmith and never regretted it."

Jane's eyes reflected understanding. "Yes, I'm sure that's true," she answered softly.

Riding home in the carriage, with Eli at the driver's seat, Clara said nothing of the scene she and Jane had witnessed. She observed that the young man never seemed to smile as broadly when they were leaving as he did when they were coming, but often could be heard humming a cheerful tune.

"Phoebe, I believe your brother will be gravely disappointed when I cease visiting Jane on a daily basis," she confided after she had changed into a cotton day dress and joined the Negro woman at her work in the kitchen.

Phoebe stood over the ironing board, working the wrinkles out of clean sheets just recently taken down from the line outside. The iron was warmed by placing it on the cast iron stove, which always had a fire burning no matter the time of year. Sweat beaded the woman's dark skin as she smoothed out the cotton sheet with a practiced hand.

"He can't hardly think straight for moonin' over that girl," Phoebe laughed. She paused, straightening and resting a hand absently on the swell of her stomach. "He don't know if he comin' or goin' for thinking 'bout when he gonna see her again. I declare he's gonna have a fit when he gots to stop seeing her every day. Though maybe both houses will see more work done!"

Clara chuckled, but her eyes had snagged on that small bump beneath Phoebe's apron. She'd never spoken of such matters with anyone before, but she felt false pretending it didn't exist.

"I guess it ain't no secret," Phoebe placed her hands on her slim hips and surveyed her new shape. "I's gonna have a baby."

"I'm very happy for you," Clara offered. "When, I mean… do you know…" she didn't know quite how to ask the question or if it was even appropriate.

"I reckon it'll come around spring of next year," Phoebe supplied with a broad grin, her eyes, brown as acorns, sparkling with anticipation.

Clara's mind raced in a hundred directions. She wondered how Phoebe felt with a child growing inside of her, and if she was afraid of the way it would enter the world. Clara wondered what the world would be like by spring of the next year—if the war would have ended by then, and if peace could ever be restored to the broken nation. But above all, Clara wondered if the Turner brothers would be home by the time Phoebe's baby came, and how the war might have changed them.

Chapter Seventeen

Colonel Wallace agreed to grant Chaplain Davies furlough to visit his son. Jeremiah convinced Phillips and Cullen to accompany him to the Colonel's office to request that the chaplain be given time to visit his family during this time of grief. Davies had been touched by their consideration for him and was eager to leave for Brandywine, Maryland where his son lived with his wife and children.

Resting his hand on Jeremiah's sleeve, Davies lifted his chin to look Jeremiah in the eyes. "That was a nice thing you did. I can't wait to see my grandchildren and have a taste of normal life. But I won't be gone too long, I promise. Somebody's got to keep you boys in line!"

Davies had been sent off with slaps on the back and words of encouragement and affection. Even the men who ridiculed him seemed to regret his departure and the absence of Sunday services while he was away.

Jeremiah wished *he* could be given furlough to visit home. He'd received word from Clara that Jane's fiancé had been killed in battle and that she was not bearing up very well. He wished he could be there to offer comfort to his sister-in-law, and to affirm to his wife that he was safe and his love for her had not been compromised by their separation.

In the wake of Lincoln's letter in the Tribune stating, *"If I could save the Union without freeing any slave I would do it,"* the President had issued a threat to the states of the rebellion. If they did not surrender and rejoin the Union within one hundred days, on the first of January, 1863, he would issue the Emancipation Proclamation. This law would be issued under the authority of his war powers and would free all slaves within the named regions, and would additionally allow colored men to join the Union Army and receive payment as a soldier in the United States Armed Forces.

"I guess Lincoln decided he had to free *some* of the slaves in order to save the Union," Phillips commented as he exhaled a gray cloud of cigarette smoke. "At least it won't affect the slave-holding states still in the Union."

"Well, if the Confederacy raises the white flag, it sounds like they'd get to keep their slaves. Maybe they'll capitulate and let us all go home," Cullen added hopefully.

Jeremiah smoothed a hand over his beard as he considered this turn of events. "I don't think they'll fall into that trap, Cullen. The abolitionists will never let them keep their slaves permanently. It's just a warning. Lincoln's changing the stakes of the war. We're not fighting just to preserve the Union anymore—it's about slavery now. His letter in the Tribune made it clear that he would do *whatever* he felt necessary to preserve the Union, even if it meant freeing the slaves. So this is his new angle. If he turns the war into a moral issue, a fight to set the slaves free, he'll have all the abolitionists on his side. His Northern supporters were running out of patriotic fervor, and this will give them a renewed zeal for the fight."

"Well, I didn't sign up for that!" Phillips declared emphatically. "It's not fair to change the game on us now!"

"Haven't you ever heard 'All is fair in love and war'?" Jeremiah returned wryly.

"Just 'cause I heard it don't mean I agree with it," Philips retorted. "I signed on for three years of military service to save the Union. Nobody said anything about fighting to free the coloreds!"

"Why don't you write the President and tell him so?" Cullen retorted, slumping wearily. "Our job is say 'Yes Sir' and fire on command. No one cares what we think."

Jeremiah thought of Louis Bland and the thousands like him

killed at the Battle of Antietam. They were merely pawns on the political chess board, moved at will by those in authority over them, replaced when they were knocked over by the enemy. Nameless and faceless, they were the means by which the political powers acted out their objectives.

In July, a second Revenue Act had been approved. The first hadn't provided sufficient funds for the continuation of the war, and so further action had been taken. A new office had been created specifically for the collection of taxes, called the Commissioner of Internal Revenue. And, in addition to levying taxes on every day goods and services, this act adjusted the income tax imposed under the previous years' Revenue Act.

Under the new law, the percentage of income tax varied according to the amount of income earned. It was a progressive rate, forcing those with more money to pay more in taxes. There were three basic categories: anyone with an annual income of less than six hundred dollars was exempt; those with incomes between six hundred and ten thousand dollars were taxed three percent of their earnings; and those with incomes greater than ten thousand were taxed at five percent.

Essentially, the citizens of the United States were not only being called upon to provide manpower for the war, they were also being required to provide funding for it, even when the goals of that war were arbitrarily changed without their consent. Deserters were shot, and those who tried to avoid the draft were arrested. As Lincoln had suspended habeas corpus nationwide, authorities could imprison anyone for any reason.

"Damn both the Yankees and the Rebels," Phillips punctuated his curse by spitting vehemently, wiping stray spittle from his mustache with his sleeve. "And damn this war!"

"I'll drink to that," Cullen lifted an imaginary glass. Jeremiah shared the sentiment, as did most of the men in his regiment.

In the still of the night, the only sounds those of insects chirping outside his tent, Jeremiah's thoughts returned to this idea of Lincoln legally freeing all the slaves of the Rebel states. It was the first move on the chess board toward the eventual end of the domestic institution known as "slavery" in America. First it would only affect the Rebel states, but eventually, legislation would be passed to force the emancipation of slaves throughout the Union.

If the President did in fact *"wish that all men everywhere could be free,"* he would use the authority granted him to work around those of opposing views in Congress and in the public to ensure that this goal was achieved.

If Maryland had successfully seceded, on January first of 1863, Old Joe, Mamie and all their children would have been set free. Clara had indicated in her letter that Phoebe was expecting a child in the spring. By law, that child would be born a slave since Maryland was retained as part of the Union.

Growing up, no one had convinced Jeremiah that black skin made a person inferior to those with white skin. He had observed it daily in the world around him. It was the way of things, acted out at home and throughout the Eastern Shore where he roamed. He had not questioned the rightness of it, accepting it as the social order decreed by his ancestors for a reason.

Now he began to consider the possibility that those who had gone before him had erred in their assumption that one race was lesser in value than another. As Chaplain Davies had pointed out, a human being, regardless of skin color, remained a human being made by the Creator God.

The Northern states had, one at a time, voted to end slavery. Jeremiah had heard it argued that it was a matter of practicality: the Northern states were industrial while the Southern states were agricultural and had need of slave labor. Negroes were predisposed to be laborers, due to their greater strength and limited intelligence.

If this were true, what did the freedmen of the North do? How did they survive? It didn't seem fair to assume the Negro race could be no more than common laborers while at the same time depriving them of an education. It made them appear to be lacking in intelligence, when perhaps what they lacked was opportunity.

Jeremiah shifted on his cot, uncomfortable with the direction of his thoughts. One day, he was certain, President Lincoln would decree the end of slavery. If that was to be, did Jeremiah wish to wait until it was forced upon him or choose to offer it to the Negroes at Laurel Hill of his own good will?

The fundamental question which all these arguments boiled down to was this: did the Negro race deserve to be free or should they rightfully be held in bondage? As he pictured the black faces of the slaves at Laurel Hill, the loyalty reflected in Old Joe's eyes and the kindness he saw in Mamie's, Jeremiah knew the answer in his heart.

~

Clara had asked Jeremiah to send her a snip of his hair, explaining Jane's new fascination with the art of hair jewelry. She had hoped this new pastime would draw Jane outside of herself, but it merely offered another form of preoccupation. Every time Clara came to visit, having reduced her schedule to twice a week, she found Jane silently standing at the tall, round table, engrossed in the process of weaving thin strands of hair into basket weave, chain, or snake patterns to be made into earrings, brooches, bracelets, lockets, or necklaces. She had advertised her new hobby to the local women, who had eagerly surrendered their own hair, or that of their husbands or children, to be converted into a keepsake piece.

Jane was so intent on her work that it was next to impossible to draw her into conversation. She took the mission very seriously, as if preserving mementos of others' loved ones was her only reason for living. Naomi took up residence on the sofa and occupied herself with needlework while offering silent companionship to her youngest daughter.

Stepping onto the porch for a moment of privacy with her

mother, Clara asked, "Aren't you worried about Jane? I had hoped she would be back to herself soon, but I see no sign of her."

"Everyone grieves in their own way," Naomi replied calmly, "and this is her way."

"Well, how long do you think it will take her?" Clara wondered impatiently.

Her mother's soft brown eyes studied Clara for a moment before she answered with a gentle reprimand in her voice, "Everyone has their own timing, dear."

Clara bit her tongue before the words in her head passed her lips. *Moping never did anyone any good.*

Naomi produced a handkerchief from her lavender bell-shaped sleeve, patting the perspiration from her brow as she continued, "You and your sister are so close, and yet you are so very different. Jane isn't like you, Clara. She feels everything more deeply, and expresses it more openly. She can't bury her feelings inside and pretend she doesn't feel them. She wears them on her sleeve."

Properly chastised, Clara bowed her head. "I don't mean to be unfair or impatient with her. I just feel like she's wasting away with her grief instead of healing from it."

"This is her way of healing. Just give her time," Naomi lifted Clara's chin, her expression kind but firm. The worry lines around her eyes and the gray streaking her hair reminded Clara that her mother had seen much more of life than she had. "Until you walk in someone else's shoes, you don't know how they will fit you."

"Yes ma'am," Clara answered contritely.

That evening at her vanity, working the ivory handled brush through her auburn hair with slow methodic strokes, Clara reflected on her mother's words. The flickering light cast by the oil lamp left the corners of the room thick with shadows, and in the mirror, Clara could see the reflection of her silhouette cast across the wedding ring quilt. The bed was empty without her husband in it, dark head upon the pillow, waiting for her.

This was the loneliest time of the day, when she had nothing to distract her from her thoughts but the exhaustion pulling her down into slumber. Tonight the gray fog refused to come, leaving her to face the voice of fear she worked so hard to quiet.

As she did every night, Clara offered up prayers for her mother and father, Eddy and Jane, Francis, Charlie, and especially Jeremiah. She comforted herself with the reminder that her husband was well away from the fighting, relegated to guard duty on Virginia's Eastern Shore. The truth was that she had learned to fight her fear of losing Jeremiah with that knowledge as her weapon.

But what if he was stationed elsewhere, sent into battle? What if she was forced to one day walk in the shoes of mourning?

Clara rolled onto her side, curling into a ball with her knees tucked into her chest. On the white pillow beside her, she imagined her husband's sleeping form. She could see his chiseled features cast in shadow, the strong nose, dark lashes fanning across his cheeks, and the thick beard which covered his cheeks and chin. A tear slipped from her eye and dampened the pillow under her cheek. "I love you," she whispered to this memory.

With morning came fresh resolve to keep her chin up and her eyes dry. Joining her father-in-law at the breakfast table, she helped herself to a short stack of Mamie's flapjacks and a link of sausage.

"You remember that Crittenden-Johnson Resolution?" Francis barked, his thick white eyebrows drawn together fiercely.

Clara had grown used to his brusque ways, accepting that she had become a sort of substitute for his sons. "I think so," she answered, trying to remember the details.

"It states that the strict purpose of this idiotic war is to preserve the Union. Now Lincoln's determined it necessary to the war effort to free the slaves of the South if the Rebels will not drop their weapons and apologize for their actions by the first of the year. If they don't—and they *won't*—he will emancipate them all."

"*All* the slaves?" Clara tried to imagine what this would look like.

"Only the slaves of the Rebel states. Not the slaves in Maryland, Delaware, Kentucky or Missouri. We're spared because we're still in the Union."

"I don't understand how this helps his cause," Clara admitted.

"The Confederate Army relies on slave labor to cook their meals, mend their clothes, dig their entrenchments, and harvest their crops back home. Once they're freed, the Negroes can not only leave their masters, they can join the Union Army and increase its numbers. And, perhaps even more critical, Jefferson Davis has appealed to France and Britain to recognize the Confederacy as a sovereign nation. Lincoln's shifting the focus to slavery because both of these nations have already abolished the practice and would be criticized internationally for supporting the South if it's associated with slavery."

"But why should any foreign nation wish to get involved? And why would they side with the Confederacy?"

Francis tugged at his cotton shirt pointedly. "The South is called 'King Cotton.' They export their goods all over the world."

"But who will take care of the slaves if they have no masters?" Clara worried.

"Either the government will or they'll have to learn how to fend for themselves," Francis downed his coffee in a gulp. "And since this is supposed to be a war measure, what will happen after the war ends, I'd like to know. He can't take the slaves' freedom back, and I don't think the abolitionists will let the four slave-holding border states get away with keeping theirs. He'll have to set them free nationwide."

Clara nibbled her sausage, which had grown cold as she conversed. "If we have no slaves, how will we work the farm?"

"The Northern farmers have a practice called share-cropping. Freedmen or white tenants work allotted acres and are allowed to keep a percentage of their crops. The land belongs to the farmer, but these share-croppers work it for them to make their own living," he sighed, forking a generous bite of flapjacks into his mouth.

"Is that what we would do?"

"I don't see what other choice we'd have," Francis answered grimly. "But nothing's happened yet. We just have to wait and see how it all plays out."

The South had proven to be a worthy foe, fighting with spunk and valor despite being disadvantaged in terms of monetary resources and weapons, as well as being sorely outnumbered. No one had expected the war to last this long. The future was anybody's guess.

Clara wondered if Old Joe and his family kept abreast of the political developments and if they knew a possibility existed—however slim—that they might one day be no longer slaves, but free men and women.

From the dining room window, she could see the acres of fields stretching out around Laurel Hill, green with corn. Behind the house was the vegetable garden and the peach orchard, and pens for hogs, chickens, and turkeys. Clara hadn't been born a Turner. She had married into the family, into the inheritance of Laurel Hill, and yet she felt a sense of ownership because of the love she held for it.

How much more did Old Joe and Mamie feel invested in this farm? They had poured sweat equity into the land, calling it home, giving it all they had. Was it fair for them to always work it, but never own even a blade of grass or a stalk of corn?

As Mamie bustled into the dining room to inquire if they needed anything from the kitchen before she began collecting dishes, Clara realized something. Right or wrong, she *wanted* them set free.

Mamie leaned her ample hip against the table as she offered a cheerful smile, her cheeks round as apples and her teeth white as china against her midnight skin. On her head, a scarlet turban bobbed with her movements. "You want I can warm that sausage for you, Missus Clara. Don't look like you hardly touched it."

"No thank you, Mamie," Clara declined graciously, "I've had enough."

"All right then, but you need to get a little meat back on them bones," Mamie retorted as she took the Wedgewood plate from the table.

Clara smiled fondly at the concern she could hear behind the criticism. She remembered the day she had fallen in love with Jeremiah. Mamie had dropped ham slices en route to the kitchen to be served at the party, and he had been more worried about the scrapes on the slave woman's hands than the loss of the food. Jeremiah had even disposed of the evidence so no one needed to know about Mamie's accident.

She wished she could talk to him about her desire to free the family's slaves, but even though Jeremiah had always encouraged her interest in politics and farming, Clara feared this would be overstepping her bounds. When she remembered the affection in his voice as he helped Mamie to her feet and studied her palms, she knew Jeremiah would feel the same as she did.

But what about her father-in-law? How would they ever convince him?

Chapter Eighteen

A year had passed since Jeremiah enlisted in the Eastern Shore Infantry. He had spent twelve months away from his home and his wife. To celebrate the anniversary of his regiment being mustered into service, they were each given a crisp new uniform, complete with trousers and socks. Jeremiah would have preferred a short leave to visit Laurel Hill.

Last fall and into the winter, the troops had marched the length of the peninsula, chasing the Rebels across the bay. They had marched mile after mile, kicking up dust behind them, their feet aching. They carried their musket, weighing ten pounds, eighty rounds of ball cartridge, a pound of powder, five pounds of lead, a knapsack, haversack, three-pint canteen, three days rations, tin silverware, cup and plate, a rubber blanket, woolen blanket, shelter tent, and whatever other additional items they desired, including a writing kit, comb and razor. Beneath this weight, their shoulders and backs ached as much, or more, than their feet in the stiff leather brogans.

Last year, they had slept the cold winter through in their tents, warmed only by the heat of the stove in its center and the blankets they carried with them. As there was no indication that they would be departing this location before another winter set in, the Colonel had given orders for shelters to be built out of felled trees and mud. While certainly lacking in domestic charm, the cabins were far cozier than canvas as the temperatures began to drop.

Jeremiah could smell a tang in the air as the leaves began to turn and the nights grew brisk, making him grateful for the woolen blanket. The forest was transformed into a magical world of colors as summer's green yielded to the vibrant hues of autumn. At home, the brown cornstalks would be cut for the harvest, stacked into shocks throughout the stubbled fields. In the garden, the pumpkins would have grown round and orange, ready to be made into pies or stored for the winter.

For the last several weeks, Jeremiah had found his thoughts circling like the hawk in the great blue sky above him only to land on the same subject every time: slavery. The more he thought about it, the more he felt convinced that it was wrong to wait for the President to pass a decree abolishing the institution throughout the Union. He was certain that Old Joe, Mamie, and their children would cherish freedom whenever and however it was given to them, but he wanted it to be a gift granted by the family they served and not an act of legislation by a paternal government.

But the slaves did not belong to him. As long as Francis Turner lived, Laurel Hill and all its properties and assets were his to manage as he saw fit. For generations, the Turners had been planters, cultivating the land with the help of Negro hands. Never before had the subject of manumission—voluntarily freeing slaves—been raised by anyone in the family. How could Jeremiah even suggest such a thing without expecting reprimand and perhaps even ridicule?

Jeremiah wondered where Charlie would stand on the issue. No doubt, fighting with the Rebels from the Deep South had only solidified his conviction of the rightness of the institution. How would Charlie feel about coming home to find the slaves had been set free without consideration of his opinion? But ultimately, the decision did not lie with either Charlie or Jeremiah. It was a decision Francis alone could make.

Taking a deep breath, Jeremiah began writing the most difficult letter of his life. Deliberating over every word, he carefully explained the events which had sparked his evaluation of the subject and how he had come to his final conclusion. He did not ask anything of his father. Jeremiah simply made his conviction clear.

He wished to talk to the chaplain about the decision he had made, but felt it best to leave it between his father and himself. Davies had returned from his furlough with a renewed perspective and was back to his old antics. The twinkle of mischief had returned to his blue eyes, and his wrinkled face was creased into a perpetually ornery smile.

"Glad to have you back, Chaplain," Jeremiah had shaken his hand in warm welcome. "I hope the time away has done you good."

"It did, thank you," the little man answered sincerely. "I spent a lot of time alone with God and He gave me a new verse to remember."

Jeremiah lifted an eyebrow in question, confident that the chaplain would recite it from memory. He wasn't disappointed.

"I do not want you to be ignorant, brethren, concerning those who have fallen asleep, lest you sorrow as others who have no hope. For if we believe Jesus died and rose again, even so God will bring with Him those who sleep in Jesus."

"He's back to himself," Phillips announced drily as he snuck up behind the chaplain.

Davies spun around, slapping Phillips on his thick bicep as he wasn't quite tall enough to reach his shoulder. "I missed you too, little buddy!" he declared with a broad grin.

Phillips' mustache turned up at the corners as he removed the chaplain's forage cap and tousled the old man's thinning hair. "Glad to have you back," he replied.

Jeremiah leaned in close to the chaplain and whispered, "Be sure to ask Cullen about his new friend."

Phillips chuckled. "If he gives you the chance to ask."

Word had spread of the chaplain's return, and he was flooded with greetings and thumps on the back. "I'm going to need to visit the medical tent after this reception!" he'd laughed after a particularly hearty thump.

It wasn't long before Cullen appeared to offer his own

welcome. Chaplain Davies winked at Jeremiah as he draped an arm around the young man's shoulders. "I hear you have some news to tell me?" he inquired, his eyes sparkling as Cullen's smooth cheeks blushed pink as an azalea bloom.

With boyish pretense at indifference, Cullen replied, "I don't know what you're referring to."

"*Emily*," Phillips sang out, placing his hand melodramatically over his heart as he released a lovesick sigh.

Cullen's cheeks burned brighter as he answered gruffly, "She's just a friend from home, that's all."

Jeremiah grinned at the young man's discomfiture. "She's just a friend who sends him letters every single week now," he explained. "Seems that she couldn't stop thinking about him after he left and finally decided he needed to know how she felt about him. She even sent him a photograph."

"Let me see it," Davies demanded, clearly enjoying the moment as much as Phillips and Jeremiah.

With a barely disguised grin, Cullen procured the photograph from his chest pocket, displaying it proudly to the chaplain.

"Now, what's a good lookin' girl like her doing chasing after you?" Davies teased as he studied the young woman's likeness.

Cullen beamed. "We've known each other since we were kids. I never thought I had a chance with her, but she says she wants to wait for me."

Davies assumed a stern expression as he took a step toward the boy and ordered, "There will be no more talk of desertion from you, or I might take it seriously and report you. I'm sensing a sudden urgency to go home."

The color in Cullen's cheeks returned as he ducked his head sheepishly. "I wouldn't mind if the war ended tomorrow."

Phillips crossed his beefy arms across his chest. "I think we might need to post a guard to keep watch on him."

Everyone laughed as Davies raised his hand. "I'll volunteer.

I have a whole bunch of scriptures I can teach him about love and marriage... and such things." He wiggled his eyebrows meaningfully.

His blush deepening to beet-red, Cullen held up both hands in surrender. "If you spare me the torture, I solemnly swear to stay until honorably discharged."

"Think we should take pity on him?" Jeremiah looked to Phillips for his opinion.

Phillips studied the blushing boy and shook his head. "Nah. I don't trust him."

~

Clara woke to the sound of the boards creaking on the back porch. In her white shift, she padded barefoot across the floor to the window overlooking the back lawn. The moon was a thin, white sliver against the blue-black of the night sky, offering only enough light to deepen the shadows. Clara pulled back the curtains, searching below for signs of an intruder.

Her first thought was that it might be a Confederate soldier traveling at night to avoid discovery by Union patrols. It could even be Charlie. But as she studied the quiet landscape, she realized there was a rhythmic quality to the creaking.

In fact, the more she listened, the more it sounded like the runners of the rocking chair as it swayed back and forth. Slipping into her boots and wrapping a shawl around her shoulders to ward off the chill, Clara cautiously descended the stairs and made her way to the rear exit. Opening the door just enough to peer through the narrow slit, she discovered her father-in-law puffing away on his pipe, rocking thoughtfully. In his hands was a letter.

The door squeaked on its hinges as she stepped out, drawing the shawl more tightly about her as a brisk wind blew around the eaves of the house.

"Are you all right?" she asked in a near whisper.

Francis' initial surprise at her appearance quickly yielded to an apology. "I'm sorry I bothered you. Didn't mean to make you worry."

Settling onto the wicker divan, Clara swung her long braid over her shoulder and rephrased the question. "What's wrong?"

A heavy sigh was his answer as he rubbed a callused hand over his weary eyes. He puffed three times on his pipe, then looked down somberly at the letter in his lap. "I guess it's foolish to think that things are going to stay the same for too long. Season after season, year after year, everything changes. From generation to generation, things change... I don't know why it's so hard to accept it."

Clara waited for him to continue.

Raking his fingers through his unruly white hair, Francis explained, "Jeremiah's young yet. He's easily influenced by the philosophies around him. He doesn't understand all the implications—all the consequences." He chewed absently on the tip of his briarwood pipe.

"Go on," she encouraged softly.

Francis held up the letter with apparent frustration. "He's got it into his head that Lincoln's going to free all the slaves as soon as he can. Not just in the Rebel states, but here too. He wants us to go ahead and free them first, so it's our choice and not something pushed on us. He's been listening to all the abolitionists talking about equality and justice. I'm not sure if he realizes that Laurel Hill is his inheritance, and if we don't have laborers to work the fields, we don't have anything."

Worrying her lip, Clara finally ventured, "I think he does realize that. Mamie and Old Joe and their children are like family to us. We've never treated them poorly, and I believe that if they could stay on and work here under a fair agreement, they would."

Thick brows drew together in suspicion. "Did he write to you about this?"

Shaking her head, Clara assured him, "No, he hasn't mentioned a word of it to me... but if he had, I would have told him I agree."

Francis harrumphed, gnawing ferociously on his pipe as he rocked to and fro.

"If they stayed and worked with us, what would your objection to freeing them be?" Clara prodded, since Pandora's Box had already been opened.

The rocking chair stopped abruptly and Francis leaned forward, removing the pipe from his mouth and stabbing the air with it. "My objection is that there is an order to things and that order exists for a reason! It's not as simple as signing a paper or even passing a law. Lincoln knows that as well as I do, he's just more concerned about saving the Union today than about what it will look like in ten years. When you change one thing, everything changes. When you upset a system which has been in place for over a century, it must be done deliberately—not as a rash choice in the name of war effort or to appease the conscience."

"Maybe there is a better way," Clara admitted, "but it's too late now. The wheels of change have already been put into motion."

Francis grunted, whether in agreement or resentment, Clara couldn't be sure. "That's true enough." He rocked some more, puffing silently on his pipe. Finally the rocker stopped and he came to his feet. "I'm going to bed. You should try to get some sleep too."

Clara also rose to her feet, hoping her father-in-law would offer some clue as to his position. But he left the matter where it stood, saying no more as he held the door open for her to proceed him into the house.

Throughout breakfast the following morning, she kept an eye on him, waiting for further commentary on the topic. But he seemed fully absorbed in cleaning the plate in front of him. Clara knew better than to raise the subject herself. She would simply have to wait for him to mull it over and come to a conclusion.

At supper, he broke the silence by declaring quite suddenly:

"I was born in 1807, not long before the United States fought England a second time for her freedom. I was just a child." Clara listened attentively, sensing that this was a preamble to his decision. Her mother had told stories about the war of 1812. A few years older than Francis, Naomi had a few vague memories of that time in history.

"As a boy, and then as a man, I thought the matter of freedom had been settled once and for all by my father's generation. I never imagined that we would fight over the idea of liberty one more time—against ourselves—coming at the idea from two completely different perspectives. The South is fighting for freedom from tyranny and for the preservation of States Rights. The North claims to be fighting to free the slaves and hold together the nation which conquered the British." Francis sighed. "The human spirit values freedom above life, no matter what the year, where you are born, or the color of your skin."

Leaning forward in her chair, Clara waited for him to issue the final pronouncement. But he returned to the task of eating, as if he had already made his position clear. "Does that mean you'll do it?" she pressed, eyes wide with hope and anticipation.

"I will," he answered gruffly. "I'll offer to pay them wages to begin with, and we can always work out something more complicated if necessary in the future."

Lowering her voice to avoid being overheard in the kitchen, Clara asked, "You do think it's the right thing to do, don't you?"

"Isn't what I think that matters. The world's changing and we have to change with it." When she continued to study him skeptically, he reached across the table to pat her hand. "I do," he reassured her. "But it's not going to be easy. This war's taken a toll on everybody. Money's scarce," he admitted finally.

"I'll make whatever sacrifices I can to help," Clara vowed, already thinking of several ways she could begin to conserve.

Francis smiled at her fondly. "My boy did well with you," he praised.

The following afternoon, Francis went to the courthouse to legalize the documents which would declare freedom to the seven slaves under his authority. He asked Clara not to speak of the matter to any of the Negroes until it was guaranteed. To prevent herself from telling Phoebe, Clara wrote a letter to her husband, applauding his sense of justice and his courage to ask for such a difficult thing.

When she heard her father-in-law return less than half an hour later, Clara suspected something was amiss. As she descended the steps to greet him, she noted with concern the dark thunderclouds in his expression.

"Follow me," he directed, storming down the hallway to his study, boots thumping loudly against the wood floor.

Once the door was closed behind them, Clara waited breathlessly for an explanation. Francis' face was mottled red and his eyes bulged with rage. He flopped down into a leather armchair and scrubbed his face with a callused hand.

"What happened?" Clara wondered.

"Just made a damn fool of myself, that's what happened!" he growled. "I should have known about it, but it's not something I've ever given thought to or heard anyone else give thought to. Law was passed in 1860 banning manumission in the state of Maryland. We don't have the freedom to release our slaves even if we want to," he fumed.

Her hand flew to her mouth as Clara reeled from this disclosure. Who among them was free to do as they wished? It seemed to her that everyone, man or woman, black or white, North or South, were all restricted by laws imposed on them by some form of government.

Were any of them truly free?

Chapter Nineteen

April 1863

Yellow daffodils danced in the breeze along the brick walkway leading to the front door, announcing that spring had come without Jeremiah once again. In the forest, the trees were budding and in the yard, the grass was lush and green. Another planting season at Laurel Hill had arrived without the Turner sons.

Clara let the lace curtains fall back into place as she stepped back from the bedroom window. On the carved walnut dresser, her eyes caught the photograph perched there in a gilded frame. Taking it lovingly into her hands, she gazed down at the likeness of her husband. He proudly wore the Federal uniform, his expression stern and his features lean. His brown hair was combed back from his face, and his beard and mustache had been neatly trimmed.

He was as handsome as ever, but there was something different about him. Perhaps it was the lack of color in the black and white photograph, or the unsmiling pose. It wasn't the man she remembered, but it was still Jeremiah.

Clara traced the contours of his face tenderly before replacing the frame on the dresser. He had sent it to her as a gift on what was their second Christmas apart. Clara had made him a red, white, and blue quilt in a star pattern, made to fit the dimensions of his military cot. Not only would it help to keep him warm in the crude cabin throughout the long winter months, it was the closest she could get to wrapping her arms around him.

The holiday season had been far less festive than any Clara

could remember. She had felt the gray chill of winter seeping into her heart, casting her inner world with leaden clouds and dismal shadows. There seemed little use in decorating with holly berries or evergreen boughs, or going through the fuss of a Christmas tree. Even if there had been extra money for frivolities, no one seemed very much in the mood. And why should they celebrate Christmas in their customary style when thousands of men would pass the day huddled around a small stove with next to nothing to cheer their hearts?

Jane had seemed to be coming out of her grief, but when the holidays arrived she retreated back into herself, shrouded in mourning as thick as her crepe veil. It wasn't uncommon during the Christmas season to have her burst suddenly into tears. But, as the bleak weather of February surrendered to the brisk winds of March and the warming days of sunshine, Jane seemed to be slowly finding her way out of the darkness.

Clara had no patience for self-pity. Whenever she was tempted to feel sorry for being deprived so long of her husband and moan about her loneliness, she told herself firmly: *"This is your life and you have to accept it. Others have it far worse. You have no right to complain."*

Still, a spark of joy had gone out inside her. She didn't complain or cry, but every day she found there were fewer reasons to smile.

The war waged on as if it might continue until every man in uniform—blue and gray—lay still beneath the ground. In January, the Emancipation Proclamation had been passed and the slaves of the Rebel States were, in effect, free. In actuality, the only slaves emancipated were those in areas held by the Union Army.

Loss of laborers had certainly impacted the Southern economy, and many of the freed slaves had joined the Union Army, but even so the Confederacy never showed the slightest indication of surrendering. Clara kept it to herself, but the truth was she admired the tenacity and bravery of the South. She had heard that Jefferson Davis imposed Income Taxes and Mandatory Conscription like the North, but no one could deny that the Rebels fought with uncompromising zeal against a substantially larger and better equipped foe.

Hatred bubbled like water in a cauldron over a blazing fire. Every battle left a new casualty report, and every death only deepened the hatred. Yankees or Rebels—one or the other was always held to blame. The greater the divide between these forces, the more impossible reconciliation became. Both North and South had dug in their heels, firmly resolved to fight to the bitter end.

In Centreville, the war seemed to be creeping ever closer to home. Arrests of Rebel supporters continued, including a school teacher by the name of Francis Carroll, and his friend J. Alfred Bryan. It was largely assumed that William Paca was behind the arrests, as he had refused to allow one of his overseers to keep Carrol as a boarder because of his political views. Paca had sided with the Union, although other members of his family were in support of the South and his nephew, Edward Tilghman Paca, had enlisted in the Confederate Army.

The schooner *Hard Times* had been caught running men and contraband goods to the South and her commanders, the Tucker brothers, were taken by Federal authorities. The guards posted to watch the *Hard Times* began carousing in the cabin and were joined by the watchman, who had come below for a drink. At this time a band of men known to be Southern sympathizers came on board and fastened the guards in the hold before setting the schooner afire. The event had been generally broadcast before it occurred, and close to one hundred people gathered at the wharf to watch it burn. Though frightened, the guards were released in time and unharmed. Shortly thereafter, James Tilghman and William Everngam were arrested for their involvement in the escapade.

The following month, Union soldiers under Captain Andrew Stafford of Colonel Wallace's regiment of Home Guards were stationed in Centreville to maintain order and keep a firm eye on the Southern sympathizers there. Most of them had been recruited from nearby Caroline County, and after spending their first night at the Sandy Bottom Meeting House, took up residence at the Courthouse.

There were multiple newspapers in town, each offering a different perspective on the war. But as the divide widened between the factions, the tolerance for freedom of speech narrowed. The State's Rights paper had written an article which fell under criticism by these soldiers, who expressed their feelings by marching into the newspaper office, scattering the type and smashing the printing press when unable to extract an apology from the proprietor of the paper, Thomas Keating.

When Captain Stafford learned of the incident, he demanded that the guilty soldiers repair the damages and assured Mr. Keating that he would not be disturbed in this manner again. Mr. Barroll in Chestertown offered his printing press, but Keating was unsure if he wished to continue publication of the paper due to the uncertainty of the times.

Another noteworthy occurrence was told as a whispered story, shared along the slave 'grapevine' until it eventually reached Phoebe's ears and was shared with Clara. Mercy, the young slave at her family's home, had originally heard the story from one of the slaves at Chesterfield Plantation. The Newmans were well known for their Southern leanings, and Mrs. Newman had a brother who had enlisted with the Rebels. This brother had become an assistant surgeon in the Confederate Army, and been captured by the Federals at South Mountain.

Being a resourceful man, he dissolved morphine in brandy and served it to the guards escorting him to Harrisburg, Pennsylvania. He was able to escape near York and made his way back into Maryland, riding through Baltimore with only a linen duster hiding his gray uniform. Reaching Booker's Wharf by boat, Wooley rode into Centreville and entered his sister's house through a window at night while they lay sleeping. He remained for a short while with them while awaiting the arrival of military equipment which his mother and sister were discreetly purchasing for him. During this time, he frequently made visits under the cover of dark to other Southern sympathizers in the area.

One such excursion was observed by a Federal spy and reported to the Provost Marshall of Centreville, Captain Joseph Goldsborough. When Wooley's brother-in-law was asked directly if he was in the house, Mr. Newman replied that he would rather the Captain search the house than merely take his word for it. The Provost Marshall obliged by sending a squad immediately to Chesterfield.

The brazen Rebel had been well hidden by the time the Union soldiers arrived. Mrs. Newman had secreted her brother in a large box beneath a canvas cover filled with potatoes. With a piece of ice to keep the air in the box cool, Wooley remained safely concealed as the Northern soldiers completed a thorough investigation of the house. When they moved on to search the outbuildings, Wooley emerged from his hiding place and stood at a garret window, laughing at the game.

Although the Newman family was known for their support of the Rebels, Mrs. Newman had another brother who had joined the Union. With so many families divided by the war, Clara couldn't understand how anyone could draw clear lines and nourish hatred against the opposing army.

No new word had arrived from Charlie. As far as they knew, he was still alive, though where or in what condition was anybody's guess.

Clara kept her chin up, but deep inside she despaired that life would never return to normal and her husband come home to her in one piece. The longer the war waged, the less likely it seemed that the Turner family could survive it unscathed.

~

Shadows flickered within the log cabin, cast by the oil lamp on the table. Cots lined the walls, and from several of them could be heard the rumbling of peaceful snores. Next to Jeremiah, Phillips sat propped against the wall, flask in hand.

"You know my father was a fisherman?" he asked, his words slurring.

Jeremiah offered a nod, having heard this particular diatribe more than once before. The inactivity and sense of uselessness was wearing away at all the men of the Eastern Shore Infantry. They read the newspaper accounts of battles fought throughout the continent, soldiers given the opportunity to fight for the cause which had moved them to enlist. Real soldiers who fired their weapons at the enemy, charged bravely with bayonets when ammunition ran out, and were awarded Medals of Honor for their gallantry in war.

The Eastern Shore Infantry felt as if they were on an extended camping trip. They faced no danger, fought no enemy, and accomplished nothing of great purpose. The restlessness and boredom affected each of the men differently. Phillips had turned to drink.

"He didn't know what else to do, so he was a fisherman. And I didn't know what else to do, so I became a fisherman too. Lived on Kent Island in a drafty clapboard house by the water. We caught Striped Bass, Spanish Mackerel, Croakers, Bluefish and Shad. And we tonged for oysters..." He pointed a finger at Jeremiah. "That was hard work. Hard work in the sun."

Phillips eyes were blood-shot and his dark mustache wet with whiskey. Jeremiah listened to the man's story whenever it seemed important to him to tell it. He wished there was a way to heal the pain buried deep within Phillips, but unlike Davies, Jeremiah didn't have a Scripture verse to offer or the belief that it could soothe the suffering of the human soul. He believed that every man was born into a certain set of circumstances, and it was up to that man how he would manage the lot he was given.

"Never married," Phillips confessed as if he'd never confided this secret before, "because all the pretty girls want a man with money. And," he sniffed his fingers disdainfully, "they don't like that smell. Still smell it, all these years later." He wrinkled his nose, then shook his head sadly. "I didn't want to be a fisherman, but I didn't know what else to do."

As Phillips fell silent, Jeremiah eased down on his cot and pulled the quilt Clara had given him up to his chin. He had just closed his eyes and felt the gentle pull of sleep when the voice next to him resumed speaking.

"Did you know that Kent Island is the oldest English settlement in the state of Maryland? It was founded in 1631. Only settlements older than it are Jamestown and Plymouth."

Jeremiah didn't answer, hoping that Phillips would forget to continue the conversation and they could both get some rest. But his hope soon proved in vain.

"My father didn't want to be a fisherman, but he didn't know else to do. He wasn't a happy man. He liked to drink, but it didn't make him any happier. Just made him meaner. Poor Mama was a mouse, quiet and nervous. He was a bulldog, and she was a mouse… You know, my grandfather was a fisherman. Guess my father had to be. Guess I had to be…

"That's why I joined the army," he admitted, pausing to take another draught from the flask. "I wanted a different life. Wanted to be something else. Soldiers marching by in their smart blue uniforms always looked so sure of themselves. Women noticed them. I thought I would try my hand at being a soldier. So, here I am…" he mumbled something more but it was unintelligible.

Glancing over at his friend, Jeremiah saw that Phillips was finally beginning to doze. The flask remained open, and as his grip on it relaxed, it tipped to the side and threatened to leak. Jeremiah flung back the quilt and quickly caught the flask before Philips' bed reeked of liquor. Searching about, he located the lid and screwed it tightly on before returning the whiskey to its hiding place under the cot. Then he pulled the woolen blanket up to Phillips' chest, where his chin rested.

No one bothered to report Phillips' drinking to the Colonel. He was a good sort, and he didn't hurt anyone. He sipped at it discreetly through the day, and only occasionally did he over-imbibe in the evenings. Jeremiah didn't know if Davies was aware of Phillips' problem, but he didn't want to make mention of it in case the chaplain felt it was his duty to inform the officers.

Returning to his cot, Jeremiah slid back under the quilt only to realize that the oil lamp still burned. With a sigh, he pushed back the blanket one more time and was just getting ready to swing his feet to the floor when Cullen's whisper cut through the silence.

"I'll get it," he offered, coming to his feet.

Jeremiah offered a grateful smile as he sank back into his pillow.

"I joined because I thought it would be exciting," Cullen admitted softly with a wry chuckle. "At least we look dapper in our Federal Blue uniforms," he added as he slipped back into his own cot. "If only there were any women around to admire us."

Darkness blinded Jeremiah, whose eyes were now open and fixed on the plank ceiling above. Every man there had enlisted for any number of reasons, though all under the guise of patriotism. And all of them had been disappointed.

As Clara's letters reported more unrest in Centreville and the arrival of the Union Home Guard to keep watch on Rebel sympathizers there, Jeremiah wondered if he wouldn't be of more use at home. His father had managed the farm without him and Charlie for long enough. Francis wasn't getting any younger and he was having to do the work his sons should have been doing for him. But Jeremiah had signed on for a three year term, whether or not he now regretted that commitment.

Clara's letters came less frequently than they had at the beginning of his military service. But then, Jeremiah wrote to her less often than he had before. There wasn't anything left to write about. He knew what life at Laurel Hill consisted of; she knew what his life at Oak Hall was like. Apart from local news in Centreville or updates on people he knew, Clara had run out things to report. And Jeremiah's life was the same day in and day out, with very little variation.

The days of romance and passion they had once shared were nothing but vague recollections, no more than cold ashes in a grate where once a fire had burned. Clara was a friend, a confidante, a letter to be opened and read. Her face and her form were hazy memories which sometimes haunted his dreams, but nothing more. He could scarcely remember what a woman's voice sounded like, let alone the softness of her skin or the sweet fragrance of lavender in her hair after she bathed.

The rough and crude ways of men surrounded him. The smells of sweat and feet and flatulence were all he knew. The gentility and refinement of his former life had been usurped by the harsh and insensitive culture of a military camp.

A year and a half of exile to the lower end of the peninsula had left its mark on all the men, but Jeremiah felt it was especially hard on the married men who had enjoyed the companionship of a wife before leaving home. That simple comfort had been exchanged for a lonely cot and a sergeant barking orders. There was no coming home to a soft-spoken word of praise and a glass of iced tea on the back porch, holding hands as the sun slowly sank behind the trees and left the sky aflame with color. There was no sweetness to balance the bitterness of life's demands.

Even if the war ended tomorrow—which it wouldn't—and he could return home, Jeremiah would have to get to know Clara all over again. She had been forced into a new life without him at Laurel Hill, finding her own strengths and weaknesses in the home of her husband while he was away. There was a difference in her tone, an independence forged of necessity and a courage discovered in the loneliness.

He remembered the night in their room, such a long time ago, when Clara confided her fear that the days of easy laughter and conversation between them were gone for good. "Not for good," he'd promised her. "Just for a little while."

Now he wondered. If the war ever ended, none of them would be the same.

Chapter Twenty

Spring passed as quick as a blink and the summer heat and humidity descended upon Laurel Hill once again. The fields flourished with tall, green corn stalks and another season of canning vegetables began. Phoebe went on about her work, appearing unhindered by the infant wrapped around her midsection with a long strip of cloth. When both she and the child were soaked through with sweat, she let the child sleep on a blanket tucked inside a basket and put close to the window where a breeze could cool him.

In the last weeks before delivery, Phoebe had grown as large as a watermelon, her face and ankles swelling as if she had been stung by a dozen bees. Clara had never before seen a woman in the final stages of pregnancy, as most women remained at home and out of the public eye during that time. She had been mortified by the changes in her slender friend, who by the end was almost unrecognizable.

Phoebe didn't complain, although an occasional sigh or groan revealed her discomfort as she waddled around the house or garden. Her dark skin glistened with sweat as she moved slowly about, her breathing heavy with the effort of propelling her uncommonly large body around. Occasionally she would lay a hand over the swollen protrusion of her abdomen, the fabric of her dress tight over the skin, and smile. "He sho' is kicking today!" she would comment.

When the baby announced that he was ready to enter the world, Clara was unprepared to be part of the moment. Lena had been called upon to work with the men planting in the fields, taking over the role for Phoebe as she was too far along to be jostled about on the wooden buckboard of the wagon. Clara had taken Lena's place assisting Phoebe with the laundry as Mamie was busy in the kitchen most of the day preparing for or cleaning up after meals.

Clara had insisted—quite forcefully—that she would perform the more difficult work of stirring the clothing in the steaming tub of lye soap and then transferring it to a second tub to be rinsed. She had assigned Phoebe the task of wringing the water from the clothes and hanging them on the line to dry. When Phoebe suddenly straightened and gripped her belly, Clara assumed the child had given her an especially hard kick.

But the wide-eyed fright in Phoebe's eyes told her that this was something different. "I think that baby gonna come today," she announced, closing her eyes as the contraction gripped her.

"I'll get your Mama!" Clara cried, running to the kitchen and calling for Mamie at the top of her lungs.

"What all that fuss?" the plump Negro woman demanded, her lower lip protruding and her hands resting on her hips.

"I think it's time," Clara gasped out.

"All right. Calm down. Babies born all the time," Mamie answered as she removed the pan from the stove and wiped her hands on her apron. "Supper gonna be late today," she stated.

Clara fluttered nervously behind her as Mamie marched outside to the washtubs. Phoebe sat on a stool, sweat beading her upper lip as she ran her hands over her enormous abdomen. "Gonna have a grand-chile today, Mama," she grinned.

Mamie patted her daughter's shoulder and smiled. "Let's get you into bed," she ordered as she wrapped her arm around Phoebe's thick waist and guided her toward the slave quarter. Clara hesitated, then followed, determined to help in any way she could.

She'd never been in the slave cabin before. She tried not to gawk in curiosity as she passed through the doorway into the small brick building. The first thing Clara noticed was how very small the space was, followed by the awareness of how sparsely it was furnished. A brick fireplace occupied the center of the far wall, which was roughly plastered to keep out the elements. Two makeshift cots, no more than wooden rectangles with ropes suspending a tick mattress, were positioned on either side of the room. A crude staircase led to the second level, where Clara presumed Eli, Lena and Silas slept. A small table with four chairs occupied the middle space. Light filtered in through glass windows on three sides of the cabin.

Mamie situated Phoebe on her bed, pulling back the woolen blankets to expose the white sheet beneath. Phoebe sat heavily on the mattress, which Clara noted was lumpy and unforgiving. Leaning back against the pillow, Phoebe closed her eyes and breathed slowly.

"I gonna go boil some water now," Mamie told her. "Missus Clara gonna sit with you, all right?"

Phoebe opened her eyes and nodded. Clara pulled one of the straight-backed chairs next to the bed and took her place by Phoebe's side. "What can I do for you?" she asked uncertainly.

"Just sit," Phoebe smiled at her. "And try to relax! You makin' me nervous!"

"Sorry," Clara breathed as she relaxed her shoulders.

When Mamie arrived, she had brought back with her not only hot water, but towels and a very sharp knife. Clara tried not to stare at it as Mamie placed it on the table.

What followed was hours of grueling labor as the contractions gained in momentum and intensity, until finally Mamie instructed Phoebe to push. Clara had taken position by Phoebe's head, leaving the end of the bed to her mother. She watched in horror as Phoebe grunted and strained, gnashing her teeth and rolling her eyes back in her head. After several such efforts, Mamie cried, "Here he comes!" and within seconds, was holding a slick little boy in her hands.

With skilled precision, she used the knife to severe the umbilical cord, wrapped the child in a towel and held him up for his mother to see. "It's a boy!" she declared grandly before handing him off to Clara. "Wipe him down," she ordered, "while we finish up here."

Clara obeyed, taking the fragile newborn into her arms and carrying him to the table. She could hear Mamie coaching Phoebe to expel the afterbirth, but Clara kept her eyes averted and focused on the chore of tenderly cleaning the squalling babe and swaddling him in a fresh blanket.

By the time she had finished her work, Mamie was returning from outside where she had disposed of the dirty linens. Phoebe lay upon the bed, the blanket modestly covering her body, waiting impatiently to hold her hard-earned prize.

Clara carefully transferred the baby into his mother's arms, noting the pride and joy which lit Phoebe's black features. Her eyes caressed the infant lovingly as she studied his every detail. "Isn't he beautiful?" she whispered.

Gazing down at the diminutive face with thick curling lashes and a button nose, pouting pink lips and dark chubby cheeks, she had to agree. He was beautiful.

"You done real good," Mamie patted her daughter's hand, white teeth gleaming in a broad grin. "What you gonna name him?"

"Henry say we can call him Joseph, after his grand-daddy," Phoebe answered.

Mamie nodded, a tear glistening in her eye. "He like that," she replied softly.

Clara came to her feet, feeling as if she was intruding on a private moment, and said, "I'll go find Henry now and tell him he's a father."

But as she swung open the door, she saw that Henry already stood outside the cabin, hat crumpled in his hands and eyes round as saucers. "He's a healthy boy, and his mama is doing just fine," she assured him as she gestured for him to enter the cabin.

Mixed wonder and eagerness reflected in Henry's face as he moved past her. Clara pulled the door closed behind him and stepped out into the cool evening air. She closed her eyes for just a moment, overwhelmed by all she had witnessed. A twinge of longing squeezed her heart for just a second as she heard Henry's exclamation of delight, but she ignored the ache in her chest and went to the kitchen to procure a quick meal for the household.

~

Jeremiah dropped the newspaper onto the table and leaned forward to rest his elbows on the surface, head in his palms. In the last three months, between April and June, thirty-five battles had been fought. Casualties continued to grow, thousands of men losing their lives and just as many wounded or taken prisoner.

The world had fallen into dark chaos, and he worried that it would never again be able to find its way to the light.

The Confederacy could claim several victories in this string of battles, but the tide seemed to have turned for the Union. Reports came that the Rebels were running short on rations and their army was growing weak with starvation. Grant had sieged Vicksburg where the Confederate Army had retreated for safety, holding out for forty days until their supplies ran out and they were forced to surrender.

This decisive loss cut the Confederate Army off from the rest of their men in Arkansas, Louisiana and Texas, hindering communication with forces in Missouri and Indian Territory as well. It bolstered the confidence of the Federal troops, strengthened with fresh conscripts.

The best Jeremiah could figure, Charlie was stationed under General Jones in the Valley of Virginia. He'd read that the First Maryland Infantry, CSA had mustered out and the Second Maryland Infantry (also called the First Maryland Infantry Battalion) had been formed with many veterans of the First as well as other Southern units, and a handful of fresh recruits. Charlie's name had yet to appear on any casualty lists, so Jeremiah held out hope that he was both alive and well.

Jeremiah desperately wished there was a way to smuggle a letter across enemy lines to his brother, to let Charlie know where he was and how he was doing. And above all, to let Charlie know how much he still loved him.

He wondered how much fighting his brother had seen and what scars he carried, inside and out, from the battles he had known. Jeremiah almost felt ashamed that his regiment had served for a year and a half without a single engagement. Of course, he kept such regrets to himself when writing letters home. He was fairly certain his wife and father would never understand such feelings.

Clara had written that Phoebe delivered a son, and that Lena was obligated to take over watering the corn as it was planted. Whenever he thought about how hard they were working at home while he did nothing more than mark time by drilling, playing cards, and talking, he felt like a failure. He had wanted to be a brave soldier but had ended up as nothing more than a man in uniform.

"Is it really that bad?" he heard Chaplain Davies ask as he joined him at the table.

Jeremiah lifted his head from his hands. "No, not really. Just reading about another battle. Seems like that's all there is to read about anymore."

"That's why I quit reading the paper," Davies quipped. "No good stories in there."

Jeremiah offered the old man a half-smile. "It's really because you're too busy reading the Good Book to read anything else."

"Well," the chaplain admitted, "the stories are a lot better. And I know who wins that battle. *'So when this corruptible has put on incorruption, and this mortal has put on immortality, then shall be brought to pass the saying that is written, Death is swallowed up in victory.'"*

"I'm going to be honest," Phillips pulled out a chair and spun it around, sitting on it backwards with elbows folded across the back and a cigarette dangling from his lips. "His head just doesn't look big enough to hold all them verses."

"I'm going to be honest," Cullen chimed in as he flopped down to join them. "I have no idea what he's talking about half the time."

Phillips and Jeremiah laughed as they admitted simultaneously, "Neither do we!"

"Allow me to enlighten you," Davies proclaimed with a flourish, his wrinkled face forming an impish grin. "'*If the dead do not rise, then Christ is not risen. And if Christ is not risen, your faith is futile; you are still in your sins! Then also those who have fallen asleep in Christ have perished. If in this life only we have hope in Christ, we are of all men the most pitiable.*'"

Chuckling, Cullen shook his head. "I still have no idea what you're talking about, Reverend, but don't let it worry you. Maybe you have more brains in that little head than I do."

"That's a distinct possibility," the chaplain agreed, a twinkle in his eye.

"Now I think I'm suddenly remembering a verse that says, 'Pride goes before a fall,'" Jeremiah pointed a finger condemningly at Davies, who only laughed in reply.

"That's actually not a verse," he shrugged, "but you're pretty close. It says: '*Pride goes before destruction, and a haughty spirit before a fall.*'"

"I've had about enough of this guy," Phillips leaned forward to grab a tin cup of water resting on the table. "I think his big brain needs cooling off," he declared, pulling off the chaplain's cap and pouring the water over his balding head.

"Hey!" Davies sputtered, water dripping down his chin.

He started to say something smart, but a ruckus on the other side of the camp drowned out his words. As one, they all sprang to their feet and dashed down the dirt streets to the source of the commotion.

Westbrook, the resident boxing champion, was pounding a smaller man by the name of Wilson with his over-sized fists. The unfortunate recipient of this outburst tried to rally a defensive stance, but met with another blow before he could gain his footing. Wilson swung haphazardly at his opponent, his fist hooking the air as Westbrook easily sidestepped the punch. With a throaty growl, the muscular private landed an uppercut to Wilson's chin, sending him reeling backward to the ground.

When Westbrook jumped on the fallen man to continue the beating, Wilson's friends intervened and took hold of the larger man, grabbing him by his thick biceps and pulling him back. One especially outraged soldier took the opportunity to land a firm right hook to Westbrook's chiseled chin, and was lucky when his friends were able to contain the revenge Westbrook had planned for him. More men jumped into the fray, pinning this brazen fellow back and shouting for the fighting to stop.

Sudden silence fell as Colonel Keene appeared on the scene. "What is the meaning of this?" he bellowed. He pointed a finger at the three men who had clearly been engaged in the misconduct. "You, you, and you, come with me. *Now*." He turned on his heel and marched away, confident the belligerents would follow.

"Everybody's itching for a brawl," Phillips muttered as he watched three men follow the Colonel to his office to receive their punishment. "Sitting around here like a bunch of old biddies at a quilting bee is bound to make a man testy."

"Well, we were needing new latrines dug. Guess I know who just volunteered for that," Davies commented.

Often called "sinks," the latrines were merely ditches dug ten to twelve feet long and about two feet wide, and six to eight feet deep. Suspended over this ditch was a board with holes cut in it to be used as seats. Each day, six inches of dirt along with carbolic acid or chlorinated lime were thrown over the waste to cover and deodorize the stench. When the latrine was filled to within two feet from the edge, it was topped off and a new sink dug for the men's necessary functions. The latrine was disguised by a small mound of brush to afford minimal privacy.

Cullen leaned in close to whisper, "I can't say who I heard it from, but I heard that Colonel Wallace has written to the powers that be requesting duty at the front. Now, I don't know if it's true or if they'll call on us, but that's what I heard."

"Duty at the front?" Phillips repeated, his eyes brightening at the prospect. "The front lines?"

"Well, yeah, but I'm not in a hurry to get killed and I don't know why you should be. I just want this war to end so I can get home," Cullen said. His smooth jaw clenched as he patted the picture of Emily he carried in his chest pocket.

Phillips' mustache twitched. "If you can't tell me who you heard it from, how do I know if it's reliable information?" he demanded.

"I told you I don't know if it's true or not. Just letting you know it's a possibility. I for one hope it *isn't* true," he repeated.

Jeremiah and Davies exchanged glances. If it was true, their peaceful respite was about to come to an end and their muskets, bayonets and ceaseless drilling would soon fulfill their purposes.

Chapter Twenty-One

Baby Joseph was three months old, with round cheeks and intelligent brown eyes. Whenever spoken to, he broke into a wide grin revealing pink toothless gums. If ignored for too long, Little Joe would remind the women of his presence with high pitched gurgling, quickly escalating into an angry wail if they failed to respond in a timely manner.

Mamie instructed the younger women that if they catered to him every time he set up to howling, Little Joe would never learn how to soothe himself. But Clara hated the way his cries pulled at her heartstrings, touched by the fear of abandonment she could hear in those plaintive wails. Phoebe sometimes gave his belly a little pat as he lay in the basket to let him know that she was close by, but she followed her mother's orders and let him fuss when she knew all his needs had been met.

Clara was the only one who dared disobey Mamie. Lena often looked at the basket containing the unhappy baby with longing eyes, but did not leave her work to hold him unless instructed. Sometimes those lusty cries were more than Clara could ignore, and she would scoop the boy up and hold him close to her chest, humming a song as she swayed back and forth to quiet him.

Feeling his soft skin against her cheek as his screams transitioned to coos brought comfort to her own aching heart. There were times when Clara wished she could be a child again, able to climb onto her mother's lap and let something as simple as a hug and song take away the pain she felt.

In his last letter, Jeremiah had warned her there was a possibility he could be sent to the front. *"I don't want you to* worry," he wrote, "*but I do want you to be prepared should it happen. If we are called up, I will try to get word to you as soon as possible. As far as I can tell at the moment, it's only gossip.*"

Every time she began to consider the likelihood that he would be sent into battle, she told herself sternly: "Don't waste your energy worrying about something that hasn't happened yet. Today has enough to worry about."

But at night when she slept the demons of fear wreaked havoc with her imagination, producing nightmares in which she and Jane both wore the heavy crepe veil and taffeta mourning dress. In these horrible dreams, which felt every bit as real as her waking moments, she saw the announcement of her husband's death and felt the word "widow" strike her heart with pain as piercing as the spear of an arrow.

Jane had taken the lock of hair Jeremiah sent and formed it into a pair of teardrop-shaped earrings. Clara had thought it was pure sentimental nonsense, but once on her ears, she found herself touching them often and feeling a strange sense of connection with the husband she had not seen in almost eighteen months.

In these terrible nightmares, the jewelry formed from Jeremiah's hair seemed to have a life and spirit of its own. They pulsed with a strange and ghostly presence, as if he had taken up residence in them. It was a hollow and empty feeling to know that these little snips of hair and a stack of letters were all she had left of him.

In the morning she awoke with a gasp of relief upon realizing that it wasn't real. As far as she had reason to believe, Jeremiah was still safely stationed at Oak Hall, alive and thinking of her. But that niggling finger of doubt pressed sharply into her side, reminding her that just because she hadn't received word didn't mean it hadn't already happened. Or might still happen.

When his father read the warning Jeremiah sent, Francis' leathery skin formed into a deeply grooved frown, his coarse white eyebrows sprouting out over shadowed eyes. "We knew it was a possibility the day he left," he reminded Clara gravely. "He's been lucky so far."

~

Excitement rippled through the camp. As Jeremiah ran to his cabin to pack his haversack and prepare for departure, he felt it charging through him. Around him, everyone raced to follow orders, some anticipating the battle to come, others dreading it, and many unable to think beyond the moment.

Hastily Jeremiah removed his writing kit and scratched a letter to his wife. He had not been informed exactly where they were headed, only that they were going north to reinforce troops in Pennsylvania. They would take a steamer across the bay to Baltimore, then travel some of the distance by rail and march the rest of the way on foot.

Adrenaline pumped through his veins, making the pencil in his hands jerk as it quickly formed the words on the paper. There was no way of knowing what they would face when they reached the front, if they would immediately be thrown into the fray or if the battle would have already been decided before they arrived. But Jeremiah knew there was a chance this could be the last letter he ever sent to Clara, and he wrote it as if it was.

"My Dearest Clara, We are being called up to active duty on the front. We leave immediately. I hope this letter will reach you before I arrive at the battlefield in Pennsylvania. Pray for me, my sweet wife, that I may fight courageously and return safely home to you. I have little time, but I feel I must try to put my feelings into words in case that is not possible. I remember the days of our courtship and marriage as if it was a faraway dream, the best days of my life. I carry you in my heart and am confident that nothing can destroy the powerful bond we share. Whatever comes, remember that I love you with all I am. Never forget, my sweet Clara. Longing to see your face again, Jeremiah."

215

"You comin', Turner?" Cullen asked, rolling his blanket into a cylinder shape and attaching it to his knapsack. He looked up at Jeremiah with round, frightened eyes hiding behind a front of bravado.

"Yeah, just finishing this letter to my wife. I want to get it to the Post Office before I run out of time," he said as he darted for the door of the cabin, rushing down the street through a beehive of frantic activity as the camp was broken down and organized for departure.

"Can you get this out?" he demanded breathlessly as he crashed into the makeshift building and slapped the letter on the counter.

The young man accepted the letter from him and nodded. "Don't worry. You aren't the only one trying to get a last minute message home. We'll get it delivered."

"Thank you," Jeremiah breathed sincerely, spinning on his heel and rushing back to the field for roll call before they moved out.

Today they were soldiers, lined up in their blue uniforms with their weapons ready for more than merely drills. Jeremiah's heart thumped in his chest as he took his place, musket in his right hand with the barrel resting in the hollow of his shoulder, ready for orders. There was a difference in their posture, backs straight and heads erect, held high with respect for themselves. No longer frauds and imposters, they were finally soldiers.

~

Clara held her apron out in front of her to carry the cucumbers and tomatoes she collected from the garden. Sweat trickled down her temples and moistened the back of her blue cotton dress. Phoebe worked beside her, humming a tune. On the porch, Lena kept an eye on Little Joe, a basket of mending in her lap.

Although it was early in the morning and the sun had yet to reach its zenith, the July heat was already unbearable. Wearing a broad straw hat to protect her face, Clara gathered the produce to be added to the menu for the day. She was grateful for the fresh vegetables even if she didn't enjoy the task of collecting them. Not everyone had the ability to grow their own food, and as the war continued without end in sight, many families in Centreville felt the pinch of the growing economic strain.

Even if Francis had been able to free his slaves, he wouldn't have been able to pay their wages. For now, things would have to continue as they had been, but Clara knew it wouldn't go on this way for much longer. Sooner or later, the war would have to end and even if the South was able to successfully break away from the Union—which Clara found doubtful—slavery in Maryland would surely be abolished.

She was glad they had never mentioned their desire to free Old Joe and his family, as it would have certainly proven a disappointment and may have planted seeds of resentment in their minds. Glancing sideways at Phoebe as she stooped down to search for ripe tomatoes near the ground, Clara wondered how Phoebe really felt about being held as property, without rights and without a will of her own. Even though they were treated well, they weren't free. And how could anyone be content with that?

"Phoebe," she said, straightening and walking to the basket at the edge of the garden to deposit the produce in her apron, "are you happy here?"

Coming to an abrupt halt, the young woman studied Clara's face carefully. She stood, one hand holding onto her full apron and the other resting on her hip, as slim as it had been before the baby. "What you mean, Missus Clara? Why you askin' me that?"

"I'm sorry, I guess I was just thinking out loud," Clara quickly knelt down and returned to her work.

"I's happy enough, I reckon," Phoebe answered cautiously. "You... You ain't thinkin' of sending me away, is you?" she worried.

"Oh, heavens no!" Clara sprang to her feet, regretting that she had placed such doubt in her friend's mind. "Never! I was only asking because I *want* you to be happy here. You've been such a comfort to me."

The wrinkles which had formed in Phoebe's brown forehead smoothed out and a smile replaced her frown. "Don't you worry, Missus Clara, I right where I want to be."

Clara offered a grateful smile in reply, but her thoughts were churning. Laurel Hill was home to Phoebe. It was where she had been born and raised, and this life of slavery was all she had ever known. Perhaps all one could do in any situation— whether bondage or loss—was accept it and make the best of it, as her sister was now trying to do.

Jane was no longer in full mourning and was free to go without the dark veil in public. She had traded her black dress in for one of dove gray and joined the Ladies Aide Society, knitting socks and rolling bandages to be sent to soldiers in need. Jane was learning how to live with her grief and it was a relief to hear her laugh again and see the spark of joy return to her eyes.

"I think that's 'bout it," Phoebe commented, holding one last ripe tomato in her hand. "Let's get out of this sun."

Clara nodded her agreement, wiping her hands on her apron. "A glass of water would be nice," she said, hoisting one of the baskets onto her hip and leaving the other for Phoebe.

Just then, the door opened and Francis emerged onto the back porch. His face was solemn as he walked toward her. "Letter arrived," he announced, extending the envelope.

Clara quickly lowered the basket to the ground and accepted the letter, knowing it must be from Jeremiah. Francis stood watching as she opened the envelope with trembling hands, his eyes reflecting the same worry she felt.

Since the war had scattered men all over the nation, an increase in the volume of mail had led to the Post Office delivering letters to homes rather than holding them for pick-up. It was a convenience which Clara appreciated, as it guaranteed she would know as soon as a letter arrived rather than having to send someone to ask after it.

As she unfolded the paper and noticed the unusually sloppy handwriting, a cold knot of fear clenched in her stomach. Clara's eyes scanned over the words, her heart slowing to a painful thud as she realized that this missive was written in the same spirit as the one Louis had pinned inside his uniform. It was the kind of letter written by a soldier going into battle, knowing he might not survive.

She handed the page to her father-in-law, though the content of the letter was easy to guess from her reaction. Closing her eyes, Clara breathed slowly. *God, keep him safe!* she prayed. *Keep him safe!*

"Sit down," Francis ordered, taking her by the elbow and leading her up the steps and onto the porch. Once Clara was settled on the divan, he took the place beside her and scanned his son's hastily written message.

"Pennsylvania..." he repeated quietly.

"Do you know where he's going?" she worried, eyes searching his intently.

Francis nodded grimly. "There's fighting at Gettysburg."

Chapter Twenty-Two

Crouching down behind breastworks made of stones and boulders, Jeremiah aimed his musket with shaking hands. The air was thick with the acrid smell of gunpowder, burning his nostrils. The Rebels hid behind trees and rocks, slowly advancing toward the Union lines. Jeremiah fired at anything that moved.

Visibility was largely obscured by a gray cloud of gun smoke, and he was certain most of his bullets were harmlessly lodged in tree bark. But he knew he had hit at least one target, the shriek of pain had followed so closely with the squeeze of his trigger. He felt a sickening punch in his stomach at the sound, but he clenched his teeth and continued firing.

Enemy bullets whizzed overhead, the Confederate Army firing relentlessly from the base of the hill below with muskets and heavy artillery, striking tree limbs and sending them crashing down. Since they held the higher ground, the Union should have held the advantage, but the Rebels were making a valiant effort to take the hill.

The First Eastern Shore Infantry had arrived at Gettysburg that morning at eight, on the third day of the battle. It was the third of July. They were attached to the Second Brigade, First Division, Twelfth Corps of the Army of the Potomac, under the command of Major General Henry Slocum. Some of their members, most from Somerset and Worcester Counties, refused to take up arms on the basis that they had signed on to act as Home Guard and not to fight outside of their state. These men were dishonorably discharged and given train fare back to Salisbury.

Those who remained were assigned the task of reinforcing Union lines on a wooded ridge overlooking a field owned by the unfortunate farmer, Culp, whose land had been turned into a battlefield. The landscape of Pennsylvania was completely unlike the Eastern Shore of Maryland, rolling with steep hills where trees grew between rocks and boulders of all sizes.

Jeremiah had been horrified to witness the carnage of the past two days of fighting before the Eastern Shore Infantry arrived. The Rebels had attacked the hill at dusk the evening before, but were forced into retreat. They resumed their advance early that morning, and the terrain between the two armies was littered with bodies, some cold with death, others moaning and pleading for help.

As his company was ordered to rotate into position behind the breastworks, relieving the company who had exhausted their ammunition and needed to reload, they paused to allow the dead and wounded to be dragged back from the line of fire. Fear tasted metallic on his tongue. Ice water coursed through his veins, his heart pounding violently, and the sound of his pulse thudded in his ears.

Kneeling down behind the stone wall covered with wooden fence rails, Jeremiah breathed out slowly between his teeth. This was the hour of testing. He had a choice to make. For the first time since he'd enlisted as a soldier, he saw firsthand the devastation of war. And although everything within him screamed to run away, he had to stay and follow orders.

This hill, they were told, was essential to the success of the Confederacy's campaign to reach Washington. If they could defend it, they could save the nation's capital and perhaps win the war once and for all.

Before the battle had begun in earnest, while the air was still fresh with the smells of summer foliage, he had been able to see the gray-clad soldiers through the woods in the distance, their colors flying proudly. The red background, with a blue X bearing white stars, fluttered in the breeze. But when Jeremiah spotted that Rebel flag waving, it wasn't the symbol of his enemies he saw. It was his brother's flag.

Despite the trembling which made his entire body quake, he managed to fire his musket at a gray uniform taking shape between the shadows and thick smoke. *Please don't let it be Charlie*, he prayed.

Beside him, Cullen was crouched below the safety of the breastworks, clutching his musket against his chest with eyes squeezed shut. Jeremiah shared his fear, but refused to be paralyzed by it. "Get up!" he shouted. "Fight!"

Cullen's face was white as a sheet, but the order penetrated his numb brain and he slowly raised himself onto one knee. Taking up position, sweat beading his forehead, he fired down into the chaos below.

On Jeremiah's right, Phillips breathed heavily as he unloaded his musket on the enemy. The sound of splintering wood, the ping of bullets against rocks, and the cries of the injured mingled into a terrifying cacophony around them. "Damn this war!" Phillips growled. Fury radiated from him, not at the enemy, but at the fight itself.

Never before had Jeremiah been so aware of his blue uniform. A line of blue at the top of the hill, they fired down at the men in gray—men who shared the same cultural heritage, whose grandfathers had fought alongside Jeremiah's in the War of 1812, who revered the name of George Washington and cherished the principle of Freedom.

Americans in gray. Americans like his brother.

Startled by a guttural cry to his left, Jeremiah saw Westbrook fall backwards to the ground, hot blood spattering the man next to him as his jaw was shattered. The big man had raised himself too high above the shelter of the earthworks and given the Rebels a clear target.

Cullen dropped down, barely peering over the top as he managed to let off another round. Jeremiah instinctively ducked below the safety of the rocks with him, cowering behind the fortification as he swallowed down a rising tide of nausea.

He gave a fleeting thought to the chaplain, assigned to travel with the medical staff and offer assistance to the surgeons and nurses tending the casualties of the battle. Jeremiah couldn't even begin to imagine what Davies would witness before the day ended.

Jeremiah almost felt relief when he pulled the trigger and realized he had exhausted his ammunition. Lowering himself to the ground, he waited until given the command to withdraw and allow another company to take over the defensive position while they reloaded.

He and his company scrambled away from the breastworks gratefully, retreating to a safe distance to take a drink from their canteens, calm their racing hearts, and reload their muskets to prepare for the next onslaught. A lull in the fighting below indicated that the Rebels were doing something similar. Jeremiah leaned back against a boulder, Cullen slumping against him.

"You all right?" he asked the young soldier.

"It's not like I thought it would be," Cullen stammered, leaning forward to rest his head in his hands.

Phillips took advantage of the break to smoke a cigarette, his hand shaking as he placed it between his mustached lips. "War is hell, my friend. No joke about that."

A report had reached the men that a civilian had been shot in a skirmish early that morning in town. A young woman by the name of Jennie Wade had been baking bread at her sister's house when a bullet penetrated two doors and lodged in her back. Union soldiers heard the girl's mother and sister screaming and entered the house to discover her lying dead upon the floor.

The house had also been struck by a shell and the soldiers insisted that the girl's mother, sister, and her children crawl through the hole it created to the other side where they could then hide down in the cellar. Jennie's mother refused to leave her daughter's body, and the soldiers were obligated to wrap it in quilts and follow the same route to the cellar before she could be persuaded to go to safety.

Jeremiah ran a hand over his beard, damp with sweat and grimy with gunpowder. He closed his eyes and tried to pray, but all he could see was the grotesque and disfigured form of Westbrook, crimson soaking the ground beneath his head.

Their time behind the breastworks had seemed like a short eternity, and although of the same approximate duration, their reprieve lasted mere seconds. Ordered back to the defensive line, Jeremiah and his company shouldered their muskets and took up position behind the breastworks.

The Rebels had resumed their onslaught with a vicious tenacity, charging boldly up the hill only to be ruthlessly gunned down. It was suicide and madness. Jeremiah blinked sweat and tears from his eyes, respecting and pitying these gray-clad Rebels even as he aimed into the hazy woods and pulled the trigger.

Then, like a band of ghosts, the vague shapes of three soldiers materialized out of the forest. Somehow these brave men had safely navigated the dangerous gap between armies, darting between trees for shelter while the smoke obscured their positions.

The clang of Cullen's musket as it fell against the rocks alerted Jeremiah that he had been struck. The young man jerked backward, a dark stain spreading on his Federal blue uniform around a small hole through the center of his breast pocket, where Emily's picture rested against his heart. Cullen turned to look at Jeremiah, but the startled pain in his eyes quickly faded into a vacant stare as he crumpled to the ground.

Seething anger boiled within Jeremiah, and he leveled his sights on the Rebel soldiers who had dared to encroach upon them and kill his friend. Phillips had used his last shot on one of them, who now lay lifelessly upon the leaf-strewn earth. Jeremiah prayed he had enough ammunition to take at least one of the other two.

They ducked back behind a tree, popping out only long

enough to fire before quickly taking cover once again. Jeremiah steadied his musket, waiting for the second when the gray cap would become visible around the trunk. But when it did, his finger froze on the trigger.

Jeremiah's grip on the musket weakened and it slowly lowered without his permission. The Rebel stared back at him with the same open-mouthed horror.

Before he could gasp out his brother's name, Charlie fired. Agony ripped through Jeremiah's hand before he had time to register that Charlie had taken aim. He had chosen only to disable him, but that knowledge was of little comfort as Jeremiah stared down at the fragments of bone protruding from the mangled flesh.

He glanced up only long enough to see the shock and regret in his brother's eyes before Charlie wheeled back into the curtain of gun smoke which enveloped the wooded hillside.

Stunned, Jeremiah looked down at the gory wreckage at the end of his wrist, dripping red in a steady stream. Searing heat radiated up his arm. Black spots danced before his eyes and weakness gripped his knees. Then the ground rose up to meet him.

When he awoke, he lay on a stretcher jostling down a dirt road with the hot sun glaring overhead. Jeremiah was dimly aware that he was being carried into a church building, which had been set up as a temporary hospital. Boards had been lain across the backs of the pews to create makeshift cots, and he was carefully transferred onto one of them.

It would have been more comfortable to have remained on the ground. The rough board was hard beneath his back and the movement had caused the shredded remnants of his hand to begin bleeding again. He lay staring at the wooden beams crossing the white ceiling, listening to the moans and cries of the other wounded as they were carried in, wondering if he would bleed to death before a nurse attended to him.

Flies buzzed around the room, moving from one injury to

another. Those who had the strength tried to shoo them away, but as the hours passed, even those not critically hurt grew listless and weak. The smell of gunpowder on their clothing was overpowered by the odors of sweat and putrefaction.

Jeremiah knew his hand was lost. But as the time passed, he began to wonder how high they would have to amputate as infection set in and flies feasted upon the black, sticky flesh.

"When will someone tend this?" he asked an orderly making rounds with a bucket of water and a tin cup, allowing the wounded to drink as they waited for medical care.

"I'm not sure," he answered softly, his gaze shifting uncomfortably.

Jeremiah lowered his voice to a stern whisper. "Just tell me the truth," he insisted.

The man was barely more than a boy, with a thin layer of peach fuzz on his upper lip. His eyes were regretful as he answered, "Maybe days."

Jeremiah sank back against the wooden platform beneath him. "What am I supposed to do with this?" he asked through gritted teeth, jerking his head at the ruined hand.

"I-I don't know..." the boy replied, and through a haze of pain, Jeremiah saw that his brown eyes were glazed with shock and horror at all he had witnessed.

"Where are the nurses?" Jeremiah wondered.

The young orderly explained that when General Meade led the Army of the Potomac in pursuit of the retreating Rebels, he had taken the bulk of the medical staff with him in anticipation of another major battle. He had left a pathetic number of surgeons and nurses to tend thousands of injured Union soldiers, not to mention the great number of wounded the Rebels had left behind.

Nearby homes had been converted into field hospitals, organized by Corps. The farmhouse of George Bushman, three miles away, had been assigned for the Twelfth Corps. As soon as men and wagons became available, these wounded at the church would be moved to the appropriate locations. If they were still alive by then.

Jeremiah's mind reeled. He stared down at the splintered bones of his left hand, which had supported the barrel of the musket when Charlie fired. It wasn't a mortal shot taken to the head or chest, and his legs were untouched. If he could only find the strength to walk, perhaps he could persuade someone to transport him to the hospital.

Pushing himself up onto his elbows, Jeremiah slowly gained a sitting position. But trauma and loss of blood made his head spin and his stomach churn. Already sweltering from the heat, perspiration from the effort beaded his brow. He fell back against the board in resignation.

The torment was inescapable in his waking moments. He was thankful for the oblivion of sleep and retreated into it as often as possible. He lost all sense of time. Minutes blurred into hours and were swallowed up in days. In his bouts of consciousness, he thought of Clara and wondered if he would ever see her beautiful face again.

A cool hand upon his forehead and a female voice wakened him. "Clara?" he opened his eyes, grateful that she had come to him.

"No, I'm not Clara," the young woman replied apologetically. Jeremiah brought his eyes into focus as she explained, "I'm Miss Cornelia Hancock. I'm here to clean and dress your injury until you can get to the hospital."

She appeared close in age to Clara, although not nearly as pretty. Cornelia had kind eyes, and judging from the stains on her apron, he wasn't the first soldier she had attended to.

"Are you a nurse?"

"I'm a volunteer. I just want to help however I can," she answered as she set a basin of warm water next to his elbow and wrung out a cloth. "This is probably going to hurt," she warned him regretfully.

Jeremiah nodded and looked away, steeling himself. He

clamped his lips together as she moistened the crusted blood and dirt which had adhered to his mutilated hand. She hummed a song as she worked, her ministrations tender and gentle.

"I'm going to wrap it now," she informed him and he felt her hand upon his elbow, lifting his left arm.

Glancing over at her, he wished he hadn't as he saw a red puddle forming beneath the mangled hand. Cornelia was no expert, and she struggled to bind his hand tightly enough to staunch the flow, while loosely enough not to make him cry out.

"Are you all right?" she worried.

Knowing it would be foolish to lie, Jeremiah grunted in reply. "Just tie it up," he instructed her tersely.

Cornelia winced as she did as ordered, her young face pinched white as if his suffering were her own.

"Thank you," Jeremiah managed, grateful to have his flesh protected from the flies. "I'm sorry this battle happened in your town," he added, though it was no fault of his own.

A faint smile curved her lips. "It's not my town. I took the train here from New Jersey."

"New Jersey?" he repeated, trying to understand.

"I want to do my part for the Union," Cornelia said. "My brother and my cousins are fighting in this war. I can't fight, but I can care for the men who do."

"I'm grateful," Jeremiah assured her, closing his eyes wearily.

Her hand rested on his shoulder as she said, "I have more wounds to dress, then I'll write letters to send home. I'll come back around when I can."

He heard the rustle of her dress as she walked away, though he was too weak to bother opening his eyes. The only comfort to be found was in the dark numbness of sleep, and he surrendered to it willingly.

When she returned later, he declined her offer. "I've already sent my letter," he told her. "But can you tell me what day it is?"

"July seventh," Cornelia replied. "If you change your mind,

let me know."

Jeremiah hoped she knew what her kindness meant to the battered soldiers. He was impressed with her calm reserve as she moved between the injured men on their makeshift cots, like an angel of mercy floating in a sea of suffering.

Five days after the battle, on July eighth, orderlies arrived to transport men from the Twelfth Corps to the field hospital designated for them. Jeremiah was nearly delirious with fatigue and hunger, having survived on hard tack and beef tea for days, in addition to the substantial blood loss he'd incurred. He knew he should be thankful the orderlies had come for him, but he also knew that more suffering lay ahead. The allure of eternal rest tempted him.

He grit his teeth and refused to groan as he was carried out on a stretcher and slid into the wagon bed beside the other wounded of the Twelfth Corps. When the horse was urged into motion, the wheels rolled forward and jerked the weak and suffering men. The poor soul next to him, his face wrapped in bandages, wept in agony.

The fresh air revived Jeremiah as he inhaled a breath that smelled like sunbaked grass, a pleasant change from the miasma of infection and rot which had filled the church. Pulling himself upright, Jeremiah leaned heavily against the boards, gazing out with glassy eyes at the fields and forests surrounding them.

A stench suddenly rose up to his nostrils, worse even than the putrid odor within the church, and Jeremiah covered his mouth as he realized its source. Gagging, he stared in horror at the bodies that lay heaped on either side of the road, dead and decaying beneath the summer sun. The sight of the swollen, disfigured faces of these unburied sent him sinking back to his cot, right hand over his mouth to prevent retching.

Jeremiah closed his eyes and tried to keep his breathing shallow until they reached the field hospital at the Bushman farm. As he was removed from the wagon, Jeremiah observed the white tents of the medical staff erected around the stone house. He was carried to an open tent and placed atop a crude operating table. From the corner of his eye, he spied a bucket covered over with a blood-soaked towel.

Slowly his mind processed that the object dangling from beneath the cloth was a dismembered hand, hanging awkwardly over the edge of the bucket as if it had been tossed carelessly aside. Deep inside, Jeremiah felt a terrible quaking begin.

Upon a small table next to him was strewn an array of medical instruments. Knives of varying sizes rested along with tourniquets and clamps. But most terrifying of all was the large saw resting at the top corner of the table, its blade comprised of a thousand vicious teeth.

The surgeon emerged from the shadows and came to stand over Jeremiah, looking more like a butcher than a doctor in his red-stained apron.

Chapter Twenty-Three

The air was cloying even though the temperature had cooled since the sun went down. On the back porch at Laurel Hill, Clara rocked a slow and measured rhythm by the dim light of the twinkling stars and crescent moon. The humidity curled the loose tendrils which had escaped her braid, and perspiration dampened her skin.

Since Jeremiah had been sent to the front, Clara hadn't slept a night through. Every time she laid her head upon the pillow and closed her eyes, her mind began racing with a myriad of awful possibilities. Finally admitting that rest was an elusive wish, she had given up on the effort and taken to passing the sleepless hours of the night in the rocking chair. At least there she could see the open expanse of the sky and hope that somewhere her husband was gazing up at it too.

"Worryin' youself sick ain't gonna help Mistah Jeremiah none," Mamie told her after scrutinizing the purple shadows beneath Clara's eyes.

"I know," Clara sighed. "I only wish I knew what I *could* do to help him."

"If you want to know, I can tell you," Phoebe volunteered, her dark eyes sympathetic.

Clara narrowed her brows curiously. "What's that?"

"Pray for him," Phoebe answered certainly. "Best thing for both of you."

With a disappointed sigh, Clara replied, "I've already tried that. It doesn't bring me any peace, and I think God has closed His ears to prayers for soldiers—Rebel or Yankee. I'm afraid we're in it alone."

"I sure glad I disagree," Mamie retorted, her purple turban wobbling as she nodded her head emphatically. But she didn't bother to argue the point, turning instead back to her work stewing tomatoes for canning.

Clara clamped her lips and turned back to spooning the tomatoes into a mason jar. How could God possibly hear the prayers of every mother, wife, sister, or daughter crying out to Him on behalf of a soldier? Providence had surely turned away, unable to watch as the people He created slaughtered one another by the thousands.

Of all the bloody battles the Civil War had seen, the battle at Gettysburg had been the bloodiest. The Union had claimed it as a victory, but with the ever rising toll of the dead and wounded, there was no glory to be found in it.

Every day the casualty list grew as the reports trickled in from the front. It had taken days for the wounded Federals to be collected and cared for, and the abandoned Rebels still waited their turn. Those not killed by cannon or gunfire were dying of thirst, blood loss, and infection. The dead were buried in shallow graves, the great number of corpses rotting in the sun necessitating the haste of this unpleasant task.

Jeremiah's name had not appeared in the paper, but that was little assurance when so many injured were still being found, and the identity of many deceased would remain forever unknown. Clara couldn't explain it, and she didn't even try, but she knew her husband had been present at the battle and was wounded there.

As the hours of the night grew long, Clara's eyes finally grew heavy. She waited until she could barely carry herself up the stairs to fall into bed, grateful for a brief escape from the suffocating black cloud of foreboding that pressed in on her.

Morning came too quickly, and Clara dragged herself wearily from the comforting oblivion to meet another day. Her mind was numb with exhaustion and she fumbled through her morning routine in a trance. The sunlight streaming through the muslin curtains told her she had already slept longer than she should have, and she felt a twinge of guilt as she rushed down the stairs.

The sound of a man's voice in the parlor brought her to a halt, heart thumping wildly against her ribs. Despite the warmth of the day, she could feel the blood draining from her face and her fingertips felt cold as ice.

"She hasn't come down yet. I'm afraid she isn't going to take it very well," Francis replied, an edge of pain layering his words.

"I'll wait so we can give her the news together," her father's somber voice replied.

Clara closed her eyes, taking a deep breath before she squared her shoulders and willed her feet to propel her forward. She dreaded hearing the words, but the truth would find her sooner or later.

She entered the parlor as if she was facing a firing squad, determined to meet the pain with as much dignity and courage as she could muster. Her father stood rigidly by the window, a newspaper crumpled in his hands. Francis sat in the armchair as if he had collapsed there, shoulders stooped and face drawn.

"What's happened to Jeremiah?" Clara demanded in a quiet, steady voice.

The men's gaze met, then shifted slowly back to her. It was her father who answered, "He's been wounded at Gettysburg."

Clara's breath left her lungs in a rush. At least he was still alive, or had been at the time the information was released to the paper. Instead of the tears they expected, Clara lifted her chin stubbornly as she announced, "I'm going to be with him."

"No you most certainly are not!" Francis insisted, coming to his feet.

"Absolutely not," her father shouted, almost simultaneously.

Clara couldn't explain the calmness she felt, and she had no idea where this certainty came from. But one thing she knew, she needed to go to her husband. And she would.

"The battlefield is no place for a lady," her father lowered his voice, laying a hand gently upon her arm. "I know you are worried for him, but it would be better for you to wait here and let the medics and nurses attend to him."

"I *am* going to Gettysburg," she repeated with a softness underscored by steely determination.

"Jeremiah wouldn't want you to go," Francis countered, compassion evident in his blue eyes even though the words were gruffly spoken. "There's dead and dying everywhere, Clara! You aren't prepared for what you'll find there."

For a brief second, Clara hesitated. Her mind had no images to conjure of what the aftermath of a battle would look like. She admitted to herself that she wasn't prepared for the reality of it. But that awareness didn't diminish her resolve in the slightest.

"Just the same, I have to go," she explained to her father and her father-in-law, searching first one face and then the other for some indication of understanding. She glimpsed a hint of wavering in George's eyes and narrowed in on it. "I need to be with him, Father. I'll face whatever I have to."

"Sir?" a voice interrupted behind them. Clara turned to see Phoebe standing in the doorway, hands clasped in front of her aproned skirt.

"What is it?" Francis asked.

"I go with her, sir. I take care of Missus Clara," the Negro woman offered, her mahogany features carved with fierce loyalty.

Clara let her gratitude shine in her eyes.

But Francis huffed irritably. "I'm not sending two women off to the devil's playground alone!"

"What if my Henry go?" Phoebe persisted.

"I don't—" Francis began, but was interrupted as George stepped forward.

"Will he swear to her safety?"

"You can trust my Henry," the slave woman affirmed

confidently.

Spinning to face her father, Francis erupted, "You can't mean to let her go?"

There was sadness and regret in George's expression as he studied Clara's pale face, chin tilted obstinately. "If that is what she needs..." his voice trailed off, and Clara suspected he was thinking of Jane's loss and the way it had defined her.

Clara stepped forward and clutched her father's hand. "Thank you," she blinked back tears. Turning to Phoebe, she whispered, "And thank you."

~

Jeremiah blinked. He felt as if he were drowning in a gray ocean of oblivion. From a distance, he could hear voices, but they were too remote and far away to grasp what was being said or by whom. He blinked again, trying to break free from the intoxicating void which held him captive.

As his surroundings slowly came into focus, Jeremiah realized he was in a dining room. An oval oak table had been pushed back against the window, and its chairs were nowhere to be seen. A painting hung on the wall opposite him above a fireplace mantle, depicting a stone farmhouse which he presumed was the one where he currently resided.

On either side of him, the walls were lined with cots upon which rested men in various stages of recovery. Some slept, others stared vacantly at the ceiling, while still others groaned in misery. On arms, legs, chest or head, each of them were dressed in medical bandages.

The buzzing of a mosquito in his left ear prompted Jeremiah to raise his hand to shoo it away. But the movement triggered a strange and terrible pain. He stared in disgust and horror at the blood-soaked linens binding the rounded stump where his arm abruptly ended just below the wrist. Tingling nerves sent sensations, cold and hot, shooting up to his elbow. His arm fell back upon the cot as Jeremiah closed his eyes, assaulted by a barrage of memories.

Charlie had shot him. Intentionally.

Cullen, Westbrook, and many others were dead.

The soldier next to him moaned and Jeremiah commiserated with the feeling. Far worse than the physical pain was the mental anguish they all must learn to live with. It could not be numbed with morphine, dulled with cloroform, or severed like a damaged appendage. This deep and penetrating ache would be carried with them for the rest of their lives.

Amputee. The word reverberated through Jeremiah's mind. His thoughts spun and whirled, moving from the gun smoke of Culp's Hill to the red-stained apron of the surgeon standing over him, and back to the remorse in Charlie's eyes.

He forced himself to look once more at the absence of his hand. It was strange to see nothing where once his fingers had stretched and opened, to find only a cloth wrapping the pathetic nub between wrist and elbow. A cone shaped towel had been placed over his nose and mouth, smelling faintly of chemicals, and Jeremiah had fallen into a cloroform-induced sleep which had spared him the awareness of the knife piercing his flesh and the saw cutting through bone.

That phantom hand dangling limply from the bucket covered over with a crimson towel floated to his consciousness, and Jeremiah felt a wave of nausea as he imagined his own severed hand flung casually on top of it.

How would he ever wield a hoe, drive a plough, or complete the other tasks required on the farm with only one hand? He was disabled, disfigured, and disgraced. What would Clara think of him?

Clenching his teeth, Jeremiah cursed the tear that seeped from the corner of his eye. How could his own brother have done this to him?

"Now here's a familiar face!" the voice of Chaplain Davies interrupted Jeremiah's internal dialogue.

Placing a hand on his shoulder, Davies leaned against the

edge of the cot. "How are you, son?" he asked gently.

Jeremiah felt humiliated. He forced his voice to come out evenly as he answered, "I'm all right, Chaplain. How are you holding up?"

"I've been better," Davies admitted. Exhaustion and heartache were etched in the lines of his face.

"Cullen's gone," Jeremiah told him, although he assumed the chaplain already knew. "And Westbrook."

Davies nodded.

"What about Phillips?" Jeremiah wondered.

"He's upstairs. He took a hit in the shoulder, and would've been a lot better off if he could have had immediate care. But I think he'll pull through just fine. Bullet went straight through."

Jeremiah let out a sigh of relief, grateful that Phillips had survived. The image of Cullen's smooth, pink face under a film of gunpowder, eyes wide with disbelief in his dying moments, would haunt Jeremiah forever.

"Did you write Cullen's mother and sweetheart?" he dragged his right hand across his face, unable to imagine the scope of grief that would grip the nation from the losses suffered at this one battle.

"I did."

"Was he... did they..." he struggled to push the words past his lips, "bury him?" The road had been lined with piles of decomposing corpses. He hoped that the young man had at least been spared the indignity of decaying in the full sun, exposed to carrion eaters of all kinds.

"He has," Davies' eyes glistened with tears as he nodded. "It wasn't much of a burial, but he is under the ground." He reached for Jeremiah's hand.

Jeremiah gripped it tightly. "This is worse than anything I could have imagined," he whispered. "We were so naïve, all of us. There is nothing noble—nothing *honorable*—about war."

The old man ran a hand through what was left of his white hair. He thumbed a tear from his eye, then sighed. "I wish I knew what to say. I've never seen anything like this in my life." He shook his head, lips quivering.

Jeremiah pushed himself onto his elbows, intending to scoot back against the pillows into a sitting position, propped against the wall. But the surgery had taken more out of him than he realized, and weakness flooded him. The sensitive stump would not tolerate even the faintest pressure, and when bumped against the mattress, needle-like pain ripped through his arm. Stifling the urge to cry out, Jeremiah compressed his lips into a hard, angry line.

Davies moved beside him, helping to manage Jeremiah's weight as he shifted into an upright posture. The heat of shame flushed Jeremiah's cheeks at his helplessness.

Raising his bandaged arm in the air, he pointed the stump at Davies as he spat, "*Charlie* did this to me! My own *brother!*" The words cut through the air, the sharpness of their reality piercing Jeremiah's heart once again.

The chaplain's eyes grew wide. "You're sure?"

"As sure as I'm Jeremiah Turner," he ground out bitterly.

Davies eased his small frame down onto the edge of the cot, bowing his head. "I'm so sorry, son. So sorry. This war has turned everything upside down. We've brought hell to earth."

"There's no way to undo what's been done. This country will never be united again, no matter who wins the war," Jeremiah predicted wearily, leaning back against the wall and closing his eyes.

"I'm afraid you might be right," Davies admitted regretfully. "This war defies understanding. We're not fighting the British or the French, strangers with strange ways. We're fighting one another—family, friends, neighbors... There's a story going around about a soldier killed there on Culp's hill. His cousin owned that hill, and he played there as a child. His name was Wesley Culp and he was a Rebel.

"When he died, Wesley was carrying a note given to him by an injured Union soldier, a long-time friend, Jack Skelly. Jack feared he would die and wanted to send one last letter to his fiancée, Jennie Wade. But she was killed in a home she had fled to for safety when a bullet penetrated the house. By the time the battle ended, all three of these friends—Union, Rebel and civilian, were dead." Davies shook his head sadly. "All this killing. It's such a waste of human life."

"And limbs," Jeremiah added dejectedly, the miserable nub of his arm resting uselessly in his lap.

Chapter Twenty-Four

Clara was grateful for Henry's presence next to her as the hired driver delivered them to the general hospital. Camp Letterman was no more than a collection of white tents, row upon row stretching out for miles. The property belonged to a farmer, George Wolf, and the site had been strategically chosen for its proximity to the railroad depot and its possession of a decent water supply, good drainage, and access to a forest which could be used for firewood.

Gawking in amazement and fascination at the hundreds of tents which comprised the camp, Clara wondered how she would ever locate her husband amid the vast numbers of wounded men. Activity buzzed around them as ambulances arrived with new patients, and surgeons, nurses and orderlies moved about between the tents.

Through the flaps, open to allow a breeze to move through and cool the suffering men, Clara glimpsed some of the soldiers within. Broken and bloodied men lay helplessly on every cot, some crying out for food and water, others whimpering in unabashed agony. Many were shirtless, bandages wrapping their shoulders where once arms had been attached. Legs were propped on pillows, feet noticeably absent. Heads and faces were wrapped in linens which had bled through and were in need of changing. Clara covered her mouth, swallowing down the bile that rose to her throat.

"Excuse me," Clara rested her hand on the elbow of an officer as he strode past her at a brisk walk.

He looked relieved to see her. "Thank you for coming. We're in desperate need of nurses. If you could just—"

"No, no," Clara quickly interrupted, suddenly ashamed that she had come only to help one of the thousands of injured men. "I'm here to find my husband. I... I just want to locate my husband."

The warm appreciation in the older man's eyes cooled. He stepped back, waving an arm at the rows of flimsy canvas enclosures behind him. "Well, as you can see, ma'am, there are five hundred tents filled with men. Good luck to you." And he spun on his heel and walked away.

Clara turned to Henry in dismay. "What should I do?" she whispered, humbled by the need she saw around her.

"We's gonna find Mistuh Jeremiah, ma'am, then we see if we can help some of these others," Henry decided for her. "You all right?" he studied her face with evident concern.

Comforted by his presence, as well as by the intelligence she saw in his eyes, Clara nodded. "Where do we begin?"

Henry looked about. "I say we just start askin' nurses and leave them officers alone," he suggested, moving toward a woman dressed in the habit of a nun, the hat perched atop her head unlike anything they had ever seen before. Starched white folds protruded like great wings on either side of her, and Clara found it a challenge to lower her eyes to the woman's face, the hat was so distracting.

"Please," she began gently, her eyes pleading, "can you help me find my husband?"

"I'm Sister Camilla O'Keefe," the kindly woman introduced herself. "And you are?"

"Oh, I'm sorry! Forgive me. I'm Mrs. Clara Turner, and it's my husband Jeremiah I'm looking for," Clara hoped and prayed that against all the odds, the name would ring familiar in the nun's ears.

"There's no one in my ward by that name, ma'am. I'm terribly sorry," Sister Camilla apologized, pity moving into her eyes. "You are welcome to ask around, but I fear you are looking for a needle in a haystack."

Clenching her fists by her side, Clara refused to be daunted. "I am aware of the challenges I face," she replied calmly. "But I *will* find him."

Respect and understanding lit the young woman's face, her hair hidden within the strange white hat she wore. "I hope you will," she replied with an encouraging smile. "What do you know that could help you find him? I would be happy to direct you, if I can."

Clara searched her mind for any information which might set her search in the right direction. But there was little she knew. "He's part of the Eastern Shore Infantry, Maryland Volunteers," she offered hopefully.

The lack of recognition in the nun's eyes answered for her. "Anything else?" she suggested gently.

Shaking her head, Clara bit her lip in frustration.

Sister Camilla rested her hand reassuringly on Clara's arm. "Do not despair. Come with me," she ordered as she resumed her purposeful march toward one of the large, white tents.

Obediently, Clara followed with Henry on her heels.

"If you can care for these men for a bit, I'll see what I can find out for you," the sister explained. She turned to eye Clara skeptically. "Put this apron on and take care with your dress," Camilla ordered, eyeing the bell-shaped sleeves of Clara's brown traveling dress as she removed her own apron and handed it over.

"It looks like the cook house has just delivered our afternoon meal. Why don't you help Thaddeus here?" Sister Camilla indicated a double amputee, both arms removed just below the shoulders. She handed Clara a plate cradling a bowl of stew and a slice of freshly baked bread.

"And you," the nun addressed Henry, "can deliver these bowls to all of the men here who can feed themselves. If anyone needs help, I'm sure you'll oblige."

Henry nodded, moving to distribute the meal.

Clara trepidatiously approached the young man named

Thaddeus. As she spread out her skirt and seated herself on the stool beside his cot, Clara observed that he was more of a boy than a man. A fine layer of hair covered his upper lip, the adolescent hope of a mustache. Brown hair tumbled onto his forehead, beneath which were a pair of green eyes filled with such hollow pain that Clara felt an ache growing in her chest as she looked into them.

"Hello," she said softly. "My name is Clara. I'm going to feed you, if that's all right," she said as she lifted a spoonful of the beef stew.

Thaddeus stared back at her despairingly. He opened his mouth like a baby bird and allowed her to give him the nourishment he needed to survive. Compassion stirred Clara's heart. How would he ever be independent again? The simple challenges of dressing and eating would be impossible. And what sort of work would he find to make a living and support a family, supposing there was a woman willing to overlook his deformity?

Blinking back tears, certain he would be offended by them, Clara tried to think of something cheerful to say. But nothing came to mind as she silently spooned the stew into his mouth, wiping his face when the broth dribbled down his chin, and broke the bread into bite size pieces for him.

When the bowl was empty, she offered him a drink of water. Thaddeus accepted it, then immediately turned away and closed his eyes.

Clara looked about at the wounded men surrounding her, overwhelmed with sympathy and grief. Henry had put himself to work, removing a bandage which had soaked through and replacing it with fresh binding. Moving toward the soldier closest to her, his pant leg cut off at the thigh and a cloth bound around his calf, she asked, "Is there anything I can do for you?"

"No ma'am," he replied, jerking his head at a man lying two cots over. "But Nelson looks like he could use a new bandage."

Clara cringed at the yellow fluid seeping through the linen

binding the older man's forehead. His pallor was closer to gray than white and his food lay untouched beside him. "Nelson?" she whispered, hoping he was capable of answering.

He blinked, his eyes focusing blankly on her face. "Yes?"

"I'm going to wrap your head, then I'm going to get you something to eat," she said as she searched about for the items she would need. Spotting a station in the corner stocked with a limited quantity of supplies, Clara left his side to retrieve the necessary things.

Squaring her shoulders, Clara began unwrapping the soiled cloth, wrinkling her nose at the foul odor that it released. What had begun as a mere gash had developed into a life-threatening wound. From the look of it, the cut had gone too long unattended and putrification had set in. His skin was hot to the touch, burning up with fever. If he survived, it would be a miracle.

"I'll take over," she was relieved to hear Sister Camilla's voice behind her. She turned gratefully to greet the nun, allowing the fullness of her shock and pity to be evident in her eyes.

The sister acknowledged it with a nod. *"Whatever is done for the least of these My brethren, it is done for Me,"* she quoted from the scriptures.

Clara watched as the nun adeptly unrolled a fresh bandage and wound it around the dying man's head. "What did you learn?" she asked, almost afraid of the answer.

"There's no Jeremiah Turner here at Camp Letterman," Camilla replied, her focus intent on her patient. "But there are still many men in barns and homes used as field hospitals. There's a chance he could be at the Bushman Farm, as his regiment was attached to the Twelfth Corps and that is where many of them still are."

"If he's still alive..." Clara whispered.

Sister Camilla lifted her gaze to meet Clara's eyes. "God go with you," she replied.

"Thank you," Clara swallowed the lump forming in her throat, "for everything." Oddly, she found herself hesitant to leave Thaddeus and Nelson and the other men behind. She cast a farewell glance in the boy's direction, where he lay staring vacantly at the ceiling above him.

Reentering the busy street, Henry and Clara decided on their next course of action. Hailing the first wagon that passed, they approached the driver and asked if he knew where the Bushman Farm was and how they could get there.

"If you walk to the depot, there might be a supply wagon headed that way," the man replied wearily. "I'm the undertaker. You don't want to ride with me," he assured her, his eyes shadowed with penetrating grief.

Clara instinctively stepped back as she glanced at the wagon bed, covered over with a tarp. "Where are the... dead buried?" she asked hesitantly, wanting to be able to locate Jeremiah's grave if he was already gone.

"There's a cemetery in the back. But there are graves scattered everywhere 'round Gettysburg. It's a good thing you didn't come any sooner, ma'am, as it's taken a good week to bury 'em all."

Henry took Clara by the arm and urged her forward, nodding his thanks at the helpful driver.

"Oh Henry..." Clara breathed. "I never imagined anything so awful!"

Beside her, Henry agreed emphatically, "Lawd, that's the truth."

By the time they reached the train depot, they were coated with dust from the road. After several inquiries, they were finally told that if they were willing to wait, a wagon would be driving out to the Bushman Farm when the next train arrived. It wasn't expected for another two hours.

"We could walk," Clara suggested, "rather than wait so long."

"You gotta take care of yourself, Missus Clara, if you thinkin' you gonna take care of anybody else," Henry retorted.

And so Clara agreed to wait. They were graciously offered a

ration of hard tack and a drink of water as they sat beneath the shade of a nearby tree to gather their strength for the next leg of their journey.

Clara didn't realize she had dozed until the sound of the train steaming down the track startled her awake. The black locomotive puffed smoke into the air, its wheels spinning, sparks flying from the steel rails as the conductor pulled the brake.

They had to wait another hour while the supplies were removed from the freight cars, then sorted and loaded into the covered wagons. Clara was awkwardly positioned on the buckboard seat between Henry and the wagon driver, her skirt, though narrow for travel, still overflowing onto both men's laps.

It took another two hours to reach their destination as the Bushman Farm was located on other side of the town proper, a little over five miles from Camp Letterman. By the time they arrived at the stone farmhouse, dusk had fallen and the sky was the color of slate.

The driver escorted Clara and Henry to the front door, where they were met by an orderly. "I've got supplies here, if you can send some fellas out to help me unload," he said. "And this lady's here looking for her husband."

"I'll be right out," the orderly promised the driver, turning to Clara. "Please come in. I'll get Chaplain Davies to help you while the rest of us unload the supplies."

"Thank you," Clara managed, longing for a drink of cool water and a soft place to sit. From where she stood in the entryway, Clara could see into the dining room and the parlor. Both had been converted into hospital rooms, crammed with cots for the many wounded soldiers.

An old man with white hair appeared around the corner, standing slightly shorter than Clara in his blue uniform. A bright smile lit his tired face when he saw her. "Well, aren't you a lovely surprise! I'm Chaplain Davies. What can I do for you?"

"It's a pleasure to meet you. I believe you know my husband, Jeremiah Turner. Is he here?" she asked tentatively, her heart constricting as hope and fear converged.

"I do know Private Turner," he grinned broadly. "He'll be delighted to see you! Come with me, he's just this way," he said gesturing for her to follow him into the dining room.

Relief coursed through Clara with the force of a rushing creek after spring thaw. She had found him, and he was alive!

Chaplain Davies halted midstride as they crossed the scarred wood floor of the dining room, staring at an empty cot. "Where's Turner?" he asked anyone who cared to answer.

"He was just here," one man replied.

"Just stepped out, I guess," another offered.

Clara could tell by the expression on Davies' face that something was amiss. His cheerful disposition suddenly seemed forced as he said, "Why don't you come this way and have a seat while I locate him. Maybe he's upstairs."

Again Clara trailed behind him, finding Henry still waiting patiently in the entryway with his hat in his hand. The chaplain waved for him to join them. "Come with us to the kitchen."

After they were comfortably seated at the table with a cup of water, Davies disappeared in search of Jeremiah. Clara looked across the sleek oak surface at Henry's drawn face. His dark skin was pulled tight over high cheekbones, eyes heavy with concern and fatigue.

"It be all right, Missus Clara," he encouraged just the same, "don't you worry."

Clara suspected nothing was ever going to be "all right" again.

She could hear the thump of Davies' boots as he ascended the stairs, and the muted sound of conversation through a closed door as he asked after her husband. When only one set of footsteps returned down the staircase, Clara knew Jeremiah had not been located.

When Davies returned to the kitchen, his expression was apologetic and his forehead wrinkled with confusion. "I'm very sorry, Mrs. Turner, but he doesn't appear to be here after all."

Chapter Twenty-Five

The cool air enveloped Jeremiah as he slipped silently through the back door of the farmhouse, pressing his back against the hard stones, heart thumping wildly in his chest. When the announcement had been raised: "Supply wagon's here! And hey—there's a woman on board!" Jeremiah had craned his neck to peer out the window in curiosity, wondering if perhaps a nurse had arrived to care for them.

The last person he ever expected to see at the field hospital in Gettysburg was his wife, with Henry beside her. Clara looked thin and tired, and she was coated with dust from traveling, but she was as beautiful as the day he left her at Laurel Hill in a jade muslin dress, looking up at him with intent devotion.

He hadn't moved about much since the amputation, and the sudden exertion of leaping from his bed and taking advantage of the other patients' preoccupation to sneak through the rear door left Jeremiah trembling and beaded with sweat. The pathetic stump of his left arm throbbed and tingled painfully.

Hearing Clara's voice carry through the open window spurred Jeremiah forward. He set off at a pace somewhere between a walk and run, hugging the injured arm against his chest as he darted for a nearby grove of woods. Safely concealed within the shadows, Jeremiah sank to the ground, resting his back against the trunk of a towering oak.

Why was she here? He wasn't ready to face her.

When Clara discovered he had purposefully evaded her, it would break her heart. Jeremiah's chin fell to his chest, the nub held against it, as he owned his cowardice. How could he let his beautiful, sweet wife see him in this condition—a weak, angry amputee?

The man she had fallen in love with was strong, capable, and confident. That man knew who he was and what he believed in. He was a whole person, able to love Clara as she deserved. The Jeremiah he had become was broken, inside and out. He had nothing to offer her.

Letting his forehead fall into his right palm, elbow propped on his knee, Jeremiah inhaled the clean, fresh smells of the forest. He exhaled slowly, trying to calm the racing of his heart. Through the canopy of leaves overhead, he could make out the fading sky, the first stars of the night twinkling dimly. He wished he could believe that beyond that vast expanse there was a God who saw him and cared about the torment of his life.

Never had Jeremiah felt so alone. Charlie's eyes, shadowed beneath the gray forage cap as he aimed his musket and blew off his brother's hand, haunted Jeremiah. His brother had shot him, purposefully and intentionally. Charlie hadn't mistaken his identity and shot him without recognizing who he was. It hadn't been an accidental misfire. Charlie had taken aim and pulled the trigger, pointing the barrel directly at him.

In the privacy of the woods, Jeremiah allowed the tears to come as he wept for everything he had lost and all his beloved country had sacrificed to the war. When the United States fought the British, they secured their independence and celebrated with national pride. What good could ever come from this civil war?

Behind him, he could hear the slamming of the door and the sound of Chaplain Davies and the orderlies calling his name. Jeremiah wondered what explanation Davies would offer Clara for his sudden disappearance. Sitting stone-still in the growing darkness, hidden behind the thick tree trunk, Jeremiah prayed that Davies wouldn't find him.

The shadows were lengthening as the sun dipped below the horizon, and soon enough Davies and the others gave up the hunt, leaving Jeremiah to himself. Coming to his feet, Jeremiah went deeper into the woods, walking until exhaustion got the better of him and he lay down upon a bed of fallen leaves to sleep. Resting his cheek against his right palm, Jeremiah tucked the bandaged arm into his shirt to secure it against his chest and closed his eyes.

Above him in the treetops, the eerie hoot of an owl echoed through the darkness. Crickets chirped and the rustling of dried leaves indicated the presence of nocturnal animals. But Jeremiah was undisturbed by any of it, bone-weary and heart-sick, he welcomed the peaceful respite of sleep.

When he awakened, the slanting rays of dawn were filtering through the ceiling of green leaves swaying in the summer breeze. Pushing himself upright with his one good hand, Jeremiah blinked to clear his head. He needed to keep moving.

As he came to his feet, Jeremiah swayed dizzily. He wouldn't be able to get very far without provisions. He had heard talk of a nearby farmhouse, and if he could locate it, perhaps he could obtain some water and persuade the occupants to share a slice of bread and a bit of meat. Glancing around to gain his bearings, Jeremiah trudged in the direction he believed it should be located. When he reached a clearing, he felt a surge of relief as he spotted a stone farmhouse much like the one he had vacated.

Jeremiah crossed a ruined field, the prints of boots and hooves leaving no doubt as to the source of the damage. Passing an orchard plucked bare of fruit, he cautiously approached the farmhouse. A large barn stood near the house, and as he appeared around the corner, he spied an older woman bent over a cast iron pump, her full cotton skirt swaying as her elbow worked up and down to draw water from the well.

At the sound of his footfalls, she gasped and spun around, eyeing him suspiciously. Jeremiah immediately raised both hands or more precisely, one hand and a stump, to communicate that he was no one she need fear.

"I'm sorry to frighten you, ma'am," he apologized. "I'm just looking for a drink of water and any food you can spare."

Her eyes narrowed on him, but at the sight of his bandaged arm, her expression softened. Her shoulders slumped as she replied, "I'm afraid I have nothing to offer. The army's already taken everything we have. We were advised to leave before the battle, and just returned home to find our crops trampled and our orchard robbed. I don't see how we're going to make it."

Jeremiah mentally added her to the list of war casualties as he nodded his understanding. "I saw your fields and orchard. I'm truly sorry."

She stepped closer, glancing again at his amputated hand. "I'm Catherine Slyder. My husband, John, is in the barn. Where are you going?"

"I'm heading home," he lied, unsure of his destination.

"Should you be traveling?" wrinkles creased the skin around Catherine's eyes as she studied him in concern. "You don't look well."

"I'm recovering from surgery," he stated the obvious, "but otherwise fit."

"You're not deserting, are you?" she challenged.

Jeremiah shook his head. "No ma'am." He supposed he'd better make himself known to the powers that be or he would be considered a deserter and pursued as such. Though how could he explain why he had left the field hospital where he had been assigned to recuperate?

Catherine Slyder searched his eyes as if looking for the truth. Finally she said, "Well, come sit on the front porch and we'll see what we can find. We don't have much, I'm afraid. Even the well's been pumped dry," she gestured to the bucket resting beneath the spigot, filled only with an inch of water for all her efforts.

"Thank you kindly, ma'am, but I don't want to take anything more from you," Jeremiah decided.

"Well, there's a stream down that way," she pointed, "and I can give you a canteen to fill."

"That would be appreciated," Jeremiah replied.

When Mrs. Slyder returned from inside with the canteen, she also handed him a biscuit. "My daughter Hannah asked me to give you hers," she explained. Jeremiah glanced back at the house and saw a young woman peering through the curtains of the kitchen window. A young man stood on one side of her, a young boy on the other.

Jeremiah acknowledged Hannah's generosity with a nod in her direction as he said, "Please tell her I said thank you."

"I will. You take care," Catherine bid him farewell with motherly concern in her eyes.

~

"I don't understand," Clara choked back tears. "You said he was here."

Chaplain Davies pulled up a chair beside her at the small table, his gaze shifting from her to Henry, then back again. "He was," he answered gravely. "But now he's nowhere to be found."

"Suh, what you tellin' us?" Henry demanded, his dark face twisted into a scowl of confusion.

Davies' expression was apologetic. "I'm very sorry. He was lying on his cot when I came to the door, and when I returned, he was gone."

"How badly is he hurt?" the question came out as a hoarse whisper as Clara knotted her hands in her lap.

"He lost a hand," the chaplain answered. "They had to cut it about here," Davies slid his right hand across his left forearm like a knife between the wrist and elbow. "But it could've been much worse."

Clara closed her eyes and swallowed. Images of the amputees she had seen at Camp Letterman rose before her. Remembering Thaddeus, she had to agree that it could have been worse. Still, it was hardly good news.

"Where could he have gone?" she scrunched her brows together in bewilderment.

"I have no idea, ma'am," Chaplain Davies answered gently, glancing briefly at Henry.

Something passed between the men, but Clara was too stunned to question it. Jeremiah had lost a hand. He was alive, but strangely missing from his hospital bed. It was more than she could fathom.

"Missus Clara," Henry's hand over her own brought her back to the present. "Why don't you get some rest and we see if we can find Mistuh Jeremiah. He might just be takin' a walk, gettin' some fresh air."

"You can take my bed," the chaplain graciously offered. "I'll show you where it is."

Too stunned by this turn of events to protest, Clara followed the old man up the stairs to a small room, the bed and washstand occupying most of the space. She sank down onto the quilt-covered mattress, her mind reeling.

Jeremiah, where are you?

She hadn't believed it possible for her mind to quiet long enough to fall sleep, but the day's ordeal had left Clara drained. She awakened to the crow of a rooster and the yellow light of dawn streaming across the unfamiliar quilt which covered her.

It took a moment for her memory to catch up with her. Clara sat up straight in bed as she recalled why she was sleeping in this strange bed. Quickly sliding from beneath the covers, she fastened the buttons she had loosened the evening before. She'd chosen not to undress in case she was wakened in the night with word of her husband's whereabouts.

Rushing down the stairs in search of Chaplain Davies, she found him sitting with Henry at the kitchen table. Both wore the haggard expressions of men who had slept precious little.

"No news?" she assumed, dropping dejectedly into an empty straight-backed chair.

"No ma'am," the chaplain shook his head grimly. "I'm truly sorry."

"I find him, Missus Clara," Henry vowed, his dark eyes

fervent. "Don't you worry none."

"Can I get you something to eat, Mrs. Turner?" Davies inquired solicitously, coming to his feet.

Clara declined, admitting, "My stomach's in knots."

"Eat something anyway, please ma'am," Henry insisted. "I promised I'd take care of you, and I aim to keep my word."

"Well then, I'll try for your sake," Clara forced a half-smile, grateful Henry had accompanied her.

While the chaplain scrambled eggs taken from the farmer's henhouse, Clara chewed absently on her fingernails. She sorted through the available information repeatedly, every time coming to the same obvious conclusion. Jeremiah had left because she had arrived.

When a plate was placed in front of her, it jarred Clara from her contemplation. She rested her hand on the chaplain's wrist as he withdrew, gripping him firmly and meeting his eyes with a silent demand for the truth. "He doesn't want to see me, does he?"

Davies' gaze darted nervously to Henry, and Clara accepted that as answer enough. "I shouldn't have come," she released his hand and slumped back in the chair, a painful ache growing in her chest. "What was I thinking?"

"Now Missus Clara, you ain't done nothin' wrong by comin' here. You just tryin' to take care of your huzband. He need you, I promise," the Negro insisted.

Clara shook her head, biting her lip to keep control of the emotions which flooded her. The sharp sting of betrayal and disappointment hurt worse than the discovery of Jeremiah's amputation. "No, he obviously doesn't. Let's go home," she insisted, rising to her feet.

"Mrs. Turner, I wouldn't be so hasty in my judgment," Chaplain Davies countered as he sat down, tugging her back into her seat and scooting the chair closer to her. Resting the elbow of his blue uniform on the table, he stared intently into her eyes as he continued. "His wounds go deeper than flesh and bone. He needs you now more than ever—he just isn't ready to admit it."

"I don't understand why not. I have right here in my pocket the last letter he sent me," Clara removed the page, waving it in front of her. "He said *nothing* could destroy the bond we share, yet now something has."

"This has nothing to do with his love for you, ma'am," the chaplain promised.

"Then why has he disappeared?" she demanded angrily.

"Pride," Davies answered simply.

"Because he lost his hand?" Clara asked incredulously. "That doesn't matter to me!"

"But it *does* matter to him."

Clara pressed her clenched fist against her mouth. As she'd traveled by train, by coach, and by wagon, she'd concocted a reunion scene in her mind. She'd imagined Jeremiah's face lighting with pleasure to see her, offering tender words of gratitude that she had cared enough to come to him. What a romantic fool she had been.

When all had been well, Jeremiah had been fully devoted to her. Now, after one battle, Clara didn't know who he had become.

"He can't have gone far. We'll find him and bring him back to you. That's a promise," Davies swore solemnly.

"I'll go with you," Clara began, but the chaplain interrupted.

"Henry can go with the orderlies to scout the area. You stay here and help me care for these wounded men."

As much as Clara resented surrendering the search, she could see the wisdom in Davies' suggestion. She nodded in resigned acquiescence. "I feel so powerless," she admitted regretfully, "and I wish there was something I could do!"

"There is," the chaplain argued certainly. At Clara's raised eyebrow, he explained: "Pray."

"You sound like Mamie," Clara ground out irritably.

"That Mamie one smart lady," Henry interjected.

"Would you mind if I prayed for you both, right now?"

Davies offered earnestly.

What could Clara say? She nodded tersely, watching as the chaplain bowed his head. His tone was reverent, though his words were simple and sincere. Clara could barely focus on them, however, for the noise in her own head. Through the din of her own inner voice, she caught such words as *peace*, *healing*, and *blessing*. Alluring ideas, but quite impossible in her current situation.

When he had finished, she thanked him just the same. Even if there was no power in his prayer, she was grateful for the chaplain's kindness.

She spent the day caring for the men who had fought alongside her husband, grieved once more by the scope of carnage this battle had left in its wake—that the war had brought to the nation. As Clara replaced soiled bandages, cleaned the oozing wounds beneath and carried food and water to the broken men of the Twelfth Corps lying on their cots, she wondered what Chaplain Davies had meant when he said that Jeremiah's wounds went deeper than flesh and bone.

Late in the afternoon, the orderlies returned from their mission. "There's another farm several miles to the east," they told her. "Mrs. Slyder said she saw Turner there just past dawn and gave him a canteen and a biscuit before he went on his way. He told her he was going home."

"Home? But why...?" Clara's brows drew together in confusion.

"My guess is he lied," the chaplain assured her. "But I have an idea where he might be going."

Chapter Twenty-Six

Never in his life had Jeremiah felt so demoralized and lost. He had no plan of action, only an ache in his chest and a painful throbbing in the stump where his left hand was missing. He needed to think, to decide on a course of action and how to achieve it, but his thoughts were plagued with images of Charlie in his gray uniform and Clara in her traveling dress, auburn hair covered with dust despite the hat she wore.

Deep down, Jeremiah knew he was running away from memories that would haunt him forever, following him as relentlessly as a hound chasing its prey. He could never outrun the truth of his experiences. He was like a treed coon, unable to race ahead to safety and unable to go back to the security he'd left behind. Jeremiah felt trapped, staring down at the snapping teeth and drooling maw of the beast which pursued him, with no hope of escape.

"Halt!" a voice demanded behind him, accompanied by the familiar click of a hammer being cocked.

Jeremiah lifted his arms, turning around slowly. A Union patrol pointed the barrel of his rifle at him, perched from atop a bay gelding which reminded him of Archie, whom he'd sold to the War Office in Cambridge.

"Don't shoot," he said, knowing that nerves were taut after the battle and not wanting to become a secondary casualty. But how could he explain why he was rambling through the woods miles from town?

"Are you a deserter?" the patrol's finger twitched on the trigger.

"No! No, I'm an injured Union infantryman. I'm looking

for Camp Letterman," he decided as he lifted his bandaged nub a little higher to draw attention to it.

"Why are you all the way out here?" the rifle lowered just a hair.

"I was… I just… It's a long story," Jeremiah was too weary and tormented to think of a creative explanation.

"I've got time," the patrol rested the rifle across his knees, curiosity evident in his expression.

Deciding to stick with the simple truth, Jeremiah let his arms fall to his side as he said, "My wife arrived at the field hospital where I was stationed. I'm not ready to see her yet. I'd like to receive care at Camp Letterman."

The patrol looked to be about Jeremiah's age. He pursed his lips before extending his hand. "I'll give you a ride there," he offered. "Before the war, I was a blacksmith. I hated it then, but I'd do just about anything to go back to it now. Can't be the same after something like this, can you?"

Jeremiah agreed, grabbing the patrol's wrist with his right hand and climbing up behind him. It was a long ride to the hospital camp and Jeremiah was grateful he'd been given a ride. His strength would have expired long before he reached it on foot.

After being delivered to the main headquarters and his information recorded, Jeremiah was sent to a hospital tent which had recently had a vacancy. He preferred not to think about why the cot had become available as he sank down gratefully onto it, the trauma of the last two days taking its toll on his compromised health.

The nurse assigned to his tent was a nun who wore a peculiar white hat with wings. The soothing tone of her voice reminded Jeremiah of the way his mother used to comfort him when he was ill as a boy. He accepted the water and bread she offered him, managing to express his thanks before he succumbed to exhaustion and slept.

He awakened to someone shaking him with a firm hand on

his shoulder. "I have some stew here for you," a voice spoke from somewhere above him. "Wake up and eat now. You'll need it if you're going to get your strength back."

Forcing one eye half open, Jeremiah saw the bizarre shape of the nun's hat leaning over him. The tempting aroma of beef called him from the respite of a deep and dreamless sleep. Leaning onto his right elbow, Jeremiah pushed himself upright. "I can feed myself," he said, blinking to push back the fog lingering in his brain. Placing a tray on his lap, the nun sat on a stool beside him to observe his capability.

"I said I can do it myself!" he repeated, frustrated by the limitations of his new body.

"I heard you the first time," she answered, nonplussed and unmoving, waiting for him to proceed with it.

Scowling, Jeremiah cradled the bowl with his bandaged arm to steady it while he leaned forward over the bowl and slowly began spooning the food into his mouth.

The nun nodded approvingly as she came to her feet. "I'm Sister Camilla. Call me if you need anything."

Grateful as her black skirt rustled away, Jeremiah enjoyed the warm meal. When he had finished, he waited until she came around to collect the empty bowl to issue a grumbled, "Thank you."

"You're welcome, Turner," she replied with a kindly smile.

Jeremiah watched as Sister Camilla moved from one cot to another collecting dishes, checking foreheads for signs of fever, and offering words of encouragement. There were at least forty cots filling the tent, arranged in rows and columns with a space large enough between them for the nun and the other two nurses, one male and one female, to walk between them. Each of them seemed dedicated in their care of the wounded, whom Jeremiah noted existed in various states of dismemberment.

If it wasn't for his upbringing on the Eastern Shore and his exposure there to sympathy for the Southern cause, as well as the fact that Charlie fought with the rebels and he could never hate his brother—no matter what—Jeremiah might be tempted to curse the Confederacy and blame them for this human wreckage. Many of the men at the Bushman Farm had seemed in a hurry to regain their health so that they could take up arms and get back to killing the Rebels. But just as many, like Jeremiah, had no desire to ever fight again.

The flap of the tent was open, allowing a breeze to pass through, but they still baked in the summer sun. Jeremiah stared absently down at his lap, wondering how his father was faring on the farm and what he thought about Clara traveling to Gettysburg. Francis' heart would surely break if he knew how Jeremiah had come by his injury.

"You look like you could use some reading material," a Bible appeared on his thigh, and Jeremiah looked up into the smiling face of Chaplain Davies.

"How did you find me?" Jeremiah's bushy brown eyebrows drew together anxiously, darting past the chaplain's shoulder in search of Clara.

Davies grinned. "You're too smart to desert, so you'd have to end up here."

Frowning, Jeremiah demanded, "Where's my wife?"

"Back at the farm," Davies assured him. "I told her I had a feeling I knew where you were, but I didn't tell her where. I thought it might be nice if we had some time to talk, man to man."

"Do you ever mind your own business?"

"Only with people I don't love," the chaplain retorted with a wink. "So talk to me, son. Why did you run?"

Pursing his lips together, Jeremiah sighed thoughtfully. He closed his eyes and tried to find the words to describe the way he felt upon spying Clara climbing down from the supply wagon. "I'm not the man she married. I don't know who I am anymore… other than a bitter, one-handed farmer."

"Who better to love you through this than your wife?" Davies asked softly, eyebrows raised in challenge.

"She deserves a strong, capable man, like the one she married." Jeremiah studied the stump of his left arm as he concluded, "She deserves better than me."

"This isn't about your hand," the chaplain argued certainly.

Jeremiah sighed. Davies was right.

"Look son, suffering is a catalyst either for wisdom and compassion, or bitterness and anger. It tests the true heart of a man and either brings out his best or his worst. It helps us discover what we're made of, and when we've reached the end of our strength, guess what we do next?"

Raising one eyebrow, Jeremiah waited for the answer. "I have a feeling it has something to do with God," he replied drily.

"See, I knew you were a smart man," Davies grinned. "When you can't do it alone, you have to face a truth that you've been ignoring all your life. Not just you, but each and every one of us. When we try to live by our own strength and resources, we wind up anxious and miserable. But when we surrender everything we have and all that we are to God, He gives us strength and peace to endure."

Grinding his teeth, Jeremiah explained, "I'm not a pastor, a chaplain, or a nun," he glanced over at the sister. "I'm just a man. When I plant my fields, corn grows. If I leave them fallow, it doesn't. I survive by the sweat of my brow and the labor of my hands. This is real life."

"*Cursed is the man who trusts in man and makes flesh his strength, whose heart departs from the Lord,*" the chaplain quoted in response.

"Any chance I could convince you to go away?" Jeremiah challenged irritably.

Squeezing his shoulder, Davies nodded. "I'll come back later. You take some time to think and pray."

~

In the kitchen at the Bushman Farm, Clara kneaded dough for biscuits with more force than was really necessary. Her mind and heart were in a turmoil. She had been so certain that Jeremiah would value her devotion to him, and instead she felt as if he had spit in her face. She had rushed to his side, eager to accept him and care for him no matter his condition, and he hadn't even give her the chance.

It was easy enough to make lofty promises and pen beautiful words when all was well. But hardship had its way of revealing the truth, pressing down the wheat so that the chaff could be blown away by a gentle breeze.

Just moments before, she had read over his last letter to her. Its very tenderness made her angry. *"I carry you in my heart and am confident that nothing can destroy the powerful bond we share,"* he had written. *"Whatever comes, remember that I love you with all I am. Never forget, my sweet Clara."*

She hadn't. He was the one who appeared to have forgotten.

Clara bit her lip to hold back tears. She wasn't sure why she hadn't gotten on the train that morning and gone home to Centreville. What was she waiting for? If Jeremiah didn't want to see her, she wasn't going to force herself on him.

Using her wrist to brush a strand of hair from her eyes, Clara leaned into the rolling pin as she smoothed out dough for biscuits and cut it into circles. Once arranged on a greased pan, Clara slid them into the side compartment of the cast iron stove. She'd had very little experience in the kitchen growing up, and now more than ever, she appreciated the work of a cook. The kitchen was an inferno between the heat from the stove and the warmth of the summer sunshine beating down on the roof. And she wasn't entirely sure how much wood to put in the stove or how to control the temperature with all the flues and dampers.

Wiping her hands on her skirt, only to realize she wore no apron, Clara sighed as she surveyed the white handprints smeared on her traveling dress. It was the least of her worries.

"Ma'am," Henry's dark head suddenly ducked around the doorway, his eyes round. "There a man here lookin' for you. Say Sistuh C'milla sent him.

266

Clara followed on his heels as they returned to the front door of the farmhouse, where a young orderly stood waiting. "Mrs. Turner?" he verified.

"Yes?" she replied, waiting for the report. Either Jeremiah was safely at Camp Letterman, or...

"Sister Camilla said you were looking for your husband. He was brought to her ward yesterday at Camp Letterman, and she asked me to give you a ride back," the young man announced.

Glancing anxiously at Henry, Clara replied, "Can you give me a moment, please?"

"Certainly, ma'am," the orderly answered. "I'll wait by the wagon."

Once the young man was out of ear shot, Clara leaned in close to Henry. "He doesn't want to see me! I can't go chasing all over Gettysburg for him. Perhaps you could go."

"I ain't leavin' you side, and that's final. We done come all the way here to see him, and the chapl'in say Mistuh Jeremiah need us now more than ever," Henry declared passionately.

Clara worried at her lip. He was right... But suddenly the thought of facing Jeremiah made her heart hammer against her ribcage. How would he look at her? She couldn't bear the thought of his eyes meeting hers with anything other than love.

"I told the chaplain I would take care of the cooking while he was away," she began to protest, but Henry cut her off, shaking his head.

"They make out just fine without you, ma'am. Now let's get goin'."

"Very well. Let me inform someone that there's bread baking in the oven," Clara insisted, heading for the dining room which now functioned as a hospital ward.

Her stomach fluttered as she bade the wounded men and the orderlies goodbye, as anxious as she was reluctant to see her husband again. Once on the buckboard of the wagon, sandwiched between Henry and the orderly, Clara clenched her fists in her lap until her knuckles turned white.

As the neat rows of white tents came into view at Camp Letterman, Henry placed his black hand over hers. She was more nervous than she had been the day of their wedding, because she had known at the end of the aisle he would be eagerly awaiting her with a smile. Today she felt like the proverbial ball and chain, unwanted but attached.

"Perhaps you should go in first," Clara suggested to Henry. "It might be better that way."

"No ma'am," Henry disagreed. "Mistuh Jeremiah like me all right, but it's *you* he loves."

Clara wished she felt as certain about it as the Negro did.

When the orderly halted the wagon, he climbed down and offered his hand to Clara to assist her. "I'll go ahead and alert Sister Camilla that you've arrived," he suggested, patting her arm in a brotherly fashion.

Clara nodded gratefully. Her insides twisted with anxious nerves. She'd rather watch her family home burn to the ground than have her husband send her away.

At the flap of the tent, the white wings of the sister's hat appeared, dipping as she nodded in acknowledgement and invitation. Fisting her skirt in her hands, Clara slowly stepped forward.

The nun hugged her in greeting, then gestured for Clara to follow her down an aisle between the wounded men. She stopped and pointed at a particular cot, and Clara had to blink twice to recognize him. He laid sleeping, head lolling sideways against a pillow, pale and thin with an unkempt beard that hid his features. Free to scrutinize Jeremiah without reproach, Clara took a tentative step toward him and peered across his chest at the amputated hand.

She covered her mouth as she saw the bandaged stump of his arm, the sight of it quite different than mere knowledge.

Sister Camilla placed a stool beside the cot, and with a shaky breath, Clara seated herself to wait for Jeremiah to wake up. As if feeling her gaze upon him, his eyelids fluttered open and her husband stared up at her in shock.

"Clara?" he whispered brokenly, raw pain evident in his red-rimmed eyes.

Chapter Twenty-Seven

W hy are you here?" Jeremiah demanded, instantly regretting the accusation in his tone as Clara cringed in response.

"Hello Jeremiah," Clara replied coolly in an unsuccessful attempt to conceal her hurt. She was more beautiful than he had remembered, her auburn hair glimmering like burnished copper in the lamplight.

"You didn't need to come," he tried to soften his rejection, but shame and embarrassment edged his words like a razor.

"Well I can honestly tell you that I wish I hadn't," she retorted, her delicate brows arching resentfully. "But I had this absurd idea in my head that you loved me and would value my desire to be here with you."

"This has nothing to do with love," he countered, feeling like a cornered animal. Why did women have to make everything about love?

The distance in her almond brown eyes as she studied him was as painful as a bullet through the chest. "What *does* it have to do with, then?" she challenged, her voice measured and aloof.

"I don't need you to take care of me! I'm perfectly capable, and there are ample nurses here without you," he insisted.

"Really?" one eyebrow lifted in question. "That isn't what I heard. But since you clearly don't need *me*, I might as well go home," Clara announced, brushing the wrinkles from her skirt as she came to her feet.

Jeremiah had to bite his lip to keep from begging her to stay. He hated treating her like this, but he felt as if a monster had been set loose within himself and he had no idea how to vanquish it.

A voice behind Clara ordered, "Sit back down. You're not going anywhere," and as she spun around, Jeremiah saw the unsmiling face of Chaplain Davies.

He had never seen the chaplain look so serious. His lips were compressed in a straight line and his eyes burned with intensity. "The reason we're in this war in the first place is because men chose pride over peace. Now, I want both of you to stop being so stupidly stubborn and admit that you need each other and want peace between you again. I'm going to step away and I want you to talk honestly with one another, without all this foolishness. And Jeremiah, I'm expecting you to take the lead. If you're the man of the house, then this is the chance to act like one." And with that, the old man spun on his heel and strode away.

Staring open-mouthed after him, Jeremiah remembered the time he had sassed the schoolteacher as a boy and been sent to sit in the corner on the dunce's stool. He felt as if he were sitting on it right now.

Slowly shifting his gaze to Clara, he searched his mind for something to say that could bridge the gap which had opened up between them. She stared back at him coldly. How could he convince her to lower the shield his harshness had forced her to erect?

Taking a deep breath, Jeremiah ventured a feeble attempt. "You didn't do anything wrong by coming. I'm just... just in a bad place right now."

"I expected you to be," she replied, her armor almost visible. "That was why I came. To be here for you."

Glancing down at his amputation, Jeremiah felt his emotions rolling inside him like the thunderclouds of a raging storm. It wasn't just that he had lost his hand, and his abilities with it, it was that his brother had taken it from him. And the pain that knowledge caused was so deep and troubling, he couldn't even begin to wade through it.

Clara removed a folded page from her skirt pocket and held

it in the air. "The man I married wrote me this letter before he was sent to Gettysburg. Now he's disappeared, even though I'm looking right at him, and I wish I could understand why."

Though it had only been two weeks earlier when Jeremiah had written those words, it felt like a lifetime ago. How quickly the heart and spirit could be broken. If only healing could come as quickly.

"I'm sorry, Clara," he managed to force the words past his lips. "You don't understand what I've been through…"

"No, I don't," she admitted, her voice angry. "I expected *you* to be different. What I didn't expect was for the way you feel about me to have changed."

"I still love you," he whispered hoarsely, missing the tender woman he had held in his arms at Laurel Hill.

"Then why are you here, at Camp Letterman?" she queried, her eyes boring into his.

He ran his right hand over the long, unkempt beard which covered his face as he struggled to find the words to frame an honest answer. "I just wasn't ready to see you," he finally admitted, lifting the nub of his arm in the air for her to see. "I feel so broken… so lost."

"Why won't you let me help you find your way?" she wondered.

"I despise my own weakness," he managed to admit, though the truth came at a cost.

"Any man can have two strong hands. Not every man is blessed with strength of character. And that is why I fell in love with you, Jeremiah Turner. You could lose every limb on your body, and as long as that man of moral courage was still inside, I would love you just the same."

Jeremiah's eyes burned with unshed tears. He was moved by her declaration, the sincerity of it evident in the firm line of her clenched jaw.

"I never meant to hurt you, Clara," he promised. "The man you married is still here, but he's changed now. After July third,

I'll never be the same again. I can't be…" His heart hammered in his chest as he relived that day in his mind. The gunfire, the smoke, and the blood as Westbrook and Cullen, and countless others, were shot down. And then there was Charlie, leveling his barrel at him as he pulled the trigger.

Jeremiah blinked to clear his vision, finding Clara studying him with new understanding. Compassion softened her expression, and she reached out to grasp his one good hand. "What do you need from me?" she asked, searching his eyes earnestly.

Jeremiah stared at her, unsure how to reply. He looked back at her helplessly as he admitted, "I don't know."

"If you need more time, I can care for other men here and you need not see me at all," Clara offered. "But you must vow that this is a temporary situation. I've loved you since I was eighteen years old, and nothing is ever going to change that. Don't make me a widow whose husband still lives," she pleaded.

Tightening his fingers around hers, Jeremiah shook his head. "Stay with me," he whispered. "Stay with me."

Lifting his hand, Clara pressed her lips against the rough skin of his knuckles. "That's all I've ever wanted."

~

The warmth of his skin against hers brought a rush of emotion. Clara was relieved beyond words that Jeremiah had asked her to stay. For a dreadful moment she feared he would send her away and she would have no choice but to give him the space she had offered. It had been a gamble, calling his bluff like that, but the risk had paid off.

Some of the tension in his face began to relax, the grooves in his forehead smoothing out as Jeremiah clutched her hand, reassured by the knowledge of her love and acceptance. He wore a woolen undershirt, rolled up to the elbows and stained yellow under the armpits from sweat. His hair and beard looked like they could benefit from use of soap, and his skin hugged his cheekbones as if he hadn't eaten well in weeks.

Checking the urge to cluck over him like a mother hen, Clara held her seat at the stool, cherishing this moment of reconciliation. Right now his emotional needs were of far greater priority than his physical. One healing would follow the other.

"Well, I'm glad to see you two acting friendly," Davies commented as he joined them, placing a hand on each of their shoulders. "This man means a lot to me," he said, "and I'm glad to see God has given him such a good woman... and pretty too," he winked.

Clara smiled warmly at the chaplain, grateful he had been there for her husband when she couldn't be.

"Now, if you don't mind, I'd like to tell you both something. Truthfully, I'm going to tell you even if you *do* mind," Davies admitted with a toothy grin. "In war, the word 'surrender' is usually a last resort. When you're outnumbered and out of options, you have to lift that white flag to the enemy and give up the fight. That word, 'surrender,' means to cease resistance to an enemy and submit to their authority.

"In life, we make God our enemy when we choose to live by our own will. He loved us before the foundation of the world, and He's just waiting for us to surrender our lives to Him and submit to His authority. But God doesn't want to make us His prisoner, He wants to make us His child!"

Opening the Bible in his hands, the chaplain began thumbing through the thin pages. "Listen to this: '*Peace I leave with you, My peace I give to you; not as the world gives do I give to you.*' The peace of this world depends on life going the way we want it, and people doing what we wish them to. But God can give us a peace that transcends both people and circumstances.

"'*If anyone loves Me, he will keep My word and My Father will love him, and We will come to him and make Our home with him.*' To get this peace, you have to love God and surrender your life to Him. It isn't an act of weakness or failure, but an act of love. When you give God your dreams, needs, and your very life, everything changes. When you surrender to God, *you* win! He'll help you carry all the burdens that are too heavy to carry alone."

Jeremiah eyed him skeptically, and the chaplain turned to Clara and explained, "He thinks that it all depends on him, the way the crops depends on his planting and harvesting them. But tell me, Who sends the rain and makes the sun shine? No matter how hard the farmer labors, it's God who makes the crops grow. There are things we can do, and there are things beyond our abilities. You can't control everything—but God can. So when you surrender your life to Him, a whole new world of possibilities opens up for you!"

Clara felt hope spark within her chest, but Jeremiah's unruly brows drew together in challenge. "What exactly is all that supposed to mean to us right here and now? I don't believe in magic and fairy tales, Chaplain. I believe in the reality of what I know and see around me."

Davies pursed his lips together as he carefully considered his answer. His eyes were filled with sympathy as he replied, "I understand that, son. Right now all you know is how much you're hurting, and all you see is the darkness in the world around you. But if you just open up your heart to God, you'll find that He can bring healing where you thought it impossible, and He can restore what you think is lost forever."

Watching her husband's eyes drift away from the chaplain, glancing briefly down at his wounded arm before gazing out into the distance through the open tent flap, Clara sensed there was more to this conversation than what she understood. There was something the chaplain knew about the pain in Jeremiah's eyes that went beyond the obvious.

"I've got one more thing to say," Chaplain Davies informed him, "and then I'll close my mouth and walk away."

"Is that a promise?" Jeremiah prodded.

Davies just grinned. "*For all have sinned and fall short of the glory of God, being justified freely by His grace through the redemption that is in Christ Jesus… And if you confess with your mouth the Lord Jesus and believe in your heart that God has raised Him from the dead, you will be saved. For with the heart one believes unto righteousness, and with the mouth confession is made unto salvation.'"*

Still gripping Jeremiah's shoulder, the chaplain put his arm around Clara. "I'd like to pray with you," he said.

"I thought you were done?" Jeremiah retorted. Clara had never seen her husband behave so rudely, and she had to bite her tongue to keep from reprimanding him.

The chaplain, however, chuckled in response. "I haven't finished my one thing yet. It was a verse *and* a prayer," he explained.

"You've got to keep an eye on this one," Jeremiah informed Clara, and she realized that underneath the insolence was both camaraderie and respect.

"You can bow your head now," Davies instructed as he closed his eyes and bent his neck, chin facing the dirt floor of the hospital tent. After a second, he opened one eye and peeked up them. This time he waited for them to join him in a reverent pose before continuing.

"Dear Heavenly Father," he began, "I pray for these two dear friends. I ask that you would reveal Yourself to them, bring healing into their lives, and bless them beyond measure. Amen." Looking up at them, Davies waited until their eyes opened to ask, "Was that so bad?"

Clara shook her head, a smile touching her lips. "Thank you, Chaplain, for your kindness to me and my husband."

"Well, you're a lot easier to be kind to than he is," Davies winked, jerking his head at Jeremiah, "but you're welcome."

"Aren't you going somewhere?" Jeremiah reminded him brusquely.

The chaplain replied by leaning over to look him in the eyes as he replied sincerely, "I love you, Turner." When Jeremiah's eyes glistened over with unshed tears, Davies announced, "I'm going now!" and quickly made himself scarce.

Swallowing down his emotions, Jeremiah blinked to clear his eyes. Clara wished she could gather him in her arms and nestle her head in the crook of his shoulder. She settled for resting a hand over his chest, feeling the strong, steady beat beneath her palm.

Clara wanted the peace the chaplain spoke of. She wanted to share the burdens she carried with One who could walk on water and make a lame man dance with joy. Lifting her heart to God, she prayed simply, "Forgive my sins, Lord. I surrender myself to You," and as the words floated upward, she sent her dreams, her needs, and her very life with them. She gave everything she had and everything she was to Him.

A strange assurance crept over her. It wasn't as if there was a promise that all the troubles she knew would be swept away, but rather a peace that the God of the Universe was with her as she faced them. Perhaps God did hear the prayers of every soldier, and of every wife and mother, after all.

Chapter Twenty-Eight

Jeremiah blinked. It felt like a dream to awaken in his room at Laurel Hill, to be welcomed by all the familiar sights and smells which had only been sweet memories for the last year and a half. Below the open window, in the yard below, the old rooster announced the arrival of a new day in a voice full and robust with optimism.

The white muslin curtains rustled in the morning breeze, and Jeremiah inhaled the aromas of home: the smell of fields filled with knee-high corn, freshly cut grass, and biscuits baking in the kitchen below. His head was nestled into the pillow, and the mattress beneath him cradled his back, offering more comfort than he had known since leaving home.

He had arrived in Centreville late the evening before, too exhausted from travel to do more than greet his father warmly and tumble into bed. After his request to be honorably discharged from the army was granted, he and Clara had immediately made arrangements to come home. Although some men chose to remain in the army after an amputation, Jeremiah felt he had done his duty and was ready to resume a life of peace.

Clara had chosen to sleep on a trundle bed on the floor for fear of rolling over in her sleep and jostling his healing arm. Sometimes it tingled and burned for no apparent reason at the site of the severed nerves, and when bumped, the pain jolted up his arm all the way to his shoulder. Occasionally he felt sensation in the hand which had been discarded like a cut of bad meat. It was a surprise every time he reached out to ease the ache, only to find it absent.

He'd shaken hands with Davies solemnly before he left

Gettysburg, grateful for all the man had given him—even if he did sometimes push into corners he didn't belong. All his Bible verses and God-talk were part of the chaplain's job, and while Clara seemed to take it to heart, Jeremiah found it all rather frustrating. While it was true that Providence provided the sun and the rain which made the crops grow, it was the work of the farmer to plant the seeds, pull the weeds, and harvest the crops. It wasn't as if corn would sprout up from a fallow field of its own accord.

A sleepy sigh from below his line of vision alerted Jeremiah that his wife was also waking from her slumber. Clara's tousled hair appeared as she sat up, her auburn braid falling over the shoulder of her white shift. While at Camp Letterman, she had shared quarters with the nuns and nurses. This was the first time they had spent a night together and Jeremiah considered that she may have chosen the trundle bed out of more than mere concern for his injury.

As their eyes met, he patted the empty space next to him and was pleased when Clara immediately climbed up onto the bed. She kept her distance, resting her head on her bent elbow as she studied him uncertainly. Even if the events at Gettysburg had never happened, they would have needed time to get to know one another again. But with all that had transpired, it would take much longer to reclaim their former camaraderie.

"It's good to be home," Jeremiah told her, his voice hushed in the still of the morning.

"I can hardly believe you're here," she whispered, her eyes caressing his face lovingly.

Rolling onto his side, Jeremiah was mindful of his injured arm as he held it against his chest. As her gaze settled on his beard, neglected for the last several weeks, he asked "Should I shave, or just trim it?"

Her pink lips pulled back into a smile. "Just trim it. I wouldn't recognize you without it…"

"What is it?" he asked as Clara's voice trailed off and a

distant look came into her eye.

"When I saw you at Camp Letterman, I didn't even know it was you until Sister Camilla pointed you out. You were so thin and pale under that bedraggled beard."

"You are as beautiful as ever," Jeremiah replied, cupping her jaw tenderly in his right palm. "I missed you, Clara. I hope you'll forgive my stupidity."

"I have forgiven you, darling," she assured him, "but I can't pretend that I understand."

Jeremiah was quite sure that she couldn't, no more than he could have understood what the men at Gettysburg faced while he was suffering from boredom at Oak Hall. Clara had glimpsed the ugliness of war in its bloody aftermath, but even that did not compare with the overwhelming blur of adrenaline, terror, and guilt which hovered around the soldiers like gun smoke. Even if that was the worst he'd faced, he would need time to process it. But that moment of recognition would haunt him forever.

"One day I'll try to explain," he promised. "But not yet."

"When you're ready," she agreed. Clara searched his eyes for a brief second before she pushed herself upright and announced, "I suppose we'd better get dressed and go down for breakfast. I'd be willing to bet Mamie's whipping up a breakfast fit for a king."

Chuckling as his stomach growled in anticipation, Jeremiah followed suit, swinging his legs over the edge of the bed. Perhaps after breakfast, he could get water pulled and heated for a bath, then tame his overgrown facial hair.

He had no sooner descended the stairs than his father appeared around the corner and gripped him in a bear hug reminiscent of the one he had given him upon his arrival the night before. "Welcome home, son," he repeated. "So glad to have you back!"

"I'm glad to be home," Jeremiah replied as he slapped his father on the broad back with his one good hand, cringing as Francis' exuberance jarred his sensitive stump.

"You better step out onto the back porch," his father told him, "as there are some folks who'd like to say hello."

Remembering the farewell the slaves had given him, Jeremiah opened the screen door to find the Negros standing in much the same formation at the foot of the porch. Stepping down to join them, Jeremiah clasped Old Joe in a firm hand shake, the big man booming, "Welcome home, suh!"

Mamie patted Jeremiah's chest, her cheeks round as apples as she grinned, "We gonna need to fatten you up, ain't we?"

Noticing the dimpled toddler Phoebe held on her hip, his hair a mayhem of corkscrew curls, Jeremiah extended his congratulations as he offered Henry his hand. "Welcome home," they chorused.

Lena and Silas smiled up at him, the young boy unable to keep his eyes off the bandages wrapping Jeremiah's amputated arm. Instinctively, Jeremiah tucked it behind his back, uncomfortable with the scrutiny.

Relieved when everyone returned to their work and he could retreat to the dining room, Jeremiah sank down into the cushioned chair. Looking around the room as if it were the first time, he realized how much he had taken for granted. The blue and white Wedgewood plates, the sleek oak table, and the painted panel concealing the fireplace, all seemed like marvels of luxury now.

He smiled gratefully as Clara poured him a glass of fresh milk from a porcelain pitcher just as Mamie appeared from the kitchen with platters of food, enough to feed twenty men. He stared at the bounty in front of him, his belly rumbling.

"Well now, I guess we better get you fed right quick!" Mamie patted him on the shoulder as she placed another platter onto the table, this one laden with sausage and cheese biscuits. Jeremiah knew he'd never be able to consume even a quarter of all she had prepared for him, but he was grateful for the warm homecoming.

"I've sure missed your cooking, Mamie," he told her

honestly, grabbing two of the biscuits.

Fried eggs, sausage links, buttermilk pancakes, sausage biscuits... Jeremiah took a sample of everything. He tried to remember his manners, but it had been so long since it had mattered that it didn't feel natural.

When his appetite had been sated, and he was eating merely for enjoyment's sake, Jeremiah looked up at his father and asked, "Any word from Charlie?"

"Why don't you finish eating, then we can talk," Francis replied evasively. He looked older than Jeremiah remembered. Thinner too. And at the current moment, he looked as if he knew something he didn't wish to divulge.

Jeremiah pushed his plate away and raised his eyebrows, as wild and untamed as his father's, only darker. "What is it?" he worried.

"Charlie was taken prisoner at Gettysburg," Francis admitted grimly. "I heard they took most of the Rebel prisoners down to Point Lookout in Southern Maryland. I'm guessing that's where he is."

The food Jeremiah had just devoured so enthusiastically now sat in his stomach like a rock. Point Lookout Prison Camp was reputed to be overcrowded, without adequate resources, and given to harsh treatment of their prisoners.

"Did you see him there?" his father asked, almost as if afraid of the answer.

Hoping the lie didn't show in his face, Jeremiah shook his head. "There were thousands of men there fighting over a vast area."

Francis ran a callused hand over his face, sighing heavily. "Thank God for that... What a horrible day in our nation's history when a father must fear his sons facing one another across the battle lines."

Jeremiah felt a gentle touch on his left elbow, and he turned to see Clara resting her hand on his arm and looking up at him in concern. "I'm so sorry, darling," she said. "We must pray him home."

He didn't reply. He had no idea what she meant, but if Charlie ever did make it back home, Jeremiah knew he wouldn't be able to welcome his brother with open arms.

~

All the long months her husband had been away, Clara had imagined that when he returned, it would be as if he had never gone. But even though Jeremiah was home bodily, there was still a part of him that seemed very far away.

There was no one she had ever been so close to in her life, not even Jane, and to have this strangely fractured relationship was almost worse than having him gone altogether. Last night, she had felt as if there was a strange man sleeping in her bedroom rather than her own beloved husband.

She saw glimpses of him, but she knew deep down that the pre-war Jeremiah was gone forever. Clara would have to get to know this new version of him, and learn how to love him for who he had become.

Hearing that Charlie had been taken prisoner had been an awful blow to Jeremiah. He had reacted quite differently to the news than Clara had expected. It was bizarre to think that both brothers had been there, fighting the same battle but on opposite sides of the war. She couldn't imagine what it had been like for her husband to be there firing his musket at the enemy, knowing that his brother marched under that Rebel flag.

Although his hand was lost, Clara was grateful that he had not been taken prisoner. If Jeremiah's brief war experience had transformed him, she couldn't begin to imagine how Charlie's life as a soldier, and now as a prisoner of war, would alter him.

After breakfast, Jeremiah requested that water be drawn and warmed for a bath. No one protested as it was obvious that a wash was long overdue.

While he bathed, Clara wandered through the trees in the peach orchard, trying to hold fast to the peace she had discovered in Gettysburg. In the green leaves that glowed vibrantly as the sun streamed through them, rustling gently in the summer breeze, and in the vast expanse of the blue sky above, Clara felt God's presence. With a certainty she couldn't explain, she felt Him holding her hand and promising to walk beside her through whatever the future brought. In this simple cathedral of nature, she lifted her heart in prayer, giving Providence all the worries that dogged her heels.

As she returned to the house, Clara spotted a man sitting on the back porch divan, gazing out at the family cemetery. With his dark hair freshly washed and curling at the neck, his beard clipped neatly back, and wearing a pale blue cotton shirt, Jeremiah was more handsome than she even remembered. Her heart thudded in her chest as his gaze shifted at the sound of her approach and his brown eyes met hers.

Clara blushed as she was overwhelmed by a desire to wrap her arms around his neck and wind her fingers through his damp hair, kissing him deeply. Sudden shyness gripped her and she took a seat in the rocking chair, spinning it to face him.

"It feels good to be clean and in my own clothes," Jeremiah sighed. "And even better to be here with you."

He patted the divan next to him and Clara joined him, feeling her pulse accelerate at his nearness. He gently ran the back of his fingers along her jaw line, his gaze fastening on her lips as if he had read her thoughts. Clara felt as if it was their first kiss as Jeremiah's hand slowly slid behind her neck and drew her to him. She melted into him, her arms encircling his neck and holding him against her.

The slamming of the screen door alerted them that they had been discovered. Heat coursed through Clara's cheeks as she looked up to find that whoever had interrupted them had fled back into the house, as embarrassed as she was.

Jeremiah winked, pressing another kiss to her lips before he came to his feet. "It's all right," he called to the mysterious interloper. "I'll kiss her again later."

Cautiously the door opened, and Phoebe appeared with a knowing grin on her face. "I don't see nothing, suh," she teased. "You got visitors. Missus Clara's fam'ly here."

Clara had sent word through Eli that her husband had returned home, and she was pleased that they had come to visit. Springing to her feet, she beamed up at Jeremiah as he held the door open for her.

She had taken extra pains with her appearance that morning, donning a pink muslin dress and carefully pinning up her hair. Not only did she want to be beautiful for her husband, Clara had suspected that word of Jeremiah's homecoming might draw any number of guests.

As Jane transitioned from deep mourning, she wore a white dress, still devoid of color and excess adornment. She greeted Clara with a wordless hug conveying her relief that Clara had been spared the same grief she endured.

"Welcome home," George extended his hand to Jeremiah and shook it firmly. "Mighty relieved you made it back safely."

"Well, most of me anyway," Jeremiah attempted at levity, displaying the amputation he knew was a source of curiosity for all.

Clara slipped her arm though the crook of his elbow, adding, "All of him that matters, anyway."

Naomi embraced her daughter first, then her son-in-law, patting his cheek affectionately. Despite the relief obvious in her expression, there was still anxiety lurking in the lines creasing her forehead. Clara knew her mother well enough to recognize it, but she bided her time, knowing the explanation would come soon enough.

As Eddy stepped forward, Clara noticed that her younger brother stared at Jeremiah's stumped arm with a combination of horror and fascination. The same troubled shadow which hovered around Naomi seemed to have settled on Edward's shoulders. He offered a tight smile as he shook Jeremiah's hand, his immaculate attire, fair skin, and good health contrasting against the rugged appearance of the returning soldier.

Foreboding prodded sharply at Clara's ribs, disrupting the joy and peace she had felt only moments before. Silently, she lifted her voice to God once more. Whatever it was, she had no way of preventing it, but Providence had power over it.

The visitors were invited into the parlor and Phoebe served tea with oatmeal and molasses cookies. A discernible strain hovered over the room, despite the pleasantries as Jeremiah's homecoming was celebrated.

Francis had been called in from the fields, and after washing off the sweat and grime, he joined the Collins in the parlor. After exchanging all the usual pleasantries, the two fathers stepped outside for a private conversation. Clara tried to focus on her mother's words, but their deep voices drifted through the open window and she strained to overhear.

Eddy also appeared more intent on the discourse taking place in the front yard than the one going on around him in the parlor. When the men returned from outside, Clara turned to her father expectantly.

"Please tell me what it is?" she said as she came to her feet. "I can tell there is something you need to tell me."

George's eyes shifted anxiously to his wife, then fell heavily on his son.

Eddy stepped forward. "I've been drafted," he announced.

Jeremiah's strong arm encircled Clara as she felt herself going weak in the knees. In March, the Second Enrollment Act of the Federal Government had been passed to replace the men who fell in battle. Enlistment had sharply declined, and even the promise of a bounty had lost its allure as more and more men succumbed either to the surgeon's blade or the cold and unforgiving ground.

Once the conscription notice was served, failure to comply would result in arrest and imprisonment. If men no longer wished to volunteer, the government would demand their patriotic service.

A fierce protectiveness rose in Clara as she stepped forward to grab hold of her younger brother's arms. Although a man of twenty years old, he would always be a little boy to Clara, with no business being ordered into battle. Eddy wasn't made for war. He had soft hands made for holding a pen and a mind bent toward business and turning a profit. He wasn't made to carry a musket or thrust a bayonet, even if he had believed in the Union cause.

Anger and resentment stirred within her. Her husband had barely made it home alive. Her brother-in-law was being held at a prison camp. And now her baby brother was being forced to risk his life for a fight which had only succeeded in deepening sectional division, violently decreasing the population, and devastating the nation.

"Is there nothing we can do?" Clara turned to her father and pleaded.

"There are essentially four choices," he replied wearily, holding up his hand as he counted off the options. "Substitution: pay someone to take his place. Commutation: pay the government three hundred dollars for his exemption. Evade the draft and risk arrest and imprisonment. Or report for duty and pray the war ends tomorrow."

Francis chimed in, "There's rioting in the streets of New York over the conscription. They're saying that it's a 'rich man's war, but a poor man's fight.' Only the wealthy can afford substitution or commutation. They're killing the Negros, burning businesses that serve them, and causing disorder and mayhem. Even up North, there's no unity of purpose. Everyone's sick to death of this war, and I don't understand why Lincoln's letting it drag on like this. If the nation was divided before the war, I'm afraid it will be forever divided afterward."

Chapter Twenty-Nine

Jeremiah knelt down on the grassy carpet in front of his mother's tombstone. He leaned the bouquet of blue hydrangeas and purple chrysanthemums against the grave marker, his eyes lovingly tracing the name Henrietta Turner, and below it the dates which marked the beginning and ending of her life: March 16th, 1811 – Nov. 7th, 1856. She had lived forty-five short years, leaving behind a husband and two sons.

He wished he could pour out his heart to her now as he had when he was a boy. She had always been good at listening to him, and even better at knowing how to respond. While Jeremiah knew his father loved him, Francis didn't have the same gift of communication.

But even if Henrietta had been with him, Jeremiah would have chosen to carry this heartache alone. He remembered the time when Charlie was eight and he was ten, and they had argued over something trivial which escalated until Jeremiah had a black eye and Charlie a bloodied nose. Henrietta's eyes, usually gentle, had sparked with anger as she grabbed hold of each son by his ear.

"You are *brothers*, you hear me? I don't care what the reasons are," she cut off Charlie as he tried to interrupt with an explanation. "You don't have to *like* one another all the time and you don't have to *agree* about everything. But God gave us family to take care of each other. And if I ever see one of you hurting the other again, I'm going to hog-tie the two of you together until you learn to get along. Am I clear?" she snapped, her eyes boring into first one son and then the other until they both nodded, "Yes ma'am."

After that, whenever they had a heated disagreement they made sure to only shove the offending brother onto his rump, where no bruises or blood would give the tussle away. The truth was that they usually got along remarkably well. Just every now and then their boyish tempers got in the way of their good judgement.

If his mother knew that this pathetic stub on his left arm was the handiwork of his younger brother, it would have broken her heart. He could imagine the way Henrietta would have covered her mouth and wept if Jeremiah had ever dared to confess the truth to her.

The only person to know who was responsible for his injury was Chaplain Davies, whom Jeremiah might never see again. He looked down at the strange nub, which was healing over and looking more like a turkey leg than a human arm, in his opinion.

What had Charlie been thinking when he pulled the trigger? That question returned over and over as Jeremiah recalled the moment when he realized his brother had purposefully taken aim. Why?

If it had been a nameless Rebel who'd shot him, Jeremiah could have cursed the renegade and remembered him with a cold and guiltless hatred. But he loved his brother. And what was more confusing still, he knew in his heart that Charlie loved him. No matter how radically opposed their political conclusions might be, they were *brothers*, just as his mother had said.

He'd once heard it said that the opposite of love was not hatred but apathy, for it was an absence of feeling while hatred is just as passionate as love. Until now, he'd never understood the saying.

He sincerely regretted learning that Charlie had been taken captive and was being held at a place as despicable as Point Lookout. If he knew a way to free his brother, he would have. And yet Jeremiah could not bear the thought of ever being in the same room with him again. He feared that his one good hand would form a fist and strike Charlie's jaw without having first asked permission.

One day, if Charlie survived the war, the brothers would have to face one another again. Perhaps by the time that day came, Jeremiah would be ready to forgive. If not for Charlie's sake, then for their mother's.

Standing, Jeremiah turned and meandered his way through the shrubs and trees toward the back porch. Spotting Clara on the divan, he realized that she had been watching him all the while. There had been a time in the past when she wouldn't have hesitated to join him, confident that she was welcome in every aspect of his life. Now she wore an expression of uncertainty, observing him instead from a distance.

Taking the seat beside her, Jeremiah thought to take her hand, only to realize that Clara was seated to the left of him. He let the amputated arm rest awkwardly in his lap instead.

It had been a week since he had come home to Laurel Hill. Jeremiah felt restless and irritable without a routine or a schedule. He'd become so used to the incessant drills at Oak Hall that he found himself enacting them in his mind out of habit. It was time to resume working on the farm, to make himself useful again. He wasn't an invalid and Jeremiah had no intention of allowing his disability to diminish his sense of purpose.

"The weeds are trying to strangle out the corn, and I'm well enough to get back out in the fields," he informed her. "I'll have to learn how to do things all over again, but the longer I wait, the harder it will be."

"What does Francis say about it?" Clara replied.

"I don't need to ask my father's permission," he retorted irritably. "I'm sure he'd rather see me sweating alongside him than sitting on the porch while he does the work."

"Of course," his wife forced a tight smile, her eyes downcast. After a pause she added, "I think I'll visit Jane this afternoon, if you don't mind."

"Not at all," Jeremiah answered, relieved that she wouldn't be watching him anxiously from the window.

He waited until she had taken her leave to go down to the barn. He wished he hadn't sold Archie, even if the money had been useful at the time. Nan was grazing in the corral, and Jeremiah whistled for the white mare, thinking he would rather ride the carriage horse than be limited to his own two feet.

But the simple task of sliding the bit between her teeth and easing the leather bridle over her large ears proved a tedious chore. More difficult still was saddling the horse one-handed and tightening the cinch. By the time he was finished, Jeremiah was drenched in sweat and his jaw ached from clenching it with bitter resolve.

Taking a hoe from the shed, Jeremiah carefully swung up into the saddle and directed the mare to the back end of the property where he could fumble his way through the next challenge in privacy. Tethering Nan to a sapling in the shade, Jeremiah marched between the rows of growing stalks and eyed the tool in his hand.

He'd spent many hours of his life hoeing weeds. It had been a thoughtless, repetitive act that freed his mind to focus on other things. Today, however, it would require all his concentration. The first hurdle was figuring out how to hold the hoe steadily with one hand. After several awkward attempts and giving himself a bruise on the shin, Jeremiah learned to tuck the handle under his armpit to give him more control over the heavy end.

While this seemed an effective method initially, it resulted in bruising and chafing under his arm as well as rubbing new blisters on his hand from having to grip the wooden handle differently. His left arm flapped clumsily beside him, the rounded stump stabbing the air as it served only to maintain his balance.

Within an hour, Jeremiah was exhausted and humiliated. He'd accomplished only a quarter of what he could have done with two hands. His right shoulder and bicep ached from their labor, while his left side had done no more than wave. He would have to find a way to exercise it or he would be grossly disproportioned. Shaking his head in disgust, he leaned heavily on the hoe.

A lot of help he would be around the farm.

~

"How is Jeremiah adjusting, dear?" Naomi asked as she poured her eldest daughter a cup of tea, handing her the delicate porcelain cup and matching saucer, painted with a spray of pink roses.

Clara accepted it, grateful for the companionship of women willing to listen to her troubles. Jane leaned forward, compassion creasing her brow.

"It's as if he thinks that since the sutures have healed, he can just go back to life as usual—except he can't. He's learned how to button his shirt with one hand, and he's still working on getting his shoes on by himself. Today he wanted to go out in the field to hoe the weeds, and I dread seeing his face when I get home and he's frustrated from the effort. I don't want him to give up on life any more than he does, but I don't know how he can do the things he used to…" her voice trailed off, her throat clogging with emotion.

"It hurts me to see him so defeated," Clara admitted. "And I feel like there's so much more than what he's telling me. I just don't know how I can help him."

"Poor thing," Naomi sighed. "Both of you, poor dears," she added. "I can't imagine how difficult this is."

It didn't fix anything, but the sympathetic words acted as a balm on Clara's heart. "I suppose it will just take time and patience," she said, voicing aloud the advice she had been repeating to herself.

"Well, he's not the only amputee the war has left us with," Jane commented thoughtfully. "In fact, my friend Abigail Sterrett was telling me just last week about her cousin who lost a hand in the war. He was fitted with a special device that attaches to his arm to help him do things. Would you like to meet them?"

Clara nodded eagerly, feeling a desperate pang of hope. "Yes, that would be wonderful!"

But as she imagined how receptive Jeremiah would be to the suggestion of a "special device" for amputees if she presented it to him, another idea formed in her mind. "What if your friend Abigail and her cousin just 'happened' to be here one evening when we arrive for supper? Then he could show Jeremiah how helpful it really is, man to man, without me ever having to say a word."

Naomi chuckled. "You're learning the ways of a married woman," she approved.

With a sly smile, Jane replied, "I'll see what I can do and let you know."

For the next week and half, Clara watched Jeremiah sink deeper into a pit of resentment and self-pity. She had to bite her tongue to keep from offering practical suggestions or words of counsel. What he needed was her quiet support, her acceptance and her unconditional love. Instead of trying to solve his problems, Clara turned him over to God and prayed that He would complete the work of healing in Jeremiah's life.

Whenever she saw her husband clenching his teeth as he struggled to perform a simple task, she looked away to spare him embarrassment and lifted Jeremiah in silent prayer once again. It was becoming reflexive, this reliance on the Creator, and Clara felt a new calm spreading daily inside her.

As the carriage pulled into her parents' drive, Clara took a deep breath. Jeremiah would know as soon as he spotted the appendage on the unexpected company exactly who had orchestrated the meeting. But she was hoping his fascination with the device would overshadow his irritation with her meddling.

Mercy, the young slave woman whom Eli had missed since Clara had ceased her weekly visits, met them at the door and invited them into the parlor. Naomi and George were pleased to see them, and Jane greeted them warmly before turning to introduce her friends.

"I hope you don't mind, but my friend Abigail Sterrett is having supper with us tonight, along with her cousin, Judson Shepherd," she announced with forced nonchalance. Clara noted that her sister wore a pink sash with her white dress, and a rose blossom had been tucked into her chignon.

Casting a sideways glance at Jeremiah, she saw him step forward and extend his hand to the young man. Judson Shepherd was a handsome fellow, with pale blond hair that tumbled into eyes the clear, deep blue of an aquamarine. He had a square jaw, and a thickly muscled physique which made him an imposing presence despite his short stature.

As he accepted Jeremiah's hand, she noticed her husband glance down curiously at the unfamiliar material against his skin. The hand which he gripped was not flesh, but rubber. Quickly bringing his gaze back to Judson's face, Jeremiah offered a customary pleasantry. But as he turned to acknowledge Abigail, he shot Clara a look which said he had guessed her intentions.

Abigail Sterrett was a beautiful young woman with dark hair and sweet, delicate features. She offered a winning smile, courteously pretending to be oblivious of the interactions between husband and wife. Her full skirt of slate blue, with vertical black pinstripes, swayed like a bell in a church steeple as she stepped forward.

After everyone was seated comfortably around the dining room table and plates were heaped with chicken and dumplings, Naomi initiated conversation with her guests. "I'm so glad you could join us tonight," she smiled graciously. "Judson, I understand you were with Burnside on what they call the 'Mud March,'" she inquired innocently.

"Yes ma'am," he replied, his left hand pausing in mid-air with a forkful of chicken. "It was that march which marked the fateful end of Burnside's career," he commented, taking a bite.

"Why do they call it the 'Mud March'?" Jane pressed, as if led only by idle curiosity.

"The plan," the veteran explained, "was to cross the Rappahannock River at Bank's Ford in late January. The weather had been seasonably mild, and we would have been fine if it hadn't been for the rain. It started during the night and by morning the ground was saturated. The river banks turned into a quagmire and the rain never let up. All the artillery and wagons were mired down, and every last one of us were drenched, freezing and filthy. It was a miserable failure and Burnside finally had no alternative but to abort the offensive."

Abigail finished the account quietly. "The Rebels had lined up on the opposite shore while they floundered in the mud, and Confederate sharpshooters harassed them continuously. That's how Judson was wounded and lost his hand."

Judson turned to Jeremiah, dropping the pretense that this was not a planned meeting. "I understand you lost your hand at Gettysburg. I heard that was some fierce fighting."

The wild hair of his eyebrows drew into a scowl as Jeremiah swallowed the food in his mouth. He looked down at his plate as he mumbled, "Yes it was."

"The Eastern Shore Regiment arrived on the third and last day of the battle, I believe," Abigail's cousin continued. "You helped turn the tide for the Union."

Nodding, Jeremiah reached for his glass and took a long drink of his iced tea. When he offered no further comment, Judson persisted, "It was your left hand you lost, wasn't it?"

His discomfort with the direction of the conversation couldn't have been more obvious as Jeremiah merely nodded again and applied his full concentration on cleaning the plate before him. Clara bit her lip, wondering if perhaps she had erred as drastically as General Burnside in her tactical strategy.

"The war's taken a lot of hands, as I understand it," George observed, blithely unaware of the underlying purpose for the dinner party.

"Yes, it has," Abigail was quick to agree. "That's why they've had to experiment with finding more effective prostheses," she added.

Clara was prepared to see steam coming out of her husband's ears as she glanced over him. His irritation, however, seemed to be slowly giving way to intrigue. She resumed eating as she smothered a satisfied smile.

"This is the latest invention," Judson attested, lifting his right arm and tugging down the sleeve of his coat just enough to reveal the wooden fore-arm to which the rubber hand was attached. "The hand looks good, but it isn't always useful. It can be taken out and replaced with an assortment of different tools. After supper, I'll show them to you," he offered enthusiastically, and Clara was pleased to see Jeremiah nod in interest.

The apparatus was an object of fascination to everyone in the room, as they had never seen anything like it before. Prior to the war and the vast number of amputees which resulted from it, anyone unfortunate enough to lose a hand or leg was fitted with a hook or a peg-leg. Not only were these unnatural in appearance, they were uncomfortable for the wearer and many preferred to go without. This new device appeared to be far more advanced.

In fact, as Judson procured the attachments from their case and lined them up on the dining room table after it had been cleared from supper, everyone leaned in close to observe this marvel of modern technology. In addition to the counterfeit hand, there were four other options Judson could use: the stereotypical hook, a fork, a knife, or a small brush. He removed his coat and revealed the cut off shirt beneath, demonstrating how the rubber hand could be removed from the socket of the fore-arm and any of the other tools inserted.

"It's been a godsend," Judson admitted. "I don't know what I would do without it." Unbuckling the straps which held the prosthesis in place, he removed the fore-arm and handed it over to Jeremiah for further inspection.

Jeremiah seemed to have forgotten his earlier pique and examined each of the individual items carefully, including the harness, held in place with leather straps. "Amazing," he said, clearly impressed. "Where did you find it?"

"There's a doctor in Baltimore that can fit you for it. He'll need to measure your arm to get everything adjusted precisely, and he'll make a cast of your other hand to make it look more natural. I'd be happy to get his information to you," Judson offered.

"Yes, I'd like that," Jeremiah replied as he continued a thorough examination of the invention.

Behind him, Abigail and Jane caught Clara's eye and grinned.

Chapter Thirty

"D id my father put you up to this?" Jeremiah wondered aloud as he sat across from Clara in the carriage.

She appeared nervous as she replied, "No, it was my own doing." Her delicate hands knotted in the lap of her full lavender skirt.

"Why didn't you talk to me about it first?" Jeremiah absently rubbed the end of his amputated arm beneath the pinned-up sleeve of his coat where the nerves tingled and burned.

"I thought it might be best for you to see it for yourself. I had only heard about it, and couldn't have answered your questions the way Abigail's cousin could."

Silently contemplating Clara's soft-spoken reply, Jeremiah let out a heavy sigh. Her eyes watched him tentatively, like a dog afraid of being kicked by its master. He had wounded her spirit in Gettysburg, and it would take time and intention to earn back her trust.

"Well, it *is* a fascinating invention," he admitted, aware that he would have protested and argued had she suggested an interview with Judson Shepherd instead of taking it upon herself to ensure the meeting happened.

"Are you upset with me?" she worried, a crease forming between her finely arched eyebrows.

How could he be, when it was obvious that everything she did for him was driven by love? "No, sweetheart," he assured her. "I'm glad you introduced us, and I think I would like to have an apparatus like that myself. All my life I never realized how valuable it was to have two hands," Jeremiah realized. "I took so much for granted…" *Not just my health, but my family.*

Pushing down boyhood memories of his brother, Jeremiah redirected the conversation. "Jane is looking well," he commented.

"Yes," Clara agreed. "She seems to have found a way to live with her loss."

Is that what she thinks I need to do? If it was only the hand he had to learn to live without, that would have been challenging enough. The greater loss was of the man he had considered his closest friend for life, and it was that particular loss which Jeremiah couldn't find a way to live with.

"I'm thankful she's doing better," he replied, unsure what more could be said.

"I'm glad we had the opportunity to meet Abigail and Judson. I think I should like to spend more time with both of them," she added as a by-the-way.

Jeremiah suspected that she did, in fact, have a sincere desire to be friends with the young woman, but he also deduced that Clara was encouraging his friendship with Judson out of a wifely concern for his well-being. Not only did she want him to obtain the means to be physically independent again, she wanted him to find a way back to himself.

He appreciated Clara's concern, as well as her efforts to make suggestions rather than ultimatums. She was stumbling her own way through this new life as blindly as he was, each of them trying to find a path that would lead to healing. The difference, however, was that Jeremiah wasn't convinced such a path existed.

That night, he was grateful for her presence beside him in the bed at last. Clara curled onto her side, her long auburn braid falling across her shoulder, hand tucked beneath her cheek. Within seconds, her breathing evened out and he knew she slept. He watched her for some time, grateful to be alive and with her at Laurel Hill.

He was unaware when he fell asleep. All Jeremiah knew

was that suddenly he was standing on that wretched hillside again, noise exploding painfully in his ears. His vision was obscured by gray smoke, and the gunshots around him reverberated through the hillside until the ground shook under his feet. Through the mist which hovered over the landscape, the shadows of Confederate soldiers glided like ghosts. His heart pounded in his chest. He felt his finger squeeze the trigger, followed by the kick of the recoiling musket against his shoulder.

Then, like an apparition, three men materialized out of the smoke. The clang of steel against rock grabbed Jeremiah's attention, and he turned to see Cullen jerk from the impact of a bullet as it penetrated his heart. His expression registered shock as he met Jeremiah's gaze, then the light went out of his eyes and he collapsed lifelessly upon the ground.

Jeremiah gritted his teeth and prepared to repay a life for life as the Rebels ducked behind the safety of a tree trunk. Oblivious of everything else, he stared intently at that tree, determined to make this shot count.

But when the soldier came into view, his heart caught in his throat. He could hardly believe his eyes. Beneath that gray cap was a face he knew better than his own, a face he had seen every day for most of his life.

He saw his brother take aim and he screamed at the top of his lungs, *"Charlie, NO!"* Then pain ripped through his hand, white-hot and searing.

Gasping for breath, Jeremiah realized he was sitting upright in his bed at Laurel Hill, drenched in sweat. His wife sat beside him, hand on his shoulder. She asked the question again and it took a moment for her words to penetrate the echo inside his skull.

"Are you all right?" her voice was frightened, and Jeremiah felt shame add to the fear which flushed his cheeks.

He wanted to answer, "Yes," but he was short of breath and his heart felt as though it were trying to hammer through his ribcage. Instead, he reached for Clara and drew her close, clinging to her for strength and comfort.

"Please tell me," she begged, tears wetting her cheeks as she wrapped her arms around his neck. "I need to know. What happened?"

Raising the stump of his arm, Jeremiah answered raggedly, "It was Charlie."

"I don't understand," Clara whispered in confusion.

"In Gettysburg. It was Charlie who shot me."

"*Charlie?*" she gasped, shaking her head in shocked disbelief.

Jeremiah swallowed down the lump in his throat. "The First Maryland Infantry of the Confederate States Army was there, at the bottom of the hill. I didn't know it was them. I saw the Rebel flag, and I prayed that Charlie wasn't down there. We were positioned at the top of the hill, behind a breastworks of rocks and timber, firing down into the smoke-filled woods. I couldn't see anything, I just kept firing. Then suddenly there he was…

"He saw me, Clara. He knew it was me. He lowered his barrel to shoot my hand. Charlie shot me on purpose…" his voice trailed off as he tried to grasp the horrible reality, his mind still not comprehending it.

"Are you sure?" she asked as if hoping he would answer with uncertainty.

Jeremiah nodded wearily. "It was Charlie."

"But are you sure he *meant* to shoot you?" she doubted.

For the thousandth time, Jeremiah relived the scene in his mind. With absolute confidence he answered, "Yes, he aimed and fired, full well knowing it was me."

She pressed her cheek against his beard, her tears mingling with his. "Oh darling," her voice broke. "Oh, I'm so sorry!"

Jeremiah held her as he wept, clinging to her as if his life depended on it. The ache which had cleaved his chest diminished just the smallest degree as he brought her into his confidence. Clara stroked his neck tenderly as he buried his face in her shoulder.

"Don't tell my father," he begged. "It would kill him."

Clara nodded in assent. "I won't."

"How will I ever forgive him?" Jeremiah ground out, the sharp knife of betrayal piercing him again with the memory of his brother's actions.

"I don't know," Clara replied honestly. "All we can do is pray..."

Jeremiah closed his eyes and leaned into her. *Pray.* For the first time the word sparked a flicker of hope within him, like a flame in the darkness. The assurance of God's presence was as refreshing as a cool drink on a blistering hot day. It may not change the circumstances, but it did bring relief and the strength to endure.

~

For the first time since the war had broken out, Clara and Jeremiah took the steamer *Balloon* across the Chesapeake Bay to Baltimore. The city had changed since their last visit, and was now occupied by "blue coats" or "blue bellies," as the southerners called them. The home of Brigadier General George H. Steuart, who had resigned his commission with the U.S. Army to join the Confederacy, had been confiscated and converted into a military hospital. This same Steuart had commanded Charlie's regiment at the opening of the war.

The property became known as "Camp Andrew," after the Governor of Massachusetts, John Andrew, although the hospital was named "Jarvis Hospital" in memory of surgeon N.S. Jarvis. The mansion which had formerly belonged to the Steuart family was converted into an administration building, and the hospital was built on a hill, with enough beds to house 1,500 patients.

The doctor Judson Shepherd had recommended was Dr. Greene, who specialized in the treatment of amputees. He was a straight-faced old man with a white mustache that protruded from his face like the bristles of a broom. What he lacked in affability he made up for in professionalism. While he did not care to dispense unnecessary pleasantries, it was of extreme importance to the doctor that the harness of the prosthesis was fitted precisely for Jeremiah's stump and that the rubber imitation he made for it was an exact reverse replica of Jeremiah's right hand.

Clara appreciated Dr. Greene's attention to detail and the commitment he felt to his patients. Jeremiah was clearly not in the mood for social banter, and the doctor's silence suited him just fine. It was Clara who was bothered by the absence of friendly chatter, but as she was only there to support her husband, she suppressed her need for conversation and sat idly through each of the examinations and fittings required to complete the prosthesis.

They were staying at an inexpensive bed and breakfast throughout the process, and the company of these two taciturn men reminded Clara once again how much she had come to rely on Phoebe and Mamie for feminine companionship.

Since Jeremiah had confided the rest of the story to her, Clara thought he seemed a little less burdened. Although the regular visits to Camp Andrew provoked a new display of melancholy inspired by the presence of so many soldiers, both those stationed as guards and those who were there to recuperate from injuries. She supposed the military atmosphere triggered memories of his war experience, and in particular, the day he lost his hand.

Clara was glad she had gone to Gettysburg so that she could have a better understanding of the trial he had endured. If she had not seen the tents crowded with wounded and suffering men, she couldn't have sympathized with the way the battle had changed him.

During the hours spent away from Camp Andrew, they sometimes walked the streets of Baltimore to the Harbor, and other times retired to their room for peace and quiet away from the hustle and bustle of the city. While they were out, Jeremiah was engaged and talkative, but in the privacy of their hotel room, he often sat in a chair by the window, silently staring down at the passersby on the street below.

Clara had brought a novel with her to read in such moments, but she frequently found herself sitting with the open book in her lap as she studied Jeremiah's profile and wondered what thoughts occupied his mind. Although she had seen the carnage of the battle, she still couldn't imagine the anguish he felt over the choice of action his brother had taken. Clara secretly hoped that someday Charlie would return to Laurel Hill and convince Jeremiah that the gunshot had been accidental. And she sincerely hoped it had been.

She watched as Jeremiah looked down at his one good hand, palm up, stretching his fingers as if fascinated with the movement of his joints and the capabilities they possessed. Then his focus turned to his left arm where the skin had been pulled over the severed stump and sewn together. It was, Clara had to admit, a strange and disturbing sight.

"I've seen the damage a grenade or cannon can do to a man," he commented thoughtfully, as if aware that her gaze was intent upon him and not the story before her. "Men with their faces blown apart, ears missing, eyes removed from their sockets, scarred into monsters. I know that my loss is so much less, but I still feel like a freak."

Clara closed the book and set it on the small table next to her chair. Coming to stand beside Jeremiah, she rested her hand on his shoulder, as strong and broad as ever. "You know it's just a hand to me," she reminded him. "But I imagine it's more difficult for you to do without it."

"This bloody war is causing so many amputees, I suppose men without limbs will become common place, as if it's the natural order of things. But it isn't. We'll be remembered by posterity as a generation of cripples, a generation of Americans who butchered one another on the battlefield," he predicted grimly.

Unable to argue, Clara remained silent. This war was indeed unlike any other.

"I'm thankful I had you to come home to," Jeremiah continued, taking her hand in his. "I feel sorry for men who have no wife to love them after an event like this, or men who have to wonder how their wives really feel about them. I'm truly sorry for my behavior at Gettysburg, Clara. I was in a very troubled state of mind and I acted selfishly." He shook his head to silence her as she opened her mouth in protest.

"You didn't deserve that. You've always been my greatest blessing, and I let my pride get in the way when I needed you most. I'm glad you were there, and I'm glad you're here with me now. This prosthetic device will help me to be useful on the farm again and to look normal when I'm away from home. I never would have known about it if it wasn't for you. Thank you for everything you've given me, Clara. I love you," he finished earnestly.

Urging him to his feet, Clara wrapped her arms around his neck and looked him squarely in the eyes. "I know, darling. But If you ever do anything like that to me again, I'm going to permanently move to the trundle bed," she replied with a coquettish smile. "And then I bet you'll learn your lesson."

The wide grin that spread over his face warmed Clara to her toes. Jeremiah pulled her against him firmly with his right arm and replied, "Well, I'll be on my best behavior from now on then." Lowering his face to hers, he kissed her breathless.

As they boarded the steamer to return to Centreville, Clara noticed a new confidence in her husband's stride. Not only was he absolutely assured of her acceptance and love, he wore the new prosthesis with the rubber facsimile attachment, and to all the world he appeared as if he had two hands. Unless one paused to give it a long and lingering look, there was no distinction between the real and the false. Once again, he could blend into the crowd.

"I think the hook will be especially handy when I'm hoeing

weeds," Jeremiah commented, eager to resume the life of a farmer which he had found so rewarding. "It will feel good to be useful again," he admitted with the first spark of enthusiasm Clara had heard in his voice since his return home.

Clara linked her arm through his elbow, blinking back tears of gratitude. *Thank you, Lord, for bringing my husband back to me!*

Chapter Thirty-One

Fall, 1863

Shocks of brown cornstalks interspersed the field like a hundred small pyramids. Their dried leaves rustled in the brisk wind which stirred the autumn garb of the woods bordering the field. Above Jeremiah, the sky was uninterrupted blue as far as the eye could see. The sun shone warm and golden overhead.

Ten year old Silas drove the mule, while the adult men cut the husks from the stalks to be deposited into the wagon. Jeremiah found that having a knife in lieu of a left hand was actually beneficial when it came working the farm. He could secure the stalk with his right hand and hack off the cornhusk with a simple waving motion, never worrying about dropping the implement or losing a finger. Instead of slowing him down, it actually increased his productivity.

Every day when he awoke with his wife beside him, in his own bed at Laurel Hill, Jeremiah was flooded with gratitude. The days of being disrupted from his slumber by the trumpet's reveille were gone and over with forever. He lived on what the farm produced, filled his days with useful work, and had the strange comfort of knowing that the thing he feared most had already occurred. It was a good life, and he was thankful for it.

He still received periodic letters from Chaplain Davies, filled with wisdom and advice. There were only a few things Jeremiah missed from his days of military service, and the chaplain was among them. Private Phillips also kept in touch, having recovered from his injuries and resumed active duty.

Whenever Jeremiah thought of them, it was painful to remember that young Cullen hadn't survived his first and only battle. Just recently his body had been disinterred from its hasty resting place and moved to the newly dedicated Soldier's National Cemetery at Gettysburg.

President Lincoln himself had been present when the cemetery was dedicated, offering a short but memorable speech which further revealed not only his determination to win the war at any cost, but to promote its redefined purpose to end slavery. As a veteran of the bloody battle, and a citizen of a border state caught between the deeply entrenched views of North and South, Jeremiah mulled thoughtfully over the conclusion of Lincoln's address printed in the paper.

"It is for us the living, rather, to be dedicated here to the unfinished work which they who fought here have thus far so nobly advanced. It is rather for us to be here dedicated to the great task remaining before us—that from these honored dead we take increased devotion to that cause for which they gave the last full measure of devotion—that we here highly resolve that these dead shall not have died in vain—that this nation, under God, shall have a new birth of freedom—and that government of the people, by the people, for the people, shall not perish from the earth."

When Jeremiah enlisted in November of 1861, his intention had not been to improve the world through the forced termination of the practice of slave-holding. He had wanted only to honor the sacrifice of those who had gone before him, like his grandfather, who had fought against the British to make the United States an independent nation, a republic, free from the dictates of a monarchy.

The President claimed that Jeremiah risked his life to preserve what his forefathers had intended for this great country to be: *"conceived in liberty, and dedicated to the proposition that all men are created equal."* Kneeling behind the stone breastworks on Culp's Hill that memorable day, such thoughts had not been Jeremiah's motivation. But now, in the tranquility of the moment as he worked alongside Old Joe, Henry, and Eli to bring in the corn, Jeremiah could agree that he did fully embrace these ideals.

The war had changed him, just as it had changed many others, and was slowly changing the world—for both better and worse. While the principle of liberty had been expanded to include Negroes, the cost was unthinkable in terms of the soldiers who died in this war, both Union and Rebel. Thousands of men had been sacrificed, and Jeremiah wasn't naïve enough to believe it was solely for the sake of an ideal.

In the history of humanity, no war had ever been fought merely on principle. There were always economic and political layers to the decision to engage in military action and to extract such a high price from the country's citizens. This war was no different. There were many angles from which it could be examined, but in the end Jeremiah could personally claim two things: his love of country and his devotion to the freedom of all men. He had made his sacrifice, and he would stand by his commitment to the Northern cause.

Would Charlie say the same? Could his brother still stand by his commitment to the Southern cause, after all that had transpired? Jeremiah might never know the answer. And while part of him wished to sit down over a meal and discuss these things with Charlie, the greater part of him still boiled with hurt and rage.

In his most recent missive, Chaplain Davies had given Jeremiah a piece of spiritual advice which he was attempting to put into practice. *"Turn your worries into prayers,"* Davies wrote. *"The blessings of a right relationship with God through Jesus Christ aren't just for heaven, but also for the here and now. If you've repented of yours sins and confessed that Jesus is Lord, you never have to face your troubles alone again. You can surrender all your worries to Providence with the knowledge and assurance that the God who orders the universe loves you as His child."*

Whenever Jeremiah found his mind drifting to the future, to the day when he might see his brother again, or to the implications of the war raging on for years to come, he tried to take the chaplain's advice. And he had to admit, it was much easier to feel at peace when trusting God than when trying to carry the weight of the world alone.

"*Is anyone among you suffering? He should pray,*" Davies had quoted James 5:13 in his typical fashion. Jeremiah smiled. The old man had, in his own unique and eccentric way, walked Jeremiah through some of the darkest times of his life and led him to God. For that, Jeremiah would always be grateful to him.

There were more dark times to come, that was certain. But Jeremiah hoped none would rival what he had endured in Gettysburg. When he considered all the nation had survived in the last two and a half years of war, and when he listened to the President's appeal that it not be vain—that the battle continue until it was won—he grieved to think of all the losses yet to come.

Over the summer, the recruiting of colored troops had begun in Queenstown and Kent Island. Jeremiah shouldn't have been surprised when Henry and Eli confessed their intention to enlist.

"We gonna wait till after harvest-time, suh," Henry assured Francis, "but then, if you say so, we like to do our part so one day my Little Joe be a free man, not a slave." His white teeth flashed against his ebony skin as he smiled, the hope of his son's freedom illuminating him with joy.

How could anyone deny his request with that light shining in his eyes?

"The white men losin' they heart to fight," Eli had added. "But we black men, we just feeling the fire grow in our chests," he thumped his chest with a clenched fist for emphasis, his dark eyes sparking with passion.

Francis consented. When the steamer *Cecil* returned to take Negro recruits to Baltimore, Eli and Henry would go with them.

Not all slaves respected their masters enough to seek permission. When the steamer had first arrived, many had taken the opportunity to run away. Among them were twenty slaves belonging to William Paca, although they were recaptured and returned to bondage.

Jeremiah hated to see Henry and Eli go, not only for the loss of their labor at Laurel Hill, but because he knew what they would be facing. In this moment, they were as clueless to the reality of war as he had been that November day in 1861 when he had mounted Archie and bade them all farewell.

It was easy to hold fast to ideals and principles when you weren't dodging bullets and watching good men bleed to death on the ground beside you. When you were staring down the enemy, heart pounding and palms sweating, it was a vastly different thing than talking of war from the back porch of your home.

Following on foot behind the mule-drawn wagon to the corn crib to unload their harvest before washing up for the noon meal, Jeremiah inhaled the cool, crisp air. The breeze carried the familiar smells of fall on the farm, the sweetness of the corn mingling with the tang of autumn leaves. It had been a day much like this one when he had left Laurel Hill to enlist in Cambridge. Not only had he been ignorant to the harsh cruelty of war, Jeremiah had been selfishly oblivious to the impact his decision would have on his wife.

Clara had been forced to step into a different role as mistress of Laurel Hill, sharing the management of the farm with her father-in-law. While she had never complained, her letters had often hinted at deep loneliness and dark fear. When Jeremiah chose to serve his nation, he had imposed his sacrifice upon her.

But from the day they met until the present time, with every trial and challenge they had faced in between, Clara had remained steadfast by his side as his greatest supporter and truest confidante. And Jeremiah swore that he would never take her for granted again.

~

Clara hummed along with Mamie as she sang, *"In the sweet by and by, we shall meet on that beautiful shore..."* as she bent over the butter churn, moving the dash up and down in a strong and rhythmic motion. The smells of bread baking in the oven filled the kitchen, and at the table, Clara and Phoebe plaited the dried tops of onions into a long braid to preserve them through the winter.

On the floor, Lena sat with Little Joe, who was now old enough to get into mischief if not closely watched. He had learned that he could go wherever he wanted on his hands and knees, and crawled around the house at lightning quick speed. Lena tried to occupy him with clapping games and songs, but the only time the boy was ever still was when he was sleeping.

Phoebe had confided to Clara that Henry and Eli were planning to join the Union Army as soon as the harvest was in. Jeremiah confirmed that Francis had given them his blessing, and that the men were eager to do their part to fight for freedom.

Clara hated the thought of anyone else she cared about going into battle. But since the war had lingered on, and the focus had shifted from preserving the Union to ending slavery, Jeremiah told her that more and more Negroes were joining the fight. With the increased number of slaves joining the "contraband camps" in the south, allowing the Negroes to join the army relieved the government of caring for such a large number of dependents, as well as compensating for the decreased number in volunteers as the white men grew jaded and weary with the fight.

When Jeremiah enlisted, Clara had hoped that the war would end quickly. Phoebe had no such delusions. The black woman also had more insight into the consequences of war than Clara had in the fall of 1861. She had watched Jane grieve, stood by as Clara pined and worried, and seen the state Jeremiah returned home in. Phoebe knew that Charlie was held as a prisoner of war, living in dubious conditions.

But for Phoebe, the reward was much greater. Clara had not been as invested in the goal of preserving the Union. Risking her husband's life to hold the seceding states captive had not felt worth the cost. When Henry marched off into battle, Phoebe knew that he was fighting for their freedom, and for the freedom of their son and all generations to follow.

If slavery was abolished once and for all, their grandchildren would grow up in a generation for whom the slavery of Negroes would be only stories and the reminiscences of the elderly. They would have opportunities and dreams never before possible because of the color of their skin. It was a battle worth fighting.

Eli was determined to gain Hattie's permission to marry Mercy before he left, and Phoebe was relatively certain she would grant it. "You can't stop young love," Phoebe chuckled. "Any of us been in love afore know that!"

Clara smiled, nodding in agreement. As foolish as she believed it was to marry a man before he ran off to fight, she would have married Jeremiah under those conditions if he'd asked her to. Love was a curious and powerful emotion, and in a world gone mad with hatred and violence, it was always a blessing to be reminded of it.

In the last few weeks, Jeremiah had grown more and more like his old self. He found satisfaction and joy in working the farm, and was thrilled and fascinated with the ability to convert his left hand into various tools. The color had come back into his cheeks from working in the sun, and the availability of meat and fresh vegetables on the farm had aided in filling him out.

It was too strange a thing to ever admit aloud, but Clara was thankful for his injury. Not only had it brought him home to her, it had given him a reason to remain at home. Without the constant stress of facing each day alone, of fearing for her husband's safety, Clara too looked healthier than she had in some time.

But until the war ended, there would always be dark clouds threatening overhead. As she sat humming along with Mamie in the kitchen, a carriage pulled up outside. She followed Phoebe to the door to find her mother, gray and ashen, standing alongside her father and sister. Jane's eyes were swollen and red, and the somber expression on George's face portended another heartbreaking loss.

"Eddy?" she whispered, gripping her mother's hand as she stepped over the threshold.

Unable to speak, Naomi nodded brokenly.

Jane encircled her mother's waist, escorting her into the parlor where Naomi collapsed onto the sofa, tears streaming down her face.

Clara turned to her father questioningly. "What happened?"

George compressed his lips into a thin line to hold back his emotions. Wordlessly, he procured a letter from his vest pocket and handed it to Clara.

With trembling hands, she unfolded the page and skimmed over the neat penmanship. Although Eddy's name had not appeared in the newspaper as a casualty, he had been fatally wounded at the Second Battle of Rappahannock Station in Virginia. It had been a decisive win for the Union, but not without some loss. The letter was written by a nurse who had attended Eddy at the field hospital before his death.

If he hadn't been able to provide his name, as well as his parents' address, they would have never known what had become of him. The nurse wrote that Eddy had been fading fast as she bent over him, but that he was determined to communicate the necessary information to ensure they were contacted and to convey one final message of love and farewell.

Clara's gaze lifted from the page to stare blankly at the orange flames licking at the crackling logs in the fireplace. Eddy, the obnoxious little boy, the doting younger brother, the well-dressed merchant's son, was gone forever. He had been struck by a grenade, with no hope of survival.

"Oh Mama," she sighed, feeling the loss deep down in her heart. "Our poor Eddy…"

Jane removed a handkerchief from her sleeve and sobbed softly into it. Clara imagined that this letter reminded her of another, written by the man whom she had intended to marry, have children with, and grow old beside. Not only had she lost her brother today, Jane had lost her fiancé and her future all over again.

Clara sank down into the armchair, allowing her mother and sister to comfort one another. They would all soon be dressed in the black of mourning, joining the many mothers, sisters, fiancées and wives the war had left behind.

Hearing the back door open, and the thump of her husband's boots on the wood floor, Clara rose to greet him with open arms. As she fell into his chest, inhaling the smell of sweat and corn and autumn air, Clara fisted Jeremiah's cotton shirt.

"Eddy's gone," she whispered as his arms encircled her. But even as anguish divided her soul, she was comforted that Jeremiah was alive and with her. *Thank you, God, for sparing my husband!*

Through the haze of her grief, Clara heard Jeremiah offer his condolences to her parents, his voice a deep rumble in her ear.

"Eddy never wanted to fight," her father ground out resentfully. "And now he's dead."

It was little wonder that patriotism was waning, that love of country had ceased to be sufficient motivation for men to sacrifice their lives. Even had George Collins shared the Yankee position, he would never have chosen to send his only son to fight for it. He clenched his fists in bitter rage, his eyes glazed with unshed tears.

Naomi gently pushed Jane away from her, gathering her full skirt in her hands as she gained her feet. Coming to stand before her husband, Naomi placed her hand on his chest and looked up into George's angry eyes.

Her voice was thick with tears as she reminded him, "No matter where we are, every one of us are in the hands of Providence. It's the only comfort to be found."

Chapter Thirty-Two

The crisp autumn breeze stirred the tassels on Clara's shawl as she pulled it more tightly around her shoulders. A contented smile graced her lips as she swayed gently in the rocking chair, surrounded by the brilliant colors of the fall leaves contrasted against an unbroken blue sky. Her heart was full.

Tomorrow the nation would unite in celebrating Thanksgiving on the same day for the very first time. Prior to the President proclaiming it a national holiday it had been observed by some of the states, but on a day of that particular state's choosing. Now Lincoln had decreed that henceforward it would be celebrated, by one and all within the Union, on the final Thursday of the month of November.

It was a day for the American people to set aside sectional differences and remember the blessings of Providence. Despite the carnage of war, the sky still yielded sunshine and rain to cultivate the earth, and new life was still being birthed into the world.

President Lincoln declared: *"They are the gracious gifts of the Most High God, who, while dealing with us in anger for our sins, hath nevertheless remembered mercy."*

While the men, more cynical from their experiences in war, questioned the motives of the President as political and manipulative, Clara embraced what the day represented. It was wise to pause and celebrate all that was still good in the world, especially when surrounded by so much death, loss, and fear.

The idea of making Thanksgiving a national holiday hadn't originated with the President, but a woman by the name of Sarah Hale. It was interesting to note that she had written to the four preceding Presidents of the United States—Zachary Taylor, Millard Fillmore, Franklin Pierce and James Buchanan—but it had been Abraham Lincoln who had granted her request. Some argued that it was a campaign strategy for reelection the following fall, legislating for something other than death and destruction to influence the people to think more favorably, both about him and about the era in which they lived.

Even if it was, Clara didn't care. It was like lighting a candle in the darkness, and for this one day, they could bask in its glow. They could set aside the many reasons to mourn, and instead remember that there were still reasons to rejoice.

Judson had brought Abigail and Jane to visit, along with a puppy which was to be entrusted to Silas' care. Abigail's pair of Staffordshire Bull Terriers, Sam and Sophie, had produced a litter of puppies which were now in need of new homes. Clara had convinced Jeremiah to let her keep one, with the proviso that it would be Silas' responsibility. The boy had accepted his new job with a wide grin.

Now he sat at Clara's feet, cradling the black and white pup in his arms, his dark face split with joy. Beside him, Lena held Little Joe in her lap, hand over his, instructing him to stroke the animal gently.

"What are you going to name him?" Judson asked Clara, smiling at the children's delight over the little creature. His hair was bleached from the sun, a blond so pale it was almost white, and his blue eyes contrasted against his tanned complexion.

"Hmm... Silas, what do you think?" she turned to the boy who would be the dog's caregiver.

Silas' dark eyebrows scrunched together as he studied the sleeping puppy. Abigail winked at Clara, enjoying the boy's serious consideration of this most important decision. Finally, he looked up at them and declared, "I think I gonna call him 'Rags,' cause he look like he gots a rag tied 'round his head."

"I think that suits him perfectly," Clara praised. The little puppy was predominantly white, with a black tail and a few patches of black on his torso, and a black band which encircled his head, covering one eye and both of his floppy ears. He did indeed look as if he had a rag tied around his head.

"I agree," Abigail smiled approvingly, her dark hair pulled back from her pretty face in a sweeping chignon. "Now I only have one more puppy in need of a home."

"I'm sorely tempted to keep it myself," Jane confessed, gazing longingly at the sweet little dog cradled in Silas' arms like a baby. "But I'm not sure Mother would let me keep it inside."

With a wink, Judson suggested, "We could bring it by for a visit. I suspect once your mother sees the little dear, she'll be more easily persuaded."

Jane glanced over at the young man and laughed, and Clara wasn't oblivious to the color which pinked her sister's cheeks. Although Jane hadn't openly admitted attraction to the young man, her eyes often shifted to his handsome figure with more than casual interest. September had marked the first anniversary of Louis' death and while Jane had moved beyond the worst of her grief, Clara knew it would take a little longer for her to risk loving again.

Clara grinned as she chimed in, "I'll go along with that scheme. If I know Mother, it will melt her heart just like Rags is melting yours." She didn't add that she believed it would be good for Jane to have something to nurture and pour herself into which could give her affection in return. A puppy would help ease the loneliness she felt, and might aid in mending the scars she still carried.

Hugging her shawl closer around her waist, Clara shivered as the November wind blew through the orchard and swept over them. Jeremiah sat in one of the wicker chairs and leaned forward to ask, "Would you like me to bring you a blanket?"

With her heart thudding in anticipation of all that was to come, Clara replied with a grateful smile. "I'm all right, darling, but thank you."

They had much to be thankful for, more than Jeremiah knew. The prosthesis had given him a second chance at life, allowing him to step back into the role of farmer which he loved so much. He had returned to his old self, strong and independent, solid and reliable. The relationship they shared was different than it had been before his military service, changed by the challenges they had faced and overcome. It was deeper and stronger, tested and tried.

The one great sorrow which cast a shadow over Clara's happiness was that Eddy would never return home to them. Jane might have been able to retire her mourning garb if their brother hadn't passed, but now all the women of the household were relegated to a somber wardrobe signifying loss.

"Would you like to hold 'im?" Silas offered Jane, interrupting Clara's wandering thoughts. Without waiting for a reply, the boy came to his feet and carried the drowsy pup to Jane, carefully placing him in her arms.

"He's so soft!" Jane exclaimed as she accepted the puppy, cradling him against her shoulder and caressing his fur with her cheek. Disturbed from his nap, Rags wagged his tail as he enthusiastically licked her ear with his wet tongue. Jane giggled as she pushed him down into her lap, "You need to learn some manners!"

Clara glanced in Judson's direction, pleased with the look on his face as he watched her sister. The strong line of his jaw softened with tenderness, and affection warmed his blue eyes. In time, Clara was certain, Jane would let down her guard if Judson wooed her with gentle patience.

And Clara couldn't have been more pleased with the idea. Judson was fast becoming a valued friend to Jeremiah, the men having much in common as war veterans and amputees. Although Jane never imagined embracing the life of a farmer's wife, Clara suspected that the handsome young man gazing at her sister as if she were the greatest prize in the world might be able to persuade her.

Rocking slowly, Clara turned to the man who had convinced her to give up a privileged life to gather vegetables, churn butter, and oversee the slaughter of hogs. Jeremiah's dark hair tumbled over his forehead, lined with new creases from the struggles of the last two years, and the youthful twinkle in his eyes had been replaced with the wisdom of suffering. Their marriage had begun concurrent with the tumultuous events of their time, but of two things Clara was certain: she wouldn't do the past differently even if she could, and whatever the future brought, it would only serve to bind them closer together.

She had once believed herself to be a strong and capable woman. Now Clara realized that these qualities, while useful, were not enough to survive the hardships of life. In Gettysburg, in that most difficult trial of both their marriage and her life, Clara had learned a crucial lesson from Chaplain Davies about relying on Providence, and it was something she hoped to hold onto for the rest of her life.

Closing the gap between them, Clara reached for her husband's hand. She was blessed. God had heard her prayers, even when she had put more faith in her fears than in the Almighty. Clara vowed to face the days to come with that knowledge to guide her, and never again to be ruled by the power of worry.

Jeremiah squeezed her hand, his skin warm and callused against hers. The rubber prosthesis rested casually on his thigh, easily mistaken for the real thing. "I don't believe Mrs. Collins stands a chance against her daughters," he chuckled. "I'm not sure anyone does when you put your mind to something."

"Maybe so," Clara agreed, recalling a certain dinner party hosted at Laurel Hill in 1855.

~

Grinning at the impish twinkle in his wife's eye, Jeremiah was grateful that she loved him as much now as she had when they were young and idealistic. These brief years of their marriage had been drastically different than anything they had hoped or imagined for themselves. But they were still together, and more in love than ever.

There seemed to be a glow about Clara as she smiled at him. There were days when Jeremiah wondered if he deserved to be loved as she loved him, but every day he was grateful for it.

Rags, having enough of cuddling, leapt to the porch floor and bounded from one pair of shoes to another, nipping playfully. Jeremiah leaned down and scooped him up, just as taken with the wet little pink nose and the lopsided markings as everyone else. Jeremiah sat the puppy on his lap and let Rags plant his paws on his shoulders and lick his chin.

When Rags sprang again to the floor, Silas carried him into the yard to let him run free. Jeremiah watched as the boy ran after the puppy, then the game reversed, and Rags chased him. Jeremiah laughed with the others, but inwardly, his thoughts took a more serious turn.

Maryland had been divided before the war broke out, but now the schism ran deeper than ever. As the state was taken and held by the Union, Yankee ideas and philosophies crept in to influence the situation. The subject of emancipation had become a frequent matter of debate, so much so that the Republican Party had separated into two groups: those for and those against.

In an election held earlier that month, the State Comptroller, Congressman, Senator, Clerk of Court, and members of the House of Delegates had all been filled by members of what was called the "Conditional Union Party," which was opposed to freeing the slaves.

However, the war couldn't go on forever, for the South was running out of manpower and resources. Its defeat was only a matter of time. Then, certainly, President Lincoln would find a way to decree liberation for all slaves within the United States. Jefferson Davis and General Lee had to know this as well as Jeremiah did, yet month after month the war dragged on and men of both sides were sacrificed in the name of "the Cause"—either that of freedom from tyranny, or that of unification and the end of slavery.

Jeremiah believed in freedom. Freedom for the Southern States to make their own laws, but also freedom for mankind of any color. He had come to believe, with true conviction, that no man should be held as property as Old Joe, Mamie, and their children were. He despised the waste of human life the war had caused, and yet he yearned for the day when this peculiar institution should be abolished.

In two weeks, when the steamer *Cecil* returned to Queenstown, Henry and Eli would leave Laurel Hill and exchange the bonds of slavery for the manacles of the military. But at least they would be present to celebrate the first national Thanksgiving Day with those they considered family.

Hattie had allowed Eli and Mercy to marry, and Francis had given permission for Eli to live at the Collins' with her until his departure. It only seemed right to allow the girl to remain with her mother, but as the Collins would be joining the Turners for this special Thanksgiving, they would all be together one last time.

All of them, with the exception of Eddy and Charlie. And of course, Jane's fiancée, Louis. Even in the midst of laughter and celebration, the shadow of grief hung over them.

Jeremiah glanced over at his father, who stood stoically in the corner watching the antics of the younger generation. The holidays were always a painful reminder of those who could not be present. One day, he hoped, peace would be restored not only to the nation but to the Turner household.

Until then he would pray, imploring God for Charlie's safety and health, as well as for a way to forgive the unforgiveable. As hatred and prejudice unleashed their horrible fury upon the earth, Jeremiah was reminded of the great necessity to choose love.

Glancing down at the manmade representation of a hand attached to his left arm, Jeremiah counted his blessings. He was alive, and he was mostly intact. All of the vital organs functioned as they should; his face was unscarred; and he still walked on two good legs. With the attachments on the prosthesis, he could continue his work on the farm. And perhaps most importantly, he still had one good hand to hold tightly to his precious wife.

As the sun set in the western sky and shadows lengthened across the lawn, their visitors took their leave and Silas carried his new companion back to the cabin to sleep at the foot of his bed. With a gruff "Good night," and a squeeze of his shoulder, Francis slipped into the house, leaving husband and wife alone on the back porch.

"Walk with me?" Clara asked, slipping her arm through the crook of his elbow.

"Aren't you too cold?" he worried, but she shook her head.

"I just want to enjoy some time alone with you," she replied. "The stars are trying to twinkle there, just beyond the fading sunset," she pointed to the pale pinpoint of light visible in the darkening sky.

Slipping an arm around her waist, Jeremiah drew Clara close to warm her with his body heat. As much as he had enjoyed their earlier company, he enjoyed this peaceful moment alone with her even more. Leading her into the shadows of the orchard, Jeremiah cupped her jaw with his right hand, feeling the softness of Clara's skin against his palm. Leaning forward, he kissed her lips gently and smiled as she sighed and leaned into him.

"I'll be happy to never leave you or Laurel Hill again," Jeremiah admitted, encircling her waist with his left arm and pinning her against him.

"That sounds just fine with me," she agreed, and Jeremiah stepped back to see the shifting shadows of the rustling leaves play across her features.

"I'm sorry Eddy can't be here tomorrow," he said, certain she was already thinking it. "And Charlie."

"Me too," she whispered, resting her hands against the wool

coat of his chest and gripping the fabric in her fists. "Sometimes I feel so torn between grief and elation. Grief for those we have lost, but elation that you weren't listed among them. I think the President is right. All we can do is choose to be grateful for our blessings, even in the face of great loss."

"Well said," Jeremiah pressed a kiss into her forehead, smoothing back the soft auburn hair which appeared black in the fading light.

Clara lifted her chin to gaze up at him, her expression enigmatic as she added, "Even in the midst of death, there is new life."

Wrinkling his eyebrows in confusion at her cryptic words, Jeremiah half-smiled as he inquired, "What do you mean?"

"What I mean, Jeremiah Turner, is that you are soon to become a father," Clara beamed, her eyes sparkling with anticipation.

Jeremiah felt an odd stutter in his chest as his heart skipped a beat. "A father?" he repeated in a whisper, hardly able to believe it had finally happened. Then, as the idea took hold, he drew Clara against his chest in a crushing hug.

It felt like a miracle, and perhaps every new life was exactly that. He had just never taken the time to consider it before. His father would be delighted, and if his mother were still living, Henrietta would have doted on her first grandchild the way Silas doted on his puppy.

Yes, even in the midst of death, there was new life. For every loss he could count, Jeremiah could also find a blessing. In life, there were seasons of sunshine and seasons of storm. There was always the interplay of light with darkness. And even as the war continued to wage with no end in sight, there was hope glimmering on the horizon.

With this child, this promise of the next generation, there was hope that mankind would learn from the mistakes of his forbearers and make the sacrifices necessary to live in peace and to respect the sacred spark of life within all humanity. As long as the sun rose and set, there was hope.

Lying on a rough board balanced across the backs of two pews in the church at Gettysburg, staring up at the cross beams of the ceiling above him as his ears were filled with the groans of the wounded, the mercy of God had seemed an absurd idea. Jeremiah had doubted he would live to see Laurel Hill or Clara again.

Yet, as proof of God's mercy, here he was.

MY BROTHER'S FLAG

On Maryland's Eastern Shore, the division of the Civil War is an inescapable reality for many households. For the Turner brothers, it means choosing politics over blood.

Although his younger brother goes south to join the Rebels, Jeremiah feels honor-bound to defend the Stars and Stripes even at the risk of meeting Charlie on the battlefield and facing a deeper conflict of loyalties.

His wife, Clara, is left behind at Laurel Hill to manage the farm with her father-in-law and his slaves. As the country is torn apart by opposing forces from within, Clara must find the strength to live in a world of uncertainty and change.

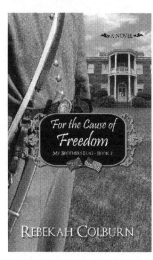

At the outbreak of the war, Charlie enlisted in the Confederate Army to defend States Rights while his older brother, Jeremiah, chose to fight for the Union.

Three years later, an emaciated prisoner of war, Charlie is determined to escape Point Lookout Prison and make his way home to face the conflict awaiting him there.

When Abigail Sterret discovers a wounded man near her home, she is moved by compassion at the sight of the gaunt Rebel soldier. Risking the consequences of aiding the enemy, Abigail shelters Charlie at Bloomingdale and nurtures him back to health. As his wounds heal, she discovers that Charlie carries more secrets than she supposed, and Abigail is more involved than she presumed.

And though war may end with the sweep of a pen, peace comes far less easily.

 Rebekah Colburn is the author of the Historical Fiction Series, *"Of Wind and Sky."*

Her desire is to bring history to life with rich stories, compelling characters and inspirational themes which will inspire and encourage her readers.

In 2001 she obtained a B.A. in Biblical Studies from Washington Bible College. Rebekah loves being outdoors and enjoys mountain biking, cycling, and cruising the local waterways with her husband.

She lives on the Eastern Shore of Maryland with her husband, teen-aged daughter, four spoiled cats, one rambunctious dog, and a whole lot of chaos.

You can contact Rebekah Colburn via:

Email: rebekahlynncolburn@gmail.com
Website: http://rebekahcolburn.weebly.com/
Facebook: https://www.facebook.com/ColburnRebekah
Twitter: https://twitter.com/RebekahColburn

Made in the USA
Middletown, DE
24 May 2016